COVENANT:
THE WITCHES OF PIONEER VALE
BOOK 3

DAVID COMBS

ALSO BY DAVID COMBS

Thieves' Honor

THE WITCHES OF PIONEER VALE SERIES

Ascension

Guardian

PRAISE FOR ASCENSION

"This book has it all...If you love magic and witches and entertaining stories, give this one a try. It will not disappoint you." - Laura D. Child of The Magic Book Corner

"I'm rooting for two awesome, badass women, instead of one. Awesome contemporary/historic fantasy cross-over with an excellent plot. Just love it!" - Astrid V.J. author of Elisabeth and Edvard The Siblings' Tale series

ISBN: 9781735003436

DEDICATION

For Emma and Libby

INTO THE REALM OF NIGHTMARES
BY DAVID COMBS

ACKNOWLEDGMENTS

This is a work of fiction. Any similarities to real places, people, or events are unintentional, coincidental, and accidental. In short, this all came from the depths of my imagination.

There are forms of address used within this story that may seem insensitive to Native American culture. The usage was meant solely for the purpose of authenticity for the time period in which they occur and in no way is a reflection of my personal views of Native American culture in general or the Nipmuc people in particular.

Dave Combs

Cover art by oliviaprodesign

Alistair Carmichael

Anne-Marie Carmichael
b.1643

Jeremiah Carmichael
b.1640

The Firstborn

The Inheritors

Aiden Carmichael b. 1661

Thomas Carmichael b. 1668

Kenton Carmichael b. 1690

Abigail (Carmichael) Hunter

Phoebe Hunter b. 1711

Devlin Hunter b. 1712

Levi Hunter b. 1736

Barnaby Hunter b. 1747

Kelvin Hunter b. 1778

Grace (Hunter) Cooke
b. 1784

Kathryn Cooke b. 1811

Renee (Cooke) Wright
b. 1813

Brooke Wright b. 1845

Jacob Wright b. 1850

May Wright b. 1880

Faye (Wright) McCowen
b. 1885

Jennifer McCowen b. 1912

Michael McCowen b. 1918

Mitchell McCCowen b. 1941

Gwendolyn (McCowen) Brighton
b. 1943

Christopher Brighton
b. 1961

William Brighton b. 1971

Angelica Brighton b. 2001

Jamie Brighton b. 2007

Carmichael Family Tree

CHAPTER 1
GHOSTS OF THE PAST - PRESENT DAY

"What have we got?" shouted Rebecca Harmon. The ambulance bay was filled with its typical chaos as EMTs and nursing staff ran from one emergency to the next. She stood clear of the nearest vehicle's swinging doors while a paramedic jumped out and pulled at one of the two stretchers crammed into the space.

"First one's a Jane Doe. Whoever she is, she's one tough lady," he said as he lowered the wheels to the ground and pushed the gurney towards the automatic doors. "Still breathing despite this."

Rebecca gasped at the broken piece of lumber that stood garishly in the air from the woman's abdomen. Blood was everywhere, seeping up the fibers of the stake and spattering the sheet that was thrown over her body. The white sleeveless blouse she wore was stained crimson, and droplets were sprayed across her neck, face, and even her hair.

Her fiery copper-red hair.

"It's her," she said. "She's the same woman who attacked the high school fundraiser and kidnapped a girl from there. Have you guys called the police yet?" Rebecca pulled her cell phone from her pocket and was about to speed dial her husband, John, when the second stretcher rolled up beside her. A weak hand reached from beneath the sheet and grabbed her wrist.

"Hold on, Rebecca," groaned Ben Hibble. His face was pale and haggard and he too was covered in blood, although she suspected not so much of it was his.

"Doc? Oh, my God! What the hell happened out there?"

"Nasty run-in with some of the local fauna." His eyes grew distant for a moment and he shivered. "But put away your phone. She's not what you think she is."

"I think you know Patient Number Two," quipped the other paramedic. "He looks like he fell into a wood chipper, but he's in better shape than that lady. He's going to need a few stitches for these cuts but I think he'll make it."

"Sorry about your luck, Nurse Harmon," Ben groaned.

"I'll take him from here," she said. The paramedic stepped aside and she wheeled Ben's gurney down the hall and into the triage area.

"Patch me up quickly, Becky. I have to get back to her."

"Hell of a time to become a company man, Ben," she said, then shook her head. "You're in no shape to get out on the floor. You're going to focus on taking care of yourself, and I'll worry about the redhead. I plan to see her fixed up just enough so that her ass can go straight to jail."

"You don't understand," Ben said. "That woman is the most important patient that you and I will ever treat."

"What I understand, Doctor Hibble," she snapped, "is that woman was caught on camera literally throwing fire from her hands and then disappeared into thin air with that poor girl in tow. The people in this town are scared and full of questions, not the least of which concern those recent deaths and disappearances that she may be responsible for. She's dangerous and I can't simply ignore that she is right here under our noses."

"I don't want you to ignore her or forget what you saw, Becky." Ben swung his legs off the stretcher and nearly toppled over. She caught him and pushed him back to a seated position. Sweat dotted his brow and he gritted his teeth. "That woman…, our very lives depend on her pulling through. She and Angelica…."

"Angie Brighton? How is she mixed up in this?"

"She's the girl from the fundraiser. Those two women are the only hope we have of surviving what is really out there." His fingers dug into her forearm and the madness in his eyes made her blood run cold. "I've seen this creature up close, and I can only hope that they have the power to stop it, Becky."

"Ben, I'm going to get you settled and then call my husband." She pulled her wrist free and absently rubbed where he had grabbed her. She didn't know if the man was crazy or just delirious, but clearly he believed everything he told her. "John can put half the precinct down here to stand watch."

"They won't be enough," Ben said. "Cops can't stop this monster. It's a true demon. This is the beast that tore apart that poor girl a couple of weeks ago, and that was just a warm-up. I'm talking about End of Days stuff here, Becky, and it's not an exaggeration when I say that if Angelica and Anne-Marie fall, we all die. Every last one of us."

His head swayed from side to side, his breathing became more labored, and his eyes rolled back in his head. Rebecca lowered him onto the stretcher and swabbed his arm to prepare it for an IV. The wound in his side still pumped blood and the loss had caught up to him at last. Or else, he had really faced whatever hell he believed was bearing down on them. She dabbed his forehead with a clean towel and nodded to another nurse who came in with a bag of saline and hung it on the IV pole. Ben moaned weakly as the needle pierced his skin, and Rebecca held his arm steady until the nurse had finished.

"Get some rest, Doc," she said softly. "Neither you nor the redhead are going anywhere soon. There's enough time to share what you know about her."

"The...wolf...Anne-Marie...Carmichael...Witch of... Pioneer Vale..." he mumbled before he finally lost consciousness and lay still.

There was that old family name again. The same one that the Brighton's farm was named after. Ben had brought it up the other day and now that he had said Angelica was involved, it connected enough dots that it couldn't just be a coincidence. Rebecca frowned then reached out and gave the doctor's hand a gentle squeeze. She pulled her cell phone from her pocket once more and gently tapped it against her chin.

"Where do we put him, Becky?" asked the other nurse. She released the brakes on the gurney and took hold of the bed handles.

"Take him down to Exam 4," she said. "Doc Hibble can be an ass, but he's still one of ours so let's take good care of him." The nurse pushed the bed down the hall, and Rebecca looked at her phone again. Before she could dial John's number, the main entry door swished open at the end of the hall and a sudden chill gave her goose bumps. Her heart sank when she saw the ragtag group that stumbled into the ER lobby.

"Dear God, not them too," she muttered. She jogged towards the doors and waved at a young intern. "I need some help over here, now."

Will Brighton had his arms wrapped protectively around Kim and Jamie stalwartly shielding them from some unknown threat. Clarissa Brenner clung to his arm while the former soldier led the battered group towards the waiting room seats. Though he stood tall and straight like always, when he looked up at her, his haggard face and bleary eyes told her just how rattled he was.

The others were in even worse shape. Their faces and clothes were smeared with blood and ash. Kim's eyes were distant and haunted as if she looked upon horrific memories that reminded her of Ben's feverish warnings. Jamie's arms were wrapped tightly around his father's waist, and the boy's face was streaked where his tears had cut through the grime on his cheeks. Clarissa searched the dark corners of the room, her head whipping back and forth, and she jumped with every crash and clatter that filled the ER.

Wordlessly, Rebecca stepped up to the huddle and guided them to some empty chairs. A flash of a weary smile flickered across Will's lips, and he eased his wife into the nearest seat. Two other nurses hurried over with blankets and draped them over the group's shoulders.

"Heather," Rebecca said to one, "I don't want my friends sitting in the lobby any longer than necessary. Find them some private rooms as quickly as you can." The young woman dashed off to see what was available while the other stayed with the Brightons, wiping their faces with a damp cloth. "Don't worry, Will. We'll get you all cleaned up and make sure there's no serious injuries."

"Thank you, Becky," Will said. The normally rich timbre of his voice was far quieter and more subdued than she was used to. Heather ran back over and nodded.

"We've got space for them, Nurse Harmon," the woman said. She had found a wheelchair and pushed it in front of her. Becky eased Kim, easily the most distraught of the group, into the seat.

"Go ahead and take them. I'll be along shortly." She knelt and wiped a streak of blood from her friend's cheek. "You can breathe now. We're safe here."

Kim's head turned slowly towards her with eyes that were clear for the first time since the family had arrived. Her neighbor looked right through her, and then slowly shook her head.

"No. We aren't," Kim said. Her voice was little more than a whisper.

The nurses led the family away, and Rebecca could only stare after them. The despair in Kim's voice had cut straight to her heart, and she felt helpless for one of the few times in her life. The growing fear around the hospital was proving contagious, and she was left uncertain of what comfort she could begin to offer to her dear friends. She hurried past the registration desk, waving off another staff member before they could distract her again. She had a call to make.

She slipped into an empty office, quickly thumbed her husband's name on her contact list, and tapped her foot as she waited for him to pick up. "Come on, John," she whispered. She was just about to hang up when the other line clicked.

"Hey, honey," he said. There was a tremble in his voice "Can I call you back? I am out at Will and Kim's farm right now and you wouldn't believe what I'm looking at."

"How bad is it?" she asked. "The Brighton's just got here a few minutes ago and they're all a wreck."

"I'm not surprised. I'm standing in a smoking crater that used to be their living room, and it sounds like they were sitting at ground zero when the thing went up. Still don't have a clue about what happened out here."

"Johnny, can you come over here to the hospital as soon as you can? You know all those really strange things that have happened around town the last couple of weeks? I think something big is brewing and it's all coming to a head. Please, John, and hurry. Maybe send a few of your guys over too."

"Jeez, Becky. Ok, sure. Let me wrap things up out here, and then I'll be right over. Baby, are you going to be alright?"

There was a lump in her throat and a chill in the air. Thunder rumbled outside the hospital, but it shook her even from this distance.

"It's probably just nerves, and all in my head. But," she said with a quiver in her voice, "it feels like I'm walking through a nightmare."

*   *   *

Anne-Marie opened her eyes and regretted it instantly. A jagged bolt of agony screamed across her stomach and ripped through every nerve. She turned to her side and retched but there was only the acidic sting of bile at the back of her throat. Cracked gray dirt reached out in all directions, and the smell of brimstone assaulted her, forcing her to dry heave once more. Black lightning flashed through the swirling red clouds of the heavens above, rekindling distant memories of her prior visit to this place that she had longed to forget.

The Realm of Nightmares.

Shade's home.

She struggled to her feet, ignoring the shrieking protests of her abdomen muscles. Her mind reeled with the flash of a piece of wood punching through the leather corset she wore, and then all had gone black. Her hand ran over her belly but found no hole. No blood. Only the staggering pain remained as a stark reminder of the terrible wound Shade had inflicted.

"Show yourself, you filthy cur," she yelled. Her voice echoed across the wasteland, and some startled carrion birds took to wing. "You have wanted me here for ages, well here I am. Let us end this feud between us once and for all."

"Do you still believe that you can defeat him after all this time?" said a dulcet voice from behind her.

Anne-Marie spun around, but the snarl on her lips faded away when she saw the young woman walking towards her. Dark brown curls framed plump but pale cheeks. The once inquisitive hazel eyes of her great-granddaughter, Phoebe, were now filled with scorn. The left side of her face was lost in shadow, but her blood-soaked bonnet betrayed the crushed bone that had caused the girl's demise so long ago. "Tell me, Grandmother. Is it sheer arrogance or blatant stupidity that yet drives you to feed your children to the wolf?"

"Begone, ghost. You are not my sweet child. Just another of Shade's painful tricks."

"Oh, you clever fool." Her dark laughter rang across the wasteland, as she glided closer. Her bloody slippers skimmed the ground and the hem of her simple homespun dress fanned out behind her. "Your deceits were far more sinister than anything the wolf ever fashioned. You convinced each of us in turn that you cared about something beyond your own ambitions."

Anne-Marie covered her mouth with a trembling hand as a ring of sparks like candle flames lit up one after another in a circle around her. Each light bore a unique color and, just as her lavender flames marked her gift, so too did each hue belie the telltale signatures of other unique magics. Each dancing ember took shape until she stood surrounded by the wraiths of her ill-fated descendants.

The Firstborn.

The shadowy figures closed around her, each one still bearing the grisly remnants of the deaths that they had succumbed to. Savage wounds still bled black ichor. Smoke still wafted from burned flesh. Muscle and bone were laid bare to the naked eye.

"We trusted you, Grandmother," said Levi. The tawny scruff of fuzz on his chin was lit by the same amber glow that had burned him alive from the inside out when she had lost him.

"You gave us hope and inspired us to stand beside you," said Brooke. Her perpetual laugh lines that adorned her lovely face were turned into a menacing scowl from the slashes that ran across her cheeks. The scars turned even more sinister when cast in the crimson light of her ambiance. "And then you abandoned us when we needed you most."

"There was no other way," Anne-Marie cried out. "Shade's corrupting influence turned you, one and all, against me."

"You dare to call yourself Guardian when you could not protect those who were most dear to you," said Mitchell, his once powerful frame now twisted and broken, ablaze in his turquoise light. "The only one you have ever saved was yourself."

"It was my duty to keep the gateway sealed. When you attacked me, I was left with no other choice but to fight for my life," she shouted back. Lavender fires erupted in her eyes. "And I'll do it again if I must."

Anne-Marie's rage blossomed, and a shroud of purple flame engulfed her with the snap of her wrists. The blaze had barely reached its peak when a bolt of agony shot through her body and dropped her back to her knees. The thud of her pulse hammered in her temples and she choked on the gout of blood that filled her throat. She trembled in the gray dust, and Phoebe's specter knelt beside her, with a savage grin on her thin lips.

"Oh, did I forget to tell you?" the girl asked. Her voice dropped to a hissing whisper. "You cling to life by the thinnest of threads in your world, Grandmother. Using your magic here will only weaken you faster at home."

Anne-Marie's fire winked out, and the crushing weight on her lungs immediately eased. She fell back on her elbow and took a deep breath but bit her lip as the circle of spirits hovered around her, threatening, yet holding their animosity in check. She shook out her coppery mane and wiped the blood from her lips. "Do you think I am afraid of death? If my life would have spared any of yours, I would have given it without a second thought."

"It was never about us," said Jennifer. "You are the collar around the wolf's neck. We were but links in the chain that bound him."

"Your war is lost, Grandmother," purred Phoebe. "It matters nothing to us anymore."

"It matters to me," Anne-Marie snarled back. "I cannot give up so easily. For too long have I suffered at that monster's hands. I have buried too many of those I love because of his schemes. I will not lose another."

"Then you will fail once more," Phoebe snorted.

"What a shame you didn't share such conviction with us in our own time," said Kathryn. "You cast us aside before we could prove ourselves in battle. What might we have done had you supported us with all of your righteous fury?"

"We would have lost." Anne-Marie shook her head and smiled sadly. "You were not the one, child. None of you possessed the strength to stand against Shade's full might."

"And so you once again hinge the fate of the world upon your latest protégé," said Christopher. "You would dangle yet another morsel before him so that her corpse in time may also be casually forgotten by you."

"I have never mourned a single one of you any less," she said wistfully. "Your final cries fill my ears every single night as I try to sleep, cursed by the knowledge that I was the cause for them. For centuries, I have shed tears in your memory. You will forever remain my lost children."

The circle of phantoms shimmered and the shadows around them deepened. One after one, the vibrant colors of their magic were replaced with the dull grayish-black of coldfire behind their pale eyes. The moans of the specters echoed like whispers in a mausoleum. At last, Phoebe chuckled and peeled the bonnet away from her head. The crimson cloth fell away and revealed the smashed bone and encrusted blood of her ruined face that glistened in the perpetual twilight of the Nightmare world.

"We are yours no longer, witch." Anne-Marie felt the deathly chill as the girl's fingertips gently caressed her cheek. She cried out when Phoebe suddenly snatched a handful of her hair and wrenched her head back.

"We are Shade's children now."

CHAPTER 2
SOMETHING WICKED - PRESENT DAY

Angelica slammed the cover shut and shoved yet another of Whisperwind's magical books away from her. The stone slab that served as the table in the cottage's pocket-dimensioned laboratory was lost beneath an ever-growing pile of mystic journals whose pages were filled with knowledge from the ether on whatever subject the reader focused. She took a long sip from the tea cup beside her, and nearly spat across the room. It was ice cold.

"How long have I been down here," she muttered. The young Guardian glanced at her watch and rubbed her burning eyes.

She had spent hours skimming histories of ancient lore ever since returning from the battle at the farm. What had started as a distraction to steal her mind away from Anne-Marie's injuries, had become a full-blown research project to try to discover some weakness about their enemies. Tales of demons and witches had adorned every page she turned. Legends and tales from foreign cultures hinted at the existence of other Guardians, and their own Demonkin, but everything she found was chalked up to folklore and myth without any real substance.

Sketches of dragons, vampires, and, she noticed with a shiver, werewolves appeared on every vellum sheet. One book had fallen open to the picture of a medieval age etching that bore the ghastly decayed visage of Shade, his unmistakable savage grin staring back at her. That particular volume had been launched across the room and now resided on the library's floor.

She stood up and stretched, enjoying the release of her muscles, before pulling another of the blank book from the shelf. When she sat back down a crackle of blue-white lightning danced across her fingertips and around the mug until steam rose from it once more.

"Give me something more than fairy tales this time. I wouldn't mind a little help here," she called. She held her breath and hoped that the Elder Guardian would appear in a burst of blinding white light and offer some supernatural insight into what she needed to do, but the chamber only flickered with the eldritch glow from the ever-burning candles that Anne-Marie had placed around the room ages ago.

The ancient being had appeared to her by the Widow Stone after the battle at the farm and had told her that the yellow crystal, the drop of the Adversary's blood that had imprisoned Shade for so long, was necessary to defeat the demon. Easier said than done, she thought to herself, since she had blasted it into dust.

She dropped the book that she carried onto the table and placed her hands on the soft leather cover. She closed her eyes and whispered, "How do I kill Shade, the Father of Nightmares." She absently bit her bottom lip and flipped it open.

The pages were blank.

"Dammit," she shouted. Lightning snapped and sizzled the air around her, and she kicked the chair away from the desk. "There's got to be a way to win. Why fight each other for thousands of years if there's no chance for victory?"

She stared into the hearth and lost herself in the dancing flames that played lazily over the logs that still looked as if they had been placed this morning although she knew Anne-Marie's magic would keep them lit without ever consuming them no matter how long they burned.

Eternally.

"I'm asking the wrong question. If Shade's a demon, then he is probably immortal," she said. She smacked herself in the forehead with the heel of her hand, grabbed the book, and closed it once more. She took a deep breath, "But that doesn't mean he can't be stopped."

"How do I defeat Shade?" she asked. This time, when she opened the cover, glittering script spread across the pages, but in sigils and runes that made no sense to her. She blew her bangs from her eyes and snorted. "Well, that's a step closer, I guess. Now if only I knew what language this was."

Angelica let her vision blur, and with a snap and twirl of her fingers, twin whorls of lightning sparked within the dark brown irises of her eyes. The runes fought against her will, but the squiggles slowly bent into English. With a satisfied smile, she began to read.

"Let our voices be raised to He whose name cannot be profaned by human lips. Praise be to the Dark Lord. Although I am but a humble servant, faithfully shall I serve as protector of this crystal entrusted to me that is His very lifeblood until I am deemed worthy of His dire blessing. May I breathe my last before the hands of the unbelievers befoul this sacred temple. The waters of life that course through this ancient valley shall run red with blood upon my Master's triumphant return. Even mighty Babylon shall quake before the approach of his terrible army."

"And thus was brown-nosing invented," Angelica joked to herself. "Pucker up, Buttercup." She sipped her tea and continued reading.

"When my time of Ascension comes," she read with a sudden shiver down her spine, *"I shall be reforged in fire and blood. Though my mortal shell shall be lost to the magic of the cosmos, I will revel in my rebirth in the image of my Sovereign. With*

wings of blackest midnight spread wide I shall send his vengeance across the world and become the Harbinger of his omnipotent will."

A pulse emanated from the book and rippled through the room. The magic candles snuffed out, and the fire in the hearth flickered and dimmed. The temperature plunged and her breath fogged in front of her. The ancient text shifted, and the words changed before her eyes. Angelica gasped as she read the next paragraph.

"Even now across the ages, I sense a heretic, watching and waiting for some indication that our dominion shall falter. Foolish child, you know not that you pave the way for the end of days and the glorious victory of my lord! Dabble in things that you know nothing about and ensure your downfall. The gateway swings wide and the invitation is cast!"

A blast of gray fire exploded from the book and hurled Angelica into the shelves if herbs and ingredients at her back. A shower of shattered glass rained down on her head and a howling gale whipped through the library's confines. Despite the wind's ferocity, the book sat undisturbed, as if the pages were held down by unseen hands. A dark mist rose from the pages and a shrill keening tore through the room. A jagged rift appeared, much like one of Anne-Marie's portals, and showered the floor with blackened ash and embers.

Angelica ignored the bruises and cuts, grabbed the edge of the table, and hauled herself back to her feet. Her hair whipped around her face, and her stomach twisted and burned. A foul miasma billowed from the hole in the air and a hollow emptiness washed over her. She peered deep into the floating void above the stone and saw a rolling sinuous movement within. The faint light gleamed off iron gray scales, and the snarl that rumbled from beyond the gateway echoed with the moans of lost souls. Slowly, two sickly yellow eyes that blazed like the hearts of dying stars opened within the depths of the swirling smoke.

Leathery wings tipped with wicked talons fanned away the drifting haze as they unfurled. Venom dripped from the tip of the beast's forked tongue, and it flickered towards her from the serpentine snout that bristled with hundreds of stiletto-like teeth. The creature beyond the veil blinked and narrowed its eyes as it became fully aware of her.

An unearthly roar shook books from the shelves and overturned the furniture that rested too close to the rift. Angelica screamed as rivulets of blood gushed from her ears and nose. Her heart thudded in her chest and every nerve was aflame with unholy fury, for this was no ruthless Demonkin that stared at her from across the dimensions.

She had awoken the Adversary itself.

The hate-filled monstrosity's eyes burned into her own, and she stood paralyzed in terror unable to tear away her gaze. A malevolent force pierced her mind, and images, or rather memories, of bloody rites conducted from across time, rifled through her darkest thoughts until the flickering images settled upon a vision of her lying upon an altar bathed in crimson and staring sightlessly up at a broken statue bearing Shade's face. Her vision exploded into a thousand shards of color as dizziness overtook her and pain beyond anything she had ever known wracked her body.

Black talons took hold of the edges of the portal, and the library trembled as the barriers crumbled between planes. The shriek of the raging wind rose into a triumphant symphony of chaos and a blackish-red glow surrounded the book on the table that grew brighter and brighter when the Adversary's snout crossed the threshold. It opened its maw and a shadowy bolt of dark fire blossomed in the creature's throat before it belched forth toward her chest.

Angelica drove her nails into the palms of her hands, barely staving off the madness that such overwhelming fear demanded of her mortal mind. By pure instinct alone, she wrapped herself in lightning to deflect the ancient power that poured through the rift. She threw herself open wide to the storm of wild magic around her, and, with her fingers spread open to the scaled snout, channeled a massive blast of blue-white fire that thundered through the gate. Arcs of electricity rolled across the creature's scales, but it pushed forward with little more than scorch marks marring the hide.

The beast roared anew and lunged his great horned head her way. In desperation, Angelica changed her target and sent the next current not at the being that loomed above her, but at the book that lay on the desk. Her magic struck the pages with a resounding clang as equal but opposite forces of ancient power collided.

The pages of the magic tome burst into flames and a whirlwind of raw force erupted upwards. Scales were ripped away from rippling muscle and left deep tears in the Adversary's flesh. Angelica took the unshaped power, and added it to her own, hurling a second bolt of lightning directly into the snarling jaws that snapped inches away from her head. The creature's tenuous grip slipped on the edge of the collapsing gateway, and she shoved with all of her will, forcing it back through the dimensional curtain which slammed shut with a deafening peal of thunder and a cloud of ash and cinders that drifted lazily to the floor.

Angelica collapsed to the ground, her body quaking and a trail of pinkish drool curling from the side of her lips. She just managed the flick of a fingertip that blanketed her in a gossamer blanket of healing energy, with faint sparks running from head to toe over her. Fragments of burned pages wafted through the air around her head and, as her consciousness fell away, a single sliver floated in front of her dwindling vision. The scintillating rainbow script upon it slowly faded into obscurity, but not before the fleeting words were emblazoned in her mind.

"...Reforged in fire and blood...."

*　　*　　*

Clarissa's eyes were open but she couldn't see a thing. The curtains had been drawn over the windows of her hospital room to help her sleep and now the only light piercing the darkness was a muted red glow that outlined the edges of the door. She slid out of the bed and whistled through her teeth as the cold tile floor bit into her bare feet. Maybe one of the nurses could find some hospital socks she could borrow. She blew into her cupped hands, rubbed them together, and hopped from one foot to the other over to the door. Clarissa fumbled for the light switch, but when she flicked it, the room remained pitch black.

"Someone forget to pay the electric bill around here?" she muttered. Uneasiness gripped the pit of her stomach, and, haltingly, she touched the door handle, but jerked back as frost spread across the metal and stung her hand. She swallowed hard, pulled the hem of her hospital gown over her fingers, and turned the latch.

A wasteland unfolded before her, painted crimson by the steady blinking of the hospital emergency lights. Papers littered the ground and chunks of drywall lay scattered across the floor. Smashed light fixtures hung askew from the ceiling while sparks rained down from exposed wiring that dangled overhead. Gurneys, IV poles, and supply carts lay tossed about, and created a mad obstacle course down the cluttered corridor. She tiptoed carefully through the debris, mindful of her bare feet. The air smelled musty, like turned earth, rather than the antiseptic aroma of a hospital, and it reminded her of the demon's cavern where Aiden had imprisoned her.

"Hello," she called out, but her voice merely echoed through the hall. The nurse's station was deserted. She wrapped her arms around her shoulders and looked up and down the corridor. Her voice caught in her throat and came out as little more than a harsh squeak. "Please. Don't leave me alone in the dark again."

"You were hardly alone, Sweetling," rumbled the shadows around her. A cascade of sparks showered over her and pierced the looming shadows for a heartbeat. Clarissa's blood ran cold at the sight of the massive silhouette that paced back and forth at the far end of the hallway. The sparks faded but the cold hellish glow of the demonic wolf's eyes still dragged the horrors of her captivity crashing back upon her. The decayed muzzle peeled back over yellowed teeth, and the low rumble became a chuckling growl. "Such a pity that our time was cut short in my shrine. However, where I merely wanted you as bait, your unblemished innocence has caught the glorious attention of one with far more grandiose designs for you.

"But, you'll still beg for death before all is said and done, though."

"No," she sobbed, squeezing her eyes shut and shaking her head. Hot tears spilled down her cheeks and she caught herself on the nurse's station counter. "No, no, no! This can't be real. How are you here?"

"The old magics impose their limitations," Shade said, "but even such safeguards falter when I would drag someone into my realm." He stepped forward and casually dragged his claws along the wall. Long gouges tore through the drywall and crumbled to sickly gray ash beneath his touch. The points of his matted ears brushed the acoustic tiles of the ceiling and the dim glow of the red emergency lighting gave him the appearance that the demon was cloaked in a corona of Hell itself.

Clarissa turned, stumbled against a supply cart, and bolted down the hall. Shade's blood-curdling howl split her head, and she staggered, nearly falling, until the heavy thud of the monster's footfalls spurred her to run faster. She grabbed the handles of a wheelchair, spinning it behind her and into his path, only to have it whistle past her head and slam into the wall.

Her bare feet skidded on the cold linoleum floor, and she whipped herself around the corner.

A wall of scale and muscle rose before her, and instead of racing to freedom, Clarissa rebounded from the massive armored body and crashed to the floor. The dim light glinted off a mouthful of iron black fangs gnashing over her head. Saliva dripped from the creature's maw, sizzling into the floor where the drops fell. Giant leathery wings unfurled and taloned hands raked furrows in the floor. A heavy tail swished beside her ear, and the low throaty growl, far deeper than Shade's rumble, rattled her teeth.

Shade slid around the corner and sauntered past her, clapping his hands together and chuckling as he walked by. He reached out and stroked the thick cords of the beast's sinuous neck, but even the fearsome creature that towered over her flinched away from his touch. The Father of Nightmares snarled and then spun back to her with blinding speed. With a heavy hand, he shoved her to the ground and the tips of his talons teasingly grazed over the skin of her stomach. Behind him, the creature rose over his shoulder, savage curiosity etched in the draconic visage.

"This isn't real," she shouted at him. Her fists glanced off of his heavily muscled arms, but her strikes were beneath the demon's notice. Shade licked his lips and leaned closer. "If this is your realm then this is nothing but a bad dream."

"But there is one beautiful, yet often overlooked, aspect to the darkest nightmares, Sweetling." The hand around her throat clenched tighter, and the maddening tickle across her belly burned with seething rage. "The most frightening among them are merely visions of horrors yet to come."

Clarissa's screams echoed through the hospital hallways when the first slice of his claws carved into her flesh.

*   *   *

Ben stood in his office and gingerly lowered a clean tee shirt over the bandages across his stomach. Everything ached, and he knew he should just sit in a bed and watch TV, but he needed to get back on the floor. He felt something more personal between him and Anne-Marie, beyond his oath as a doctor. There was some deeper inexplicable responsibility he had to keep her alive now.

A piercing shriek from down the hall shook him from his daydreaming, and he bolted from the room. He shoved past the startled staff who stood idle and threw open the door to Clarissa's room. The girl was doubled over in bed, with a second silent scream frozen upon her lips, and her bloodless knuckles tangled in the sheets. Her breath came in short agonized gasps and sweat plastered the clothes to her body.

"He's coming for us," she gasped. Convulsions overtook her body, and her eyes rolled back in her head. Ben tried to grab her wrists, but she bucked and fought against him. An errant punch to the side of his head made his ear ring. He pushed her hands down and threw his arms around her in a bear hug.

"You're ok, Clarissa," he said. He pulled her tightly, yet gently, to his chest. "It's Ben. You're safe." She struggled briefly against him but then eventually quieted down. Sobs shook her shoulders, and she hugged him back. He rocked back and forth with her as tears soaked through his shirt. She leaned away from him and wiped her eyes. The light from the hall seemed a comfort to her and he noticed she breathed a little easier, but then she shook her head.

"It isn't over yet. We're still in danger, Doctor."

Ben nodded. "I know. Your friends sent the wolf running with his tail between his legs, but he's still out there. Anne-Marie may be down for the count, but I'm on my way to take care of her, and Angelica is still looking for him."

"Not Shade," Clarissa said. She shook her head and shivered. "Something ancient. Something...worse."

"I don't even want to imagine that. Let's hope your buddy has another trick up her sleeve. We may be down a witch right now, but that girl has got some serious fight left in her." Ben ran his fingers through his hair and studied the young woman. She had folded her arms around her knees and blankly stared into what could only be the bad dreams that lingered in her thoughts. "Tell you what. Why don't I send in a nurse with something to help you sleep?"

With the way her eyes suddenly widened, he knew he had said the wrong thing.

"No, please don't," she cried out. "He'll find me again if you knock me out."

"OK, OK," Ben said. He squeezed her hands gently. Her fingers were ice cold. "I'll only leave it as a standing order if you change your mind, but let's at least get you a blanket." He quickly found one in the small linen closet in the room and wrapped it around her shoulders. The girl pulled it tight and pressed herself as far into the corner of the bed as she could manage.

"I'll see you soon, kiddo," Ben said. Clarissa said nothing, but only nodded absently. With a sigh, he left her room and gently closed the door behind him. He made his way to the nurse's station and wrote out an order for a mild sedative, but, after a moment, he balled it up and threw it into the trash can.

After all they had been through, he didn't think anything could help them sleep soundly ever again.

*   *   *

The room plunged into darkness once more as Hibble left. Clarissa shied away from the encroaching shadows as they fell across the room, but as the gloom touched her skin, a slow teasing agony crept across her stomach. With a whimper, she stumbled over to the bathroom and flipped on the light, scratching at the maddening burn that spread over her abdomen. She pulled up the edge of her shirt, and Shade's throaty laughter echoed hauntingly in the back of her mind. A fresh wave of tears rolled down her cheeks, for emblazoned on her skin she saw the demon's mark tattooed in wispy black flames.

A terrible winged dragon, coiled and ready to strike.

* * *

The pungent scent of brimstone filled his nostrils. Every muscle burned and his tongue played across the jagged edges of his broken teeth. His mouth was dry but he licked away the iron tang of blood on his lips. With a groan, Aiden Carmichael opened his eyes. He didn't need to study the crimson skies or blasted landscape to recognize the world that had been his prison for over three centuries of his unnaturally long life.

He knew the Realm of Nightmares intimately.

Aiden pushed through the myriad pains shooting through his face, ribs, and muscles. He stood slowly, wobbling at first but his growing anger turned quickly to strength. He threw back his head and screamed to the shifting sky.

"Why am I returned here?" he shouted to the void, but there was no answer. He kicked a rock and sent it skittering across the broken cobblestones. "I will not be banished again."

The shadows recoiled from his rage in silent deference, but he was seized by an unusual chill. Something lurked nearby, a presence both foreign yet familiar, and he knew that he was not alone. He scowled and turned around, as his master's throne room took shape around him from the darkness. He spit a stream of blood from his broken lips.

"Given the results of your most recent battles, you may want to save every last drop of that." A flash of lightning melted away the inky gloom and briefly illuminated Shade perched on the edge of his macabre seat of bleached bones. He casually rested his chin on his balled-up fist, and a sneer adorned what remained of his black lips. "More of yours has been spilled than of our foes."

"Do you lay this failure at my feet? You have made no greater strides than I." Aiden scoffed and waved his hands around at the swirling chaos around them. He bit his tongue before any more scathing words could slip free, for Shade's savage glare and the rumble from the demon's throat set his hair on edge. Black claws raked against the skulls that adorned the throne's armrests, and a storm of coldfire billowed around his master. A greenish-black mist enshrouded the demon, and once the fog drifted away, the dais stood empty. A heavy slap from behind drove him to his hands and knees.

"Take care to remember who serves between us." Shade dropped into a crouch, with his slavering maw mere inches from his face. His flesh stung from the demon's foul breath that blew upon him. "I am not the one whose usefulness may be outlived."

"Forgive me, master," Aiden sputtered. He dropped his eyes before the demon could interpret his own gaze as a challenge. "I did not mean to overstep my bounds. I spoke only from frustration, not disloyalty."

"Whelp." The demon rose and paced along the broken sculptures and stonework that adorned the ethereal hall. "The battle drained my magic to a point where maintaining my presence in your world so far from my temple grew difficult. I felt it prudent to fall back and let the damage we caused take its toll. We stand closer to victory than ever before."

"But the Guardians still live. I can sense them through my bloodline. Battered and faint, yes, but still vigilant. How have we advanced our position against them?" Aiden scrunched back against the dais steps as his master towered over him.

"You bowed out of the fray without witness to my final stroke of the fight." His lips pulled back in a sneer and the demon capered and pranced before him, excitedly hopping from one foot to another before howling into the sky. The echoing roar slowly gave way to thin barking laughter. "Your mother's body lies broken and her life's thread is but a gossamer strand. The hasty vow she made those long years past, now binds her to this realm and to me. Her soul is mine to torment until she draws her last breath."

"Should she recover…"

"She won't," the demon snapped. Talons grabbed the front of Aiden's shirt and lifted him from the ground. Shade paused, the smile returning once more to his lips, and then gently returned him to his feet. The black claws pretended to brush away lint or dust from his shoulders. "I have already put pieces in play to harry your wayward mother. Even now, the ghosts of your fallen relatives nip at her heels. Their constant torments shall keep her off balance long enough until she succumbs to the wounds I inflicted." The demon took a goblet from a nearby spectral servant and raised it in the air. Black ichor sloshed from the cup as he lapped it up with his tongue. He wiped his muzzle with the back of his hand, absently peeling away more of the decayed flesh from his jaw

"And while on the subject of my accursed family," Aiden said as he choked back the rising bile in his throat. He covered his disgust with a small cough. "What of my cousin? Have you designs for her end as well?"

"The last Guardian is both alone and fearful." The Father of Nightmares leaned forward and the deep rumble in his voice became a languishing purr. "Her efforts are scattered and she overextends herself in the belief that she can still protect all of those she holds dear. Thus do we have our choice of prey to strike first at her heart, and then we rend her soul."

"We have a bad habit of underestimating her," Aiden said. He tapped his fingers against his lips and then sighed. "Even you must admit that her power is unlike any that we have ever faced before. She may even be mightier than my mother. Angelica is no mere child playing at magic."

"Neither am I," Shade growled. "The girl is undisciplined and reckless. She wields her power like a sledgehammer."

"You would prefer a scalpel, then?"

"Oh, no," said Shade. A wicked smile creased his lips. "I simply swing a larger mallet."

"You lack a certain finesse, my master." He tried to stop his eye roll, but the scowl of his dark master was all too telling.

"And you lack conviction, Apprentice."

"Make no mistake," Aiden shot back. He clenched his fist and enshrouded his hand in rolling coldfire. "I want nothing less than to make that little bitch scream."

"And so you shall." Shade rose tall above him and held his arms out wide at his sides. Gray flames burst around the demon's body, fanned by an infernal tempest that rose with the wolf's simmering rage. Lightning flashed and struck the ground nearby, forcing Aiden to shield his eyes from gale and glare. Showered with grit and ash, he scrambled back on his hands and knees, and an eerie chill rattled his bones.

A living shadow rose behind the demon, dwarfing even the wolf's imposing form. Leathery wings with spined tips spread wide and tore the air with gouges of fire. The buffeting winds threw Aiden against the dais steps, while obsidian claws ripped through the cobbles and crushed the buried stones to gravel. The godlike figure's mighty tail slammed the ground and sent a shockwave rippling across the barren plain. Blood streamed from his eyes when a pillar of flame, full of power unlike anything he had ever known enveloped the Father of Nightmares. Shade's head lolled back, his tongue dangling from the corner of his toothy maw, and basked in the seething energy. Slowly, the demon turned back towards him.

"In her foolishness," Shade roared, "your cousin has awoken that which slumbered for ages past and has given us the key to her undoing. Are you worthy, Aiden Carmichael, to receive the blessing reserved for only the most faithful?"

"I will not fail you, my lord. Grant me whatever portion of your majesty you see fit and I shall finish the Guardians once and for all in your name." Aiden knelt and lifted his head to the shadowy form of the Adversary that towered above them both. With his hand over his heart, he dared to meet the dire gaze of the ancient creature. "Make me the instrument of your dreadful vengeance."

Shade stepped towards him with lips pulled back over his yellow fangs. Coldfire surged through the demon as his muscles swelled and popped under the strain of the coursing power that ran unchecked through his frame. The serpentine neck lifted to the heavens and the Adversary's roar mingled with the wolf's howl into an unbearable dissonance that burst Aiden's eardrums. Gray-black flames fanned out from the demon's outstretched hands and bathed him in primordial magic as he cowered on the ground at his master's feet.

The pain that swept over him was so intense that he couldn't even cry out. His face blistered and peeled as demonic energy ravaged his mortal body. Chunks of his flesh fell away in smoldering coals. His muscles twisted with such force that his bones snapped from the convulsions, and his shoulder blades erupted in a spray of blood as twisting protrusions punched through his skin. The liquid in his eyes boiled yet his vision saw his two masters shining like the noonday sun against a backdrop of darkest midnight. Leathery tissue slithered around his limbs and the flow of the demonic fire flickered away. Aiden writhed in pain, his frame torn apart and remade in the ebb and flow of ancient energies. His mind slowly drifted away into oblivion, but not before he heard Shade's throaty purr.

"No, my son. You shall be something far worse."

CHAPTER 3
PASSING THE TORCH - PRESENT DAY

A sliver of light from the hallway spilled over the life support machines as the hospital room door silently swung open. The relentless hums and pings muted the soft footsteps as a shadow settled over Anne-Marie's still form. Slowly, the silhouette widened, as if wings slowly spread over the unconscious woman's form, and plunged the helpless redhead's face into darkness.

Kim lowered her arms as she wrapped the blanket back around herself. Her emotions warred with one another as she studied the lines of tubes and wires that kept the woman alive after the surgery had removed the piece of wood that had pierced her ribcage. Rage and relief, hope and fear, all fought together because of this strange woman who had slipped into her life so recently. She dragged a chair over from the nearby table and sat down beside the bed.

"I don't even know what to wish for you," she said softly. "You stole my daughter from me and brought literal monsters to our doorstep, which is nothing more than charcoal and splinters now. A part of me really wants to turn these machines off."

She looked at the heart monitor and watched the jagged little twitches that were so weak that they barely registered. The oxygen pump billowed up and down. She sighed, then winced as the aches and bruises in her own body gave a grim reminder of what could have been.

"And yet if not for you, I would be the one lying there. That ...thing wanted me dead." She rubbed her eyes, still stinging from both the smoke of her destroyed farmhouse and the torrent of tears that had followed so often since then. "So what are you? Our savior or our damnation?"

"She is a candle holding back the darkness," said a soft voice from behind her. "Just as she has done for centuries."

Kim spun around and saw Angelica standing in the doorway wearing her worn gray Pioneer Vale sweatshirt. Her daughter closed the door gently behind her, lowered the hood, and shook out her black ponytail. She rushed over and threw her arms around the girl, then realized that she was holding her breath. She let it out in a relieved sob.

"Are you ok?" she whispered against Angelica's cheek.

"I should be asking you that," she replied. They held each other tightly in silence for a few heartbeats, measured out by the beeps of the machines in the room.

"Well, I'm wearing clothes bought from the hospital gift shop because what I had on was covered in blood. I've also taken two showers but still can't get rid of the lingering smell of smoke that is all that remains of our house." She held her daughter at arm's length and wiped her eyes. "But we'd all be a lot worse off if you two hadn't come along when you did."

"I brought all of this on us." Angelica's shoulders slumped. She padded over to Anne-Marie's bedside and squeezed the woman's limp fingers. "Everything that has happened to this town recently is because I let the monster out of his cage."

"Angie, don't. You can't take that guilt on yourself."

"How can I not, Mom? People are dead because of my stupidity." Her daughter blew her bangs out of her eyes. "She tried to forge me into a weapon, and instead she handed a loaded gun to a child. She tried to guide me and share her knowledge of what we were up against. Prepare me for the fight that she knew was coming. I rushed off on my own because I thought that I had everything under control when all I had to do was listen to her."

"You are young, and everyone believes they are bulletproof at your age, honey. That includes me, and I can promise you that Anne-Marie did too. We all make foolish mistakes. That's the price we pay for growing up."

"Did any of yours open a gateway that nearly unleashed a dark god from the dawn of time into your mentor's library while you were looking for ways to kill a demon?"

"Mine were probably more of a truth or dare variety," she said. Kim put her hands on her daughter's shoulders and watched the bluish sparks that crackled behind the girl's hazel eyes. "Listen to me, Angelica. I don't know squat about magic and monsters, but I have a special superpower of my own. I may be just a local girl who married a handsome farmer and raised a family that means everything to me. Same as her," she said as she jerked her thumb towards the bed, "but the one thing that she and I have in common is a mother's wisdom, so let me give you the same advice that I think she would offer you."

"Should I take notes?" Angelica asked. Her grin was infectious and Kim tousled her daughter's hair, her fingers trailing along the white streak that now ran down the right side of the girl's head.

"Always heed the advice of an older and wiser woman," she replied. "Do you remember last winter when we found that fox lurking around the chicken coop? Your dad spent days trying to trap it so we could relocate him."

Angelica laughed. "Yeah. The fox stole the bait, sprung the door, and got away. I thought Dad was going to lose it."

"He …vented a little bit when you and Jamie weren't around, but he never gave up. He took the setback in stride and reset the trap after he fixed the broken latch. We caught the little guy and turned him loose miles away from us. That's where you are now. Find a way to fix the trap."

"This one's a little more complicated than what a few bits of wire and duct tape can repair." Lost in thought, her daughter folded her hands behind her back and slowly paced beside Anne-Marie's bed. "It's a crystallized drop of blood from that same Dark God I mentioned a second ago, and I didn't just break it. I smashed it into a million pieces."

"So is there some way to get more demon blood? Maybe magically glue the pieces back together?" Angelica stopped suddenly and spun around to face her.

"Or reforge it," she whispered. Kim's breath was knocked from her as her daughter threw her arms around her neck. "Oh Mom, you might just be a genius. That damn book told me how to win after all."

"Let's pretend for a moment that I know what you are talking about," Kim groaned.

"Reforged in fire and blood. Those were the words some ancient demon worshiper wrote down. We hurt Shade at the farm, and the history of the Demonkin says that all of the monsters of legend were spawned from the blood of the Adversary."

"Which means, what, exactly?"

"If I can wound Shade in his home, a fiery hell in its own right, and soak the crystal shards in his blood then just maybe I can remake the crystal. And if I pull that off, then maybe that will seal the gateway and put him back to square one where he can't threaten the world again."

"There's a lot of 'if's' and 'maybe's' in your plan."

"Well, I was kind of hoping you might try to talk me out of it."

Kim studied her daughter's face. Her little girl was gone, her place taken by this fierce and determined young woman before her. "I'll never talk you out of doing the right thing, Angie."

"I know you wouldn't." Angelica winked at her. "I was counting on that even more."

An awkward silence hung in the room, broken only by the steady drone of the life support equipment. Finally, Kim swallowed hard and squeezed Angelica's hands gently, fighting back the quiver in her voice.

"Can you beat him? By yourself, I mean?"

"Shade's gotten so strong now, and the divider between his realm and ours is falling apart. That's why he was able to show up at the farm." She pulled away and lightly brushed her fingers over Anne-Marie's crimson-stained bandages. "I have been dragged into a war that has been raging since caveman times. In the time it took for a broken two-by-four to get thrown across our yard, thousands of years of fighting have fallen on my shoulders. I can't let anyone else that I love get caught in the crossfire again."

"Angie," Kim said, "you have a strength in you that has nothing to do with throwing lightning bolts, and you're the type who will go down swinging before you ever let anything threaten those you care about. You may not have understood what you were getting into at the time you accepted this mantle, but you wouldn't have done it lightly if you truly thought that you couldn't face whatever risks came your way. This magic isn't a curse that you have to grapple with. It's your birthright."

"So, this is my destiny? Now you really sound like her." Angelica wiped a tear from her eye. "I'm scared, Mom. This isn't like losing a track meet. There is no prize for second place here. The world can't afford for me to screw this up."

"When was finishing second ever an option with you? I've seen you suffer through all those twisted ankles, broken toes, and leg cramps and you've always gritted your teeth and pushed through the pain with everything you had to give. You have always played to win, and I couldn't be more proud of the woman you have become. The stakes are higher than you've ever dealt with before, but in your heart, you know exactly what has to be done."

"She and I were supposed to make this last stand together." Angelica pulled two crumpled wildflowers from the pocket in her sweatshirt, one of deep lavender and the other a deep blue streaked with white veins. She rolled them between her fingers and held them in the palm of her hand with the stems now intertwined. "We were going to fight side by side and slam shut the door on the Demonkin for good."

"Sometimes the parts we play aren't what we originally thought." Kim placed her hand on the unconscious woman's leg. "She's still alive, and from what I've picked up on, that allows her to hold the door shut against that creature. It may be your job, however, to turn the lock for the safety of us all."

"I should go." Angelica squeezed Anne-Marie's hand once more. Then her daughter lowered her head, but Kim knew it was not in defeat, but rather in summoning her strength. With shoulders back, sparks crackled around her curled fist, and her lips were set thin and tight. "I'm still supposed to be missing and I have some work to do before I jump into a world of living nightmares to hunt down a demonic wolf and a 350-year old homicidal warlock."

"Give them hell, sweetheart." Kim wrapped her arms around her daughter and held her tight. "Make that son of a bitch regret ever crawling out of whatever hole he came from."

"Tell Dad and Jamie that I love them," Angelica said before giving her a quick peck on the cheek. She headed to the door and pulled her hood back up over her head. "Thanks for getting my head back on straight."

"That's part of my job description, kiddo. Moms will always be there for you crazy kids when you need us most."

Angelica nodded and slipped out the door. As it swung closed, the shadows enveloped the room once more. Kim's knees buckled, and she slumped into the chair beside the bed. Trembling, she reached over and took Anne-Marie's hand.

"Just send her back to me in one piece," she whispered into the darkness.

*   *   *

"And that's when this wolf-demon-thing blew up your house?" asked John Harmon. He had rushed to the hospital after leaving Will and Kim's farm, only to find his friend staring blankly at a wall in an exam room. Becky had found the two men a private place to talk, although the conversation had remained largely one-sided except for the offhand nod or grunt from his neighbor.

They were more than just that, though. The two of them had grown up together, played football for Pioneer Vale High together, and hunted the hills around their farms together for years. After graduation, he had decided to join the local police force, while his friend had enlisted in the Marines. Now, decades later, Will was still built like a linebacker, where the last few years of sitting behind a desk had softened him up.

"You don't have to say it like I'm crazy, Johnny. I know how it sounds." Will sipped the coffee in his hand and looked up at him. "But have I ever lied to you?"

"No, of course not, buddy." He tapped his pen against the notepad absently. "It's just a hell of a tale to swallow."

"Then go talk to Kim or Jamie," Will sighed. "Ask Clarissa. They'll all tell you the same thing."

"Becky already tried for me. Your family is shell-shocked and Clarissa's an absolute basket case right now."

"That's because a prehistoric werewolf as big as my truck decided to hold a grudge match against my however-many-greats grandma on my damn front lawn!" The big farmer threw his styrofoam cup against the wall and jumped up, kicking the flimsy folding chair across the room. John's hand dropped to the taser on his belt, but Will had already stopped and held his hands out to him. "I'm sorry, John. You didn't deserve that. It's just that I've never felt so useless in my life."

"You got nothing to apologize for. You guys have been through hell today." John scratched at the stubble on his neck, a nervous habit he had developed over the years. "So let's talk about this wolf. I showed those photos you sent to me the other day of that animal carcass to my guy, Mike, over in the morgue."

"What'd he say?"

"That it wasn't one animal hunting another. It was too savage. Too deliberate."

"It was just out for blood. Killing for sport."

"Mike also said that some of those claw marks looked similar to the ones on that poor girl a couple of weeks back, as well as those two missing roughnecks we found pieces of in a dumpster a few days ago. You think your monster is behind them all?"

"Wouldn't surprise me." Will placed the chair back at the table across from him and plopped heavily into it. He ran his hand over his buzz-cut before he leaned forward to steady himself. "I saw some pretty horrifying stuff overseas. I mean downright inhumane and I shook it off. A lot of guys never could. When I saw that monster come out of the trees towards me and my boy, I damn near pissed myself."

John looked at his notes. "That's when Angie and the redhead down the hall showed up?"

"Anne-Marie. Yeah. The Witch of Pioneer Vale," Will chuckled.

"Thought all that mess was just stuff we told ourselves around the campfires when we were kids to spook each other."

"Well, pass me a s'more, my friend."

"You know, Becky's granddad was a full-blooded Native American, one of the local Nipmuc folk. He used to tell us all of these tall tales and old legends at family reunions. I do remember one about an evil spirit that took the shape of a black wolf and hunted unsuspecting children."

"Kinda sounds like your suspect."

"Yeah, but there was a good spirit too. Called it the Lady of the Forest, who watched and waited. Protected their tribe, and was supposed to have a final throw down one day with the monster."

"Anne-Marie said she has been fighting this battle for about 400 years, so that fits too."

"Well I hate to break it to you, Will, but I don't think she is going to be standing up to much of anything anytime soon."

"Which means my daughter is all alone out there chasing after this... thing."

"So let's figure out how we can offer her a little backup. Let me get some cars out on the back roads to look for this creature and his accomplice." He reached over and put his hand on Will's shoulder. "Maybe the guys at Animal Control have some suggestions on how to corner it and tranquilize it."

"I appreciate it, Johnny, and I know you mean well, but this monster isn't going to go quietly into a cage. Thinking like that is only going to get good people killed. I watched it shrug off bullets. Darts may not even sting enough to piss it off."

"OK, so what if we find Angie and bring her here? We circle the wagons at the hospital and make the monster come to us. You said she ran off after the fight. Any idea where she would hole up?"

"Yeah, but we'd never find our way there. Place is covered by granny's magic so nobody stumbles into it. We'd just walk circles in the forest until we gave up." Will stood, pulled a couple of paper napkins from a dispenser, and knelt beside his discarded coffee cup. He sopped up the spill and then tossed the mess into a nearby trash can. "I'm scared to death for her, John. Not going to sugarcoat it."

"Spitballing at you here, but what if the torch has been passed on? Could be a new sheriff in town."

"How so?"

"Well, what if Angelica is the Lady of the legend now? Destined to save us all from this demon. Do you think she has that kind of power inside of her?"

"I hope and pray she does, Johnny. Because we sure as hell don't." Will slowly shook his head. "Yesterday, I watched lightning streak from my daughter's hands just before she reached up and shattered the sky. She pulled down a hailstorm of diamonds that cut through that son of a bitch. If that's the kind of stuff those ladies can muster when they are expecting a fight, I'd hate to see how strong they are when truly desperate."

CHAPTER 4
UNCERTAIN SANCTUARY - 1671

The air trembled and folded in upon itself. With the clashing ring of a thousand mirrors shattering at once, a ragged hole of lavender flame ripped open in front of the Carmichael farmhouse. Like the lead ball firing from a musket, Anne-Marie was thrown through the tear and roughly tumbled across the grass. The fiery gateway slammed shut behind her, but the backlash of such a powerful use of magic demanded retribution.

The wash of embers and sparks from the collapsing portal stung her skin like a thousand wasps, and the recoil of arcane energy wracked every bone in her body as compensation. Her breath seized in her chest and her pulse, staggered in its rhythm, thudded in her ears. Her insides twisted and blood sprayed from her nose and mouth. However, the punishment of ancient magic paled beside the threats implied by the inferno that ravaged the barn ahead of her. Tongues of flame reached angrily into the sky and the shrillest of screams pierced the night even above the roar of the towering column.

Plumes of thick smoke rose against the pale backdrop of the moon, sinuously churning time after time into the shape of a leering wolf's head looking down at her. The demon's cold laughter rang through the back of her mind, and the air suddenly filled with the stench of rot and sulfur. The fields and farmhouse flickered amid the swirling tableau of cinders and shadow that surrounded her, replaced for the briefest moments with the rocky barren landscape of Shade's nightmarish realm. The crushing weight of an unseen predator landed heavily upon her back and drove the air from her lungs. A hot wind, like the demon's own fetid breath, blew against her cheek.

"I will not be denied, Guardian." Thick fingers grabbed her hair in a grip of iron and sharply jerked her head level with the blazing building. The razor points of deadly claws lazily teased along the skin of her neck and Shade's threatening purr hissed in her ears. "Tonight I shall rip out your heart, and bathe in the tears of your anguish. Now, watch them burn."

Flickering shadows entwined her wrists like shackles, and the scar from Shade's handprint, given to her in the vision of this moment during her trek into the Realm of Nightmares, smoldered beneath her wrist guard with gray fire. The bones of her forearm screamed in protest and her fingers curled in wrenching spasms, but, determined of purpose, a ball of lavender flame filled her hand.

"You will not take my children, you bastard," she growled. Magic mingled with fury, and the fire in her palm rolled down her arm and erupted all around her body like the wings of a phoenix reborn. The oppressive force that held her down fell away with a hollow cry, and she flipped over, blindly unleashing a dual blast of flame into the encroaching shadows. With a fading shriek the darkness melted away, but the deafening crack of breaking timbers from the barn left no time to savor her victory over the demon. Wiping a crimson smear across her cheek, she rose on unsteady legs and lumbered through the smoke towards the frantic cries of her children.

"I'm coming, boys," she shouted hoarsely, choking and blinded by the conflagration. The barn doors loomed ahead at last, held fast by an ax threaded through the red hot iron handles.

"Mama, hurry," cried Thomas. His thin wailing voice drove her forward, but so intense was the heat that even she couldn't get close enough to remove the ax. Exhaustion gave way to panic, and with a wide sweep of her arms, the crimson and orange flames licking around the edges of the door turned an angry purple. Lavender sparks scattered on the winds with every clench and twist of her fists. The sturdy oak doors creaked and hinges squealed as she wrenched the slabs from their moorings and hurled them across the yard in a blaze of slivers and cinders. Undaunted by the billowing mundane flames that drafted back through the open doorway, she charged forward, swathed in a halo of her fiery power.

Two still forms lay huddled together beside a fallen rafter while a slow shower of embers from burning hay bales rained down from the lofts above. Aiden's arm was protectively draped over Thomas, but blood from his scalp ran down the side of his head. Smoke and flame had stolen the air from the room, leaving their faces a pallid bluish-gray highlighted by the firestorm all around. She dropped beside them just as another deafening crack sent a deluge of sparks and embers from above.

The center ridge beam sagged as flames ate through the wood, and Anne-Marie knew that time was against her. She drew her shroud of purple fire tightly around them but her magic sputtered and her protective dome fell away in a flurry of sparks. Agonizing knots twisted through her, and battered from such use of her power and the blistering heat, she simply wanted to cradle her boys and lapse into unconsciousness beside them.

The faintest twitch of a tiny hand in her own dragged her back to her senses, and she scooped her children into her arms. Though only a dozen feet separated them from the wide doorway of the barn, the distance might as well be miles away with the fiery debris all around. She tried to rip open another doorway in the air, but she lacked the strength to shred the fabric of the world again. More likely, her magic would tear her apart before letting her cross the space ahead. She laughed at the bitter irony, for here she sat, a mistress of fire magic about to die by the very flames that, with the flick of her fingers she could create.

Or suppress.

The Elder's Whisper thrummed in her head and visions of Henna's earliest lessons flooded her thoughts, where her first mishaps had nearly set Whisperwind alight. Her mentor had taught that she could not only ignite flames with the magic at her disposal but could just as easily quench them, and with far less strain on her body. She ignored the groaning timbers overhead and threw herself open to the swirling eddies of power around her. Mystic energy coursed through her once more and she shaped the magic to her bidding.

The ferocity of the natural fires fought back against her, but her eyes blazed with lavender might, and the amethyst pendant around her neck flashed with a brilliance of its own. The surrounding flames wavered, flickered, and then fell away, quenching the pathway out to little more than glowing coals and embers. With steps unsteady and faltering, she grabbed her boys by their shirt collars and dragged them outside. The cooler air was a welcome reprieve and she found strength enough to reach the corner of the farmhouse's front porch before she dropped to her knees and crumpled face down into the dirt.

With her magic released, the inferno that she had held back surged skyward again with a roar of primal fury. The last rafters of the barn gave way and the high peaked roof collapsed under its own weight while a column of flame and sparks lit up the night sky. The backwash of heat buffeted her, and Anne-Marie lifted her tear-filled eyes in time to watch the oak walls fold inward upon themselves. Fond memories of her husband and his father, Alistair, building the barn blew away on clouds of black smoke, but it was a small loss compared to what might have been. From beneath the protective sprawl of her arms, Thomas and Aiden both stirred and coughed as fresh air filled their lungs once more.

"Oh, thank God," Anne-Marie gasped. Her voice was choked with blood and ash, but she showered each of their heads with kisses. She hugged them tightly to her breast and fought back the sobs that welled up within her. Thomas let out a squalling cry, but Aiden merely squeezed her hand and stared into the flames.

"Mama," her oldest said softly, "it was that bad man from town with the eye patch. He kicked open our door and took us to the barn. I tried to fight back but he was too strong for me." Although she could barely hear his voice, the iciness in his tone was deafening. Despite the sweltering conflagration so close to them, Anne-Marie shivered.

"He's gone now, Aiden," she said. Shade's vision had shown her a rider leaving the scene in that horrific dreamscape, and her son's words confirmed that he could only have been Patch Erickson. Preston's brutish henchman had already murdered her husband, and nearly her children, but justice for them would have to wait a little longer. "And we should be away as well."

"Are we still in danger, Mama?" asked Thomas. He threw his trembling arms around her neck. She cupped his chin and kissed his forehead.

"I will not lie to either one of you. Yes. There are those who have ill intentions towards our family, but I will do everything...," she paused as the implications of her next words hit her, "within my power to protect all of those I love."

She wrangled Thomas onto her hip and groaned as she stood up. Every muscle ached and streaks of crusted blood ran from her nose, her lips, and her ears. She took one final glance at the ruined barn and shook her head sadly. Aiden's small fingers took her hand, and her shoulders quaked, but she had no more tears to shed.

"Come along, boys," she said. "I know of a place where the bad men will never find us."

"But, Mama, our home?" sniffed Aiden.

"Our home will still be here for us when the sun rises anew. When things have settled once more, and all the dangers are past, we will rebuild all that was torn apart. Now, follow me closely. We've a bit of a walk ahead of us."

She whispered a silent thanks to the Elder Guardian and wondered for a brief moment if there was a significance to upsetting the intended outcome of Shade's nightmare. With the dancing flames at their backs lighting the path ahead, she led her children, the most precious treasure left to her name, into the protective shelter of the ancient forest.

*   *   *

"The pathway behind the falls can be slippery," said Kitchi. He stepped behind the deafening curtain of water with surefooted precision and glanced over his shoulder at Henna. "Mind your step."

"Ye've others far more important than I to concern yerself with, lad," said the old woman with a chuckle. "Just hold that torch steady as we go and Old Henna will do just fine."

"Could your powers not light the way and dry the path ahead of us?"

"Aye, it surely could, but I hold back," she replied in a hushed whisper, "for them." The old woman pointed a gnarled finger and drew his eagle-eyed attention to the huddled and shivering shapes in the cave ahead. "Your people bear enough scars after today's events. The last thing they need is an old forest witch strolling in all aswirl with green motes of magic."

Two shadows broke from the assembly, one a massive hulking shape, the other lithe and winsome. Kitchi's torchlight first washed over Chogan, an older bear of a man who clutched a thick war club adorned with sharpened antlers in his still bloodstained hands. He had been a protector of their people since Kitchi was a child, but the streaks of gray shot through his hair, had taken no toll on his heavily muscled frame, nor did the thick bandage wrapped around his upper arm soften his fierce countenance.

"Hold your swing, Chogan, my friend," called Kitchi. "I haven't enough fight left in me today to defend myself."

"Kitchi, is that you?" The big warrior paused and lowered his club. He clasped Kitchi's forearm tightly. "Thank the Great Spirit that you survived."

"I was lucky today. How many others have made their way here?" Before his friend could answer, the smaller figure rushed up to him and caught him in a tight embrace.

"Kitchi!" cried a melodious voice. Hot tears splashed against his bare chest. "I thought I'd never see you again."

"Alawa," he cried out and returned her hug with equal strength. He looked deeply into her doe eyes and smiled. Gone was the shy girl he had grown up beside, replaced instead by this proud and strong young woman. Without thinking, he pulled her close and kissed her. "I am so relieved that you are safe."

"Not to dampen such a fond reunion," Henna said and gently cleared her throat, "but we've wounded to tend and plans to make. Chogan, yer leader asked a question. How many able bodies survived the raid on your village?"

"I do not answer to outsiders, crone. Who are you to question me?" the warrior asked. He puffed his chest out and stepped toward the old witch. "Has Chieftain's Son brought us a second prisoner?"

Kitchi reached out to keep his warrior friend in check, but Henna stopped the man in his tracks with the flick of her wrist and the point of the steel dagger she carried in the leather bracer she wore on her forearm. The blade dimpled the skin of the man's bare belly and Chogan froze.

"I saw ye take some of yer first steps, little Blackbird. I'd prefer not to be the cause of your last ones."

Alawa stepped between the two and gently pushed the knife blade away with two fingers. "Please, old one. We've already seen more than enough blood today."

"I have not been called that name since I was a boy, and there was only one outsider who ever knew it. A fierce warrior maiden with hair of honey wheat, and eyes of blue steel."

"Good to see you again too, lad." Henna lifted the knife and waggled the handle before him, the carving and decorative workmanship a trademark of the Nipmuc people. "You're tribe and my own folk once shared a long history, and this won't be the first time I've fought beside ye. I dare say that I'm as akin to you as any outsider could be."

"Then I welcome you with what little hospitality we can offer," said Alawa with a bow.

"What's this about a prisoner?" asked Kitchi.

Chogan stepped back from the tiny woman with a respectful nod and then turned to him. "We found one of the raiders wandering nearby and captured him."

"He surrendered himself," Alawa corrected and the big warrior scowled at her.

"None can understand his speech to get any information. I would have ended his life already, but some here," he said with a sidelong glance to Alawa, "do not believe he is of the men who assaulted our village."

"He does not wear the uniform of those who attacked us," said Alawa. She crossed her arms over her chest and lifted her chin to the warrior.

"Throwing a sheepskin over a wolf doesn't make it less dangerous," Chogan replied. Henna's knife slipped from her fingers and clattered to the stone. Kitchi picked it up, and handed it back to her, certain that the shock on her face mirrored his own.

"I would speak with this man before we strike any blows. Please, my friend. Lead me to him." Chogan nodded then headed into the darker depths of the cavern. With a wave of his hand, Kitchi beckoned Alawa and Henna to follow along after him.

Scared eyes found Kitchi's own, as dirty faces streaked by the tracks of running tears watched him. He squeezed every beseeching hand that reached towards him, and he gave whatever shallow comfort he could offer to his people. Sadly, though, there were far fewer hiding in the cavern than he had hoped to see

"He is here," said Chogan as they entered a second chamber and waved him forward to where an old, balding man in the simple clothes of the local farmers sat with hands tied behind his back. Kitchi knelt beside him and motioned Henna closer with a nod of his head. He studied the man before him and noted how the stranger's eyes were full of hope and determination rather than fear.

"Will he understand my words?" he whispered.

"I should probably widen the range," muttered Henna. Chogan and Alawa had edged closer to the small group. "We've other ears about that will want answers and I don't feel like repeating every blasted word ye two trade." Her eyes sparkled like emeralds and Kitchi felt a familiar prickling of his skin.

"I am called Kitchi," he said in a low voice, "and these few people here are all that survived today's attack on my village. I ask you to speak plainly to me, for although I wish you no harm, your life may depend on your next words." He pulled a strip of cloth from the man's mouth and reached for a water skin that sat nearby. "Your face is familiar to me. You are one of the local farmers?"

"Aye. Name's Abel Harmon." The old man drank deeply from the proffered skin. "Thank you."

"You've known our language this whole time?" roared Chogan. "I knew you were not to be trusted. How many of my friends did you slaughter today during your raid?"

"Be still, Chogan," said Kitchi sternly. "We will decide this man's fate once we know the truth of who he is."

"Harmon?" asked Henna. "You are one of Anne-Marie's friends?"

"That I am. Friend and neighbor," he said. The old man puffed his chest out defiantly and glared at the brawny Nipmuc warrior who still brandished his war club. "And should any of you stand otherwise, then be glad these cords bind my hands."

Henna rolled her eyes. "You foolish men and yer idle threats," she muttered. "The lass is my...student. If ye are who ye claim then ye know of what I speak." The farmer's eyes grew wide for a moment, and Kitchi smiled.

"Aye, so you pull from a similar bag of tricks." The old man nodded towards him. "Guess that explains how we understand one another then. I thought perhaps your people had been visited by one of our missionaries."

"Our village was visited some time ago, but we found their teachings and our own Great Spirit held many of the same truths. We decided to hold to our ways and let the Elders provide when needed." Kitchi jerked his thumb towards Henna. "They often guide us on the most prudent courses of action."

"Indeed they do," said Abel with a bow of his head to the woman.

"But what brings you alone and so deeply into our woods, Abel Harmon?" Kitchi continued. "Your safety in our territory has never been guaranteed even under the best of times."

"I had hopes of keeping your people from making a grave mistake. I heard the drums of war," the farmer said, "but the attack on your folk was meant only to draw you into a battle that the Nipmuc are ill-equipped to fight. Your retaliation will only give those who orchestrated the assault the justification and support they currently lack to finish the job."

"Why attack us in the first place?" asked Alawa. "We are a peaceful people and have done nothing to provoke such hostility."

"It shames me to say that there are those among us who seek only wealth and power and bargains have been struck to take your lands by force." Abel lowered his head and looked at the stone floor.

"Mathers," scoffed Henna. "That scoundrel has wealth enough to last him, yet still he opens his door to a hellfire that he understands precious little about. Stealing away a few acres of land will be the least of our troubles, mark my words."

"So what would you have us do, Abel Harmon?" Kitchi drew a small knife and cut through the man's bonds. The old farmer smiled and rubbed the chafed skin of his wrists. "We are too few to fight even the small force of soldiers that attacked us today, but I do not wish to surrender our homes to these marauders and flee."

"Nor should you. Reach out to the neighboring tribes and convince them that they too will be butchered by these same men who attacked your folk if they don't stand together against them."

"The neighboring tribes are not likely to just take in those of us who survived the attack." Kitchi sheathed his knife and scratched his chin thoughtfully. "We may all be of the Nipmuc nation but that only grants an uneasy truce. There are some who would be quick to finish the job that those soldiers began today."

"And why do you care about our people?" growled Chogan. "You encroach on our lands but now seek now to extend your hand in friendship?"

"I served in an army many years ago across the great sea." The man lowered his eyes. "I have seen things, done things, in my life that have caused the same expressions that are etched into the faces of your people now."

"You are a soldier, but one who does not enjoy the fight," Henna said softly. It was a statement, rather than a question.

"I would spare as many from further bloodshed as I may. I can no longer stand idly by. We must find allies against the darkness."

"Then I will lead you to them," said Kitchi. "Perhaps together, you and I may rally our neighbors to stand beside us against the ones who attacked us." He shrugged. "Or else we will have our backsides dotted with arrows."

"Either way, at least I will know that we tried to make amends for what happened to your people today." The farmer turned to Henna. "Anne-Marie has other friends in town that we should let know what we are about. They are resourceful folk and may have means at hand to help us from inside the town walls."

"Leave that to me," offered Henna. "I've ways to pass along messages that no watchman could even suspect."

"Then we are decided," said Kitchi. "Allow me a short time to attend to my people here and then we can be away once more."

"You've only just arrived, and are leaving us again," said Alawa. Her lips trembled and he took her hand.

"One day all of our fiercest warriors will not be able to drag me from your side, but there are greater dangers that I cannot ignore for now."

Henna cleared her throat. "Rest easy, lass. I shall stay behind and help how I can. Ye don't get as old as I am without learning a few tricks along the way."

"We trade two warriors for an old woman," snorted Chogan.

Henna flicked her wrist and her flashing dagger zipped within a hair's breadth from the big man's brow. It struck the center of a dream catcher that had hung over the sleeping area. The sentry jumped, but the older woman merely pointed at the quivering blade in the lazily spinning target.

"Ye should graciously accept whatever help ye can find, my friend. The Black Wolf does not sit patiently, and you'll need more than a few arts and crafts to ward off the real nightmares that come with his rise.

"Woe to us all should the beast recruit even more dangerous allies to his cause before we are prepared."

*　　*　　*

Patch's horse trotted along the road that ran between the outlying farms and the town. The light of the Carmichael's burning barn still climbed into the night sky behind him, and a grim smile crept to his face. Something in the back of his mind murmured that his actions today had been met with some sinister approval.

The peak known as Alistair's Climb rose like a fist into the night sky standing in silent silhouette before the full moon. The main road forked into a side trail that led up the side of the mountain, but was soon swallowed by the overreaching trees. Still, the hairs on the back of his neck bristled. Something lurked in the shadows there, watching him. He snatched his pistol from his belt and peered into the pitch-black forest to his right.

"Whoever you are, either step forward or turn aside," he shouted into the woods. "You'll find no easy prey here."

"Precisely why I would speak with you, Master Ericson." The deep snarling voice shook the brush and gave way to a satisfied chuckle. "I have need of a man with your certain, shall we say, moral stripe to further my ambitions."

"And I do not make deals with anyone afraid to show me his face. Step closer where I can see you." A cold breeze, fouled by the stench of carrion and brimstone, hauntingly whistled down the mountain trail between him and the stranger. His horse bucked and shook beneath him, but he clasped with his knees and kept himself seated.

"You'll hope for more than that paltry weapon should we come to blows, my friend," purred the dark shape that rose from the undergrowth. A towering shape with shoulders broader than his own stepped from the brush onto the edge of the road bathed in pale moonlight. A threadbare cloak draped the powerful frame, but Patch was entranced by the cold and gleaming eyes perched above the wolf-like creature's maggot ridden muzzle. A mouthful of razor-sharp teeth gleamed from blackened gums stretched thin over yellowed bone.

His horse reared without warning as gray flames erupted around the looming creature, and Patch was thrown from his saddle. He landed with a thud on the dirt road, the wind knocked from his lungs, and his pistol sailed from his grasp. He bolted upright when the shrill scream of his mount was suddenly cut short by a feral roar followed by a wet tearing noise. Patch rolled to one knee, and drew his knife from its sheath as the figure hunched over his lifeless horse. One taloned hand threw the cloak back from his shoulder, while the other stuffed a dripping chunk of meat into its toothy maw.

"I know you," Patch said. Slowly he regained his feet, and, for the first time in his memory, he shivered, finding his usual merciless resolve wavering before the immeasurable power that enshrouded the beast before him. "Preston has told me of you, but I thought his tales were little else than brandy-fueled delusions."

"Do you find me real enough now?" The apparition paced the edge of the road, slight hints of a snarl crossing his rancid lips whenever his feet pressed too closely to the worn trail. It leaned forward, but a barrier of gray fire sprang up against his skin as he pushed closer. He fell back into the bushes and snuffed out the embers that singed his pelt. The monster snapped his teeth at the air as if he could bite the barrier, and then rolled his cold stare back to him. "A pity that I remain confined within this terribly limited vicinity due to your benefactor's lack of urgency to my cause. As such, I must remain little more than a ...shade... of my true magnificence. You can change that."

"What would you have of me?" Patch swallowed and took a step back, confident that the creature's inability to close the distance between them would keep him safe from the gnashing teeth and rending claws.

"I would bring stronger predators to my pack. Your employer is a man of cunning, but he lacks the razor's edge that I expected. His actions, or rather lack thereof, should have allowed me an escape by now, but he has proven unfit for the task. My captors were recently within his grasp, but he tucked his tail between his legs and fled. I believe you are made of sterner stuff, and more deserving of the accolades he seeks."

"You would have me betray Preston?"

"I would have you supplant him. Remove the restraints upon me that his failures have left intact, and reap the rewards that were once promised to him."

"And all I need to do is let the hound off the leash, so to speak?" He smiled at his own joke but froze as a sinister growl rumbled from across the road.

"You would mock me with whispers of your own aspirations, Master Erickson? The folk of Pioneer Vale sees you as nothing more than Mathers' lackey, and the beast within you aches to bare its teeth." The demon extended his hand, studying the iron claws before brushing his knuckles against the fabric of his cloak. "Assist me, and together we will both forge our empires. Your rewards shall exceed your greatest... dreams."

The creature extended his hand, beckoning him to take his open palm. Patch hesitated only a moment then stepped forward, grasping the wolfish paw in his own firm handshake. He gasped as the monster's crushing grip shot a bolt of energy that ripped through his arm and ignited every nerve of his body with exquisite agony. His back arched, his chest bowed out, and Patch reveled in the unfettered strength that ran wild through his frame. He bristled with renewed vigor as all of the fatigue from the day's efforts washed away. Gray flames wrapped around him and the demon's teeth pulled back in a feral grin.

"There are lives that I would have you take in my name, Erickson. Accept my sovereignty and the power to destroy all of our enemies will be yours."

Patch met the monster's gaze, the dancing flames of hell itself gleaming in the cold embers of his eyes, and he managed to nod through the ecstasy of the might that coursed through him.

"I am yours to command."

"Of course you are." The wolf's eyes flashed and a halo of coldfire enveloped his body. A crushing force seized his chest, but the dark magic held Patch like a warm blanket. Like a living serpent, the flames slithered through his veins, and glorious rapture was replaced by wrenching pain as his muscles and bones twisted and popped. "You will all be mine, eventually."

Patch's scream echoed all the way back to town.

CHAPTER 5
HIDDEN ALLIES - 1671

Marcus Brenner skimmed once more through the short note that had mysteriously appeared on his desk. He crumpled the paper in his meaty hand and gave it a backhand toss into the fireplace where it vanished in a puff of smoke and a twinkling shower of green sparks. Someone knocked faintly at his study door, and the barkeeper rose from his chair and threw back the shot of whiskey from his private stock that he had poured.

The door creaked open and his daughter, Alison, peeked around the corner. She wrung her hands in her apron and bit her bottom lip. Her eyes darted back and forth between him and the stairs that led to the taproom. The normally boisterous atmosphere was ominously quiet.

"I don't imagine you come bearing good news, Allie," he said.

"The Reavers are returning, Papa," said the young woman. "They're covered in blood."

"And likely not enough of it their own, from what I'm told," Marcus muttered. "Take your sister and busy yourself in the back room or cellar. Probably better for you to keep out of sight of that lot. I'll take a look for myself and let you know when things are safe enough." He gently brushed past his daughter and his heavy boots thudded on the wooden stair treads that led down to the taproom of the Hirsute Huntsman.

A crowd of scowling patrons crowded around the front door and windows, barring his way. Marcus cleared his throat and a grizzled trapper clad in leather and furs looked back over his shoulder and shook his head.

"Far too many of those cutthroats made it back, if you ask me," the man growled. "What do you make of this, Marcus?"

"If only ye were as concerned with settling your overdue tab, Josiah," said a voice at Marcus' elbow. His wife, Dorothea, stood beside him with her arms crossed. Though small in stature, her commanding presence carried a tenacity that had even sent him scurrying for cover when her hackles were up. It had been said, ever so quietly and out of earshot, that if Dorothea Brenner didn't take a liking to you, wiser folk found a watering hole other than the Huntsman for their leisure. "And in something other than skunk hides, if you please."

Marcus raised an eyebrow at his wife who simply shrugged and then shoved some of the townsfolk out of her path to the front door. He patted the fur trader's shoulder and fell in behind her until they reached the front porch. The crisp evening air carried with it the unpleasant tang of iron, gunpowder, and blood.

A grim column of mercenaries rode in tight formation down the main thoroughfare of Pioneer Vale. There was no fanfare or celebration as they poured through the newly constructed town gate. Crimson sprays streaked the flanks of the men's horses and dotted the faces of the hardened soldiers. Theirs was a grisly parade, marching in solemn and terrible triumph.

"My God," Dorothea said in a horrified whisper. Her trembling hand covered her mouth. Never before had Marcus seen his wife so shaken. He wrapped his arms around her and pulled her back against his chest. "Do you think any of the Nipmuc survived?"

"Aye," Marcus said with a nod. "I have been told through some unusual channels that our wayward soldier found those that escaped in a hidden sanctuary. Already, he is working with our neighbors to gather an army that might run these brigands out of the valley."

"That's a relief. I saw Nell and their boys some few hours ago," said Dorothea. "They settled into the growing refugee camp, and she was visibly upset. Said only that Abel had rushed them all off to town and then looked like a man with a mission as they drove away."

"Good to know," said Micah Robillard, the town smith, as he climbed the stoop and stood beside them. "We'll need the Nipmuc, our militia, and a dose of good luck to stand a chance against this lot. These men are seasoned killers, one and all."

Marcus watched the townsfolk nearby and ignored the soldiers' procession. Women buried their faces in their husbands' chests, while those same sturdy men looked on in horror at the blood-spattered brigade. He turned away from the mercenaries and led his wife and their friend back into the taproom.

"I can't disagree with that," he replied as he poured mugs of ale for them all. "Sending these farmers and shopkeepers against trained soldiers would be leading lambs to a slaughter. Even if Abel returns at the vanguard of a Nipmuc war party, their weaponry won't compare with what the Reavers have at their disposal."

"I've plenty of spare parts and broken pieces that I could cobble together into serviceable weapons given enough time," Micah said. The smith scratched his head. "Hopefully, the old man knows to tell them to attack only those wearing the mercenaries' yellow livery."

"I've known Abel since before you were born," said Marcus. "Though he may stumble around here deep in his cups some nights, he ranks highly on a short list of men I would make damn certain was on my side when the fighting starts. Still, it would be nice to know that we have some firepower of our own should things go sideways and his efforts to find help fall short."

"Don't suppose you've tucked away a few big guns in an ale cask in your cellar, have you, husband?" said Dorothea as she threw back her drink. "Now'd be a grand time to fetch them."

The door to the kitchen creaked softly, and a broad smile broke through Marcus' bushy beard as a flash of coppery hair fell away from view.

"I just spotted one," he said softly. "I think there may be a little more magic on our side than we realize and it's right under our very noses."

*   *   *

Madeline Pritchard stood beneath a great oak tree away from the road where the procession passed by. The stench of blood and sweat in the air made her already delicate stomach churn and she stumbled to the cover of some nearby bushes and emptied her dinner into the foliage.

"Butchers, one and all," she muttered. "May such hellspawn burn ever after." She coughed lightly and dabbed the corners of her mouth with a handkerchief.

"Would you say the same of me?" said a voice behind her. The shadows melted away as Corbin Reynolds, the town preacher, slid from the darkness between the houses. He wrung the barrel of a pistol in his bony hands and glanced at the passing mercenaries. "Their souls are no less damned than my own."

"Corbin," she hissed. She whipped around frantically to see if anyone looked their way, but they remained unnoticed and she shoved him back into the alleyway. "You cannot come up on me unannounced like that. You risk us both with discovery."

"Oh, I suspect that my multitude of sins shall be discovered soon enough, and perhaps such confession would best serve the greater good."

He turned towards her with a wistful smile. His gaze was distant and his eyes were bloodshot. Drips of blood from a dozen scratches adorned his face and his clothes were stained with grass and dirt.

"Why does it seem that your words intend far more than our shared predicament? Whatever else you may have done, I cannot imagine you did so with any evil intent." She shivered at the bitterness and self-loathing in his laughter.

"Today, I led a good and decent man to his death. Though I did not commit the deed, my hands remain stained by his blood because I cannot help but tread upon the road of cowardice."

"Oh, Corbin," Madeline gasped, and her hand flew to her mouth. She then laid her shaking hand upon his arm. "The fault is not yours then, if another committed the crime. Even if you are somehow accomplice to the act, do you not preach to us that there is always a means for atonement?"

"Atonement?" His laugh was wild and his sunken eyes bored into her soul. He snorted and pushed her gently away. "What apology may I extend to the widow of a dead man who has already suffered unjustly by my deeds? No more than I may offer you words of comfort that might lessen the burden that my lust has inflicted upon you. Oh, there are few indeed that walk the earth that are as wretched as me, my dear."

"What guilt lies between us is not yours alone." She absently rubbed her stomach and stepped towards the faint light that pierced the alleyway. "And, besides, you will be absolved of all responsibility soon enough."

"What do you mean?"

"My husband will not risk being known as a cuckold among those he has lived beside for so long." She bit her lip and glanced again to the thoroughfare to make sure no stray eyes or ears stood close at hand. "He intends to take us away from Pioneer Vale where I may have the child without disgrace to either him or me."

"You're leaving town with him? And yet, when I asked you to run away and start a new life with me, you refused." He scoffed and shook his head. His laugh was both mocking and malevolent. "Tell me truly, Madeline. Did you ever really love me or was I merely a dalliance until your benefactor returned from his patrols?"

"How could you say such a thing to me?" Heat rose in her cheeks and she couldn't swallow. She folded her hands in front of her abdomen and looked at the fabric of her dress that clung ever-so-slightly tighter than it used to. "If you ever thought for a moment that my affection for you was uncertain, Corbin, then you brand me as nothing less than a brazen whore."

"I didn't mean that." Corbin leaned his head against her shoulder. His body shook, and her dress grew damp. "Please forgive me, but you take our child away and into the care of a man whose only virtue is an ability to provide for you that exceeds my own."

"The man who is my lawful husband," she said softly. She stroked his hair until he lifted his head again and wiped his cheeks. "This child might have been his, were it not for my feelings for you."

"Would that I had the courage to squeeze this trigger but once." Her lover tapped the barrel of the pistol against his forehead and slumped against the wall of the house at his back. He coldly regarded the weapon in his hand. "What further trouble might I spare the world with a single report of this dark instrument."

"Don't speak like that!" She slapped him and then cringed as the crack of her hand echoed in the small alley. "I could never bear the thought of even attempting to hide away such pain. I gave you my heart, Corbin, not just my body. Even should our paths never again cross, you have that for all time."

"Well, my dearest Madeline, we know not how many hours remain to each of us. Trust that should you soon enough hear the thunderous echo of a lone gunshot in the dark of night that I have at last found my misplaced courage." He slinked away into the alleyway behind them, and spared her a glance over his shoulder. "Perhaps in the end, I shall undertake at least one token gesture to make amends to all of those I have wronged in my life."

Madeline stood in shocked silence as the preacher disappeared into the shadowy twists and turns of the back streets. Left alone in the courtyard, she folded her hands and prayed softly.

"Please watch over him, and let him do nothing rash. For although we are none of us perfect, I know there is yet some role for which the world needs him."

*　　*　　*

In the dim glow of the Huntsman's cooking fire, Anne-Marie stepped forward and lowered the shawl that she had wrapped around her fiery red hair. Her clothes were streaked with ash, soot, and blood. Dark circles rimmed her green eyes and her warm smile did little to hide the lines of pain and fatigue that were etched into her face.

"Oh, thank the powers that be, girl. I was worried sick for you." Dorothea raced over to the younger woman and threw her arms around Anne-Marie's neck. The renowned cook of the Hirsute Huntsman crinkled her nose. "Ye smell like ye slept in the fireplace."

"It's been a long night," the younger woman muttered, "and sleep has yet to find me."

"Does Jeremiah know you're here?" asked Marcus and he watched the steel set of her shoulders slump. Her weary facade crumbled and tears welled up in her eyes. Her knuckles whitened as she squeezed Dorothea's hand a little tighter.

"My husband is dead."

"What?" Dorothea cried out. Marcus grabbed the edge of the table and fell heavily onto the stool beside him while Micah solemnly bowed his head.

"How did it happen?" asked the young blacksmith.

"Ericson ambushed him in the woods. He tried to disguise it as a Nipmuc attack, but he was seen in the act. His description was given to me by the witness."

"And we all know that one doesn't act on his own initiative," muttered Marcus.

"No. Mathers used him to send me a message. Strike out against those I love most and flush me from hiding. After he was finished with Jeremiah, the bastard went to our farm and trapped the boys in the barn and set it ablaze. I narrowly reached them in time." She raised her arms and waved to her clothes. "Hence the soot and smell."

"That black-hearted son of a bitch," growled Dorothea. She grabbed a cloth and dunked it in a pot of warm water, then began wiping the grime from the woman's face. Marcus rose from the stool and found an empty mug. He filled it from one of the many ale kegs in the kitchen and gently placed it in front of her. Anne-Marie nodded in silent thanks before Dorothea pushed between them and fretted over her some more. "Where are your boys now, dear?"

"They're safe. I know of a place hidden from stray eyes. They cannot be found by chance." She took a long sip from the mug and simply shrugged her shoulders. "There's a bit of old magic at work in those forests."

"Mathers has gone too far," said Micah. "We should march to his estate right now, and drag him before the town."

"Small good that would do," said Dorothea. "Mathers owns the magistrates."

"Oh, I have no thoughts of letting a court decide his fate." Anne-Marie took another drink and wiped her mouth with the back of her hand. "I intend to walk down the street wreathed in flame and burn him alive for all he has done to my family."

"Easy, lass," said Marcus. He started to reach out, but the raging glimmer of purple fire that sprang to life in the woman's eyes stayed his hand. "I would remind you that you remain a fugitive from a witch trial, and there may still be those in town who stand swayed by Preston's rumor-mongering. You'll do neither yourself nor your sons any favors should you rush off and get yourself tied to the stake."

"Shade moves closer to victory with each passing moment," she snarled back. "Every tragedy the Vale has recently seen has been part of his carefully masterminded plan to strengthen his foothold on our world. He has sown fear throughout the region with bloodshed and intimidation using Mathers as his puppet. I could take that all away from him tonight in one blast from my hand, and you would have me do nothing, Marcus?"

"I would save you from becoming the monster that some already fear you've become," he said. This time, Marcus did reach over and laid his hand on her forearm, sighing as the lavender flames sputtered and the green of her eyes slowly returned. "We know you're hurting, and ye've every right to the justice you seek, but Mathers holds the leashes of some particularly vicious hounds."

"Erickson and that cutthroat mercenary captain," Dorothea spat.

"Aye, the very same. You know it as well as any in this room that those two would tear the town apart fighting each other over an empty seat of power. Mathers is despicable and deserves every torment that you might visit upon him, but without him to restrain those men, there's no telling how many innocent heads might get cracked."

"We need a way to pull that snake's fangs," said Micah.

Marcus looked around at the faces of his dear friends and then slapped his knee. He grabbed three more mugs and filled them each in turn, offering one to his wife and one to Micah. He sipped on his own and mulled over the stampede of thoughts whirling through his mind. He stroked the braids in his long salt and peppery beard then looked into their waiting eyes.

"Your wheels are turning, husband." Dorothea scowled at the mug in front of her and crossed her arms. "Quit playing yer games and tell us what ye have in mind."

"We send them a message of our own. One so terrifying and wicked that the Reavers lose all resolve and will to fight."

"What do we have that would frighten them like that?" asked Anne-Marie.

"Why, you, of course." Marcus drained his cup and laughed at the stunned silence of his friends. "We'll turn the Witch of Pioneer Vale loose upon them."

"Didn't you just caution me against taking any direct action?" Anne-Marie arched an eyebrow.

"Against Preston, yes," he said. "I never said anything about lashing out at the mercenaries though. And besides, the true beauty of my plan asks precious little of you at all." He looked in turn to Micah and Dorothea. "You are going to leave the dirty work to your coven."

Anne-Marie stared at him with eyes wide and her mouth hanging open. After a moment's pause, she shook her head. "No, I cannot allow any of you to risk yourselves for me any more than you already have. This is not your fight."

"Like hell, it's not," Micah snorted. "Freeing Pioneer Vale from Preston's grip is as much our fight as any. If we sit idly by, he has full reign over us all and those soldiers can take whatever they want, hurt whomever they want, with impunity."

"But that is all the more reason to let me face them." She dropped her face into her hands, her voice muffled. "I cannot bear to lose any of you."

"Hush, lass," added Dorothea, holding their friend against her shoulder. "Although we can never replace what these bastards have taken from ye already, once we can get inside their heads, the battle becomes much easier for us to win."

"These men are bullies and are likely to fold when anyone pushes back too forcefully," Marcus said. "We can hit them with something unexpected and outside of their experience."

"But with my help, we could stop the Reavers in a day."

"And you'd risk tipping your hand to the wolf to what we are about," said Micah. "The true danger to us all can only be defeated by your hand."

"He's right," said Marcus. "Your job remains more difficult by far. We can square off against a bunch of hot-headed loudmouthed brutes all day long, but it falls on you to stop that beast from the mine. I saw him up close, and iron and steel won't scratch such a creature. We need your unique abilities where they matter the most."

Anne-Marie rose and turned towards the fire, folding her arms around herself. Marcus laid his hand on his wife's shoulder and stopped Dorothea from rushing to comfort her. He smiled when the young woman's shoulders squared up, the strength and resolve within her rekindled, and she looked over her shoulders, eyes aflame once more.

"Let me draw attention away from you so that you may have the freedom to work your schemes in secret, and together we shall rattle the Reavers' cage."

"We'll steal a page from your demon wolf's book and leave these thugs shaking in their boots." Dorothea smiled wickedly.

"I've some thoughts of my own as to how we can cause further unrest among these mercenaries," added Micah.

Marcus bowed his head as Anne-Marie stepped forward and warmly hugged him.

"I want you to credit whatever rumor and mishap to my name," she said to them, "for your own safety if nothing else. Let the soldiers' superstition prey upon their courage and steal away their will to fight.

"Together, we will make The Witch of Pioneer Vale a legend to be feared."

CHAPTER 6
WITH HACKLES RAISED - 1671

Brandy sloshed all across the sideboard as Preston struggled to pour himself a drink. His flight from the mine had been harrowing, and he had watched over his shoulder for the two witches so often that was fortunate not to have been knocked from his horse by a low-hanging tree bough. He threw back the snifter in one gulp and savored the slow burn down his throat. His hand steadied and he started to pour himself another round, when a hulking shadow fell across the wall. He spun around and snatched the pistol tucked into the front of his trousers.

"Hardly the warm welcome I expected, Preston," said Patch. The brawny man leaned on the doorframe with arms over his massive chest, eerily silent for one of his stature. Logs popped in the fireplace and the gloom that hovered about him melted away from his grim face. His one good eye glittered as if flames danced from within, and the angry scar that creased his visage flowed like a rivulet of blood in the firelight. There was something different about his already imposing figure tonight, as his enforcer drifted closer with a smooth, easy gait. Almost like a wolf stalking its next meal.

"Is it done?" Preston asked. He lowered the pistol and tucked it behind the decanters along the sideboard. He finished pouring the drink and held his glass out to his man. Patch took it and swirled the amber liquid around then smiled. Given how rare such an expression was, that leering grin would have been enough to justify the chill Preston felt down his spine, but the unusual gleam and sharpness of Erickson's teeth made him shiver.

"It would seem that the local Nipmuc uprising has claimed the lives of both Jeremiah Carmichael and his children," he said with a smirk. The brutish Erickson threw back the drink and laid the crystal glass down with a heavy thump. "The town should rally and strike back to avenge these poor lost souls."

"Well done," Mathers said. He folded his hands behind his back and paced thoughtfully before leaning against the edge of his desk. A single question burned within the back of his mind and he was unable to hold it back any longer. "And what of her?"

"Who? Anne-Marie?"

"Yes, that damnable woman. Did she fall as well?"

"Never saw her." Patch shrugged. "I thought you were taking care of that one."

"I had her in my sights, but was overtaken by unexpected circumstance, and my opportunity was lost." Preston shook his head and couldn't hold back the exasperated chuckle that welled up. "I sought only clear ownership of the gold that sits on her land, and yet now have I embroiled myself in a contest of wills that surpassed my estimations."

"What the hell are you talking about, Preston?"

"Deals with the devil gone awry, my boy. The forces of an even deeper darkness now stand upon my stoop." He plopped down heavily into his chair and steepled his fingers. "Oh, what delicious irony. Had I but known how truly close to the mark my scheme to discredit her had struck. For all my twists and turns, my every contingency laid forth, never was I prepared to run afoul of a true witch."

"Such is the problem with playing by the rules," Patch replied. "Need I remind you that at one time, you had that little bitch in a cage and yet still she lives to thwart your plans?"

"Cold-blooded murder would have proven detrimental to my ambitions. I can't rule over people who believe they may be executed at a whim." A strange scent, like rotten eggs in the air, caught his attention, and Patch leaned closer to him with his hands almost clawing at the wood top of his desk.

"All the more reason our mutual benefactor has asked me to do what you could not."

"Our mutual…" Preston's eyes narrowed and he leaned back in his chair. "So he has approached you as well. Am I so readily cast aside then?"

"Not at all," Patch said. His teeth flashed white in the candlelight, and the air around his frame shimmered, like the air on a hot summer's day. "The demon simply continues to recruit allies. Nonetheless, his faith in you has been shaken."

"I am cautious and take the necessary time to position my pieces upon the board, but I shall remove 'the queen' in time. Lord Shade forgets that strategic and devious planning has ever been my strong suit, just as breaking bones is yours." He rose and poked Patch in the chest to emphasize his point. "You would do well to remember who holds the leash. The wolf cannot run free without help. Perhaps you can remind him that he first required discretion before damage."

"He has waited long enough," Patch said and the big man slapped his hand away. Corded muscles twitched, tensed, and coiled like springs ready to unleash. "The difference between you and I, Preston, is that I can deliver the wolf the results he seeks. Perhaps you've gone soft?"

Preston stepped back and rubbed his hand where he had been struck. A smirk crept to his face. "And perhaps you have underestimated what this new dalliance shall truly cost you, my son."

A hoarse cry rose from outside and a flash of purple fire filled the front window. Patch pulled back the curtain and together the two of them peered out as mercenary soldiers and townsfolk alike ran amid some new brewing chaos. The man's lips pulled back in a snarl, and he jerked his knife from the sheath on his belt.

"Then why don't we find out together?"

*   *   *

Cyrus Forrester bit down on the handle of his knife and nodded. His breath hissed through his teeth as Albert Jansen, Pioneer Vale's surgeon, pushed the flint arrowhead through the other side of his thigh. He pounded his fist on the tabletop when the doctor snapped off the exposed piece of the thin shaft and slid it gently from his leg. The blade fell from his teeth with a clatter on the floor and he wiped the sweat from his brow.

"There's the hard part," scoffed Jansen. "Now, with all due respect Captain Forrester, if you fancy not walking with a limp until the end of your days, may I suggest that you leave the heroics to the more able-bodied men of your command."

Cyrus leaned forward and picked up his knife. With a deft twirl of his fingers, the razored tip touched skin and left the slightest indentation on the surgeon's throat. A thin drop of blood welled up under the point and stained the doctor's white shirt collar.

"I don't recall asking anything of you other than your professional services, sir. If you are done advising me on military matters, finish the task to which you have been summoned."

"I…I…I need only to wrap a clean bandage around it, and then I am finished," he stammered. Jansen leaned away with his hands held up beside his head.

"I can attend to that myself. Get the hell out." He slammed the point of the knife into the wooden tabletop as the doctor gathered his tools, stuffed them into his satchel, and rushed for the door. As he swung it open, he collided with the young officer who was reaching for the knob, and Jansen's bag crashed to the floor.

"Leave, oaf," shouted Cyrus. With the toe of his scuffed boot, the younger mercenary shoved the leather satchel through the doorway and shut the door after the frazzled doctor as he guided him outside. "Nate, please tell me something good."

"You should have let Levens tend you," said Lieutenant Carter as he leaned his lanky frame against the wall. "He's undoubtedly more skilled than that backwoods butcher. These simple folk are more accustomed to carving livestock than sewing them back up, I'd wager."

"I only called upon Jansen as a demonstration of my goodwill between our company and the town. I need these sheep to trust us. For now, at least." Cyrus grimaced as he tied a knot in the white linen bandage he cinched around his leg. "Besides, Levens has our own wounded to care for."

"A few bruises from bar fights, maybe," Carter said with a shrug. "Not much else going on in this town."

"How did our men fare after the Nipmuc operation?"

"I'd say you suffered among the worst of it," Carter said, nodding towards the bandage already showing a crimson bloom. "We had few serious injuries during the attack. We lost three of our own but dished that out nearly tenfold. By all accounts, that was less than half of the savages' number, but those few that escaped were mostly women and children. No concerns of retaliation from them. They've scattered into the forest rather than face us."

"I want them found," he said. The throb in his wounded leg pushed aside thoughts of mercy. Cyrus tested his weight and grunted, but was satisfied that he wouldn't be out of the action. "Send our best trackers and spread the word that I shall offer a bounty to the man who discovers their hiding place. That young upstart who shot me is most likely among them, and I want his head on a plate. I will lead the charge myself once they are located. I want you to call in our outliers."

"Already?" his second-in-command asked. "Seems a bit premature, doesn't it? Why tip our hand so soon?"

"Because I don't trust Mathers." He limped over to the window and gazed into the darkness. Shadows danced and shifted as if things just out of sight teased him with their presence. "When we first came to town, did you not feel it too? There is a wickedness about the man."

"No more unsavory than some others we have worked for in the past, Captain. What sets him apart?"

"He showed no fear of us yet he has no other means to deny us from taking every last coin to his name. Does that not seem suspect to you?"

"He has that hulking cyclops of his," said Carter. His man shifted from foot to foot, and Cyrus' lip curled up in a smirk. "I would caution you against crossing that one more so than Mathers. There's something not right about Erickson, sir."

"He is one to be wary of for certain, but in the end, he is still only a man." He pulled his knife from the table and twirled it in his fingers again, before sheathing it. "And anything made of flesh and blood can be killed. No, I believe that our benefactor has other hidden allies, and I'm not open to sharing the spoils earned from our efforts. Am I wrong to think as such?"

"No, sir. Our men deserve what we have fought and bled for."

"Precisely." Cyrus threw his arm around Carter's shoulder. "We have earned a greater share than what our meager arrangement with Preston has secured and I believe the man has wealth far beyond reckoning. Given his ambitions to become the new sovereign of these lands, I believe a show of our true strength gives us a certain leverage to renegotiate terms."

"I understand, Captain." The young officer chewed absently on his lip. "It's just that…"

"Speak your mind, Nate." Cyrus stepped away from the young officer and poured a cup of tea, handing it over to the man. "You have faithfully served under me long enough for that."

"Well, sir, it would mean the Reavers reneged on a contract." Carter stepped away from him and stared thoughtfully into the crackling fire. "We fight for profit, of course, but we've never openly turned against an employer. There are some of the men who may not feel entirely at ease with that notion."

"Yourself included, I take it?" He chuckled and poured a second cup for himself. "We have found ourselves in a country both rugged and untamed. Its people should be governed by men of that same cut, don't you think? Mathers is neither, despite whatever darkness he surrounds himself with. He doesn't deserve to rule this land if he cannot hold it without us. Bluntly stated, those who elevate him should be graced with land and titles of their own. Duke Nathaniel Carter has a nice ring, don't you think?" He sipped his tea, studying the man over the rim of his mug. His lieutenant stared at him, and then slowly nodded.

"I think I like it just fine, sir. If you believe my service is worthy of such a title, I would be honored. But what of Mathers? Do you think he would turn over authority so easily, especially if he has something else hidden up his sleeves?"

"Mathers," he scoffed. "I would guess that so long as coin flows into his pockets, he wouldn't care who tended the sheep."

"The townsfolk speak in hushed whispers against him already. They may feel they have been handed a beast of a different stripe."

"Make no mistake, Lieutenant." Cyrus set down his cup and stepped close to the officer. Carter started to step back, but his gaze held the man at rapt attention. "I will ask graciously, but I'll take what I want by force if I must. I will not shed a tear for any who stand against me, nor am I overly concerned with whose toes I tread upon."

"Understood, sir." A long silence hung between the two men before Carter eventually cleared his throat and set his mug down on the mantle. "Yours would be a reign of iron, Captain. None would dare threaten your dominion."

A sudden flash of purple light flashed through the window and the courtyard outside filled with the startled cries of his men. Cyrus drew his pistol and flung open the door. Battle-honed instincts served him well for he ducked just as a splash of lavender flame slammed against the frame beside his head.

"What fresh hell is this," he muttered. Carter pushed past him and stood shielded him from the bonfire in the middle of the makeshift garrison that writhed like a wild serpent. Violet flames spouted into the sky in a geyser of sparks and ash. A slow keening wail ripped through the chaos of scrambling soldiers and tongues of fire lashed out at any man who dared stand too close. Pistol shots rang out in the night as the mercenaries tried to ward off the encroaching flames but there was no target of substance to strike.

"Show yourself, charlatan," Cyrus shouted. He stared into the twisting flames. Twin points of blazing amethyst glared at him from within the heart of the inferno, fierce and full of rage. "I've seen such parlor tricks before."

"Heed my warning, cur, for it shall be the only one you receive," said a crackling voice that echoed from the nearby buildings. "I am Guardian here and Pioneer Vale is under my protection. Take your men and leave at once or face my fury."

"Look alive, men," he called out. Dozens of panicked eyes searched the courtyard and looked to him for guidance. The fear in his soldiers' faces spoke of desertion and mutiny without, and he would have none of it. "Whoever is behind this farce must be close at hand. Find them and bring them before me."

"You oppose me at your peril, Captain," hissed the flames. "Once your soldiers feel the wrath of my will, you shall see where their loyalties lie."

"I'll not be intimidated by flash powder and looking glasses. Begone yourself." He raised his pistol and fired his shot right between the glowing eyes. The inferno surged into the air again while tongues of violet fire lashed forth and set tents, supply crates, and camp furniture ablaze. The wind shrieked through the streets and a hot breeze raked across his face. With a final rumble, the flames spiraled into a tight ball before winking out altogether.

"What the hell did we just see, Captain?" breathed Carter at his side.

"Nothing more than someone is playing an elaborate game that would take us for gullible simpletons."

"The greater fool is the one who doubts that Pioneer Vale is plagued by a true witch, Forrester," called a voice to Cyrus' left. The shadows melted away from Mathers with the hulking Erickson in tow. "There have been developments with the enemy common to our mutual arrangements that we are need to discuss."

"Fortuitous timing, indeed, Preston." He rolled his eyes at Carter, but his man's face was riveted on the dwindling flames, Cyrus pushed aside the pain in his leg and drew himself up before the newly arrived men. "As it turns out, old man, I've got more than a few questions for you."

"Let us retire to my study, then, Captain Forrester," Mathers said. The hint of a wicked smile teased from the corners of his mouth. "But I must give fair warning that you may not like the answers I have to give."

Cyrus met the man's beady eyes and then cleared his throat. "Carter, see that the troops get these small fires out. I expect order to be restored to the camp by the time I return. I'll not have such haphazard discipline within my ranks."

"Yes, sir," the man said. He quickly holstered his pistol and stepped down from the porch. Cyrus looked at the burned circle in the dirt and then silently started to follow Preston toward his manor at the end of the road, but then paused.

"And, Lieutenant?"

"Yes, sir?"

"Remind the troops that the only permissible excuse for tremors of voice or hand is reserved for my reprisals alone."

*   *   *

"Mind yer nose, dear. You've got a bleeder."

The room spun somersaults around her as Anne-Marie pitched forward and rested her forehead on the Huntsman's kitchen worktable. Her friends all huddled close and Marcus' meaty hands steadied her by the shoulders while Dorothea handed her a handkerchief. She dabbed away the trickle from her nose and scowled at the crimson stain on the cloth. She balled it up in her fist then sighed. Her whole body ached from the enormous outpouring of magic she had used recently, but there was no help for it.

"It has begun," she said. "The common soldiers are shaken and threats of the Witch's Curse shall play hell with their minds. Their leader, however, was not so easily swayed."

"Let us do our part and we'll make a believer of him as well," said Marcus. He waggled his fingers menacingly in the air then shook with silent laughter, betrayed by the broad smile on his face. "He has never faced the likes of the dreaded coven of Pioneer Vale's witches."

"Be wary, I beg of you," she said. "I have seen into the heart of this Captain Forrester. You mustn't take him lightly. If he discovers your ties to me, he will send his soldiers against you and your families without mercy."

"Our mishaps will be discrete enough that he'll not suspect our hand in them. He'll not have the chance to move against us," said Micah. The smith bowed out his chest and put his fists on his hips. Though still a young man, years of learning his craft had forged a mighty frame, nearly as bearlike as Marcus who stood with brawny arms crossed beside him. She smiled at the sight of them.

"And, I'm certain that he would think twice before tangling with either of you two." She yawned and covered her mouth with her hand.

"You are long overdue for a nap, girl," said Dorothea. "Come upstairs and you can hide out in Allison's room until you find your second wind."

"Thank you, but I should leave. Although my boys are in a safe place, I still would rather they weren't unattended. Also, I still need to find my teacher and the Nipmuc warrior that I left behind. We will better coordinate our defenses once I locate them."

"Best be on your way then before there is too much light in the sky," Marcus said. "With the Reavers shaken up, they're likely to keep a more watchful eye for anyone creeping about." The barkeeper drained his mug and slapped it heavily on the counter.

"But may they never suspect what's about to hit them," he added.

*　　*　　*

"And just how much of that brandy have you two shared tonight?" Forrester snorted. He looked away from Preston and over at Erickson who loomed large in the shadowy corner of the study. There was something different about him tonight. Something almost feral about him as if the smile on his face was more akin to a beast baring its teeth. The brute's single eye gleamed in the flickering candlelight and he suppressed the shiver that ran down his spine. "You both truly believe this Carmichael woman is a witch?"

"Guardian," growled Patch. Preston's thug slowly circled behind the chair that Cyrus sat in. "There is a distinction."

"You may call her the Queen Mother for all I care," said Preston. A gold coin danced across his knuckles as he sat behind his desk. "You saw her devilish fires with your own eyes, Captain."

"And I've seen swindlers who can pull doves from their coat sleeves. Perhaps she lacks the stains of bird droppings upon her clothes, but I think her no less a charlatan than they were, nor do I think much of her claim as the Vale's protector." He rose from his seat and stabbed his finger against Patch's chest. A trick of the firelight illuminated Erickson's single eye with a dancing gray flame and he took a half step away from the man. "The woman dares to threaten my men and me, and we only impede our enterprise by lending credence to whatever title she gives herself."

"Our enterprise?" Deep laughter shook Mathers' belly. "You are a merely the help, Forrester. Your services end when I decide you aren't worth the gold."

"And how necessary are my services now that you have had us start a war with the Nipmuc people? Should the savages rally against your Vale folk, will your only other 'hired hand'," he said with a jerk of his thumb to

Patch, "be enough to save you from the angry mobs? My original asking price was given too cheaply."

"Your orders were to drive the Nipmuc people from the surrounding lands," Patch sneered. "Were your men too incompetent to strike fear enough to discourage retaliation?"

"Your local tribe is all but exterminated." He shot a wicked grin back at Erickson. "Their kin were not part of our deal."

"Enough," shouted Preston. The moneylender rose from his seat and paced over by the fireplace with hands folded behind his back. "We do ourselves no favors by bickering amongst ourselves. Captain Forrester, Anne-Marie Carmichael remains my concern, and you are under no obligation of our contract to engage with her. However, should the opportunity arise for you to drop her in her tracks, then, by all means, I shall see you rewarded with a handsome bonus. I shall see you rewarded for it. However, focus on securing the valley as you were contracted to do."

"Go and mind the savages. Leave the witch to us," said Patch. The bestial man took a step toward him, and Cyrus once again saw the gray flames in his gleaming eye. He tried to be as nonchalant as possible, as he spun around and took the brandy decanter from the sideboard. He pulled the stopper with his teeth and took a long swig, the jangle of his nerves lessening as the amber liquid heated his throat.

"Let me know if your sweet talk entices her to pull gold coins from your ear, rather than wherever else you are getting them from."

"I don't think you would care for what lurks in the depths of the hole where our resources are found, Captain," said Preston. "Would you dare enter the gates of Hell itself?"

"And here I thought that we were the devilish ones," Cyrus said. He cradled the bottle and leaned back, taking the weight from his throbbing leg. "Spare me your ghost stories, Mathers. I am not cowed by the prestidigitations thrown at you by a frightened young woman who has managed to escape your custody repeatedly."

A blur of movement flashed in the corner of his eye and Patch's mighty hand slammed down on his shoulder. The strength in Erickson's fingers closed with crushing force and Cyrus could hear his bones grind against one another. He reached for his pistol but the brute's other hand snapped forward and grabbed his wrist in the same vice-like grip. Preston ambled up beside him and bared his teeth in a wide grin.

"You can mock my wariness all you like, Captain." The portly man leaned forward and snatched the brandy bottle, placing it lightly on his desk. "There are things in this world beyond your experience. Up close, I have seen this woman wield her fiery magic, and in the face of powers far darker than her own whose presence she still stood undaunted by."

"Let go of me," he spat through gritted teeth. Cyrus groaned as his wrist bones ached from the unnatural chill that flowed through Erickson's hand where it gripped him.

"Patch, release him." Preston chuckled and returned to his seat. "I think we have reminded the good Captain where his loyalties should lie."

"Perhaps the Reavers could do with new leadership," said Erickson.

"They'd never serve the likes of you, Patch." Cyrus yanked his arm away and rubbed his wrist to restore the feeling lost from the man's crushing grip. On the walls behind the two men, tricks of the firelight twisted the shadows into menacing shapes. "My men are handpicked and even the lowest among their ranks I would trust with my life. I doubt they would afford you the same courtesy."

"Do as you are told, Captain, and we won't have to find out."

Cyrus grasped the cold brass knob. With a final glance over his shoulder, he said, "I hope for both your sakes that this Carmichael woman is not as fearsome as you believe her to be.

"I'd hate to hear that nothing of you was left to be found but piles of ash."

CHAPTER 7
PICKING UP THE PIECES - PRESENT DAY

The straw target exploded into flame as a bolt of lightning blasted it from the bough upon which it hung. Angelica leaped over a fallen log and nimbly dove into a tuck and roll. She sprang back to her feet and raced down the twisting forest path. Blue-white brilliance engulfed her fist and she punched a tree that leaned across the trail. Her strike blasted the mighty oak into kindling and pent-up thunder boomed from the blow. Ancient roots were torn from the ground as if the tree were no more than a dandelion being yanked from the ground by a child at play. Without breaking stride, she bolted down the forest trail without even appraising her handiwork.

She ran the practice course behind Whisperwind with renewed vigor, and bursts of her arcing magic bolstered her speed as her feet skimmed the hidden paths. She dashed from one target zone to another and unleashed precise bolts of power that shattered every obstacle along the way. The end of the course loomed ahead, while behind her the mystic nature of the forest began to heal the smoke and fire damage that had been scarred by her passage.

She burst into the final clearing and dropped to the ground, sliding through the leaves on her knees. One last effigy, specifically shaped like a snarling wolf, popped into view and Angelica threw her fists out to her sides. The heavens screamed in harmony with her primal, almost barbaric, howl. Surrounding the grove, trees shook and rocks cracked. The air around her burned in the storm of raging magic that coursed through every fiber of her body. Arcs of lightning twined around her, cradled her, and lifted her off the ground.

A blue-white pillar of raw energy blasted into the sky, weaving through the air with supple grace. The clouds gathered in the otherwise cloudless sky, rolling above the glade in anticipation of her call. When Angelica threw her fist downward, a trail of white fire sizzled behind and the angry heavens answered with a sheet of lightning lashed down from the angry heavens. The straw target was engulfed in the elemental fury and blew apart under her onslaught.

Glowing embers drifted lazily away as the savagery of nature's wrath subsided. Her feet slowly touched back to the earth, and she closed her eyes. The fading thunder drew a grim smile to her lips, and a warm breeze fanned the sweat on her brow. She blew her bangs out of her eyes and scowled at her watch.

Far too slow.

It wasn't enough that all of her targets had been hit perfectly by her uncanny aim or that the course behind her lay in smoking ruins. This was the fight of her life and nothing less than perfect form would do. Every heartbeat mattered. She needed to run faster. Think faster. Unleash her magic faster.

Faster than Shade.

A gentle fatigue settled into her muscles rather than the wracking spasms that she had expected upon unleashing so much power. No gout of blood, but only a faint trickle, ran from her nose. The white scars on her stomach, the vivid reminder of the first fight of an inexperienced girl from the High School duel against Aiden that seemed so long ago, gave merely the faintest tingle and the gut-clenching nausea that had dropped her to her knees in the past was the flutter of butterflies. Gone were the usual consequences of her magic and that could only mean one thing.

She was growing stronger.

Anne-Marie had told her this would happen as she became accustomed to her newfound abilities. Just as she had trained for the track team by running mile after mile, her magic took less of a toll on her body the more she practiced, but she had also learned that the ancient energy was far more than just a force for her to manipulate and wield. The lightning that flowed through her veins was a part of her now and marked her as a true soldier in the grander battle that the Guardians had waged for thousands of years.

She only wished she wasn't alone.

Angelica shook her head and dusted the grass from her knees. No point even going there, she thought to herself. Her grandmother had defended this corner of the world by herself for nearly 400 years and was currently in no shape to help. With Anne-Marie out of the fight, Shade and Aiden were her responsibility now. There was no one else.

The pervasive quiet of the encroaching forest drove that sentiment home. Her whole life she had been surrounded by her family, her friends, and familiar faces of the town. Now she was hidden away in this ancient place of power and presumed dead. She watched the world from the very same shadows that she expected to come alive at any moment and attack her. She was caught in the calm before a storm of unimaginable strength, but around her, the forest waited for the spark to ignite.

She brushed an errant leaf from her hair and started back along the trail that led to Whisperwind. The scents of jasmine and lavender filled the air while bees buzzed and floated in lazy little circles. Squirrels scampered and chittered nervous greetings to her. With her hand on the cottage's door latch, she closed her eyes and let the peaceful backdrop burn into her mind because she knew that she might not see it again.

The door swung open on silent hinges and the ever-present fire in the great hearth sprang up when she crossed the threshold. It crackled only for a moment in the customary sparkling purple hues that Anne-Marie was so fond of, before shifting into a distinctive blue-white flame. It was as if the old cottage was aware enough of her to say hello, grasping her signature power in greeting, but it also cast a darker thought through her mind. Did it recognize her now as its keeper?

Was she now the Witch of Pioneer Vale?

"It doesn't matter," she told herself. She didn't want to even consider those implications right now. She grabbed a broom from the kitchen pantry closet. "Bigger things to worry about."

The hearth fire danced merrily, but the warmth of the blaze was a small comfort. With a roll of her wrist and snap of her fingers, twisting arcs of lightning danced around her open palm. The faint outline of intricate runes glowed above the mantle, and they blazed with a fiery radiance under the presence of her telltale magic. Her fingertips glided over the hidden sigils and the stone wall and mantle faded away to nothingness, revealing the short hallway and spiral staircase that led deep into the extra-dimensional pocket space of Anne-Marie's own making. A second snap sent a spark darting from wick to wick along the series of candles that lined the walls in equally spaced alcoves along the descending corridor. Like a wisp leading the way, an eerie blue-white glow beckoned her to follow into the receding shadows before her.

Her descent was swift and sure-footed, despite the dizzying steepness of the winding stairs. She slowed her steps, however, when she reached the landing that branched off to the library. Ever since she arrived at Whisperwind, Anne-Marie's secret little sanctum had been a place of solace and comfort in the absence of her own home. Now, the cold memory of the Adversary's near intrusion kept her from crossing that threshold. She shuddered and continued down the spiral.

Down and down she went into the depths so far below the hearth entrance. Soon enough, the air chilled and her breath puffed out in white plumes. She stepped out onto another landing, where thick cobwebs draped like curtains around a heavy oak door at the end of the short hallway. The thick iron bands on the wood, intended to keep what lay beyond sequestered for all time, belied their heavy enchantment as a shimmering rainbow of power glimmered in the candlelight. Shadowy forms played around the edges of her sight, vanishing whenever she tried to look directly at them. Even through the stone walls, there was a malevolence inside that defied even her grandmother's power to drive from this place after so many years.

The Holding Chamber.

Her hand shook as she pulled the heavy door open. Unbidden memories of her last time here, where, in the throes of her terror, she had shattered the ancient crystal that was the single drop of blood of their ancient enemy, flooded her thoughts. Since the dawn of time when it was first spilled, the droplet had burned away at the veil that separated her world from the realms of demons, eating away at that fragile curtain like a ravenous moth. The gem was both portal and prison, a doorway that the Guardians were sworn to protect with their very lives.

And she had blasted it to bits, setting Aiden free and giving Shade the foothold into our world to enslave humanity.

She crossed the threshold and was immediately assaulted by the horrific visions and memories that Aiden had tormented her with of how the Firstborn who had come before her had met their grisly ends. Whispers hissed in her ears, and the taunts and cries of her fallen predecessors whittled away at what resolve she had left to stand here.

Angelica covered her ears and squeezed her eyes shut, but the shadows in the room dove and swooped around her. Icy fingers clutched at her wrists, tugged at her hair, and dragged the tips of talons like pinpricks along her skin. She knew, or hoped at least, that like all things that served the Father of Nightmares, these apparitions could only hurt her if she gave them power over her thoughts.

"Get away from me," she screamed. The tempest in her voice scattered the spectral beings, and she, showered the room with a fan of lightning. The cold fingers left her skin, and the encroaching shadows burned away beneath the fury of her magic. She flooded the chamber with her power and caused the ethereal torches that flickered so slightly in the wall sconces to burst forth in brilliant light that pierced even the deepest shadow of the room. When her thunder faded away, the creatures were gone.

Her sneakers crunched across the glittering floor with each step she took toward the pedestal in the center of the room. The dust and shards of the fragmented crystal were everywhere, even embedded in the stone walls. She looked at the broom in her hand and leaned it against the wall with a shake of her head.

"Don't think this is gonna do the trick," she muttered. Angelica looked around the room and raised her hand into the air. Tendrils of light raced down her arm in a scintillating gauntlet of electricity. Her head rolled back and the power spread across her entire body to enshroud her in an armor of electricity. Blue-white arcs rolled around her and as the magic attuned to her every cell, she sensed the lingering malaise within every piece of the broken crystal, like a million grains of sand scattered to the wind.

She stood in the center of a spinning maelstrom of magic that radiated throughout the chamber. Ropes of lightning combed every surface within the room and plucked shards of crystal from the floor, the rug, and every crack in the walls. Fragments drew together into a floating orb that hung lazily in front of her. When the last specks merged with the rest, Angelica pulled a battered leather pouch taken from an old armoire upstairs from her pocket and dropped the fragments of the broken gemstone inside it.

Her lightning faded away with a soft rumble of thunder in its wake. A soft keening wail began to seep from the stones and the shadows began to push once more at the edges of the candlelight. She spun on her heel and pulled the door shut behind her with a loud bang then hit the stairs two at a time back towards the magical doorway at the hearth. The flickering firelight blazed in excitement at her return, and she found herself emboldened, as if the dancing flames heralded the end of the Demonkin's menace.

It was time to cast the darkness back where it belonged.

*   *   *

Darkness and pain. That's all there was.

She dug her fingernails into the palms of her hands and bit the tip of her tongue until she tasted blood, but she couldn't tell where one agony began and the next ended. Ethereal whispers buzzed in her ears, full of promised torments yet to come. In the distance, a slow rumble, like the purring growl of some faraway beast, rose into an ear-splitting roar, and then all went silent. The chill air grew steadily warmer. The ache in every bone and muscle of her body slowly eased, and then a familiar voice called to her.

"Wake up, Annie. It's almost over."

Anne-Marie squinted into the growing light and heard the rasp of steel on a whetstone. The stars twinkled at her through the rose and violet clouds lit aflame by the setting sun. She forced herself up on one elbow, and, through the clearing fog in her head, the familiar eaves of her farmhouse rose tall and proud against the evening sky. The whetstone rasped again, and there on the porch, in his customary place on the front stoop, sat Jeremiah sharpening the edge of his hatchet. He looked up from his work and lost her in the warmth of his smile.

"Tell me this isn't a trick," she dared to breathe. She dragged herself over to him on hands and knees, and he reached down and drew her gently to her feet. She leaned against his warm chest for only a moment before she threw her arms around his neck. "Please tell me that you aren't another of Shade's torments for me to bear."

"The demon has no hold over me." He smiled, and lavender flames danced merrily in his eyes. "You're home, Annie. It's time to rest. After all this time, I'd say that you've earned it."

"I wish that were true," she sobbed while he pressed his lips to her forehead. "Angelica is still out there. She needs me."

"You have taught her everything that she needs to know. Lay aside the mantle, and let Angelica carry on the fight now. This burden is yours to bear no longer." He waved his hand towards their home, as pristine as the day they had set the last timber together. "When we built this place, it was meant for us to share forever. That time has come at last."

Anne-Marie listened to the steady drum of his heartbeat. The cornrows in the nearby field waved at her in the lazy breeze. The smell of wood smoke brought a familiar comfort to her. Languishing here with her love was everything that she wanted.

And precisely why she couldn't.

"I can't leave her to deal with Shade alone. She is more powerful and courageous than I ever was, but she is still young and headstrong. If I stand aside now, one mistake born from inexperience could cost us everything we have fought for, and I have already lost too many that I loved to this infernal war."

"I'm well aware. Was I not the first?" He pushed away from her and jumped lightly down from the porch stoop, pacing restlessly in the grass. "How much time were we cheated out of because of your duty?"

"My oath still binds me, Jeremiah," she said. She followed after him and placed her hand on his shoulder. "As long as my heart beats, I am honor-bound to fight Shade. Surely you understand that."

"And what of your bond to me? How long must you keep me waiting, Sweetli-?"

Anne-Marie stiffened as he stopped mid-sentence and a sheepish grin found his lips. She shoved him backward, hooking his ankle with her foot, and sending him to the ground with a thud.

"Ahh, to be undone by so simple a slip of the tongue." Coarse black fur sprouted across bare skin and his bones snapped and popped. Gray smoke rose from his body. When the figure's head swung around to face her, Jeremiah's handsome visage had been replaced by Shade's rotten muzzle. He shook with laughter from where he lay on his back while the farm backdrop fell away into the barren wasteland of the Realm of Nightmares once more. "To think that I nearly had you seduced into giving up."

The agony in her stomach roared back to life as Shade's illusion fell apart, and she dropped to her knees. Her teeth clenched, and pain gave way to rage as multicolored sparks sprang up from the gray mists. The leering faces of the Firstborn wraiths glared at her, but she was so focused on her nemesis that she paid them no heed.

"For 350 years I have thought of nothing except destroying you, bastard, but to see you profane my husband's face and memory is the final insult. Come along and let me spend my last breath burning your miserable hide to ash." She braced herself, ready for the exquisite anguish that the open conduit of magic would deliver, but, a boot heel stomped down onto the back of her hand.

"Silence, witch," snarled Phoebe as she twisted her foot. The bones in Anne-Marie's hand gave a sickening crunch and she pounded the ground with her other fist, but she bit back the shriek that rose in her chest. The girl's mangled visage returned to the demon who rolled back onto his feet. "You said this would break her, and we would be set free at last. Has she proven resilient beyond even your abilities?"

"She'll not last much longer," Shade purred. He knelt beside her and caressed her cheek, the tips of his claws teasing across her skin. "Why should I waste my strength when hers is waning? I wouldn't even give her another day as things stand."

Anne-Marie wrenched her face away from the monster's touch, but she feared he wasn't wrong. And while the wolf's feral smirk drove her blood to boiling, she held back. If she had any chance to assist Angelica further, she would have to make whatever magic she could summon count.

Thunder rumbled, and the wraiths stirred restlessly. They looked around the wasteland, their stares lost and distant, and then looked to their dark master expectantly. The demon stiffened and whipped his head to the sky, his eyes rolling back into his head. Lightning flashed and Shade's furry frame rippled with a momentary shudder of pain. Anne-Marie smiled.

"Angelica is moving against you back home, isn't she? And you're frightened." Her mirth was short lived for Shade lunged forward and grabbed her neck. Her feet dangled from the ground as he effortlessly hoisted her into the air. He pulled her face close to his. She choked on his rancid breath and the cold points of light in his eyes blazing with fury.

"You are not beyond the infliction of whatever torments I would throw upon you, witch. Never forget that." Shade threw her back to the ground, where she landed with a thud. She groaned, sat up, and dusted herself off with trembling hands. She then rubbed her throat and scowled. Phoebe skipped up and knelt beside her.

"She hasn't the faintest notion of what real torment is, I assure you." She leaned in and gave a quick peck on Anne-Marie's cheek with her cold bloodless lips. Her granddaughter snorted. "Lord Shade's lessons on the subject, however, have been beyond thorough. Far more enlightening than anything you ever taught to us."

"You should have paid better attention," she replied.

"Headstrong to the last," snarled the young woman's ghost. Phoebe batted her eyelashes at the Father of Nightmares, "Shall I break her other hand, now?"

"I have suffered far worse than broken fingers, child." She searched the faces of her lost children and her soul ached for only hate-filled eyes stared back at her. The anguish of each loss crashed upon her in a tidal wave of dredged-up memories that she had thought long buried. Remembrances of days when she had watched over them from afar before she had dragged them each into the war with the Demonkin. Their voices were little more now than the distant echoes of childish laughter from their innocence that was forever lost to the winds of time. "I failed you all and this monster ensnared you with his lies. And that is a pain I have lived with every day of my life."

A blast of teal light punched into her gut and rolled her along the ashen landscape. A burst of crimson fire spawned a horde of centipedes, scorpions, and spiders that crawled across her flesh. A thousand needle-like bites and pinches pierced her skin and venom wracked her muscles, but a fleeting wisp of fire raced down her body and crisped the swarm. Her head throbbed and she could only see the blurred shadows of her remaining students closing in. She tried to rise but the strength in her arms gave out and she planted her face in the dirt. Phoebe rolled her over and dropped a heavy knee into her chest.

"Oh, Grandmother, I simply cannot wait to hear you scream for mercy before we have finished with you and your little darling."

"You can't kill me here," she said. Anne-Marie groaned as she wiped the ash and blood from her lips. "I have to die in my world, remember? And I as yet remain beyond your reach. All of your taunts serve only to entice me to use my strength and weaken me further." She gave a dry bitter laugh. "As injured as I am, you are still powerless against me."

Shade pushed through the line of specters and dropped onto all fours, crouched to spring. "Rest assured that I intend to slake my thirst on your blood when your heart beats its last. And then there will be only the girl."

"You won't defeat her, wolf. Angelica is stronger than any of these children that you have forced into your service. She is more than just a witch. She's a warrior," she said with an almost feral smile of her own.

"Then she shall die by tooth and claw."

Shade's lips curled back in a vicious snarl. His taloned hand traced sigils of coldfire in the air that burned with an unholy light, but Phoebe placed a hand on his shoulder. With a growl, he whipped his head back to her.

"I've another suggestion," the wraith hissed. "When the girl arrives to fight, for we all know that she is on her way, give her a real battle."

"And what, pray tell, did you have in mind, little one?"

"Release Kenton."

Anne-Marie watched as Shade merely stared at Phoebe, slack-jawed. She searched the faces of the Firstborn, and for the first time realized that one indeed was missing. "What have you done to him? Where is my grandson?"

"What a delicious idea," howled the demon. He capered and pranced like an excited puppy, bounding away and pouncing back. "Would you like to see one of your earliest failures at play, Sweetling? I don't often let the Betrayer out, so I am sure that he is restless. And hungry. His cravings tend to be somewhat insatiable, but such was the price he chose to pay for his...talents." Shade rose to his full height, his writhing shadow blotting out the faint sunlight that struggled to show itself in this realm. "Phoebe, you have done well, my child. How can I reward you for such a chilling suggestion?"

"Let me stand beside her until the end." Anne-Marie's heart lurched in her chest when her granddaughter knelt in front of him. "I would see her face up close as the end arrives."

"I am not so rude of a host that I would leave such a distinguished guest to lie here and bleed alone. I know how your hatred for her burns almost as intensely as my own." His grating chuckle echoed throughout the wastes. "Phoebe, feel free to torture her as you will. The rest of you, come with me."

"Nothing would please me more, Lord Shade." Anne-Marie felt hot tears run down her cheeks as Phoebe's cold eyes turned her way. "I almost pity that you'll miss all the fun."

"I will taste her anguish in the air, and once you manage to rip that scream from her throat, I have little doubt that it will be loud enough that I may still hear." Anne-Marie recoiled as Shade leaned forward and his muzzle lightly brushed against her nose. She stared into those baleful eyes, her inner flames rising to match the coldfire within his gaze. "I've a few final preparations of my own to attend to, child.

"I'm expecting company soon."

*   *   *

A silver spear of moonlight pierced the canopy of leaves and bathed the quiet clearing in soft light. The towering trees stood as sentinels around the Widow Stone, keeping watch over the glossy marble slab. Something moved between the mighty pines and oaks, slipping down the worn path to finally cast a slender silhouette over the lush carpet of grass.

Angelica stepped from the shadowy trail that led back to Whisperwind and breathed in the fragrance of the wildflowers. She listened to the muted chittering of the curious woodland creatures. She could taste the faint burn of lightning in the air. The sparkle in her eyes had changed from one of childish impetuousness to that of steely determination. Gone was the whimsical girl who had been bedazzled by the recent discovery of magic. Here stood a strong and confident warrior maiden, fierce and terrible in her purpose.

Tonight there would be blood.

She had forsworn her favorite hoodie and jeans and instead wore the slick black leather jacket and white linen blouse of her Guardian battle garb. Leather pants were tucked into the tops of her sturdy boots. Her hair was held back by her navy-blue hair clip shot through with white veins, like lightning in the dark heavens above. The shock of white that streaked through her hair added to the impression that she was a living tempest raging in the night sky. On her hip, jingling with every step, rested the battered leather pouch. A dull hum vibrated against her thigh as if the gemstone suspected her intentions and knew fear. She looked up at the full moon overhead, half expecting to hear a distant howl, but only the soft chirps and hums of the forest spoke to her.

It was time. No more stalling.

With arms outstretched, the blue and black sky slowly gave way to roiling clouds of pink and purple. Flashes of lightning shot through the air and the misty patter of rain became thudding droplets, pounding out a rising tempo on the fallen leaves around the clearing. Angelica felt the hairs on the back of her neck stand up, and goose bumps ran along her arms. The might of the Elder magic coursed through her. Even with her eyes closed, she could sense the rising storm and knew that the primordial power swirling through the grove awaited her command.

The branches overhead thrashed back and forth, and dust fell away from the large rocks as the air quivered with anticipation. Even from the depths of the brush, wild creatures stared at her in reverential awe as a globe of brilliant scintillating magic surrounded her. With the next knell of thunder, the Guardian opened her eyes.

Crackles of lightning had replaced her doe brown irises while arcs of power raced through her frame. The world shuddered with every breath she took, setting the air aflame with her gathering might. Her very core burned from the rising magic. Angelica reached her hand to the heavens and grabbed the waves of energy that flowed through the skies like reins.

The thunder was deafening and with a downward slash of her fist, a massive bolt of white fire pummeled the polished marble of the Widow Stone. The slab surged and lit up as the magic from the dawn of time that rested within was summoned forth. A prismatic rainbow shimmered through the entire spectrum as the raging crescendo echoed through the valley. The voices of spirits long gone filled the air with a powerful chant that reverberated in her mind.

The Guardians of ages past sang to her in triumph.

A hole ripped wide in the air above the ancient monolith and the currents of magic around her carried Angelica towards the swirling door between worlds. Tumultuous gray-black clouds billowed on the other side in warring contrast with the vibrant flashes of the Guardian storm in her world.

"I'm coming for you," she whispered, but even she was uncertain if she spoke to Shade or Anne-Marie. She stepped forward onto a floating disc of lightning and floated through the gateway.

The portal slammed shut behind her, and the booming thunder slowly faded away to a distant rumble. The clearing of the Widow Stone fell silent once more, save only for the patter of the falling rain.

CHAPTER 8
SHADOW PUPPETS - PRESENT DAY

Anne-Marie watched Phoebe pace back and forth in front of her like a wolf sizing up its prey. Or trapped in a cage. The girl's gray eyes never left her, nor did the snarl leave her lips.

"You're as much a prisoner in this hellish place as I am, aren't you, my dear? That bastard continues to make a puppet of you."

"You were the one who pulled the strings. What choice were any of us ever given by you? It was your war to fight. Your vow. Your ...covenant." The last word echoed across the wasteland, even though there was little enough for the sound to rebound from. "I should have suspected your intentions from the moment I learned of my predecessors' endings. You imprisoned your own son and allowed Shade's dark magic to drive Kenton insane. Yet, I was the first one that you murdered yourself. Do you find it fitting that I shall be the teacher in your final moments of life to show you one last lesson on the subject of vengeance?"

Anne-Marie groaned and pushed herself away from the hard-packed ground. Gray dust fell from her skirts as she brushed herself off. She looked at her granddaughter and sadly shook her head. "I had already learned the harshest lessons before you came along, child. Aiden taught me the pain of betrayal. Kenton showed me the price of my arrogance. You were my hope that we could find a way to end the darkness. Shade knew that you posed the larger threat to him and he used his cunning to strike at you where he knew he could hurt you the most. How many nights did I soothe the nightmares that he used to prey upon your mind? Once fear was all that remained, the demon turned you against me."

"Fear was all I ever had," screamed Phoebe. A surge of coldfire flashed around her body and the wraith shoved her back a step. "I needed you! I was lost and alone after Mama died. You were all that I had left in the world once Papa didn't have time for anything other than that damnable farm."

"Your father was desolate and trying to raise four children alone. I called for you sooner than I ever intended, but I had hoped to ease the burden on all of you."

"Yet instead, you filled a naive girl's head full of fairy tales and fantasy. Told me how the magic in my blood would save the world," Phoebe sneered. The wraith spun on her heel and looked off into the bleak landscape. "I looked up to you. I wanted to be you. So strong and fierce."

"And so you are, Phoebe." She reached for the girl but Phoebe slapped her hand away. "But you turn such anger against me, when Shade remains your enemy, even now."

"The stories about you were not so ominous then. I know now that the hushed whispers of the witch in the woods failed to do you justice. Never did I see the monster before me until you bashed my head into a stone wall."

"I saw through eyes keener than your own that there was no longer a way to save you." She hung her head and shook it slowly. Sadly. "You were lost to the darkness. I fought for my life against a ferocity that was instilled by the demon's own hatred."

"Oh, and how you struck back," Phoebe growled. "Well, now it is my turn."

The wraith balled her fist, enshrouded in a gray-black mist. The girl threw out her hand with fingers splayed out, and a spray of fiery missiles flashed forward. Instinctively, Anne-Marie raised a shield of lavender flame, but searing pain flashed through her body, and her fires sputtered out. Only the first few bolts splashed against her defenses, but the two remaining streaks of dark magic punched through and slammed into her side. She staggered and her hand felt the sticky warmth of blood leaking from under the edge of her corset.

"That one wasn't in your repertoire before," she coughed.

"Lord Shade has inflicted many new tricks upon us all over the ages. Let me show you another of my personal favorites." The girl's hands twirled in a slow circle above her head and the air grew thick with a scything whirlwind of blades that spun into being around her. Razor-sharp blackened steel of all shapes and sizes whirled in an ever maddening frenzy and Anne-Marie threw herself to the ground just as Phoebe hurled the wall of knives at her. A burning line of blood opened on her shoulder and the girl's backhand swipe tore another cut along her thigh. The barrier spun faster and the blades scraped against one another in a deafening clash of steel on steel.

Anne-Marie slapped her palms together and caught the descending weaponry in a grip of magic. She howled as her guts felt torn asunder, but she buried the agony deeper and ripped apart the deadly spell. Blood spilled from her lips and sweat poured off her brow, while coldfire filled the spirit's eyes once more.

Phoebe made a swift lifting motion, raising her hands skyward. A pillar of stone erupted from the ground, and Anne-Marie, too weak to react, was launched into the air by the very bones of the realm striking out beneath her. She tumbled off the side of the jagged precipice, shaped not unlike Shade's fangs, and her teeth clacked together when her head slammed into the hard ground. She groaned and rolled over on her stomach in a futile attempt to get back to her knees.

The scuffing steps of light skipping came closer but she knew it was all for show since Phoebe's feet hovered above the ground. The girl crouched down beside her and folded her eternally blood-stained fingers in feigned innocence under her chin. The wicked curl of the girl's smile belied her charade all too clearly.

"Do you know what I remember most clearly of that night, Grandmother?" Icy fingers dug into the wound on Anne-Marie's shoulder and her granddaughter threw her over onto her back once more. "It was the look in your eyes right before you ended my life. I watched those lavender flames dance with hatred and contempt."

"Yes, you did. I cannot deny that I felt nothing in that moment but fury and disgust." Anne-Marie spat a splatter of blood into the dirt. "But none that was directed at you."

"Of course not. Let me guess. Your enmity was only for the wolf? Was I one more innocent caught in your crossfire?"

"No, my hatred was not even for him." Anne-Marie shook her head. "I loathed myself for what I knew I must do. I was left with no other choice but to give you up."

"Such unsung nobility," Phoebe said as she clucked her tongue. Raw savagery adorned the once-beautiful cheek. Her snarl, twisted even more by the torn flesh of her head and face, pulled back over her broken teeth. Her eyes smoldered with gray embers. "How many of us might have been spared had you not spent nearly four centuries trying to redeem your...firstborn? What lives might we have lived had you simply let Aiden die first? He alone survived your failure to stop the demon."

"Are you truly defeated, child?" She crossed her arms over her stomach, hiding how badly she wanted to just crumple into a ball on the ground. "You stand here threatening vengeance upon me, but what if you one and all turned against the wolf? Marshall your strength and help Angelica defeat Shade. While we cannot save you, I would pray that we could at least allow you to know peace at last."

"An untrained girl," the wraith scoffed. "You have spent less time with her than the least of us and you hold on to the hope that she will stand toe to toe against both the Father of Nightmares and your wayward son? How delightfully brutal shall her end be." She turned slowly and rose to her full height. Her arms spun in a lazy circle in front of her. Where Phoebe's magic had once surrounded her with a vibrant golden glow, it was now cold and lifeless, tinged with the gray cast of coldfire into the shade of dead autumn leaves. The dark energy sapped the vitality of the once carefree young woman and threw a baleful pallor over her features.

A pinwheel of flame slowly irised open before her to show a shadowy figure wandering along the wasteland. Anne-Marie shook her head sadly when, with the flick of her wrist, a burst of lightning revealed Angelica walking through the dark heart of Shade's realm. She reached feebly towards the window across the void.

"She's already here," she whispered.

"Come and see your protégé's last stand, Grandmother." Phoebe's eyes narrowed. "Your final moments will be spent watching your nemesis rip apart one more of your descendants. Another lamb brought to the slaughter by the Witch of Pioneer Vale. Enthralled by your honeyed words and then, in the end, left powerless and alone. Just like the rest of us."

"Angelica is nothing like the rest of you," spat Anne-Marie. "She is the warrior that we have been waiting for." She watched her student through the swirling window of flame and Phoebe sat down cross-legged in the dirt beside her. The coldfire raged behind her eyes and stole away whatever humanity the girl still possessed.

"For her sake, I hope you are right."

*   *   *

Ben gently opened the door to Anne-Marie's room but froze when he saw Rebecca scowling at the heart monitor tape in her hands. The Head Nurse glanced over at him and gave him a small shake of her head. At the redhead's bedside, a young woman wearing a volunteer's badge wiped the patient's brow and stepped back when he entered the room.

"Alright, who's in charge here," he said with a corny gangster accent. He winked at the volunteer. "You there, Candy Striper. You got a name?"

"I'm Vicky Robillard," she said with a nervous laugh. "I volunteer here a couple times a week, Doctor Hibble."

"And we're grateful to have you," he said, dropping back to his normal voice. "Why don't you take five? Go grab a cup of coffee."

"Is that alright with you, Nurse Harmon? I have a break coming up soon anyway."

"Sure, Vicky. Don't wander too far though."

"I'll stay close. Just give a shout if I can help." The young woman nodded to them both and left the room.

Ben's grin melted away. "What's the story, Becky?"

"Tape's been faint but steady all evening. Last hour has seen a lot of erratic spikes, and then the beat gets a bit weaker after each one. Like something is agitating her and leaving more damage behind. It's not looking good."

Ben took the ribbon of paper and studied it, biting his lip as he saw the feeble rhythm drawn out. He stepped over to the bedside and studied the woman's pale face. "Can I let you in on a little secret?"

"Why do I feel like I don't have a choice?"

"I'm terrified right now, Becky. If I told you what I have seen these last couple of days, you'd have me tossed in the psych ward."

"If only I had the authority, Doc." He ignored the jab.

"That...monster... out there that wants this woman dead and it will stop at nothing to make that happen. God help us if he finds his way here."

Becky raised an eyebrow at him. "You're acting weird again, Doc."

"Things feel weird. I don't know how to explain it, but something big is going down, and it all revolves around this woman and her family. Hell, maybe I am going crazy." He paused when the nurse stifled a yawn. "When does your shift end, Becky?"

"About an hour ago," she said as she looked at her watch. "My son is with some friends, and John is around here somewhere still trying to piece together what happened with the Brighton's. For the record, I don't think you're crazy, Ben. I feel it too. Something is brewing and about to blow up. It didn't seem right for me not to stick around."

"I'm grateful that you're here. Truly."

"And I think that you're still really shaken up from your injuries. Go get some rest, Doc. We've got officers on every floor, and locked steel doors that require security clearances to get past." She waggled the badge on the lanyard around her neck. "You're guy needs one of these to get on the floor, remember?"

"Yeah, but I don't think he's inclined to knock gently and wait for someone to open up."

"Stop worrying about thugs roaming the hallways," Rebecca said. "You'd have to be quite the badass to walk through a place like this uninvited."

*   *   *

The Realm of Nightmares stretched endlessly outward, recalling to mind a similar vista from her previous trip here. Angelica watched a dust devil lazily twist around before it showered her with a fine mist of grit.

Before, she had been greeted by an apocalyptic vision of Pioneer Vale town laid to waste. Now, there was nothing but barren plains broken by rocky outcroppings scattered across the horizon. She spun around in a slow circle but stopped and shook her head.

"Not going to make it easy for me to find you, I see," she muttered. "Let's try to get a sense of you then." She closed her eyes, but when she opened herself to the flow of magic, the jolt of power hit her as if she had grabbed a live wire. She staggered as whorls of lightning swirled unbidden around her, but she clenched her teeth and dragged the surge back under her control before it could run unchecked. Back home, she had become a force to be reckoned with. In this place, she could level mountains with a gesture.

"Your power is impressive, Guardian." Haunting whispers, both male and female, echoed all around her and blended into a sinister chorus. "But the might of all who wield such ancient magics here find them far more intimidating."

Angelica dropped into a crouch as wisps like candle flames of all different colors ignited and swirled into the ghostly figures of men and women. Each was clothed in a myriad of styles from throughout history as if all of the fashions from the last few centuries were on display for some macabre show. A few of the faces belonged to the same ghastly phantoms that had tormented her during the terrifying trip to the Holding Chamber, where she had set into motion the events that had led to this place. Others, while new to her, bore distinctive features beneath the gruesome wounds, blood stains, and pale skin that caught her attention. A jawline here, the tip of a nose there, or the familiar curve of the eyes. Similarities she had seen every day in the faces of her father, her brother, and even in her own mirror. A chill ran through her as the threatening wraiths of her ancestors circled. These were the Firstborn who had come before her, forever scarred by the final moments of their brutal deaths.

"You should not have come here, girl," hissed the ghostly apparition of one of the men. Gray coldfire burned through the slashes across his cheek and smoldered within the depths of his empty eye socket. His clothing was far more contemporary than the others that fell into place behind him, and, although muted and washed out by Shade's dark magic that fueled their strength, the deep crimson hue of his magic gave away his identity to her.

"You must be my Uncle Christopher," she said. "Anne-Marie keeps a very detailed family tree in the library, including the color of your gifts. Have to say though, that I didn't recognize you from the family photos with half your face gnawed off. You might want to mention that to the Furball in charge next time you see him. If you're still on speaking terms after I kick his ass, I mean."

"Have you brought more to bear than sarcasm and bravado, child?" asked May. The wraiths fanned out around her, drifting along in a sickly rainbow full of bristling hatred. "Your time here before you join us will be brief indeed."

"Don't worry. I came ready to fight," she said. Angelica turned a slow circle, keeping all of the ancestral ghosts in her sight. A blanket of electricity rolled in waves around her body. Thunder rumbled in her voice and she saw some of the figures waver under the power of her words alone. "I'll ask you only once to stand aside. This battle doesn't have to be between us."

"Of course it does," said Levi. The young man's body leaned to one side, twisted and misshapen from the snapping of his entire skeleton during his last night at Whisperwind. "A welcome death by our hands will prove far swifter and more merciful than what the Wolf would visit upon you, cousin."

"Spare me the big, bad wolf threats." Angelica rolled her eyes. "I don't have time for this. Nothing personal, but the world you once swore to protect is in danger. You all had your chance and blew it, so get out of my way."

"We cannot," said Jennifer. "But neither can we allow you to leave."

The air lit up in a kaleidoscopic display as the spirits each summoned their magic. Each wraith in turn armed themselves with some weapon drawn from their respective eldritch arsenal. A spear of simmering lava stretched forth within Levi's grasp. A swirling globe of inky purple smoke formed between Mitchell's fingertips, and the bladed tips of icy daggers floated around Kathryn's head. They stood as silent sentinels, a wall of magic standing between her and them, and true to her distant relative's words, Angelica knew that she would have to punch her way out of this confrontation.

Gray lightning flashed across the sky. The ground shook, and Angelica staggered from the unexpected tremors, yet none of the spirits around her made a move against her. The air was split by a hollow gleeful cackling that sent even the ghosts around her looking anxiously from one to another. A swirling purplish black spiral began to iris open in the air, not unlike the portals that Anne-Marie created, but a foul reeking blast of air emanated from the darkness within.

"Yes, hold her for Kenton," boomed a screeching gravelly voice. The deranged laughter rang through the air again. "It has been so long since Kenton has fed."

"Forgive us, cousin," said May. "We had no say in what must come."

Something shifted from within the void, but not even her heightened senses, so acute with the overwhelming magic of this place, could see into the depths. Like a whirlwind, a filthy man in ragged clothing dove through the tear in space and pounced onto his hands and knees. His wild hair was matted against his scalp, and the flesh of his muddy face and arms were covered in the scars of scratches, too small for the likes of the demon wolf, but just the right size for his split and jagged nails.

The man bounded forward and slammed against her hastily conjured lightning shield that Angelica threw between them. The brutal impact of the blow rattled her teeth and knocked her back a step. Gritty fingers clawed at the edge of her defenses, and a piece was torn away with every swipe. The air grew pungent with the smell of burning flesh, but her attacker didn't seem to notice how his skin blistered under the streaking arcs. Blindly, she kicked at him, but her foot barely found purchase on his thigh, and only caused the slightest stumble in his frenzied attacks.

"Yes, feed Kenton," the thing shrieked, for there was no trace of humanity left in the eyes that glared out from under the tattered hood. Corrupted by Shade's evil schemes and then cast aside, Kenton's teeth dug into the crackling rim of the barrier. His lips charred and split, but this creature that had once been her ancestor paid no mind to whatever pain he may have felt. She reached deep within herself, and pushed back against Kenton's relentless assault, but knew that she couldn't hold him at bay forever.

A black mist enveloped Kenton's hand and it left behind a trail of ash in its wake as he punched down. Angelica's shield splintered in a flash of sparks, and Kenton's fist plowed into her chest. The force of his strike threw her to the ground and an icy cold stole her breath away as his hand bloodlessly phased through her skin and ribs. Her heart lurched, skipped a beat, and convulsions swept through every limb. His teeth, chipped into needle points, buried into her collarbone. She tried to scream but a numbing cold swept through her, and her muscles locked up tight.

Coldfire raged through her body, sapping her strength, but breaking against the magic within her blood that leaped to her defense. In that heartbeat, the brilliant cores of each of the wraiths, even Kenton's own, blazed forth with a brilliance that drove back the cold. Their connection to the Elder Guardian remained buried deep within them, suppressed but blinding nonetheless. Shade's power grappled against their radiance and bent their gifts to his bidding. They were nothing more than frightened children, the prey that the wolf favored most of all, and Angelica realized that she wasn't fighting this war only for the sake of the living world.

The dead needed her to win as well.

Angelica reached past Kenton's head and fired lightning into the rolling sky. The bolts reversed, as if hitting a barrier, and streaked back towards her, diving down like the talons of a swooping eagle. She clenched her teeth as the blasts struck them both, but shaped the arcs of electricity so that they spread into a living harness around Kenton's back and shoulders. With a great heave, she yanked him off of her and hurled him into a roll across the ground where he landed in a smoking heap.

"Take her," shouted Levi, and one by one, the wraiths fell into nervous stances with their magic at the ready.

She scrambled back to her feet and lowered her head. The Whisper of the Elder fueled her once more, and her senses were so dialed up that she knew exactly where each of the Firstborn stood without so much as a tilt of her head. She saw them without vision. Heard them without sound. Magical energy roared through her veins, and although each of her cousins had been granted their own arcane gifts, there was one thing above all of which she was certain.

None of them compared to her power.

"Let's do this," she said. A shield of blue-white fire deflected Kathryn's hail of ice knives that flashed through the air. A slash of her hand split Mitchell's stream of acid, and when she clapped her palms together a blistering shockwave sizzled through the air. The resounding thunder sent the two spirits reeling.

Angelica spun into a crouch and punched the ground. A spray of lightning leaped through the rock and ripped the ground apart into jagged scars. Three other advancing wraiths were caught in the upheaval of her miniature earthquake and burst into wisps of smoke as bolts raked across the battlefield.

The tears in the ground bubbled with lava that sprayed towards her face. Hours of running Whisperwind's practice course, however, had honed her reflexes to lightning speeds of their own. She threw herself into a backward handspring and came up with her hands already guiding the jet of molten rock into Levi's face when her wayward cousins strayed too close. The specter vanished in a flash of greasy black smoke.

Angelica ducked as an aquamarine shower of sparks exploded above her head. Embers fell to the ground and thorny vines sprouted from the ash around her feet. Tendrils wrapped around her legs and bit into her thighs, climbing up to her waist to ensnare her. To her side, May's hands swirled with sickly ochre light.

"There can only be one ending for you, child," called her ancestor. There was sadness in her eyes, even as the vines under her control squeezed tighter, pinning Angelica's arms across her chest and crushing the air from her lungs. Black spots in her eyes blurred the light that enveloped the ghost. "You see too late that Lord Shade will win in the end. The last lesson you will learn will be one of pain, unlike anything you've ever known, just before he ends your life."

"Here's the last trick your master showed me," Angelica gasped. She fell into the deluge of magic, and the air swelled with power. She ignored the stinging pokes of the thorns that dug into her body and boiled their venom from her blood. Her mind raced back to the battle at the farmhouse, and to the moment right before the demon had blown her home into rubble. With her arms still pinned across her chest, the magic spilled over within her and her eyes burned once more with the now familiar white-hot fury behind her closed lids. Lightning roared through her body, and an explosion of electricity blasted forth with her at its center.

The entangling vines writhed in spasms, split down the middle, and then crumbled to ash at her feet. Crackling electricity washed over the spectral bodies of the wraiths, and they were flung about like paper dolls on the burning winds. Angelica threw her arms out wide and tears streamed down her cheeks as she unleashed all of her pent-up enmity, torment, and remorse in raging torrents of raw magic.

Her onslaught ravaged the dark bonds of Shade's magic that confined the Firstborn to his domain. She ripped his tattered bindings apart and blasted them with everything she had within her. The demon's hold over each of them snapped free from their hearts, and the surge of the Elder's magic rekindled the luminous cores within them. One by one the wraiths wisped away in a flash of colored light until the only remnant of their presence was a fleeting impression of gratitude as they vanished from her sight. Smoke drifted across the battlefield, and Angelica rubbed the dry sting from her eyes. The oppressive heaviness in the air lifted, and for one brief moment, hope seemed to punch through the dismal gray landscape.

But something lingered.

Like tar on a hot summer's day, a puddle bubbled at the base of a rocky outcropping. An inky tendril slowly rose out of the muck, swelling as it pulled itself upright until arms and legs sprouted from the ooze. Crazed feral features took shape under the coal-black cowl of the robes that fell around it. Kenton, still snarling like a rabid animal yet more cautious and fearful this time, lifted his head and glared back at her with eyes of crimson fire.

"Still couldn't get rid of you, I see," Angelica sighed. She circled slowly, and his eyes followed her every step, but he held his place, fists clenching and unclenching, his breathing heavy and deliberate, but from pain or simply because he was more beast than man now, she couldn't tell. "Kenton the Betrayer. Do you even know that was how we all referred to you afterward? The only one of all the Firstborn that Shade didn't have to trick into taking his side."

He said nothing. Didn't move. He just stood there looking back at her and dug the balls of his feet into the ground. Like getting set in the starter blocks, she thought to herself. Sizing her up. Ready to spring.

"Are you even still in there? You only wanted power. You didn't have the patience to learn what Anne-Marie wanted for you, so you threw in with Shade, and now, here you are. A walking shadow damned to this place. Your mind shattered by whatever hell he put you through. I could have freed you just like the others." She stopped moving and his knees bent ever so slightly. Teasing him. Making herself look like a flat-footed target. "You picked the wrong side."

Kenton threw his head back and screamed into the dusky sky, then launched himself at her, black smoke trailing behind him like a comet of ominous portent. Lightning flashed in her hands and she threw her palms skyward. A pillar of stone shot from the ground and the resounding thud of Kenton's face slamming into the rock made her smile. She spun in a pirouette and blasted a second time, shattering the column, and burying him in a deluge of rubble. Coldfire blasted rocks and gravel into a shower of dust as he stood up, staggered, and shook his head.

A crackling blue-white whip of energy rolled from her fingers, and she deftly snapped it in a wide swath, the blistering coils wrapping around his neck and jerking him towards her. Off balance, he fell to his knees, and Angelica pressed her hand against his chest. A bolt of white fire burst forth, and blasted a hole through his body, driving him flat on his back through the loose stone.

"Stay down," she yelled, but Kenton's hand snapped out and took hold of the flowing magical tether that bound him. Smoke rose from his tattered robes and his hair burst into flames, just as a numbing chill shot through her. The fires in his eyes grew brighter and her strength was torn away as her ancestor began to draw her power into himself. Reluctantly, she released the whip and stepped away.

"And here Anne-Marie said I was the stubborn one," she muttered.

Kenton gnashed his teeth, threw his head back, and cackled. Lost in his madness, the spirit charged suddenly, his filthy fingernails snatching at her through the charged air. Gauntlets of crackling energy wrapped around her hands and she caught him in mid-swipe, bracing her feet as he tried to push her backward. She fought back with fingers intertwined, knowing that her life now hinged on the results of a mystical game of "Mercy."

Coldfire pushed against her with staggering force, reaching out from the void within Kenton's black heart and leeching not only her arcane might but her physical strength as well. She strained against Shade's dark influence with her own formidable will, and her arms trembled as she held his gnarled hands at bay. Sweat broke out on her brow, but she knew that she couldn't relent or she would be clawed to shreds. Her knees quaked and the encroaching shadows howled in triumph as her feet slid back through the gravelly dirt. With a snarl that matched his own, she gave in to one last desperate idea.

"You want my magic," she said through gritted teeth, "then you got it."

Angelica let the full force of the intensified arcane energy in the realm sear through her until her own body burned from the incredible flood of power that coursed through her. Instead of resisting the pull of Kenton's hunger, she made herself an open conduit and poured raw magic into his frame. His eyes went wide, and he tried to jerk away, but her grasp tightened and she drew him closer.

"Time to cry, 'Uncle', you bastard." Angelica gave a lightning fueled twist of her wrists, and Kenton's fingers cracked. He kicked and thrashed as the vicious outpouring of electricity ripped through him and shattered his gnarled hands into splinters of charred bone. He tried to shove her away, tried to shield his eyes from her blinding white magic, but she grabbed his robe and hugged him against her chest.

Frantic to escape, her ancestor struggled within her powerful grip and slammed his face into the bridge of her nose, but not even the dizzying pain and crack that rang through her head could stop her now. Angelica threw one fist up high and thunder split the air in answer to her call. Kenton's mouth hung open in silent terror as a bolt of pure white fire crashed down and engulfed them both. The wraith burst into flames and his final wail dwindled into a somber harmony with the roll of thunder. When her blast had faded away, all that remained of Kenton's body was a flurry of ash and a few scraps of scorched cloth between her fingers.

Angelica dropped to her knees and a light rain pattered against her skin only to mingle with the tears that streamed down her cheeks. The battlefield around her stood empty. She sucked in her breath, grimacing at the taste of the air, now metallic and full of soot. Angelica brushed the dirt from her fingers, and absently wiped away the familiar crimson smear of blood from her nose. Her body ached and she knew that Shade still awaited her, but she took solace in the fact that she had at last freed the spirits of the Firstborn.

A cold breeze ruffled her ponytail like icy fingers giving it a gentle tug. Thunder rumbled in the sky above, and she reached to the sky and called down a gentler strike of lightning from the clouds. The energy settled over her shoulders like a comforting blanket and the restorative magic eased the aches of the battle. She climbed to unsteady feet and found on the horizon a cobblestone pathway lined with torches held in iron sconces that meandered off into the distance. With eyes ablaze, Angelica started down the pathway to the heart of Shade's realm.

*　　*　　*

"Nooooo," roared Phoebe. The air around her blazed with gray fire. "That's not possible."

"You continue to underestimate what power Angelica brings to this fight." Anne-Marie watched through the window as Angelica faded away into the mists and smiled. "She is the tipping point that the Guardians have waited for all these centuries. Shade would do well to hide before he learns what true wrath really is."

Phoebe spun around and scowled. Her fists were clenched tightly at her sides. Her granddaughter's eyes locked with her own, but Anne-Marie's will, even when so grievously wounded, proved the stronger. At last, the specter's resolve failed her and she turned away.

"She is formidable. I'll give her that. I still wonder, however, if she will be strong enough."

"She will be the one to save us all." Phoebe's head made the slightest turn and her shoulders slumped. "Including you, my dear child."

"She'll have to save herself first, Grandmother." Phoebe tapped her chin with a think bloodstained finger as the shadowy figure in the portal slowly retreated. A grim smile crossed the phantom's lips and the hellish tinge of Shade's coldfire simmered within her fearsome eyes as she turned back.

"Her greatest struggles are yet to come."

CHAPTER 9
WHERE ANGELS FEAR TO TREAD - PRESENT DAY

The cobblestone pathway snaked its way through burning rubble, swarms of flies, and creeping shadows all drawn from the stuff of nightmares. Cracked and broken pillars lined the sides of the walk and stretched up to the sky lost in the mist with no ceiling to hold aloft. Leaves swirled around her feet, blown by the chill breeze that raced through the citadel. Angelica's footsteps echoed hollowly in the gloom reminding her of an old empty church. It reminded her of walking through an old empty church, except there was no comfort or sanctuary here.

The solemn atmosphere was instead ominous and threatening and sparks danced reflexively along her knuckles. The swirling fog parted and Shade's massive throne loomed on the dais ahead. She scowled back at the grinning skulls that adorned the armrests for the seat of her foe's dominion sat empty.

The weathered boughs of a long dead tree leaned over the crumbling walls of the demon's otherwise undecorated throne room. Soft languishing creaks and groans whispered under the tremendous strain of a large leathery husk that hung suspended from the branches. Dull red veins pulsed beneath the thick leathery skin and, when she stepped closer, ripples of agitated movement coursed through the surface of the disgusting cocoon.

The faintest glimmer of movement at the edge of the shifting mists was her only warning, and Angelica threw herself into a forward roll just as

Shade's claws flashed past her face. His ferocious roar burst in her ears, and his heavy footfalls cracked the stone behind her. With a twist of her hips, she changed the course of her tumble to one side as the cobbles were uprooted by his second swipe. She and the demon rose as one from the stone and faced off against each other. Shade's snarl turned into a mocking, toothy grin and he held his arms out wide, his threadbare cloak flapping in the acrid breeze.

"'Will you walk into my parlor?' said a spider to a fly?" The wolf giggled, and he pranced wild and gleefully like a clown at the county fair. The gleam of his eye, more sinister than she had ever seen from the Demonkin before, ran her blood to ice. "How desperate you must be, indeed, to come here alone, Sweetling."

"Speaking of alone," she said, giving a little huff to blow her bangs out of her eyes, "Did you finally send your errand boy packing? I'm impressed. It only took you 400 years to realize just how useless Aiden was." She crossed her arms over her chest, but she reached her heightened senses into the nearby shadows waiting for Anne-Marie's son to try to sucker punch her.

"Oh, your cousin will be along soon enough. In fact, I suspect that he eagerly awaits your little family reunion." Shade howled and Angelica winced from the reverberating wail, enhanced in volume by the magic of this realm. She covered her ears until the cry slowly turned into a deep hollow laugh. "I know I do."

"Sorry that I didn't bring anything for the potluck. I didn't plan to stay that long."

"Neither shall your precious mentor. The Elder's Champion," he scoffed. Saliva dripped from his savage grin and the droplets smoked and sizzled where they hit the ground. His coal-black hand flexed and the demon regarded the way his razored claws glinted in the torchlight. He tilted his eyes back towards her and sneered. "Her strength fades with every passing moment and she clings to life by the most tenuous of threads."

"You should be more concerned about your own mangy hide." Angelica snapped her wrists and felt the reassuring strength of her magic flow through her arms. The comforting weight of the pouch of shattered crystal rested against her hip. "Anne-Marie may be a little worse for wear, but she's alive and in good hands, while you are still stuck in this cesspool you call home. I guess it just hasn't sunk into your thick skull that you are the one who is out of time, Shade."

"Oh no. The instrument of my doom has arrived at last," he said in mock panic. The demon laid the back of his hand against his brow and gave an exaggerated tremble of feigned terror. Lazily, he swung his fist in a circle and watched the gray streak of coldfire that trailed along behind it. "Her heart still beats, but her mind wanders lost among her nightmares. Four centuries of tortured souls will play havoc upon one's conscience."

"Yeah, I met them already. Shame that I broke your hold on their eternal souls. Well, all except for the nut job who thought you were the better deal. I had to burn him to ash for you." She dropped into a mocking curtsy. "You're welcome."

"The courage of youthful bravado is a thin mask for your lack of experience. Fool yourself with the facade that you can stand tall against any obstacle as long as you may, child." He bared his teeth once more. "You shall you stand long against me."

"Well don't expect me to kneel, you son of a bitch."

"Oh, child. I expect you to scream," the demon snarled.

Shade's legs tensed, his muscles coiled, but Angelica was ready for him. She had trained for this, and when the demon sprang at her, they moved together as one. The monster's powerful leap carried him through the air with his wicked claws outstretched, but she fell into a somersault with practiced ease and tumbled under him. As the wolf passed above her, Angelica's hand filled with lightning and blasted it into his chest at point-blank range. The fur of his pelt tickled her knuckles as the electricity made it stand on end. The thunderous explosion catapulted Shade through the air and he crashed into the side of his throne, knocking the seat from the dais and showering the air with chips of bone.

Undaunted by the smoking crater in his chest, Shade scrambled to all fours and made a chopping motion with his hand. The ground split between her feet, and Angelica leaped to one side as a fiery chasm ripped open. She tucked into another roll, coming up on one knee, wary of the demon's muzzle that swiveled to track her movement. Lightning flashed once more in her eyes, and she flicked a spray of sparks from her fingertips that streaked like tiny missiles and peppered the demon's hide. Shade grunted and doubled over, as her volley struck him, but he merely shook like a wet dog, brushed away the embers from his fur, and lazily fanned the wisps of smoke that rose from where each bolt had landed.

"You'll need to sting me harder than that," he growled. "If that's the best you can do, then your blood will wet my lips far sooner than I expected."

"It's your blood I'm here for, Shade." Lightning arced down her legs, and she dashed forward with unearthly speed. Angelica drew a blade of crackling energy from the air, and swung wide and fierce, like a baseball slugger aiming for the fence. The demon, however, sidestepped the attack and then entangled her arm with a spin of his cloak. The breeze from the swipe of his claws brushed uncomfortably close to her cheek was.

Angelica twirled closer to the demon, like a dancer twirling into her partner's embrace, but rolled under his arm so that she stood beside and slightly behind him. Shade's elbow whipped back, and cracked into her temple, dazing her in an explosion of lights. She lashed out instinctively, driving her heel into the back of his knee, and buckled his leg before he could follow up. The demon craned his neck, jaws snapping at her, but she remained just out of reach. His eyes flared gray and a lance of coldfire raced along his cloak, breathing life into the garment that constricted around her arm and jerked with crushing force.

Her shoulder groaned with a sickening pop, and she bit back a scream of agony. With her free hand, she drove a supercharged fist between the monster's shoulder blades. Her arm tore free from the grasping fabric in a concussive blast that sent them both rolling across the ground.

Angelica turned the momentum into a graceful handspring and lightly hopped back to her feet with her hand resting casually on her hip. On the other side of the throne room, Shade lumbered along, his chest huffing and tongue lolling as he dragged himself up with the help of one of the columns. Something was off in the way he fought against her now. She had seen him move faster. Punch harder.

"What's the matter, Furball? Slowing down in your old age?"

"Not at all, Sweetling." His eyes burned with a wicked gleam in their depths as he looked beyond her. The demon pointed a long claw beyond her shoulder and said, "I was merely stalling."

The deafening crack of a tree branch boomed over the demon's laughter. Angelica whirled around as the leathery cocoon crashed to the cobblestone in a hail of rock, bone, and dust. The ripples of movement inside the membrane were more agitated now and stretched as the creature inside pressed against the slimy tissue. Clawed fingers punctured the skin and an oily ichor spewed out. The sky darkened and she shielded her eyes as a storm of black ash carried upon the rising gale blinded her. She grabbed her temples as a terrible roar ripped the air asunder and a thud of agony drove her to her knees. Her magic blazed to life, throwing up a wall of shields around her out of pure self-preservation. Through her own dazzling light, the shadow of a monstrous figure loomed above her. Lightning flashed in her eyes, struggling to pierce the blistering flames that cloaked the creature's body. Slowly, it leaned its head closer and Angelica stared into the razored teeth of Hell itself.

Glistening fangs bristled in the leering smile. Iron black horns spiraled back like a crown towards the broad scale-covered shoulders. Dull yellow eyes burned around slitted pupils, and the beast's forked tongue slowly tasted the air, savoring the heavy sulfurous stench. The creature ripped away the tattered vestiges of the shirt he wore, unfurling great silvery black wings tipped with vicious talons that spread wide and blocked out the feeble light of the sun.

"Couuuussssiiiinnnnnnn," the creature hissed. It dropped to all fours and idly tore chunks of cobblestone as it stared at her.

"Oh, my God," she whispered breathlessly. "Shade, what have you done?"

*   *   *

"Come and watch your little protégé die," cackled Phoebe. She clapped her hands in childish glee, and a malevolent smile burned across her scarred face. "Shade has stolen the last of what remained of your son, twisting Aiden into a living embodiment of the Adversary's vengeance and corruption. Even your vaunted warrior witch cannot stand against their strength combined."

"Angelica, get out of there! Run," Anne-Marie cried out, although her voice lacked force enough to carry across the realm. She watched helplessly through the shimmering window as Angelica scrambled back from the two malevolent foes. Shade gnashed his teeth, prepared to lunge, and the misshapen half-dragon-like creature that had been Aiden circled behind.

"Don't worry, Grandmother. You won't have to mourn for long," purred Phoebe. The wraith draped an icy arm across her shoulders. "When they finish with her, you'll be next."

*   *   *

"I have tipped the scales, Guardian," Shade said with a sneer. He threw back his head and howled in triumph, until his booming roar tapered into a hoarse laugh. He capered and pranced and his cloak flared out as he spun gleefully. "Behold my Harbinger."

"You channeled the power of the Adversary into him." Angelica gasped. The thing before her that had once been her cousin growled and wisps of smoke curled from its nostrils. A wave of hopelessness, not unlike what she had felt in Whisperwind's library when the Adversary had nearly broken through, washed over her as she met Aiden's eyes. Whatever evil force he may have been before, he was now something far more sinister.

And deadly.

"Your Elder Guardian left one tiny loophole when he imprisoned the Demonkin all those ages ago," Shade snarled. "While we immortals may not cross the threshold between worlds while our respective Guardians bar the way, I have imbued my apprentice with the greater share of my power. His body, still made of mortal flesh and blood, may carry my strength and carry out the final strike against the witch that binds me here." His bared fangs gleamed, slick with the acidic drool that dripped over his mangled lips. "Right after we rip the life from you."

As one, her enemies sprang at her, Shade lashing out with grasping claws, and The Harbinger swooping down like a bird of prey, but Angelica didn't waste a breath. She dove under the two airborne foes, and snapped her palms outward, ensnaring them both in bands of coiling energy. She crossed her arms across her chest in a swift motion and slammed them together in a blast of sparks and blue-white embers.

Shade's putrid muzzle smacked into her cousin's scaly chest, and the demon fell into the loose sand with a thud. Aiden, however, shook off the blow, and tucked his wings tightly around his powerful frame, snapping through the net she had cast around him. Barrel rolling past his master, the twisted beast landed heavily behind her. The shadow of his wing flashed over her head right before the back of the head exploded in pain and a burning slash split across her back from the claw on the tip. She crashed to the ground and tried to crawl away, but Shade's heavy feet pulverized the marble where she was headed to dust.

"Stay still, Witch," growled the Father of Nightmares.

"What? And make this easy for you?" With a wide swirl of her arms, gale-force winds peppered them with a tornado of gravel, dust, and splintered bone. Thrown back on his heels, Angelica dashed past Shade and mounted the dais stairs where his grisly throne had been wrenched from its ancient moorings. Lightning flashed in her hands and she seized hold of the upended throne with arcs of blazing energy. She spied Aiden, buffeted by the ferocity of her wind wall, and whipped the chair into the side of his head. His wings fluttered and he spiraled into the ground, but she hadn't finished yet. She crossed her wrists, snapped them downward, and tore the bones of the macabre seat into pieces. With a thunderous clap, she stabbed down with jagged daggers of bone that deeply pierced into the creature's hide.

A crack of marble behind her drowned out his shriek, and a giant pillar toppled her way behind the force of Shade's shoulder into the base. Angelica sprung away, coughing on the dust thrown out by the broken stone. The demon vaulted lightly over the rubble, and she timed a perfect spinning kick as he landed near her. Although her aim was true and her strike backed by the power of her magic, she might as well have kicked a tree trunk for all the impact Shade showed. Instead, he raised an eyebrow mockingly, and then simply shook his head.

A heavy fist hammered her shoulder from behind and she tumbled across the stone, narrowly dodging the snap of the Harbinger's dagger-sharp teeth. She crossed her forearms in front of her as Aiden fell upon her, bracers of lightning alone keeping his wicked fangs from her throat. Her skin burned from the acidic mist of his breath and sparks of coldfire and lightning sprayed embers across her face as her magic flickered and winked out.

* * *

Anne-Marie watched through the glare as Angelica struggled to hold back Aiden's maw, while Shade crept closer, his clawed hands clenching in anticipation. Every flicker of the girl's dwindling magic made clear that she needed help now.

"Elder, grant me strength," she whispered. Her chest felt as though it ripped open as her magic swelled within her, and a crown of lavender fire blossomed around her head. Phoebe spun around, her brow furrowed ad head tilting to one side.

"What are you doing?" the wraith asked.

"I'll not lose another of my children to this damnable fight. For all that you have suffered, dear Phoebe, I am sorry." She gritted her teeth as a column of fire swirled larger and larger around her, shining brighter than the hottest summer sun at its zenith. Flames roared with a primordial might, and even the ghost of her granddaughter had to shield her eyes from the intensity of the glare. Anne-Marie stood tall within the fiery maelstrom, and smiled sadly.

"Forgive me, my love, but this is going to hurt. Both of us."

* * *

Sirens blared at the nurse's station, but Ben dashed down the hall without even looking. He already knew what room the emergency was in. He bounced off the door frame as he skidded into Anne-Marie's room. Violent convulsions seized the redhead and the frame of the bed rattled under her thrashing. He ran over and grabbed her shoulders, but jerked away as a wreath of purple fire coursed down her body and scorched his hands.

"Dammit, woman, I'm trying to help here," he muttered. Anne-Marie shuddered one last time, and the lavender flames winked out and she lay still. The heart monitor that she was hooked up to resumed a steady rhythmic beeping, but Ben frowned when the spikes were less pronounced and further apart than they had been before. A shadow fell across the floor, and Ben spun around.

The young volunteer he had met earlier, Vicky, stood in the doorway, trembling and her mouth agape. Wide-eyed, she tore her gaze away from the patient and looked up to him. She pointed to the scorched sheets.

"What …what did I just see," she whispered.

"Don't freak out," he replied. "There is so much more to this case than you would ever believe. I'm still trying to grasp it all."

"Things have felt strange all night, like something in the air. When I heard the alarm I felt like I belonged here." The young woman stepped to the other side of the bed and folded her hands in front of her. "How can I help, Dr. Hibble?"

"Thank you, Vicky. Just do me a favor and stay close to her." Ben wiped away the sheen of sweat from Anne-Marie's pale skin and marveled at the lines of concern that furrowed the brow of the unconscious woman's face. He couldn't explain it but somewhere, this woman still fought for the sake of them all. "It's been a hell of a last couple of days. I suspect that, all too soon, she's going to need all the help we can give her."

*   *   *

Pure anguish wracked her body as twin bolts of flame erupted from her hands, but Anne-Marie drove it down and ignored it. Her lances of fire punched through Phoebe's chest and roared through the open portal behind her in a twisting spiral. The arcane bonds that held Phoebe to the Nightmare plane unraveled and snapped, and a silent scream adored her lips as the searing flames engulfed the girl.

Tears rolled down Anne-Marie's cheeks as the surprise and agony that plastered the girl's face dredged forth the terrible memories of her previous clash so many years ago in a heart-wrenching moment of déjà vu. This time however, as the last shreds of Shade's leash melted away, Phoebe's eyes softened with a haunting look of both forgiveness and gratitude just before her ethereal form burst apart into a rolling cloud of smoke and ash.

Her blasts streaked on and raged through the gray window like a spear thrown by a wrathful god. Anne-Marie poured everything she could muster into the devastating attack until her battered body faltered from the deluge of power. She collapsed to the ground, and the dark magic gave way to her fiery onslaught. The viewing window shattered in a storm of coldfire embers.

The world spun, her insides twisted, and her ribcage felt like it was being cracked open. A gout of blood spewed from her lips and pooled in the gray sand as smoke rose from her body.

"Rest at last, sweet Phoebe," she muttered. "I fear I may join you all too soon."

*   *   *

Angelica struggled to push Aiden's maw away from her throat, and blood ran freely from her nose and ears. The Harbinger's relentless force drove her back one step after another, while Shade pounced along behind them, biding his time to strike. Without warning, her cousin's serpentine tail swished between her legs and swept away what precarious balance she fought to maintain. The lightning gauntlets around her wrists faltered, and her magic was ripped away as she slammed onto the cobblestones.

Aiden's crushing weight blasted the wind from her lungs, and his teeth clamped around her arm with a gleeful snarl. More of her blood sprayed hot against her cheek, and her gasp rose to a scream when the flash of fire in his eyes was followed by a crunch of bone. Foul venom ran the veins of her arm to black, but the searing pain lasted only a moment before it went cold and numb. Shade's shadow fell across her face, and the demon crouched low in the reflections of the gray light of her cousin's coldfire. The wolf's fangs glistened, and the tips of his claws clicked in a teasing staccato that carried the promise of spilled blood.

"You are lost, Guardian," the demon purred. "While I must grudgingly respect your fortitude, your stubborn struggles only delay the first of many deaths to come this day." Shade's hand rose high above his head, with claws spread wide. "Hold her still for me, Apprentice."

The heavy hands of the Harbinger pinned her shoulders against the cobblestones, and she fought against him although his strength far outmatched her own. Blindly she jammed her thumb into one of Aiden's eyes, drawing breath when he reared back with a cry of his own.

The air crackled with a shrill whine like an incoming meteor, and a spear of lavender flame burst through Shade's chest as he towered over her. The demon was hurled head over tail across the barren throne room, while the bolt punched further still into Aiden's ribs with a grisly crunch.

"Anne-Marie," Angelica gasped. Her lightning roared to life once again and twin beams blasted from her eyes. The searing storm slammed her monstrous cousin in the chest and threw him across the ground in a tangled ball of lashing tail and crumpled wings. She slowly got back on her feet and tucked her savagely mangled arm tightly against her waist, but before she could enjoy the smoke wafting from Aiden's back a frustrated snarl spun her around.

"WITCH!" Shade bellowed. His eyes searched the distant horizon from where the flame blast had come. The demon clenched his fists and stomped around in a circle. "Why won't you just die already?"

Shade's antics were comical, like a child in the throes of a tantrum with his mouth hanging open and his tongue lolling from the side of his face, but the black ichor in her veins, far more potent than Kenton's venom from earlier, left little strength in her loosely clenched fist. She sent a pulse of magic through her arm, and the viscous poison dripped from her torn flesh, pocking the stone where it fell. The pain eased, although her arm still hung all but useless at her side.

"Even stuck in that hospital bed, she is still fighting you," she yelled at Shade. Unbridled fury smoldered in the demon's cold eyes as turned his rancid gaze back to her. From behind, the Harbinger's talons scraped against the stone, and she circled around so that both were in her view. Coldfire blazed within slitted pupils, and powerful muscles coiled to spring, but she met their yellow eyes unflinchingly and a ball of raging electricity hovered over her hand as her palm fanned out. "And neither will I."

"Leave her," snarled Shade. He made a slice in the air with his hand and a portal of coldfire ripped through the air between her and Aiden. The stark white hallway of Pioneer Vale General lay beyond the gateway, serene and unsuspecting of the three of them gazing through the veil. "Find your mother and end her life while she lies helpless. I will deal with this whelp myself."

Aiden's wings fanned out wide, and he leaped into the air. He made a lazy circle and then dived towards the portal. Angelica fired a blast at him, but he rolled into a tight ball, dodging the bolt, and then swooped through the doorway. Raw magic boomed through the air and both she and Shade tumbled to the ground. Angelica landed hard on her already wounded arm, and the world spun from the pain that shot through her body. The tear between worlds shimmered and began to slowly spin closed as the greater magic of the realm healed the rift.

"No," she screamed, and showered the gateway with a fan of lightning. She strained to hold the door open while the ghostly shadow of her cousin drifted around a corner of the hallway. His destination was certain, and if she couldn't get back, Anne-Marie was doomed. She scrambled back to one knee, ready to sprint, just as a host of skeletal hands erupted from the ground. Bony fingers clutched at her legs and ankles, latched on to her wrists, and painstakingly dragged her streaming magic away from the gate.

"Oh, Sweetling, stay a bit longer, won't you?" Shade had casually propped himself up on one elbow, and held out his massive fist wreathed in his dark power. On all fours, the demon crawled over to her and grabbed her face in his mighty hand. Behind him, the portal's spiral grew smaller and smaller. "I want you to have a front-row seat to the end of the world."

"No time to stay and play fetch with you, Furball," she growled. Blue-white fire coursed through her body and shattered the bony fingers to splinters and ash. So strong was her pulse of magic that Shade slid back across the cobblestones from the sudden strike, but he dug his claws into the ground as he fought to maintain purchase against her blow.

Angelica snapped her hand skyward, reaching towards the ever-present clouds of the dim sky. Lightning roared through her body and a massive bolt from the heavens crashed down onto the demon's sprawling form. With a twist of her hand, the tendrils of electricity became fiery ropes that entwined his thrashing limbs and lifted the demon from the ground. Held aloft by her power, his feet kicked helplessly in the air. She glanced over her shoulder at the gate, now nearly closed, and then punched downward, her fist cracking the rocky floor. Just as sharply, Shade smashed into the dirt with such force that a dusty crater formed around him.

Angelica sprang to her feet and dashed forward, throwing herself through the coldfire portal. A tingle of magic burned along her body as she crossed the eldritch threshold, and back into her world. With a resounding whumphf, the ring of fire slammed shut, sealing the way behind her, but not before the faint sound of Shade's laughter echoed in her ears.

CHAPTER 10
TELLING FRIEND FROM FOE - 1671

The rushing waterfall thundered ahead, and sunlight glinted like sparkling diamonds in the misty spray. Ancient boughs arched overhead like the beams of a forest cathedral complete with a choir of chittering squirrels and skittish birds that scolded her as Anne-Marie stepped lightly across the slippery rocks. A thin shroud of lavender fire flickered around her. Though light and airy, they were yet able to hold the cascade from drenching her clothes, but equally enough to turn her woodland observers' innocent curiosity into nervous agitation.

"Excuse my flames, little ones," she whispered. "They hold no threat to you." This place held a natural peace within it, but the hairs on the back of her neck prickled all the same, for their remained some underlying turmoil that even the sanctity here could not suppress. The grass before her showed signs of wear, and her keen eyes spotted the unmistakable stains of dried blood spattered among the wildflowers.

Embers danced across her fingertips, but she heard the dulcet song of a familiar energy. The unmistakable presence, subdued to avoid notice, but clear as a clarion bell, told her that Henna hid behind the curtain of rock and water with the few survivors of the tribe. She stepped boldly forward, steam rising from each surefooted stride as she followed the trail behind the deluge.

"Hold where you are," shouted a voice from behind the water's veil. A hulking shape lurched from the side of the pathway, but, before the figure's thick fingers could close around her arm, reflexes honed by arcane flames sprang to action. Anne-Marie slipped beneath the grasping hand, twirled a half circle, and took the brawny Nipmuc warrior down to the dirt with a sweep of her foot. His breath whooshed out as her knee drove into his stomach.

"That's hardly a proper greeting for someone who has come to help you," she quipped. A young Nipmuc woman, little more than a girl, held a spear in trembling hands, and Anne-Marie scowled. "And you, young lady, had better point that stick somewhere else."

"If you side with those who attacked my people," the young woman said, swallowing hard as she clenched her weapon in a white-knuckled grip, "then you will not leave this place and reveal our sanctuary." The warrior at Anne-Marie's feet groaned and scuttled away like a crab, placing himself between the two women, although his heavy club lay beyond his reach.

"Fear not, Chogan and Alawa. This daunting firebrand would not have come so softly if she meant any harm," said a cackling voice from the depths of the cave. A stooped shadow ambled forth into the dim circle of daylight that pierced the falls, and Anne-Marie breathed a sigh of relief when the age-worn face of her teacher melted away from the darkness. Henna broke into a wide grin. "Fortunately, she is a dear and beloved friend to us all."

"Strange way of showing it," muttered Chogan. The man pulled himself back to his feet and eyed her warily as he reclaimed his weapon. He rubbed his head where he had struck the ground.

"Henna," Anne-Marie sighed. She pushed past the two sentries and threw her arms around the old woman. "You're safe. I feared that Shade's minions might have caught up with you." From the corner of her eye, the Nipmuc woman stiffened at the demon's name.

"Never was I in harm's way, child," Henna said. Her teacher warmly returned the hug and then held her back to arm's length. "I don't feel as though you can say the same thing though. Ye've a bit of wear and tear about you, and there is weariness and pain etched in your eyes. Tell me, lass. Are your children safe?"

"I reached them in time," she replied with a nod. She lowered her voice so that the Nipmuc folk would not hear. "But even still the effort nearly ended me. The toll such power took upon my body was no easy thing to bear."

"Did ye think tearing a hole in the veil between realms would be child's play?" Henna clucked her tongue. "Don't mistake me, my dear. I am indeed relieved to hear that yer boys escaped harm, but what ye did was beyond reckless."

"What other choice did I have?" she snapped back. Heat rose within her and she fought down the flames that surged within her heart. She stepped away from Henna with her nails digging into her palms. "This damnable war has already cost me my husband. Would you see my sons sacrificed as well?"

"If duty calls for such, then yes. How many more might be lost had the wolf, or worse yet, the one he serves, found his way through?" Henna leaned against her walking staff and the sparkle within her eyes was less whimsical than Anne-Marie was used to. Not vibrant and mischievous, but solemn and contemplative, much like the air before a summer storm.

"He is not here. Not in full anyway, but his power grows all the same." Anne-Marie took a deep breath and relaxed her balled fists. "He sows such chaos within the Vale, that I've no doubt you can feel it as well."

"Aye," Henna said with a nod. "His allies distract us from the true threat he brings to the table."

"You do not face this threat alone." The young woman named Alawa cleared her throat and stepped forward. Her escort, Chogan, fell in behind her. "Kitchi and Abel Harmon travel alone on a dangerous task, but they will return at the head of an army of our own fierce warriors."

"And I for one await the chance to repay the wolf's soldiers for what they have done to us," said Chogan. He folded his arms across his brawny chest.

"Are you so quick to risk more of your loved ones' lives?" Anne-Marie asked. "Your people have already suffered well beyond reckoning."

"And you have not?" The young woman stepped closer, and Anne-Marie marveled at the steel in her doe-brown eyes. "You are the one Kitchi called Firehair. He spoke of you before he left, and said that you are a woman of tremendous power who could tear a hole in the sky."

"Are you frightened of me, child?" Anne-Marie tilted her head.

"I am," the young woman said. She stood tall and raised her chin. "But I am inspired as well, for you would still boldly stand against Maheegan despite all that he has taken from you."

"Bit of an understatement there, lass." Henna snorted. Anne-Marie scowled at the old woman but turned back to the Nipmuc girl and crossed her arms.

"I am a Guardian of the Vale and I have sworn to protect the people of this valley from the demon's assaults on our world."

"No less our home than yours," Alawa replied, "and ours to defend as well. I fear what lies ahead, but I hold to the hope that together our people will withstand and overcome these hardships."

"With someone like you to watch over them, how can we fail?" Anne-Marie placed her hand on the girl's shoulder and an unbidden wisp of fire flowed through her fingers. Her hair ruffled as if by an unfelt breeze. "There is vast strength within your people. And within you. Do not doubt that you possess the wisdom and courage to care for them. After all," she said with a glance at Henna, "there is a certain magic to this place that will watch over you."

"Thank you, Lady Firehair." The young woman smiled. "I will leave you and Henna to speak together. Come, Chogan. We have preparations of our own for when Kitchi and Abel return." The girl bowed her head, a slight blush on her cheeks, and retreated towards the cave mouth.

"Farewell, Alawa," Anne-Marie called after them.

"She will lead the Nipmuc well one day," said Henna. The old woman tapped her long fingernails on her staff and watched the retreating figures with a tear running down her leathery cheek.

"You aren't returning to Whisperwind with me, are you?" Anne Marie asked softly.

"Ye called it yerself, girl. These few folk are all but defenseless." Henna took her hand and squeezed it gently. "I have a history with these people from long before I took up our mantle. The glamour in which I have enshrouded this place will prevent Shade's scouts from finishing the savagery the Nipmuc have already suffered through. I will lend what help as I may until Abel and Kitchi return. My place is here for a while longer."

"I'm sure the comforts of this cave far exceed that of your little hovel."

"As much yours now as mine, dearie," Henna cackled. "Whisperwind comes with the job. Just mind how much redecorating you do while I still live."

Anne-Marie joined in her friend's laughter and she gave her one final hug. She turned and picked out the way across the stony path, but paused a moment and took in the natural beauty of the Nipmuc sanctuary once more.

"This truly is a beautiful place," she whispered. "Jeremiah would have loved to have seen it. I can't fault you for wanting to remain here."

"Shade shall not go unpunished for what he has done. The pure of heart shall rise against him and he shall suffer in the end." Henna's hand fell upon her shoulder.

"Nothing we might do shall be enough in my reckoning. I ache to hear that bastard cry out under my flames."

"Then keep yer furnaces stoked for we two shall stand before him in due course."

"I'm relieved to know that you'll be by my side. I don't think I can face him alone."

"Ye should take to heart those same words of strength you said to Alawa, dearie." Henna tapped the amethyst pendant around Anne-Marie's neck. "Your magic is far more primal and suited for such battles than my own. You were not made Guardian by chance, lass. We each have our parts to play in the upcoming fight, and we shall know precisely when and where our gifts are best suited. I suspect that we all are hurtling toward a moment that will define us all."

Anne-Marie lost herself in the droning thunder of the waterfall behind her. The older woman's words weighed heavily upon her. The icy fears of doubt began to rise but were just as quickly pushed away in a sparkle of sunlight that gleamed from the gem that dangled around her throat. She brought the stone to her lips and then tucked the chain back into her blouse.

"And what happens after the dust has settled?" Henna's eyes trailed off, looking vacantly into the distance.

"Either we send Shade away howling in defeat, or you shall be reunited with your lost love sooner than we would like."

*   *   *

"I do not know what sort of welcome we will receive, my friend," said Kitchi as he and Abel walked along a game trail in the deeper woods. They were two days away from the safety of the waterfall sanctuary. "You might find that being bound and gagged was more to your liking."

"Your people have always seemed reasonable." Abel snorted but absently rubbed the still-raw skin of his chafed wrists. "I hope that they would at least hear us out before jabbing us with the point of a spear."

"It's not my hide I am concerned about, farmer." Kitchi looked over his shoulder at the older man and grinned. "It would be a long walk back to Deer Run Hollow alone."

"I shall endeavor not to upset the Nipmuc hospitality, then. I'd hate for your return trip to be a dull one."

The brush ahead of them gave way to an open clearing, filled with timber huts in neat rows. The smell of cookfires and wood smoke filled the air. Children laughed as they chased one another, while the women and men of the tribe worked side by side at their daily tasks. Kitchi choked back a sad smile and his heart ached with wistful memories of recent days. The farmer placed a hand on his shoulder.

"Your folk will have this again," Abel said softly. He pointed out two burly Nipmuc warriors. "Our moment of truth is upon us."

"Let me do the talking. You do not know our customs," he whispered. Kitchi waved at the two men and held his arms out wide, showing his empty outstretched palms, and then nodded for Abel to do the same.

"Hold where you stand, travelers. You trespass on our lands here." The two sentries cautiously approached, yet held their spears loosely. The larger of the two looked at Abel and scowled. "And would you add still more insult to us by bringing one of these settlers along, or is he meant as a peace offering?"

"I am Kitchi, Chieftain's Son of the Vale tribe, and we have come to ask a favor from your people. An ancient evil has come to our lands and threatens to overtake us all, Nipmuc and settlers alike, if we do not join together against it. I have brought this man," he gestured to Abel, "to vouch for my words. I implore you to let us meet with your chieftain."

"I am sure you know that we have no quarrel, yet no love, for your Vale folk. You must be truly desperate, or simply foolish, however, to think we would believe his words," said the bigger sentry. "Go back the way you came, before I count to three, for if I can still see this man in that time, may you both pray to the spirits that my throw falls short."

"You must understand," Abel began, but his words were drowned out, cut off by a ferocious roar from the nearby treeline. They spun as one just as an enormous grizzly bear burst from the undergrowth, its claws tearing the ground and shaking the trees as it lumbered into the clearing. Terrified screams of those nearby erupted all around the beast and startled it long enough that it broke its charge, although it reared back on its hind legs, towering over a woman and her child who huddled closest to it.

"If your arm is as mighty as you claim, then prove it now," yelled Kitchi. He broke away and ran past the guards without a second thought. His bow slid free from his back and he had one arrow in the air and a second shot nocked before he had even taken three steps into his dash. From the corner of his eye, Abel unslung his rifle from his shoulder and dropped to one knee. The crack of the farmer's gunshot interrupted the bear's deafening snarl as the animal's shoulder burst open in a spray of blood. Kitchi closed the remaining distance in a slide, and unleashed his arrow into the bear's belly at a range so close that the tiny missile plunged deep and doubled the mighty predator over. He hopped back to his feet, spun back around, and scooped up the little boy.

"Behind, you Kitchi," yelled Abel, just as a massive shadow loomed over his own on the ground.

"Run," he yelled to the young mother whose frozen stare was fixed on the beast that closed on him. He shoved the boy into her arms, and but only fell a few steps back. Kitchi threw himself into a forward roll, but the burning agony of the bear's claws tore across his flesh. Only his quick reflexes kept the mighty creature from ripping his head from his shoulders.

The crashing boom of Abel's gun rang out again, and through a haze of blue-tinged smoke, Kitchi saw the farmer running forward, steadily reloading even as he charged. The two Nipmuc warriors who had stopped them chased behind with spears ready to throw, but he knew from the angry roar behind him that they would never arrive in time. Time slowed to a crawl for him. With the bear's breath hot on his back, he smoothly drew his antler-handled knife from his hip. He nodded to the farmer as Abel raised his rifle once more and squeezed one eye shut.

"Stay low," the farmer shouted, and Kitchi dropped down on one buckskin-clad knee. His heart hammered in his chest and he held his blade in a tight two-fisted grip as the grizzly lunged forward. The dull echo of Abel's rifle cracked once more, and a hot lead ball grazed his cheek as it zipped by.

The shot blew another bloody hole in the beast's thick pelt, and its enormous head rocked back from the staggering impact. With its throat laid bare, Kitchi's legs drove him upward, his blade leading the way, and he plunged his knife into the bear's neck with driving force. The deafening roar turned into a wet gurgle that slowly faded to a whimper, and the great animal toppled to the ground with a thud.

Kitchi bowed his head as the bear breathed its last. His back was aflame, and pulses of pain wracked his body with every beat of his heart. He dimly heard Abel's pounding footsteps, and the lingering smoke from the farmer's rifle barely dragged him from the edge of unconsciousness. Still his legs betrayed him and he collapsed across the mighty animal's back. The farmer's callused hands caught him and lowered him gently to the grass.

"Rest easy, son. That old fellow got his hooks deep in you," Abel said. His friend called over his shoulder. "Don't just stand there slack-jawed. Find your healer at once."

"You know that a little more to the left," groaned Kitchi, "and we wouldn't be speaking right now."

"I saw what ye had in mind with your knife," Abel said with a grin. "Don't question my aim, lad. I knew right where to place my shot, but just so we're clear, I get half the credit for this giant."

The press of bystanders soon broke as several more Nipmuc arrived, led by a large man who stood a head taller than all the others. Scars across his chest peeked out from under the leather vest he wore and the scuffed war club in his hands had equally seen its share of battles. Several onlookers, including the two warriors who had first met them, fell to their knees. The boy that Kitchi had snatched away from the bear ran to the Chief, for he could be no other, and was scooped into a tight squeeze in the brawny man's arms.

"Fetch Sooleawa," the chief shouted as he put his son down and knelt at Kitchi's side. One of the women raced away, pushing through the gathering crowd in his path. "I owe you my son and wife's lives, my friend. Rest now, and later when you are well shall we discuss whatever matter bears such urgency to the Vale folk."

"There is no time to waste," said Kitchi. He struggled to sit up, but his hand slipped in the widening pool of blood beneath him. His vision swam and he grabbed the man's vest leaving a crimson stain on the leather. He tried to swallow, but his mouth may well have been full of sand, for his words struggled to come forth, but at last, he managed to speak his message.

"Maheegan has come," he said. The chief's eyes widened in shock just before the world went black.

*   *   *

Frightened eyes watched him from behind curtains and from the depths of shadowed alleyways as Patch walked down the center of the main street through the Market Square. The knapsack slung over his shoulder, stuffed with a few days worth of food and other wilderness supplies, bounced jauntily with each step. His course led him past the Reavers' encampment where the clack of bootheels on the cobblestones behind him made him stop and slowly turn.

"Slinking away to hide, Erickson?" Cyrus called out. The mercenary captain walked toward him with a cocky smirk on his face. "You should stick around. Some big changes are coming to Pioneer Vale soon."

"That may be the first thing you have ever said that I agree with, Cyrus," he growled back. His fingers played over the handle of his knife, while Forrester's hand hovered over the butt of his pistol. The clouds overhead rolled across the sun, blood red in the western sky, and painted the long shadows along the streets with a crimson tinge. The visceral urge to tear out Forrester's throat flitted through his mind for just a moment before he shoved the thought back into the dark recesses. The mercenary captain still had a purpose to serve.

Pity.

"You're headed out to look for that Carmichael woman?" Forrester said at last. The man spat on the ground. "Waste of your time, if you ask me."

"I don't believe that I did, Captain." Sarcasm dripped from the title.

"She is scared and on the run. Probably halfway to Boston by now. And if not, then just give her enough time. She'll slip up and fall right into your clutches. Work smarter, not harder."

His blood boiled through his veins and he closed the distance between him and the cutthroat mercenary with strength and swiftness that belied his imposing size. One would think it almost … supernatural, he mused as he grabbed the man's vest before Forrester could so much as twitch.

"My errand may keep me away for some small time, but I assure you, the hunt will be worth the chase. Anne-Marie Carmichael will not simply stumble through the front gates. She is a clever girl, that one, but she remains close by and I know the area where she lairs. Once the little mouse sticks her nose out, I will strike without mercy." He licked his lips unconsciously, like a wolf cleansing the blood of recent prey, and glanced down at the pistol Forrester now clutched in his hand. "A lesson others may wish to heed before their time runs out."

Patch stepped away and unconsciously bared his teeth at the man. Then, with a curt nod, he tugged his knapsack into place once more and spun on the heel of his boot. The shadows swallowed him up as he stormed through the gate and into the dark woods that surrounded the town.

*   *   *

Cyrus smoothed his vest as the brute disappeared into the dusk, and he eased the hammer of his pistol back down. He had fearlessly faced trials in his life that would make most men soil themselves, but there was something about Erickson that sent an unbidden shiver down his spine. Still, a vicious smile crossed his lips.

"Prepare for lessons of a different sort upon your return, Master Erickson," he whispered. The echo of boot steps came up behind him, and the newcomer gently cleared his throat. Forrester holstered his weapon and glanced over his shoulder, where Carter stood in a parade rest with hands neatly folded behind his back. "What is it, Lieutenant?"

"Sir," said Carter. "I have just received word from the field. Our reserves are in position."

"Good. Tomorrow at noon, then, see to it that all the townsfolk within Pioneer Vale are brought to the square."

"Of course, sir."

"And Carter?"

"Yes, Captain?"

"Make clear to the men that I will tolerate no hesitation to crush any who would stand against us."

*　　*　　*

"This fight has not come to my people."

"Maybe not yet, but how long do you think you'll have before these same soldiers come for you? They will prove as merciless to your folk as they were to Kitchi's tribe. You put your kinsmen at risk if you ignore this threat."

Kitchi squinted as the men's raised voices pierced his pounding head. He was shirtless and on his stomach, and his chest was gently tickled by the soft pile of furs he rested upon. Lines of fire blazed across his back, but the tightness in his muscles was soothed by a damp coolness, and the cloying fragrance of herbs hung in the air about him.

He groaned as he pushed himself up, slowly turning towards the arguing men, but spied instead an old Nipmuc woman with muddy brown skin, weathered and cracked like old leather, regarding him with a toothless grin. Stringy white hair hung loosely to her scalp, and the beads and polished stones that decorated her aged doeskin dress sparkled in the low light. Her eyes twinkled from deep within the heavy creases of her face beneath stark white eyebrows that were so bushy he was given to thoughts of caterpillars searching for their winter rest.

"Mind you move gently," she said in a raspy voice, "or the stitches and poultice on those fresh badges of honor you've earned won't do you much good. I am Sooleawa, healer for these folk."

"And I am deeply grateful for your presence here," he said. He wobbled as he rose and the woman offered her walking stick. Kitchi bowed his head to her, and steadied himself, although he leaned more heavily upon the stout piece of hand-carved oak than he would have liked. "How long have I been out?"

"Long enough for us to add fresh bear meat to the cooking pot tonight," she cackled, "but not enough for those two to quit their bickering. They've been at it since you were brought to me."

The two men broke off their conversation once they saw him on his feet and hurried over. The powerful Nipmuc warrior's dark eyes studied him and then he gave a quick nod before he crossed his arms over his broad chest.

"You heal quickly," the man said. "That and your unquestionable courage speaks well of you."

"I am in your debt. My wounds already feel like they are on the mend."

"Your quick action spared my wife and son," replied the brawny warrior. "It is I who owe you, my friend. I am Rowtag, chieftain of our people here."

"And I am Kitchi, Chieftain's Son and speaker for those few of the Vale tribe who yet survive. If my friend and I have done anything that has earned your favor, then we would redeem it without delay."

"We have spoken at length while you rested and he has shared with me the reasons for your visit. You would have me commit to a war with the settlers that has not threatened us here. That is more than just redeeming a favor, Kitchi of the Vale."

"The coming fight is not with the settlers, but with soldiers who march beneath the banner of the Black Wolf."

"You said as much before you blacked out. You believe Maheegan comes for us?" the chief asked. The man's eyes darted to the old medicine woman and he frowned when she cackled gleefully. She stuck a long clay pipe between her lips and leaned heavily on her stick.

"You are not the first to caution this old fool, Chieftain's Son," Sooleawa said. "I have shared my visions of the darkness that the beast would spread across the land and I have seen naught but suffering wherever his shadow falls. Too often, my warnings fall on ears that hear even less than my own."

"You should address your chieftain with more respect, mother."

"There are those enough who grace you with honeyed words. I am too old for such flattery, my son." She grinned her gap-toothed smile at him, and when the big warrior turned back to him, Rowtag could only shrug. Kitchi cleared his throat.

"Mighty Chief Rowtag, my village was burned to the ground and the small handful that escaped with their lives, while hidden and safe for now, are not enough to fight back. These soldiers are but the vanguard of the true enemy. The Black Wolf is on the prowl, and if we fail to stop his threat, our brutal end is assured."

"Our legends are full of fallen heroes. How can mere men dare to stand against the old spirits?"

"They cannot," answered Sooleawa. "Maheegan will only be defeated when a light shines through the beast's darkness and lays down such a challenge that he falls prey to his own cowardice. Only then will his hold over the Vale be broken."

"Would it be presumptuous to hope that light was made of purple flames and green sparkles?" asked Abel. Kitchi placed his hand on the farmer's shoulder.

"Anne-Marie and Henna," he said. He turned to the old woman again whose eyelids drooped and she pursed her lips.

"Warriors chosen by the Great Spirits themselves, yet their struggle will be in vain if Maheegan summons his full might to bear against them. His attention needs to be drawn away so that they may find the strength to prevail."

"And we can give them the distraction they so sorely need," said Kitchi. He faced the chief. "Should we clash against his legions at Pioneer Vale town, the Guardians may attack him where he is most vulnerable. You must join us!"

"Our ancestors settled these lands and we have held them for generations, but never have we faced such a foe." Rowtag drew his hand slowly down the length of his face, and, after a silent moment, bowed his head. The chieftain gestured to Abel's gun leaning against the wall. "We do not have the weapons to stand openly against these men, and yet I fear that if our warriors do not join your cause, there will remain nothing but ashes for our people should the Black Wolf reign over us all."

"We can steal away his chance of victory," Kitchi said, "but we need your voice to unite our neighbors, Rowtag, for you are most respected among all the Nipmuc nations. With such a force assembled, we will strike from the forest, blend into the bushes, and ambush Maheegan's soldiers when they least expect us. One powerful strike and we could drive away Maheegan's men for good."

"And give the Guardians the opening they need to trap and skin our wolf," added Abel. The chief folded his hands behind his back and paced slowly, lost in thought. At last, he gave a low whistle, and one of the men entered through the doorway.

"Light the signal fires and fill the skies with the blackest of smoke. Let all of the Nipmuc who may see send their bravest and strongest warriors." The man placed a fist over his chest. "And send our own messengers to meet them en route. Tell them that Maheegan has come to Pioneer Vale but Rowtag will lead them into glorious battle against his minions."

"Our deepest thanks," said Abel with a bow as the warrior hurried from the chief's lodge. The farmer extended his hand and after a moment, Rowtag clasped it.

"You and your ways are largely unknown to me, Farmer, however, I recognize a man of spirit and honor when I see one. I will be proud to fight beside you."

"Likewise, and I think you'll find there are others who share my contempt for these butchers we face," Abel said. "These mercenaries are a lowly sort of rabble hired by a wicked man who is in league with the beast and who even now holds much of Pioneer Vale beneath his thumb. I have known such cutthroats in my day, and my greater fear is that Mathers holds sway over them with a shakier hand than he knows. We will be hard-pressed to measure up should these hounds slip the leash and set their own will loose upon us."

"And your people would call us barbaric." A grin cracked through Rowtag's stern demeanor, but Abel could only shake his head.

"Among my folk, there are those who have dealt most unfairly with your own," the farmer said. "I can only stand before you as one who never wanted anything but peace between us all. If it is within my power, I would always treat the Nipmuc as friends and allies."

"Let us hope that this comes to pass." Kitchi cleared his throat as the chief turned towards him. "I knew your father, Kitchi, and I gave offerings to the spirits when I heard of his passing. He was a brave and wise leader of our people. I see his strength in you and know he would be proud of the man you have become. Be wary, though, that you do not embrace war with such open arms."

"Never with open arms," he replied softly, "but with heavy heart. I do not wish to see any man placed in danger, whether it be one of our people or Abel's, and certainly not standing in my stead. If we must fight, then it shall be shoulder to shoulder as brothers."

"Then rest and eat, my friends," said Rowtag. "I will see that preparations are underway for our march back to your sanctuary." The chief left and the old shaman shuffled over to them.

"Our thanks to you as well," said Abel. "I fear that we could not have convinced him without your help."

"Thank me once the battle is won, Valeman. Victory over Maheegan will not come easily or without a cost." She reached out and grabbed Kitchi's wrist, and her touch sent a jolt through his arm. "Tell me, Kitchi, son of Keme, you have offered much in the service of our people, but what if there is something more precious that you must give?"

"I will do whatever is asked of me."

"You stand in the shadows of a proud heritage, but for the Nipmuc to thrive, I see that the life of Chieftain's Son must end."

He stared at her for a moment, and then nodded. "If such is the price for our people to survive, I am prepared to pay it."

"And you, Abel Harmon, have been a good and brave man all of your life, but you'll live longer still if you keep your valor closer to your heart."

"You'd have me run and hide? I'm not one to shy away from a fight."

"Never did I say that you should. The clarity of my sight will reveal itself in due time. For now, find whatever respite you may. Your people, Nipmuc and settler together, must become one if Maheegan is to be stopped. Only through the leadership of you both working side by side will differences and past grudges be set aside."

"You are the latest in a series of wise women I have been graced to meet recently," said Kitchi with a grin. "Are all of you so burdened with knowledge?"

"The burden comes from dealing with the men folk who cannot see the forest for the trees," Sooleawa cackled. "Heed the words of old women, boys, for they have forgotten more of good sense than most men ever learn."

CHAPTER 11
INSIDER SECRETS - 1671

Corbin was numb. The street in front of the Pritchard household was lined up with an assembly of well-wishers, friends, and neighbors who had come to say their goodbyes to Horace and Madeline. Congratulations echoed throughout the square, but the cheers and laughter were little more than a dull buzz drilling through the fog in the back of his head.

"My friends," bellowed Horace, "I can't tell you how much it means to us that you have all gathered here to see us off on our new lives in Boston. Although we have been graciously blessed with such wonderful people in our lives, we feel that this frontier town is no longer the ideal place for us to continue given my recent injuries and Madeline's news of the forthcoming addition to our family. It saddens me to say farewell, but know that we shall think fondly of our time here and will undoubtedly miss you all."

The crowd laughed amiably and pressed closer to the couple. Gift baskets were placed into the cart already loaded heavily with their belongings while several ladies of Pioneer Vale each, in turn, hugged Madeline. When her eyes found him, the false smile collapsed and tears welled up in her eyes.

He drew in his breath and dug his nails into his palms to drive down the ache in his chest. The hidden truth between them boiled just below the surface, and a cry rose in his throat. All he had to do was shout, but before he could brand himself before the crowd, Preston Mathers pushed his way through and stole away the attention of the crowd by pressing a jingling coin purse into Horace's hand. He waved his hands into the air and the murmurs fell silent as all eyes turned to him.

"Horace and Madeline," he said. His voice was deep and carried through the square, but Corbin shivered at the buried malice in his timbre and his knees threatened to give way when the moneylender smiled directly at him. "Truly our town is lessened by your departure. Your time and service to our community have brought comfort to so many. Please accept this small sum to help you land on your feet upon your arrival in Boston."

"Why…, thank you, Preston," said Horace, clearly as puzzled by Mathers' generosity as any. "This is most unexpected, but certainly appreciated."

"As no doubt your own blessed news was." Corbin understood the true intention of Preston's pageantry that lurked beneath the cunning leer. "Clearly the little scrapper takes after you already, Horace. See how much prominence he demands already when you are only so recently …how do I put this delicately…returned to service after your recent injuries?" Coarse laughter from the crowd made Horace shift uneasily, and Madeline hung her head with cheeks aflame.

"I do but jest and hope for nothing but blessings to rain upon your growing family," Preston continued. "In fact, I spy Parson Reynolds nearby. Who better than our proverbial father of the flock to shower the happy couple with some divine benevolence before they depart?"

Several townsfolk echoed the request, and Corbin was gently grabbed and pushed through the parting crowd until he stood side by side with Preston. The throng waited in anticipation, staring expectantly at him, and he swallowed hard. He couldn't read Horace's face, but his dear Madeline trembled and the fear behind her eyes was as obvious as the swell of her belly.

"What are you waiting for?" hissed Preston in his ear. "Time to say your farewells."

"I hope you burn in Hell, Mathers," Corbin whispered. He glared at the man, but Preston's lewd grin only widened.

"I'll keep a seat warm for you, my boy," he chuckled softly.

"Come on, Preacher. Say a prayer for them," called another, one of the town militiamen.

"Yes, Parson Reynolds. Give them a few parting words!" called one of the ladies, a seamstress if he recalled correctly. He turned and forced a smile to his lips raising his hands high above the crowd. Horace wrapped his arm around Madeline, drawing her close to his side, and her hands fell unconsciously to her abdomen before she folded them together in prayer and closed her eyes.

"I cannot express how greatly it pains me to see such dear people leave our little fold," Corbin began, his voice catching in his throat when Madeline's lips trembled. "Our time together in this wild place has made us a family, and I shall miss watching us continue to grow as one. Although we may never see your dear faces again, I can only ask that you receive all of the blessings that you deserve."

He smiled sadly as Madeline looked up at him, her eyes now wide open, and Horace crossed his arms over his broad chest, clearly uncomfortable. "Thank you, Parson," the young woman said softly.

A chorus of "Amen's" rose from the crowd, and Corbin found himself roughly caught up in handshakes and slaps on his back. He broke free from the whirlwind of adulation and was spun face to face with Horace who silently reached out his thick hand to him. Corbin grasped it and squarely met the man's cold eyes. The militiaman's lips were pursed tightly, and no words were spoken. It was clear in the unnecessary firmness of Horace's handshake, however, that the man understood the thinly veiled truth of his words.

"Take care of her," Corbin said. The crushing grip slowly eased and his hand was freed.

"Finish your goodbyes, Madeline," Horace said. He stepped away and pulled himself into the seat of their cart. "We've many miles to go and we are losing daylight."

"Madeline," he began. Corbin took her hands in his own, his knees nearly failing when she returned the most gentle squeeze to his fingers. She lowered her head, unable to meet his gaze, although he could not ignore the tears that spilled over her eyes and ran down her cheeks.

"Goodbye, Parson Reynolds," she said softly. "I have faith that you shall one day know what greater good still awaits you."

"I shall think of you often," he blurted. It was all he could think to say. She pulled her hands from his, gave a quick nod, and hurried over to the cart. Her husband helped her up into the seat beside him, and with a sharp crack of the reins, their wagon lurched forward. Cheers and goodbyes followed in their wake as they passed through the town gate.

"If only all of our troubles could fade away into the dust so easily, eh, Corbin?" Mathers nudged him with an elbow, but an icy wind whipped around the man. "One less thing to worry about, if you ask me."

"Do not speak to me ever again, Preston," he snarled as he spun around and grabbed the front of the man's jacket. He ignored the gasps from the bystanders from his congregation. "Unless you care to see exactly what hellfire I may bring forth."

"I have already looked into the face of pure evil, Parson." Mathers peeled his fingers away from his lapel. "Trust me when I say you bear little resemblance." He gave a curt nod of his head and then melted back into the crowd.

Corbin stumbled down the street and leaned heavily against the nearby wall of the Hirsute Huntsman. In a daze, he watched the receding cart round the bend in the road that led deeper along into the forest. When the last clouds of dust had settled back to the ground, he fell to his knees and wept as one painful truth set in.

She had never once looked back.

*   *   *

Cyrus stood tall and proud on the platform that overlooked the bustling town square where his Reavers shoved whimpering townsfolk until they stood shoulder to shoulder practically at his feet. The frightened faces that stared up at him brought a cruel sneer to his lips that widened when Preston Mathers was roughly dragged to the bottom of the wooden steps. The moneylender shook away the soldier's grasp and straightened his waistcoat, glaring up at him.

"What's this all about, Captain?" snarled Mathers. "What gives your thugs the right to drag us all from our homes?"

"Here, here," cried one of the many people corralled into the square. Anxious whispers began to grow into shouts of outrage, and Cyrus raised his hands in the air gently waving them in a futile attempt to quiet the townsfolk. With a sigh, he drew a pistol from his belt and placed it atop of the railing, and the mutterings quieted immediately.

"Now that I have your attention," he said calmly. He paused just long enough to hear his voice resonate around the square. The way all eyes were upon him as he stood above them all brought a blaze inside of his chest that he found almost intoxicating. "If you will be so kind as to lend me your ears long enough for me to make my statement, and provide your fullest cooperation, you may all be about your business soon enough."

"What sort of statement, Forrester," said Preston. "And cooperation for what? Has Pioneer Vale not already accommodated the needs of your men with our most gracious hospitality?"

"Indeed you have, and we are not ungrateful for it. Quite the contrary." The crowd stood enraptured, he mused. Just like the sheep that they were. "In fact, as a show of our appreciation, I am before you today to let one and all know that I intend to save this town from the single greatest danger that it faces. Namely, your own pathetic weakness."

"You must be joking," Mathers said at last, breaking the stunned silence. "Have you merely called us forth just to belittle us?"

"You have done that yourselves. I have seen the likes of Pioneer Vale before," Cyrus continued. "You lack strong and decisive leadership and waste too much time in pointless committees and public debate. The local savages could stroll through those gates while you spend time squabbling over who should load the first rifle. Therefore, in the best interest of the common good, I will henceforth assume complete authority over both the town and outlying farmlands."

"You would rule over us," called Jordan Lucas, the town magistrate who stepped up beside Mathers. The man was nothing more than a mouthpiece, another lackey in Mathers' pocket.

"To ensure the town's continued survival, yes."

"You were hired to protect us from the Nipmuc menace," retorted Preston. "Not set yourself up as a despot."

"Necessity would require the two to become one and the same, sir. Consider our contract renegotiated."

"And what loyalty do you hope to command from our townsfolk given this brash display, Captain Forrester?" Lucas snorted and preened before the crowd, and Cyrus felt his blood boil. A cold rage welled up from somewhere inside him and his vision clouded in a curtain of gray fire that vanished as quickly as it came. "Frankly, I find your arrogance nothing short of vulgar."

His hand moved with supernatural speed and Cyrus snatched the pistol from its place on the rail. He fanned the hammer and the crack of the shot echoed throughout the square. Lucas jerked and then looked up at him with wide-eyed surprise as blood trickled from the corner of his mouth. A drop fell in a crimson spatter beside the smoking hole in his white linen shirt. Without so much as a whisper, the magistrate fell to the cobbles amid shrieks of terror from the people standing near him. The rasp of blades leaving scabbards and dozens of flintlock weapons being cocked and readied cowed them just as quickly.

"Any other dissenting votes?" Cyrus shouted. He blew the smoke away from the barrel of his pistol and tucked it back into his belt. He towered over Preston, who could only shrink away from the weapons that bristled all around him. "I thought not. This was such a waste. I would have greatly preferred no objections to my generous offer."

"You'll have precious little to rule over if your handful of men treat the rest of the townsfolk with the same generosity as you have shown Magistrate Lucas," said Preston. "Once the stench of gunsmoke clears the air, there are those among these hardy folk who will rise against you."

"A possibility already considered, and one with contingencies already in motion." Cyrus nodded to one of his soldiers standing nearby who carried a battered brass horn under his arm. "Allow me to provide crystal clarity for you all as to why surrendering the town to me is your only choice."

The bugler raised the instrument to his lips and blew a long, bellowing, baritone call into the air. From beyond the town's fence, not so far into the dense woods, a second note answered, and then a third. In the distance, a horse whinnied, and a distant rumble slowly built like rolling thunder until the leaves of the trees began to tremble and quake. Doors rattled in the frames of the homes nearest the gates. Tools tumbled with a clang from their pegs along workshop walls and neatly planted flower gardens shook in primly groomed beds, their petals floating lazily to the ground in an unseen onslaught.

Cyrus lifted his hands skyward as if the columns of dust that rose and blotted the hills on the horizon were called forth by his might. That cold fury overtook him once more and his eyes flickered to certain faces in the crowd, belonging to the most irksome of the Vale's townsfolk. Mathers cowered at the foot of the stairs. The stubborn young blacksmith, Robillard, wrung his hands together, and the insufferable Brenners held tightly to one another as the ground quaked under their feet. The old woman turned to him, and Cyrus saw in her eyes the moment that revelation dawned upon them.

"We're under attack," cried Dorothea.

"Close the gates," yelled Marcus. The big man started to push through the crowd, but Carter and two of his Reavers blocked the tavern keeper's way with pistols drawn.

"Stand down, Master Brenner," shouted his second in command. "There is no need for either of us to regret our next moves."

Two ranks of mounted soldiers split through the underbrush and erupted from the forest with an exultant whoop. The road was pounded into a muddy ruin as they charged forward through the open breach town gate. Dozens upon dozens of men on horse and foot, armed ruffians one and all, surrounded the townspeople packed into the central square within the defenseless town.

The seasoned mercenaries broke into flanking patterns, and cut off avenues of escape, even going so far as striking with the butts of their rifles and lashing out with sharp kicks at any man or woman who tried to bolt for the safety of their homes. With the citizenry subdued, the full force of Forrester's Reavers leveled their musket barrels at the helpless townsfolk.

"This was your intention from the very start," said Preston. Cyrus clapped his hands in slow applause as he hobbled down the platform steps, and threw his arm around the man's shoulder.

"Come now, Preston," he said. "You should know better than anyone that a shrewd businessman never reveals all of his secrets. Now that you see our true numbers, it should seem obvious that I sold our services for a bargain, sir."

"You're a madman."

"Says the one who looks for witches because the shadows told him to do so. I do not wish to see anyone injured as a result of this changing of the guard, however, make no mistake." He gestured broadly at his troops but caught Preston's arm in a crushing squeeze that made the man wince, and he raised his voice so that his words would carry throughout the square. "My command carries little room for mercy or gentle leniency. Refuse to submit to my authority, and I will not hesitate to crush all of you beneath my bootheel. Pioneer Vale belongs to me now."

Cyrus roughly shoved Preston away, and the crowd parted for him as he spun on his heel and headed toward the command tent. He could smell the fear as hushed whispers and muffled sobs filled the wake behind him. Even his own men pulled back a respectful distance from his path as his steps led him to where Carter still held his pistol steadily aimed at the tavern master. His second saluted his approach.

"Shall I disperse the crowd now, sir?"

"If you please, Lieutenant. Our tavern master and his wife here are immediately needed to ensure that our additional men are adequately provisioned." He sized up the bearish man and the little shrew that clung to his arm. "Congratulations, sir and madam. I have deemed you necessary, for now."

"Relieved, I'm sure," muttered Dorothea.

"Hush, woman," Marcus said, placing himself in front of his diminutive wife.

"For your own sake, I trust you will remain so," Cyrus replied. He noted how her husband's eyes darted towards the magistrate's corpse in the street and a snarl found its way once more to his lips.

"Now get to work."

*　　*　　*

"Is this what this backwater town considers a smithy?" barked a gruff voice from the door. "Might serve for nails and horseshoes, but I'm not sure I'd leave my sword here, Gregor."

Micah set down his hammer and wiped the sweat from his brow with a rag. Three burly mercenaries filled the narrow entrance to his forge and stepped around the growing pile of weaponry that had overtaken his workshop in the two days since the Reavers' main force had arrived in town. The scent of oiled leather and sweat accompanied them, and the soft jingle of their weapons rang with their every footfall.

"Master Robillard is as fine a smith as your sorry lot would find in a bigger city," called Anders. Micah's young apprentice dropped the tongs he carried with a clang and balled his fists. "You'd do well to treat him with the respect he deserves."

"Maybe you should get the boy to fix your blade," laughed one of the soldiers. He drew a knife from the sheath at his belt and stepped towards the young man. "This one appears to have some steel in his spine, although his tongue might get him in trouble."

"If you'd trust your work to a boy who just took up the craft, then I wish you well," said Micah as he quickly stepped into the man's path.

"Instead, I'd ask you to forgive my apprentice. I assure you we want no trouble here, sirs. I have worked at this forge for a decade now. First with my Da, and then upon my own merit when he passed on. How may I be of service?"

"Can I know that if I drop a blade here I'll not get a butter knife back from you?" growled the one called Gregor. In the crimson glow of the forge, there was a savage gleam in his eyes, but Micah crossed his thick arms over his chest and held the mercenary's glare.

"Anders," he called. "Go and fetch some wood for the forge, if you please."

"Yes, sir," said the young man and he hurried out the side door.

"Now, gentlemen," Micah said with a bit of a sneer on the word, "Your brothers in arms have already provided tasks enough that I can justify turning away jobs for which I haven't an interest in taking on. I leave the decision to you if you believe I am an honorable man of my craft. If not, then I would bid you good day, so that I might not have more of my day wasted."

The soldier's savage grin melted away and with a smooth pull, drew his saber from the sheath at his side. Micah struggled not to flinch when the man flicked the tip of the blade under his chin. The soldier deftly twirled the weapon around and dropped it onto the table with a clang.

"Cutting down those savages took the edge off of my steel. Be a good lad and get her sharp enough to shave with again. I don't want to see so much as a scuff on that blade when I get her back, understand?"

Micah picked up the weapon, tested the heft, and closed one eye as he squinted down the blade. As the three gruff mercenaries spun and walked back towards the door, the young smith replied with a smile and nod.

"Rest assured sir. You won't see a thing."

* * *

"Get some more of this slop out here, woman," roared a rowdy nameless soldier. The Hirsute Huntsman's main room had never been busier, but Dorothea couldn't wait until her husband's select ale stock dropped these obnoxious fools on their arses. Before she could respond with a scathing reply, her daughter, Allison, shot past her with a pitcher in hand and gave her a subtle shake of her head as she hurried over to the table of ruffians.

"Meat pies are in the oven now and second helpings are coming shortly, gentlemen," she said as she quickly filled their outstretched mugs. "We're not accustomed to having quite so many mouths to feed at once."

Dorothea flushed with pride as her daughter nimbly deflected groping hands and inappropriate jibes, always with a pleasant smile on her face. She jumped when a slab of roast boar slammed down on the counter beside her and Marcus wrapped his beefy arm around her waist.

"Our girl probably just saved those bastards from the fiercest tongue-lashing they'd ever have taken," he whispered in her ear. His beard tickled her face when he kissed her cheek.

"Startle me like that again, and you'll catch it in their stead. I might just hang yer hide over our mantle instead of that mountain lion."

"Turning your wrath on me might just save us all from a skinning, or maybe something even worse."

"They'll know worse the next time my work is called 'slop'. They keep that up and the lass is only delaying the inevitable."

"We've weathered harsher storms. Remember the plan. We need endure them only long enough for Abel and Anne-Marie to rally whoever they can."

"Let's hope that the wait is nearly over. How ye abide this rabble in our home, I'll never understand, but since ye find a way, then so shall I."

"Don't underestimate these brutes, love. They are bloodthirsty killers one and all. I shudder to think about what they could take from us, should they have a mind to it." Her husband looked towards their daughter and she wrapped her fingers in his own, comforted by the familiar rough calluses of his hands as he gently squeezed back. Dorothea frowned, but her heart still fluttered whenever she looked up at his weary face. Tough as nails, he was, but there wasn't a more kindly soul that she had ever known.

"I'd better get another pot a-boiling." Dorothea peeled his arm from around her and retreated through the door to her kitchen. The heat of the cookfires warmed her, and the fragrance of herbs filled the sanctuary where these ruffians and sellswords could never bother her. She pulled down one of her canisters from the shelf, but knew from the heft that she had used the last of the secret blend of seasonings that it once held.

"Woman's work is never done," she muttered and grabbed her gathering basket from its hook beside the Huntsman's heavy rear door. With a grunt, she pushed it open and stepped into the yard.

The heady perfume of the dozens of herbs used in her renowned menu filled the air with an almost intoxicating aroma around her carefully cultivated garden. Dorothea dropped to her knees among the neat little rows and played with the rich soil between her fingers. With the small blade she kept tucked away in her basket, she deftly sliced through the stems of the sage, rosemary, and thyme plants within her reach, and stacked them in neat little piles.

The breeze shifted ever so slightly, and a different smell, one faintly more pungent and cloying, carried on the wind. Without rising, she made her way to a second bed of plants. Few in Pioneer Vale knew half as much about herb lore as she did, and fewer still would understand why she kept these buds and flowers separate from those she cooked with. The back door creaked open and the raucous sounds from the taproom reached through as Allison leaned out into the yard.

"Mama? Da says you best hurry for these soldiers are getting rowdier by the minute. He's telling them tales about witches and ghosts, but I think he's doing more harm than good."

"And sowing the seeds for our deception," Dorothea said under her breath. She grinned and the small knife in her hands danced neat somersaults along her knuckles. "Go and roll out the crusts for another meat pie, love," she called to her daughter.

"I've only a few more sprigs to gather."

*　*　*

"Abel, I had once wondered how we would make ourselves known to our enemies when the fight began," Kitchi sighed, "but now I am certain that you shall herald our arrival long before my people do." He had winced with every twig that snapped under the old farmer's boots, and even the roar of the thundering waterfall ahead barely muffled the footfalls to his ears.

"I am not the one who will need to stay hidden, lad. They won't be shooting at me. At least not at first, but I'd not concern yourself with the tread of my steps." The farmer's words were cut short when a heavy shape slid from the concealment of the underbrush and wrapped a thick arm around the man's shoulders. With a jovial shake, Chogan's booming laugh filled the forest as he shook the startled farmer.

"Let us reserve heavy feet for the throats of our enemies," the sentry said. Kitchi returned the respectful nod that Chogan gave him. "I am happy to see you safely returned, my friend."

"Good to see you too, Tiny," muttered Abel. The old farmer freed himself from the Nipmuc man's bearlike grasp. "And I am fine as well, thanks for noticing."

"You're back!" Kitchi turned, the excited squeal affording him just warning enough before Alawa slammed into him and threw her arms tightly around his neck. The wounds along his back shrieked in protest, but he welcomed the young woman's embrace nonetheless. From behind the curtain of falling water, Henna ambled along the path trailing after the young woman. He returned the aged Guardian's smile, as she leaned upon her staff, and looked the two of them up and down.

"You'll forgive me for not greeting ye likewise, Master Harmon," she said with a wink, "but I fear your wife would disapprove."

"And you are a wiser woman for it, madam," Abel returned. "I would not wish my Nell's wrath upon you."

"So how went your journey?" asked Chogan. "Will the other tribes join us against the marauders?"

"We will not face Maheegan alone, my friend," replied Kitchi. He looked over his shoulder and called out. "Chief Rowtag, you may bring forth your men."

The bushes rustled then parted as the brawny chieftain marched out before columns of Nipmuc warriors, emblazoned with different stripes and symbols distinctive to their various and respective tribes. Kitchi smiled broadly and clapped his slack-jawed friend on the shoulder. The region had answered Rowtag's call without question and, within hours, the ranks had swelled with their brave kinfolk brave from across the land.

"So many," breathed Alawa. "I never expected such an alliance." Rowtag smiled and bowed deeply to the young woman.

"Kitchi proved most persuasive," said the Nipmuc leader, "especially while covered with the blood of the bear that would have killed my son and wife."

"I helped a bit with that too," mumbled Abel. Henna cackled merrily and elbowed the man in the ribs.

"Of greater help still, my friend," said Kitchi, "is the plan that you shared on our return to the sanctuary." He raised his voice so that all of those gathered could hear his words. "Under Master Harmon's guidance, we can get inside the barricade that the mercenaries have built around Pioneer Vale town. Once the walls are breached, we will meet up with other brave and true folk among the settlers who will stand with us."

"And together we will drive back Maheegan's black-hearted soldiers and restore peace between us all," cried Rowtag. Cheers erupted from the assembled Nipmuc warriors as the chieftain turned to Abel. "What do you need from us?"

The farmer scratched his stubbled chin and marched down the line of men with his hands folded neatly behind his back. Kitchi followed close behind his friend, watching him size up the warriors at the front of the line. Abel stopped abruptly, the scowl on his face clearly for show, as a proud smile tugged at the edges of his lips.

"I need two brave men, with steel in their hearts and fire in their blood. Men who can move like the shadows, but can fight like mountain lions. Who've you got?"

The Nipmuc men within range of Abel's bellowing voice all looked at one another and murmurs buzzed throughout the contingent. As one, the entire group stepped forward and a chorus of war cries filled the clearing, drowning out the raging waterfall. Kitchi doubled over with laughter while his friend ran his hand down his face and then rolled his eyes at him.

"I think you may have to select them yourself, Abel," he shouted over the enthusiastic whoops of the throng. "There isn't a soul here who fails to fit your description."

"And I'm certain that I'd be well served by any of them," the older man replied. A shadow fell over them, and Kitchi turned to see Chogan, towering over Abel with arms crossed over his chest. He elbowed the farmer who regarded the sentry, and huffed, but not before shooting a wink his way.

"What about you, Tiny? Are you willing to follow an old soldier into battle?"

"Without hesitation," said the brawny Nipmuc warrior, "but I still have one concern, Farmer."

"And what might that be?" Chogan smiled and hefted his club.

"That our enemy won't have enough men for all of us to fight."

CHAPTER 12
BEFORE THE STORM - 1671

"Where the hell is everyone," growled Cyrus.

The training yard was empty except for a single pair of his men half-heartedly sparring. The watch tower was deserted and a blossom of fury filled his chest as he saw an unclaimed rifle leaning against the post. He pressed his eye against one of the firing slots cut into the perimeter wall.

The natural smells of the forest boldly struck his senses, and the very weight of the crisp evening air pressed down and chilled the light sheen of sweat across his brow. The eerie silence of the wilderness set him on alert as if something watched back from beneath the dusky twilight canopy.

"Begging your pardon, Captain Forrester," whimpered one of his Reavers who stumbled forward and halfheartedly saluted him, but quickly buried his head in a nearby bush and retched. The young soldier rose a moment later, and wiped his mouth on his sleeve with a trembling hand. "I only left the stand to relieve myself. Seems quite a few of us have come down with stomach trouble."

"Where is your squad commander?" Forrester demanded. "I should have him horsewhipped for leaving these posts so undermanned."

"That's just it, sir. I reckon that he's either in bed or the latrine. Same as most of the company. Camp's full of frightened whispers. Men talking about…." The young mercenary paused, quivering with fear and nausea.

"Frightened whispers are about to give way to enraged shouts, son. Out with it."

"Well, Captain, some of the men are saying there was more to the witch's curse than we gave credit for. Word going round the garrison suggests that your treatment of the town has brought her supernatural wrath down on the lot of us."

"Spread this rumor to your compatriots, boy," Cyrus snarled. With teeth bared, he grabbed the surprised mercenary's throat. "The next man who utters another word about witches or other such local nonsense will discover what a wrath born of this world feels like."

He shoved the soldier away, and the man snapped off a salute, before he tripped over himself fell to the cobblestones.

"Yes, sir," he croaked. "I meant no disrespect, Captain."

"Get somebody in that watch tower before I return," Cyrus spat. The sudden clash of shattering metal followed by a torrent of swearing behind him drew his attention away from the cowering soldier. "By the maker, now what?"

The two men who were engaged in their sparring match stared dumbly at the hilts of the sabers in their hands, the blades themselves lying at their feet in glittering shards. Cyrus' blood boiled as he stormed over to the mercenaries and it took all of his considerable force of will to not backhand the man before him.

"What must I do to get a little discipline in these ranks? Maybe once you have paid the cost to replace those weapons, you'll learn to save the hard strikes for an actual battle."

"With all due respect, sir," said one of the men who stepped forward and saluted him, "we weren't even swinging that forcefully, and such breakages aren't ours alone. Steel all around the camp has been going sour these last couple of days. Ever since…"

"If you say one word related to that purple bonfire, soldier," he said, raising his hand to cut the soldier off, "I swear to God that I will shoot you myself."

"Yes, sir." The soldier gulped and nodded.

A cold breeze blew through the yard and the men before him shivered and nervously fumbled with the broken weapons in their hands. The hairs on the back of his neck stood up, and for half a heartbeat, a grim shadow passed over their features that cast a pallor resembling the waxen appearance he had seen on so many dead men throughout his career.

"Carter," he yelled, "front and center, now." He rubbed his eyes, easing the burn that nested behind his lids, while his lieutenant rounded the corner of a bunkhouse, trotted up to him, and snapped a crisp salute.

"Here, Captain, and ready to report."

"You are a model soldier, Nate." He lowered his voice so that the others in the yard couldn't hear him. "Lieutenant, just how depleted is the garrison? Are the other watch posts so deserted?"

"We've had a lot of men report to the infirmary in these last couple of days, sir, although Levens hasn't been able to cite a cause."

"Something catching?"

"I couldn't say, sir," Carter replied with a shrug. "Doesn't appear life-threatening, but whatever the case, our numbers have surely been cut down. Should I enforce a quarantine until we have a better idea of the source?"

"Make it happen, but I want every able-bodied man on these watch posts. Anyone who can stand with a rifle and can see past the end of their nose. Should trouble come from these woods, we will not be caught unaware, Lieutenant. Do I make myself clear?"

"Of course, Captain. Before I go, however, I need your seal to purchase additional equipment." He nodded to the two sparring partners.

"Those lads weren't deceiving you. We've seen an unusual number of breakages, misfires, and the like recently. Our Quartermaster was flooded with requisitions, but he hasn't enough to replace all that is needed."

"Commandeer what you need from that local smith, and tell him that he is under my orders to work through the night if need be. Bleed the town dry if you must, but I want our men provisioned with every available resource."

"Of course, sir. Will there be anything else?"

Cyrus turned away and closed his eyes, listening for any of the usual sounds that the surrounding forest should provide, but still, he heard nothing, not even the whisper of the leaves. "There is something afield tonight. Something heavier in the air. More oppressive."

"How do you mean, Captain?" His second stepped closer, furtively glancing at the closest mercenaries. "Sir, you aren't starting to question if that Carmichael woman is what Mathers claims, are you?"

"No, not that." He snorted. "Our trials are far more mundane in nature. However, I suspect the time to earn our salary comes due. You have your orders, son. Get moving."

Carter saluted and hurried away, already calling out instructions to the men within earshot. Cyrus turned his imperious glare on the few nearby soldiers, resting finally upon the young watchman that still wobbled unsteadily. The boy's face went green once more, and with a vicious heave, hurled his supper upon his boots.

*　　*　　*

"I'm bored," whined Thomas. "There's nothing to do."

"Well, Mama told us to stay here. She said if we got lost in these woods we might not find our way back," said Aiden. He drummed his fingers on the rough wooden table in Whisperwind's kitchen. His brother wasn't wrong though.

"What if we kept close by? We won't get lost if we just chase fireflies in the yard, or maybe we could pick some pretty flowers for her. I bet she'd like those blues and purples we passed on the trail from that big rock."

The fire in the big stone hearth crackled and danced through bursts of different colors. Dishes floated through the air to the washtub when they had finished eating. The faint jingle of bells rang from time to time from the corners of the room but they stood empty whenever he looked. It wasn't scary, though. It reminded him of when Mama wrapped him in a warm blanket when he got sick last winter. Still, as magical as she had told them that this place was, there wasn't even so much as a set of wood blocks to play with.

"Alright. We'll go outside and play, but we must keep the cottage in sight at all times. Understand?"

No sooner had the words left his mouth before his little brother clapped his hands and dashed to the door. Thomas threw it wide open and raced into the yard. Aiden rolled his eyes but hurried after him. When his hand touched the door latch, the fire behind him flared up. The multicolored flames grew brighter, and flashed almost frantically through its palette of lights. Almost like it was afraid of something. Warning them not to go.

That's silly, he told himself, and yet, as his feet crossed the threshold, he shivered. It wasn't just that stepping into cold air after being beside the cozy fireplace, but something seemed…wrong. The feeling that they were being watched wasn't gone, but it changed suddenly, almost as if someone different watched from the shadows now.

Thomas jumped into the air and slapped his hands together. He peeked inside his clasped fingers and giggled. Aiden walked over to him, and in the setting sun he saw the dim shine of a firefly peeking through his brother's small fingers.

"I caught one! Have a look, Aiden."

"We should have brought something to put them in," he said. His eyes searched the woods, but there was nothing but chirping bugs and trees that swayed lightly in the gentle breeze. Jumping at shadows, his papa used to say, whenever he scared himself like he was doing now. Thomas opened his hands and the bug flew away, joining its fellows although its light seemed a little more frantic.

"Let's make Mama a bouquet," the younger boy said and he raced down the trail. "She's been sad lately. I bet I can pick the best ones to cheer her up."

"I think not. You always pick droopy ones." Aiden ignored the chill in the air and chased after his brother. Soon enough, flower picking gave way to a game of tag, and neither boy noticed how the quaint and cozy cabin was gradually swallowed up by the forest behind them.

*　　*　　*

Anne-Marie knelt in the shadows of the Widow Stone. She swept her hand over the blades of grass that still bore the crimson specks where Jeremiah had fallen. When she closed her eyes, the warmth of the setting sun nearly convinced her that his body still rested under her fingertips.

"What more will your war demand of me?" she whispered. "I know you can hear me, Elder."

The raspy rustle of leaves and the gentle chirp of nearby crickets hidden away in the tall grass were her only reply.

"In so short a time you have driven me from my home. Endangered my friends." She ripped loose a handful of the stained grass and hurled it at the stone monolith. "Broken my heart. How many others dear to me will pay for a conflict that they know nothing of?"

She rose from the ground and brushed pine needles from her skirt. From the trees, birds sang their soft songs in a mournful chorus, soft and lamenting, that brought a choking lump to her throat.

"I don't know how much more I can bear, and too often recently have I wondered if you are as terrible as the demon you would have me fight in your name. Am I truly your champion, or just a pawn in a game that shouldn't be of any concern to me? Why has such terrible responsibility fallen on my shoulders?"

A breeze blew through the glade, and gently ruffled her hair, almost like a lover's caress. The wind stirred the sweet fragrances of the scattered patches of blue and violet wildflowers and carried to her ears the gentle ring of Aiden and Thomas' tinkling laughter. Though distant, but growing closer, a wistful smile creased her lips and a flood of fond memories of her life before she had first set foot in this place filled her thoughts.

"And so you have answered me," she whispered. "The struggle is all for them, and those children who would come afterward. If I don't stand against Shade, then everything that I have lost, and what we will come to lose, will have been in vain."

The sun touched the horizon and set the sky awash with streaks of lavender. Anne-Marie lost herself in the swirling vibrance of the rolling clouds and clenched her fists tightly. The amethyst pendant at her throat blazed with the reflected fires above, and, with her resolve strengthened once more, she opened herself to the rush of power that surged through the clearing.

With a downward snap of her wrists, her hands filled with her fiery magic. Her feet lifted from the ground as the eddies of energy swirled down her body, wrapping around her in a sinuous dance. The simple farm dress she wore burned away but the ashes wreathed her skin and became the corset, blouse, trousers, and boots that were her Guardian accouterments.

Her feet settled back to the earth once more and the flames dissipated. The violet in the clouds slowly faded into a deeper blue as the sun fell behind the hills.

"Off to war, then," she said. She spun on her heel and headed into the forest depths.

*　　*　　*

Preston snuffed the last candle with a quick pinch of his fingers and languished in the exquisite agony of his seared flesh on the hot wick. Darkness swallowed his study as the dancing flames in the fireplace alone lit the room.

Shadows writhed along the walls while he dragged a heavy armchair before the hearth. He ignored the grating scrape of the wooden feet against the floorboards. Impulsively, he started over to the sideboard where his snifter sat, but held back and decided against draining another nerve-bolstering shot of liquor.

For the next few moments, it was likely better that he had all of his wits about him.

"Come to me, Shade," Preston said as he slowly lowered himself into the chair and gazed deeply into the flickering fires. "I would speak with you."

The flames crackled, but there was no sign that the demon was present.

"You may dispense with your indignation, wolf. Need I remind you that it was I who found the gemstone's strongbox in that dank hole? That had I not broken the ancient seals therein, you would remain incarcerated in your shadow realm, rather than having even so light a reach into this world as you currently enjoy?"

A log popped in the fireplace sending a shower of angry embers up the chimney, and he smiled.

"As children, we are taught to beware the enticement of a devil's dealings, and yet you are the one who has seemingly forsaken our arrangement. You have lured away the loyalty of my trusted watchman and left me burdened with that brutish cutthroat who would now lay claim to my reward for your release. Though I may not possess their affinity for violence, you would do well to remember that neither possesses the wicked edge of my keen mind." He steepled his fingers under his chin. "I am the serpent that hides in the grass, and whosoever crosses me shall feel my venom in due course. For example, it would be a shame if that yellow crystal that binds you was once more lost to the ages. Perchance vanishing overboard at sea?"

The temperature of the room plummeted and his breath blew out in a fog. The orange embers within the fireplace turned a dull gray and drew the heat from the room. Preston blew on his meaty hands and rubbed them together.

"Good to see that I now have your undivided attention." The air shuddered and a heaviness rattled the furniture. The floor creaked and the crystal that he was so fond of squealed with a high-pitched whine. A palpable malevolence washed through the room, but Preston shrugged it off.

"We two still share a common enemy, and to the core of my being, I would see her destroyed, albeit for reasons different from your own. Anne-Marie Carmichael is one of a short list of those who hold incriminations against me that, should they come to light, would force me to flee my position gained here. That will not do."

The flames in the fireplace twisted around the logs and Preston would have believed they for one moment drew down into the shape of a furrowed brow.

"I am owed. Owed still the lands upon which her farm sits. Owed my vengeance for what a pain in my arse she has become."

Rhythmic bursts of fire sprang skyward not unlike the rolling breath of a chuckle.

"Your conquest demands allies, and all you can rally to your side. Like you, I appreciate the secrecy and discretion that lurking in the shadows affords us, and it is from that sanctuary I would prefer to strike. Tonight I would renew my bond with you, Wolf. Let the ruffians draw the fire from the townsfolk and the local savages for you, but with regards to that accursed woman, whatever she may be, I would see the deed finished myself, and ask only that you grant me your will to do so."

Gray fire thrashed violently in the hearth, leaping beyond the fireplace in a sudden frenzy that scorched lines across the mantle. A low howl echoed through the room, and crystal cracked behind him. In a cascade of sparks, the flames rushed back into the confines of the fireplace and lazily resumed the proper reddish glow and the normal dance of a crackling fire. Preston nodded.

The bargain had been sealed once more.

He walked over to his desk, opened the center drawer, and lifted out the finely made pistol that rested therein. The heft of the weapon felt uncommonly comfortable in his hand and he set it gently upon the sideboard. Aside from Anne-Marie, there was but one other whose words could topple all that he had built, but he would deal with Parson Reynolds in due course.

But first, it was time for that drink.

*　　*　　*

Corbin stared out the window of his study. He looked past the burnt orange, gold, and lavender beauty of the dusky sky and saw instead the haggard reflection that looked back at him. It was the face far more akin to a vagabond beseeching grace rather than a man of the cloth who could grant such a boon. With a sigh, he smoothed his unkempt hair, buttoned the collar of his shirt, and decided he would shave later. He further ignored the stain of spilled wine on his lapel as there was no remedy for such an insult to his appearance.

A log popped in the hearth and broke the silent reverie he had become lost in. He turned away and fell heavily into the chair beside his desk, pushing aside the bowl of cold stew that he didn't even remember preparing. A half-eaten apple was a paperweight for the papers spread out across the wooden top. He picked up the oft-studied sheaf that detailed all of the sins and transgressions of his life that yet weighed on his conscience, and as he peered through the account of his misdeed over his years, his despair turned into something darker.

Stronger than his jealousy over Horace Pritchard stealing away with Madeline. More intense than his grief for the blood of Jeremiah Carmichael that stained his hands. More fierce than his guilt over how he had been lured by Preston's sinister plots that had left Anne-Marie a fugitive.

The words branded upon the pages laid bare his soul as a hypocrite, a coward, and a charlatan hidden behind a veil of false pretense and misplaced good faith. The brutal truth was that his had been a life devoid of purpose, but he laughed as he took up his quill and grabbed a clean sheet of paper from the stack at hand. He knew not what devil possessed his mind, but his words flowed, driven by the rawest emotions that had ever poured from his heart. Penance. Remorse.

Revenge.

He at length blew on the wet ink and reread what he understood to be the final entry he would ever make into his confessional. Corbin saw both his redemption and damnation intertwined within the single opening line. He folded the papers and stuffed them into his jacket pocket and then headed to his bedroom and threw open the trunk at the end of his bed.

The pistol that had been issued to him, by Horace no less, gleamed just as it had when he had thrown the weapon within. Hidden away so that he could never invoke the possibility that someone might mistake him for a martyr were he to turn the instrument upon himself.

He was no soldier. No hero.

But one way or another, his suffering ended tonight.

*   *   *

The cloying fragrance of lavender and honeysuckle hung in the air, with a lighter wisp of soot and ash trailing after that set his blood aflame. It was her scent, and she was close by. A low growl, not entirely his own, rumbled from deep within his throat, and he fought back the urge to throw back his head and howl at the rising moon.

Patch dropped to the ground and lapped water from the babbling stream. The act seemed somehow more natural to him now. He had always embraced a certain streak of savagery in himself, but the raw power that flowed through him now brought out something even more feral. The demon had granted him strength, unlike anything he had ever known before.

He dug his fingers into the loose soil of the bank, feeling the thrum of the insects and vermin of the earth rushing away from the coldfire that blazed within his veins. The living rock shared its memory with him of blood recently spilled by his hand, and though the vision seemed distant as if from another lifetime, the scene that played in his thoughts was as vibrant and vivid as if he had just left the kill.

He sprang to his feet and crashed through the brush. Deeper into the heart of the ancient forest he raced. Branches whipped past his head, and his instincts told him that he had passed this way recently. Although shrouded by the enemy's magic, he now knew the path that led back to the glade with the ancient fallen monolith.

He would find that hallowed place once more.

It was there he would hunt her. Trap her.

There he would make her scream.

*   *   *

"And so it was said that the Great Bear ran into the woods with his hindquarters aflame," said Henna. The laughter from the Nipmuc children at her feet reminded her of days long past when she was a young woman living in a since-vanished fishing village far to the north. Telling tales around the fire had always been a pleasant pastime once the evening meal was over, and the memories of heartily bellowed drinking songs, bawdy jokes, and feats of strength among friends and family still brought a wistful smile to her face.

"Tell us another, Henna. A story of your folk," pleaded one wide-eyed boy.

"I think that we've had enough tales of the great spirits buffoonery for one evening," she said and ruffled the child's hair. "There are still some chores that need finishing before you small warriors must be away to bed."

They pouted and whined as children were wont to do, but they were dutiful and knew their places among their people. They had been through so much in so short a span of time, she thought. Spirits, let us keep them safe.

As if in reply to her prayer, an icy wind howled through the cave and she fell against the rock wall at her back. A terrible pain seized her chest and she squeezed her eyes shut. A sense of dread swept over her, and the primordial magic within struck a clarion call that echoed through her veins. It could mean only one thing.

Shade was on the prowl.

She wiped the sweat from her brow and clutched her walking staff. With a groan, she pulled herself to her feet, wrapped her shawl a little more tightly around her shoulders, and hobbled toward the cave entrance. She ignored the stares of the folk who watched her striding forth with steadfast purpose in every step. The cool spray from the falls had just begun to dot her forehead when a light hand touched her elbow.

"I've asked everyone to stay within the cavern at night. These woods are untamed even in the best of times," Alawa said. A fleeting smile gave way to a respectful bow of her head. "It's not safe to go out."

"There's a change in the air tonight, child," Henna said. She reached out and lifted the girl's chin, drawing the young woman's gaze to meet her own. "And far more dangerous to us all if I stay."

"You're leaving to face Maheegan, aren't you? Stay with us and we shall make our stand together. We would do our part to protect our home. We are few but those that remain are fierce and proud."

"And woe to any who would dare underestimate the strength within you," Henna laughed. She hugged the Nipmuc woman tightly. "You will lead them well, Alawa. Your people recognize within you an inner strength that you have not seen yourself."

"I am barely more than a child playing as chieftain. I know nothing about how to lead them," Alawa scoffed. "But you? You are 'Viking's Daughter' and the deeds of your younger days are whispered among us. I would learn from your guidance that I might become more like you or even…the Fire-haired Maiden."

"Anne-Marie would have a laugh, I think, to hear herself so addressed, but I'll tell you a little secret about her." Henna leaned in closer. "She too was forged in the fires of these recent days, and I think that perhaps ye two are not so different at heart."

"I am nothing like her. She is proud and savage like the warriors of legend. Kitchi spoke to me in whispers of when he first met her. Just before you and he found us here. He said that she had powers that should not belong to normal folk." The girl swallowed hard. "She frightens me."

"The old wolf isn't so fond of her either."

"Is she... a witch?"

"Such accusations often closely follow headstrong women who dare to defy those with small minds and large agendas."

"But can we trust her?"

"Child, I would put my life in her hands without a second thought," Henna said with a heartfelt grin. "And because of that, my duties lie elsewhere tonight. Just as yours remain here with your people. You have your own ferocity, Alawa, that will take you far. Ye only need to figure out where to look for it." Henna hugged the young woman once more, then turned and stepped lightly across the glistening stones behind the falls.

"Henna, be careful," Alawa called after her. "The old legends say that those who fall in battle with the black wolf are hunted in the spirit realm for eternity."

"He may think me easy prey, my dear," Henna replied. "But soon enough he will learn that I am simply the bait for a far grander trap."

CHAPTER 13
CLOSING IN - PRESENT DAY

Becky was surprised to see light streaming from under the door of the small hospital room. This late in the shift, the only people not fast asleep were the night staff making their rounds, or the ones like her who couldn't bring themselves to leave. She gently pushed it open and peeked inside.

Every light in the place had been turned on, even the ones in the bathroom. She looked at the empty bed, but a flutter of movement revealed wide eyes hidden beneath the depths of a pile of blankets huddled into one corner of the small loveseat.

"You alright, Jamie?" she called. She smiled at him as he wriggled out from the covers, hoping to bring some comfort to the traumatized boy. He was her son's best friend and he had become as dear to her as one of her own, and it pained her to see him so scared. Although Jamie had told the same story as his parents, Clarissa, and Doc Hibble, she found the tale frighteningly easier to swallow coming from him. "Why aren't you in bed asleep, young man?"

"I tried earlier, but I kept...having bad dreams."

"It must be lonely for you here. All of us hospital folks popping in and out all night probably doesn't help either." She reached for the light switch inside the bathroom door and flicked it off.

"No," he cried out. His lips trembled and he reached towards her. "Please, leave it on."

"Of course," she said quickly. Becky clicked the light back on and sat down beside him. He pressed tightly against her and she put her arm around his shoulders. "Tell you what. I don't see why you can't get released tomorrow morning. How about I talk to your parents and see if they are okay with you camping out over at our house until things get back to normal? Billy has been worried sick ever since he heard that you were here. I know he'd be glad to have you around." She lifted his chin. "Might do you some good too, kiddo."

Jamie looked off into space, his eyes staring blankly, but nodded his head. "When we get to your house, is it ok if we leave the lights on?" he whispered, and Becky hugged him tightly.

"If that's what you want, sure, but I promise you, no monsters are allowed at my house." She felt him tense up suddenly and she bit her lip. Nice going, Beck, she thought. Figure out the perfectly wrong thing to say. Goosebumps sprang up on her arms and their breath started wisping out in white puffs as the air grew chilly.

"Too late. They're already here," he replied.

*　　*　　*

The shroud of coldfire bent the light around his twisted frame so that he drifted down the hallway unseen. A young man in blue scrubs nearly brushed against his scaly hide and paused. Oblivious to his presence, though, he simply shivered and hurried along.

A hunger, deep and ancient, rose within him and urged him to feast upon every last one of them. But Lord Shade wanted these cattle for himself. Blessed by his Dark Master with this form, there was but one that he was permitted to play with.

Allowed to tear to pieces.

His mind was a maelstrom of hazy images. Smoke rose from a ruined farmhouse and the trailing echoes of his own cries fueled the rage harbored within his breast. Familiar names and blurry faces that must have meant something to him a lifetime ago burned in his tangled memories. They all seemed so far away now that they might as well be from a dream, yet there was a presence close at hand of someone who had dared lash out against him. Within these walls, he would find those who had hurt him.

Acidic drool ran from his maw and pocked the tile beneath his heavy, taloned feet. They would all pay. One by one, he would tear the screams from their bodies while he snapped their bones like twigs between his fingers. He would rend their fleshy husks like a child tearing a paper doll, and devour their eternal souls, for such was promised to him once he had completed his task.

Lord Shade had taught him this.

He rounded the corner and followed a single blossom of flame that glimmered at the edge of his awareness, feeble and faltering but still brilliant enough to hold the shadows at bay. A candle that was his sole purpose to snuff out. A single chain that yet bound his master confined to his own realm, unable to savor the delights of crushing these frail shells around him.

More remembrances of another place and time flurried through his thoughts as if they tried to distract him from his goal. Through those copper tresses, his quarry looked down upon him as she cradled him in her arms. Smiled at him. Sang to him. But he saw through her lies. The love she had bestowed upon him was nothing more than a charade. She loved only her formidable power and cared nothing for him, or any of the others who had the misfortune to come along after. She had discarded each of them at her whim to maintain her mantle and dominion.

Lord Shade had taught him this.

The scent of her blood from the other side of the closed door was maddening. With a flutter of one leathery wing, a gust of wind forced the door to slowly swing open. In the dark center of the room, she lay still, helpless before him with all manner of wires and tubes connecting her to strange machines with another sort of magic that, while beyond his comprehension, remained powerful enough to keep her alive. The gossamer thread of her life force shimmered in the gloom and taunted him. Teased him. Dared him to snip it in two. How ironic that where he had once been her precious little angel, he had now become her Angel of Death.

"Mooottthhhhhheerrrrrr," he hissed.

His tongue snaked out like a serpent's, slavering over his gleaming fangs, and hungrily dripping with black spittle. His claws clacked above the bare skin of her throat and coldfire danced along the razored tips. One simple slash and the last anchor that tied him to the weak shell of who he used to be would be severed. With her life ended, he would bask in the power of his master's glory.

Lord Shade had taught him this.

He hooked his talons under the silver chain around her neck that peeked out from under the gown she wore and drew out its length. The amethyst pendant slid out from under the hem and bounced lightly against the side of his scaled palm. An angry, pale light flared within the heart of the gemstone and a burst of lavender fire seared his flesh. With a snarl of pain, he raised his claws high above his head, ready to flay the skin from her bones, when a strange breeze drifted through the room.

The wind carried with it a fleeting scent that tickled the depths of his foggy memory. He whipped around just as a young woman with dirty blond hair walked past the narrowly opened door, continuing down the hall. He knew this one from his time before. Through his coldfire limned sight, he remembered this same girl, once his prisoner, standing over his pain-wracked body as she had dared to oppose him. Rage twisted inside his breast, and when the fiery haze parted, his seething wrath conjured up a name.

Clarissa Brenner.

His teeth flashed like a thousand blades in the soft light of the room. His master's instructions were clear, his will without question, but how could Lord Shade begrudge him one simple act of retribution first? He spared a glance over his shoulder to his mother lying helplessly near him. She wasn't going anywhere, and after so many centuries, surely his master's bloodlust had been tempered by patience. She could wait a few minutes longer. Instead, let his first kill in this realm strike against this girl who had so brazenly attacked him. With the echoes of her cries, in his ears as he ripped her flesh, the eternal torment he would then inflict upon her enslaved soul would taste sweeter still.

Lord Shade had taught him this.

*   *   *

Clarissa stopped and cracked open the soda she carried. She stifled a fierce yawn and rubbed away the burn in her eyes. Her hand shook, but at this point, she didn't know if it was from caffeine jitters, aching fatigue, or this ridiculously freezing hallway. The ice-cold can was her security blanket, warding away the sleep that she desperately needed, but didn't dare give in to. The dullness of her hospital room lulled her senses even worse so she had taken to wandering the lonely hallways. At least being on her feet kept her blood moving. She raised the can in a toast to no one in particular.

"'What dreams may come'," she muttered and threw back a gulp. She jumped as ice burned her tongue, and she spit the sip out. There was no way the fridge could have gotten it that cold. She peeled her fingertips from the frost that climbed up the sides of the can and her breath came out in wintry wisps.

The hidden lines that now adorned the skin of her stomach spasmed with a shock as if a live wire had been pressed against her body. Overhead, the bright fluorescent lights flickered and the air shimmered around her. The few late-night staff workers faded into ghostly apparitions of themselves, going about their tasks but oblivious to the rime of ice that scaled across the walls. Their voices, already soft, grew hollow until their muted words were lost within the harsh guttural whispers murmuring around a swirling shadowy portal that hung in mid air just around the corner from where she stood.

The overhead lights flickered like strobes and caught in slow motion an enormous figure that emerged from the doorway of Anne-Marie's room. Even the shifting shadows did little to hide the massive frame of the midnight-scaled horror that leered at her. Its eyes seethed like pools of lava, and the hellish glow within them melted away the darkness. Long talons scraped against one another with the sound of knives on a whetstone and the drywall turned black with corruption everywhere they touched. Great leathery wings unfurled from the creature's back as it forced its way back into the hallway, and the claws at their tips tore gouges across the ceiling tiles.

"Heelllllllllllooooooo, Clllllaaaaaarrrriiiissssssaaa," the fiend snarled in a hissing whisper. Its hellish laughter rang through the halls and her heart clutched in her chest.

Despite the otherworldly hollowness and pounding reverberation in her head, the cadence of the voice fanned a spark of instant recognition. Every trial of the past few days, starting with the rally at the school, her imprisonment in the ancient demon's shrine, and the fight at Angelica's farm crashed over her once more. Her knees wobbled and the soda can slipped from her grasp to the floor with a loud clang. This twisted and misshapen thing that stood before her was Aiden Carmichael returned to this world for vengeance.

And he was starting with her.

She backed away, but he matched her step for step. The greater strides of each heavy footfall shook the floor and closed the distance between them, slowly and deliberately. Her back touched the wall and Aiden crouched to eye level with her, confident that she had nowhere left to run.

A glass vase shattered against the side of his head, and a young woman dressed in a volunteer's uniform dashed behind the nurse's station desk. Aiden screeched and spun around toward her. His chest expanded and a coldfire blaze gathered between his teeth. The muscles of the behemoth's legs tensed, coiled and ready to unleash its fury on the frozen across the hall. Clarissa slipped down the hall behind him and hoped in that moment that Aiden's hatred for her was enough.

"Hey, Aiden," she yelled. Clarissa gulped as the draconic snout whipped back towards her. "Thought I was the one you wanted to play with."

A gout of gray flame from his mouth raked across the nurses' station, sending a firestorm of burning paper into the air. Aiden turned the fiery blast upon the lights above them and a cascade of exploding fixtures crashed all around. The emergency lights switched on and bathed the entire corridor in the reddish glow.

Clarissa evenly met his burning glare. His eyes narrowed, and, within their depths, she saw the promise of a thousand agonies borne upon his vile magic. When next Aiden's legs coiled and those black wings spread wide, her resolve faltered.

"Run," she screamed. Her sneaker squeaked on the tile as she turned and sprinted down the hallway. Behind her, the thud of his steps thundered along, slowly at first, but gaining ground all too quickly.

*   *   *

Vicky slumped to the floor and cowered beside the smoldering nurses' station as the monstrous creature lumbered away down the hall after the blonde girl. She stifled a scream that rose within her chest, in case the monster turned its attention back to her. She crept around the corner on her hands and knees, but stopped and stared at a shrinking black hole that slowly swirled in mid-air. The air around it crackled with flashes of blue and white light that arced from the depths. A burst of thunder shook the walls as a young woman with a long black ponytail tumbled through the gateway and collapsed on the ground.

She was wreathed in lightning and flashes of smoke rose from the back of her leather jacket. Her clothes were stained in ash, soot, and more than a little blood. The acrid stench of sulfurous smoke filled the air. Her sleeve was torn and her forearm buckled when she tried to push herself from the ground. She groaned, but her eyes blazed, lost in blue fire that watched the strange gateway iris shut and vanish.

The woman's blinding power flickered away, and Vicky slowly crawled closer. This newcomer's breathing was labored and even, but she looked fit despite the state of her injuries. She rose from the floor on unsteady legs but determination and willpower alone kept her moving.

"You're hurt. Let me help," Vicky called out.

"Thanks, but I got it." A crackle of radiant light coursed down the girl's arm, and the bloody gashes sealed over with fresh pink skin. "That'll have to do for now."

"Wait. I know you," she said. "You're Angelica Brighton. That girl who went missing a few weeks ago. There's a flyer in the break room with your picture on it. So many people thought you were dead."

"Let's hear it for dumb luck," Angelica replied. "Where is he? Which way did that thing go?"

"It chased another girl down the hall," Vicky breathed. She tried to keep her hand steady as she pointed down the debris-strewn corridor.

Angelica staggered over to the same room the monster had come from and pushed the door open. Her shoulders slumped in visible relief before she turned back around. A loud crash and deep howl echoed from down the dim hallway and the other woman stood taller as she stepped over a pile of rubble.

"I need you to find Doc Hibble and tell him to stay close to Anne-Marie. Tell him that Aiden is back. He'll know what that means."

"Hold on," Vicky said. She grabbed Angelica's wrist, but a shock zapped her hand and she let go immediately. "You're going after it? You can't hope to fight that thing."

"I'm not going to fight him. I'm going to blast Aiden Carmichael back to the hell he crawled from," Angelica said. Electricity raced up and down the lengths of her arms and her lips pulled back in a snarl. She gave a curt nod and the air around her shimmered. There was a flash of brilliant light and she vanished down the hall in a blinding streak.

Emergency alarms screamed throughout the unit. The air shimmered and the ghostly form of a nurse grew solid once more. The awestruck woman's mouth dropped open as she regarded the destroyed nurse station that had been whole but a moment before. A security guard burst from the staff stairwell with taser in hand, but his frantic questions fell upon deaf ears.

Vicky clutched the edge of the charred desk and just stared at the door where the red-headed patient lay. She had no idea what she had just seen, but she wasn't about to question the woman cloaked in lightning that had just chased after some kind of a dragon that stalked the hospital hallways. She swallowed hard, pushed past the security guard, and rushed off to find Doctor Hibble.

*   *   *

Clarissa didn't dare glance over her shoulder. She sprinted down the hallway while Aiden's heavy treads already closed the gap between them. Thankfully, the halls in front of her were empty, although a few curious and terrified faces peeked through windows and doorways as she raced by.

The long corridor broke to the left a few strides up, but the flashing 'Exit' sign over the door to an emergency stairway straight ahead gave her an idea. The wide-open hallway favored Aiden's size and speed, but the tight turns in the stairwell might slow him down and improve her odds of surviving. With his breath hot on her back, she pushed herself to move ever faster.

Claws cutting the air hissed behind her and scraped along the fabric of the back of her shirt as she reached the turn of the hall. With a prayer on her lips, she juked left then spun right in a move that Coach Bradley would have applauded had she pulled it off on the basketball court. She ducked under his outstretched arms and his twisted muzzle slammed into the wall. Aiden crashed to the floor, and she raced back towards the door, but before she could hit the bar, his barbed tail lashed across her shins and she stumbled into the frame. Her ruse had bought her the moment she needed though, and she regained her balance and bolted into the stairwell's narrow confines.

The emergency lighting here was dimmer still, and her footing even more treacherous than the rubble strewn hallway she had just left. Clarissa almost tripped and tumbled down to the first landing, but held tightly to the railing and swung herself around to the next flight of steps. The squeal of metal overhead was soon followed by the slam of the steel door against the concrete block wall, and she paused to look up through the center of the stairwell.

A winged shadow blotted out the light from above, and Aiden's cold eyes gleamed as he looked upon her. His teeth glistened and his serpentine tongue played across his lips as he stood tall and spread his wings. A fierce wind rushed past her from below, and too late she realized that the swell of his chest meant that he had sucked in his breath once more. The simmering glow of gray fire kindled deep within his throat, and before she could fall back into the safety of the sheltering stairs, a plume of coldfire washed across her.

The force of the blast threw her against the wall and she tumbled down the concrete steps. Her head smacked against the steel service door at the bottom and her teeth clacked painfully on her tongue Warm blood filled her mouth and the world wobbled when she opened her eyes. Needles ran down her left arm from elbow to wrist, and her fist refused to close. Her knee throbbed where it had caught the brunt of her fall and her torn jeans turned crimson from the ripped skin under the denim.

Raspy breathing became a deep chuckle, and Aiden's rumbling bellow rattled the handrail in its moorings. The slow and steady tread of taloned feet scraped against the metal stairs, each clank and groan carrying with it the promise of pain and death. Clarissa fumbled for the lever handle above her head and yanked it down. She shoved with her legs, threw her shoulder against the door, and fell through into a cavernous room. She rolled aside and kicked the door shut, then reached up and flipped the lock as deftly as she could with her thumb.

Her labored breathing was lost within the droning hum of heavy machinery. Steam hissed from seams and valves along a maze of twisting pipes, and shallow puddles of standing water dotted the floor around the room. A heavy thud hit the bottom step in the stairwell, and ripples fanned across the surface of the nearest pools, just before the door at her back rocked against the frame from the sudden impact of some immense weight thrown against it. Clarissa scrambled away as quickly as her injured leg would allow, and searched for a place to hide before Aiden broke through.

Wind gusted from the rusty grate of a small crawl space nestled between two of the large machine cabinets. She slipped her fingers through the mesh and pulled, but the wire mesh held fast.

"Come on," she sobbed. Another boom and screech metal came from the doorway. Placing her foot against the wall, she leaned back, pulling with all her strength until at last the grate broke free with a clattering snap. Steel slashed through the meat of her palm, and blood poured down her wrist, but she squeezed between the curtain of wires running through the tight chase. She reached out and pulled the screen back against the opening, holding it in place.

The door shuddered again after another teeth-jarring strike, far louder than before and followed by an almost exasperated, but muffled, growl. One final strike and the battered service door sailed across her field of vision. The dim lights flickered as the winged shadow lumbered across the floor. Aiden's head came around the corner, sniffing the air and swinging his head slowly from side to side. A snort of gray fire rolled from his nostrils, and his wings stretched out lazily to the fullest extent of their terrible span. He dropped to one knee and tasted a splash of her blood that had dripped on the floor.

Clarissa's head throbbed, and dark memories of the shrine swam through her thoughts. She squeezed her eyes shut, but the visions grew stronger and more graphic in their tortured promises of what awaited her.

Flames raked her body, blistering and blackening her flesh. Thousands of worms swarmed over her, the myriad bites and stings making her tremble from the venom. Her bones snapped one by one as dark creatures who dwelt on the edges of the darkness twisted her limbs. Although her mind screamed that these were only Aiden's illusions, the intrusion into her deepest fears was relentless.

"Cooommmmeeee ouuutttt, Clllaarriiissssaaaaa," Aiden called in a hissing singsong voice. He ambled off into the darkness, and although she couldn't see him, the dull clang and thump of his massive frame knocking against the network of mechanical pipework was near enough that she couldn't try to escape. Caught in the small cramped crawlspace, the slightest unbidden whimper slipped from her lips.

It was enough.

A frigid rush of air flowed past her and Aiden's hellish slitted eyes suddenly filled the small space beyond the screen. He flippantly waved his hand in the air, but then his taloned fingers snapped shut sharply into a fist. The machines beside her hiding space imploded in a shower of sparks and rending metal, and when he threw his hand to one side, the steel cabinets ripped away from their bolted moorings and flew across the room. His other hand darted forward and ripped away the top of her sanctuary like it was made of tin foil.

"Leave me alone," she screamed. She tried to scramble deeper into the chase, but there was nowhere for her to go. With her back against the cold metal, she stared wide-eyed as the creature knelt down on his haunches, his arms resting on his knees, and drummed his claws against his thick hide. His tongue flickered like a serpent. His wings fanned a gentle breeze over her.

But his eyes promised her death.

His hand snapped forward, and claws ripped into her ankle. The wicked tips scraped bone and her veins burned as his demonic fire pumped venom into her blood. With every nerve aflame, Clarissa clamped her hands over her ears and screamed until the coppery taste of blood welled up in her throat. She scratched at the sides of the duct just before Aiden's glowing eyes flashed once more with their sickly gleam. Her hip exploded in pain as the monster yanked her from the cramped crawlspace and hurled her across the room like a rag doll.

She skidded to a stop against a chain link partition. Her back and elbows burned where her skin was scraped away against the rough concrete. Her leg was just a bolt of fire and she feared that if she looked she might see it still in his clutches. She rolled to one side, and found it still attached but limp and laying at a disjointed angle. She whimpered and tried to get on her back but Aiden's towering shadow fell over her.

A wicked smile creased Aiden's toothy drooling maw. Steely fingers closed around her throat and he lifted her effortlessly from the ground. She scratched at his hand, but his unearthly grip was too strong. Acidic mist from his breath burned her nose as the creature drew her closer to him. His tongue caressed her cheek teasingly as the pressure around her neck tightened.

"Please," she croaked. Her sight grew dark, but in her plea for mercy, flashes of light from across the room popped and brushed away the shadows, reaching out like a comforting hand. Aiden's head turned away from her, glancing over his shoulder as he held her aloft. His eyes widened and the razor tips of his talons glinted in the beautiful blue-white brilliance that fanned towards them both.

And then a deafening boom of thunder blew them both to the floor.

CHAPTER 14
HANGING ON BY A THREAD - PRESENT DAY

"Get away from her," screamed Angelica. She planted her feet and white fire wracked the scaly horror that her cousin had become. Coiling tendrils of lightning burned trenches in his hide, all the while tumbling him across the concrete floor until she smashed his head against a steel beam and he fell motionless to the floor. She released the current and ignored the rivulets of blood that dripped from her nose. The dull thud in her skull was lost within the fading rumble in the air around her. While keeping an eye on The Harbinger's smoking form, she dashed over to her friend and slid the last couple of feet on her knees to where she had collapsed to the floor.

"Clarissa," she gasped. Her friend lay crumpled on the concrete floor, her body covered in cuts, bruises, and burns. Gingerly, she brushed the tousled blonde hair away from the girl's face and cradled her friend's head in her arms. "Please, wake up."

Clarissa groaned, and ever-so-slowly opened her eyes. Her eyes wandered, vainly trying to focus on something, but then her face scrunched up, her sucked in her breath in a hiss, and she clawed at the leather of Angelica's jacket. The spasm passed, and her friend hugged her back once the fog of pain passed.

"Angie," she sobbed. She tensed and tried to scramble away when she saw the monstrous fiend lying close by. "That thing…it's Aiden. He's after me."

"Clarissa, it's ok. You're safe now." Out of the corner of her eye, a wing fluttered. "But listen to me. I have to get you out of here."

"I can't feel my leg, Angie. I thought he had ripped it clear off."

"Ok, just hold still," she said. Angelica gently pulled the bloody cuff of her jeans higher and frowned. Bad enough that her friend's hip was twisted at an unnatural angle, but a sickly road map of black veins sprawled out from the slash in Clarissa's calf. There was a scuff to her side as the Harbinger's foot scraped across the floor. They were running out of time. "Let me see what I can do."

Angelica placed her hands on either side of the garish wound. A thin sleeve of electricity wrapped like a fishing net around Clarissa's leg, and then sunk into her body in a shower of sparks. Her friend stiffened and bit her lip when the energy popped her disjointed leg back into socket, but Aiden's foul poison was the real threat. The venom fought back like a living creature born of his malice and hatred.

Fine, she thought. In her mind, she envisioned it like a serpent, grabbed it by the throat, and channeled all of her voltage into it. The current crackled along, entwined the sludge, and wrangled it back towards the open slash in her flesh.

Angelica's magic bolstered Clarissa's own natural defenses and they fought against the dank infection. With a resounding splat, Aiden's toxin dripped from the wound and lay in a smoldering puddle on the concrete. When the brilliance of her lightning faded out, the terrible cut had knit together until only a faint dimpled scar remained.

"Good as new, Bumpkin," she said and flashed a faint smile, but Clarissa's eyes went wide and were lost over her shoulder. She spun around and threw out a blinding shield from her hands just as The Harbinger's slavering fangs clamped down on the crackling edge mere inches from her face.

Lightning burned along his jaw and ravaged the fleshy inside of his dragon-like maw. This time, the smoke that curled from his nostrils was not his own. His claws raked against her shield, but she could give him no chance to get past it. She shoved him with a ferocious push, but where she had intended to launch him across the room, Aiden's talons gouged the floor and he skidded to a stop only a short distance away. He panted in a rhythm that matched her own heavy gasps, and Angelica braced herself for his next relentless strike.

"Clarissa," she shouted over the crackling sparks around her fingertips. "Get the hell out of here. I don't want you caught in the middle when I open up again."

"But Angie," Clarissa yelled back, "you're hurt too. Do you think you can stop him?"

"Only one way to find out," she muttered. Angelica swallowed hard as Aiden's muscles rippled beneath the scaly hide. Coldfire wisped beneath the cuts and scrapes that the roll across the floor had opened up, and the dark magic stitched him back up again.

She sighed and snapped her wrists in time with the scuff of Clarissa's shoe on the concrete. Blue-white flames coiled around her arms and enshrouded her in a cloak of lightning. Her eyes burned with raw power, and her rolling thunder drowned out Aiden's vicious snarl.

"Come and get me, you bastard," she said.

The Harbinger stomped his feet, and the concrete shattered under his weight. With mighty wings unfurled, he sprang forward with his claws grasping towards her. A twin blast of lightning caught Aiden in flight and she dragged him down, but the shock from his landing still drove her back half a step. The bony edge of his wing swept under her chin in a surprising uppercut and clacked her teeth together. Angelica was launched through the air and slammed against the nearby machinery, slumping to the floor.

"SHEEEE ISSSS MIIIINNNNNEEEEEE," Aiden hissed at her. With another leap he soared through the air on his leathery wings and devoured the distance to her fleeing friend. There was no way to reach Clarissa before him.

Her cousin's claws flashed down and although he struck only a glancing blow across the girl's back, his demon-infused strength slammed her to the ground with escape just beyond her reach. The fiend landed and kicked her squarely in the ribs before planting his massive foot on her. The muscles in his leg tensed, and his talons slowly, teasingly, dimpled the fabric of her shirt.

Angelica's tongue ached where she had bitten it and she spat blood to one side. Rolling up to one knee, she swirled her arms like a tornado above her head, and a lash of lightning lazily fell from her hand. With a sizzling crack, she snapped her electrified bullwhip around Aiden's forearm, and barbs of piercing energy dug into his thickened hide. Like the surge of a raging storm, she dragged him away from Clarissa in a spray of ichor and chipped scales. Her cousin thrashed like an angry fish on a line, but she twisted and rolled along with him, bracing her feet in the torn-up concrete.

"Move, Clarissa," she groaned. "I don't know how long I can hold him back!" She fired another jolt down the tether and then slung the makeshift lead over her shoulder. Her legs drove her forward, dragging him further away from his prey with each hard-won step. The coil went abruptly slack and she went down hard on one knee, clenching her teeth at the sickening crunch when it struck the concrete floor. A winged shadow soared overhead and Aiden's feet slammed down in front of her. She lifted her head and met the gaze of the monster that towered over her.

His eyes burned brightly with four centuries of pent-up hatred limned in the coldfire flames. His hand shot forward and grabbed the front of her jacket, effortlessly lifting her into the air. She clawed at his fingers as his cracked lips peeled back from dagger-like fangs, and a gray blazing plume seethed in the depths of his throat, a mere breath away from her face.

Angelica crossed her arms in front of her, hiding behind a wall of lightning without a moment to spare. The cone of gray fire broke around her shield, although the air was still filled with the scent of burned skin and singed hair. When the fiery breath fell away, she snapped her hands down, and a boom of thunder rocked the Harbinger's head back. When his grip on her jacket loosened, she planted her foot on his chest and somersaulted backward. Her boot struck under his chin with an enhanced kick, and she landed in a kneeling position in front of him. A blade of pure crackling energy erupted from her closed fist, and she lunged forward, driving the weapon deep into his stomach. The creature shrieked as she twisted the sword, and he crumpled to the floor.

She released the weapon, arched her back, and held her arms out to her sides. For once, she stood taller than her enemy, and, with the flick of her fingers, the power that flowed through the nearby machines answered her call. Blinding currents arced her way and coursed into her body until she glowed like a star there in the depths of the hospital's basement. A rising tempest burned within her, and Aiden cowered before her majestic power. She swung her outstretched palms forward, the tips of her thumbs touching and fingers fanned out with the Harbinger sighted in between.

"You've lost, Aiden," she said.

"Noooottttt yyeeettttttttt," he growled back at her. Before she could unleash her stored up energy, the Harbinger's tail snapped first. Barbed spines along the bony ridge tore deeply across her calf and yanked her off her feet. Her head smacked the floor and the magic within her surged wildly forth in a single concussive bolt that streaked across the basement and hammered through the block wall, carving a crude tunnel away and upwards into the cool night air. Spots danced before her eyes, but Aiden's wings spread open and he glided towards the opening.

"Angie, he's getting away." Clarissa's frantic cry was little more than a hollow echo in her ears but the urgency in her friend's voice cleared away the cobwebs in her aching head. She rolled over onto her stomach and raised a net of twisting coils that filled the tunnel entrance. Aiden plunged into the net in his desperate attempt to flee, and Angelica squeezed the magic around him, searing his body and entangling his wings as he struggled to escape.

"Like...hell...he is," she said through gritted teeth.

Aiden thrashed in her net like a captured fish, and her head throbbed from the force she needed to use to contain the intensity of his strikes. His claws dug into the broken cinder block wall, and he tore away chunks of the cracked concrete. Even though wounded, his strength was immense, but when he stopped fighting suddenly, Angelica's eyes went wide.

Thrashing in her net, a curtain of gray flame swirled around Aiden's body like a wildfire and fought against the strands that bound him. She struggled to hold him inside her snare, but his magic ate away at hers until the net burned away like paper. He spun around on her and threw his hands forward, firing a double lance of coldfire, but his bolts went far too wide around her, rending metal and grinding the gears of nearby equipment instead.

"Just a bit outside," she quipped, and wound up like a baseball pitcher with a summoned ball of lightning between her hands. The Harbinger's pointed teeth gleamed and his eyes burned above a cruel smile. Crouched at the hole in the torn basement wall, Aiden's hands clenched the air, and long vines of coldfire threaded throughout the ruined machinery all around her. The smell of fuel filled the air, and as sparks rained from her fingertips, she understood that she had never been his intended target.

"Oh, you son of a …." she breathed.

"Goooodddddbbyyyyeeee, Cooouuusssiinnnnn," Aiden hissed.

Coils of coldfire ripped pipes, cables, and heavy machinery from the floor, while setting alight the spray of gasoline and oil. Klaxons blared from distant parts of the hospital as power failed throughout the building. The blossoming fireball spread across the room in slow motion, and Angelica hurled her lightning beyond the swell of flame, wrapping Clarissa in a wreath of crackling energy. Shrapnel ricocheted against her shield, but she wasn't sure if even her reflexes were fast enough to protect them both.

The roiling explosion hit her first, followed by the crushing weight of hundreds of pounds of mangled steel that slammed into her from all sides.

*　　*　　*

Ben fell against the nurse's desk outside of Anne-Marie's room as the building was rocked by a violent quaking several floors below. The wail of the sirens died off and the emergency lights went dark. Only a handful of flashlights weaving back and forth lit the corridor. Vicky tumbled against him, and he caught her by the shoulders, steadying her.

"What the hell was that," he muttered, but one look at the frightened volunteer's face answered his question. After the girl's rapid fire report, it seemed as though the battle from Carmichael Farms had followed behind them far closer than he would have liked. Not for the first time, he wished he'd never met Aiden Carmichael in that dingy bar.

"Do you think Angelica can stop that creature?" Vicky whispered.

"We'd better hope so. That young lady packs some serious firepower, but I suspect that she is in for one hell of a fight. Nothing we can do for her right now. We have our own job to do." He pushed through the redhead's door and his heart sank. Where before the hums and beeps of the machines had greeted him, Anne-Marie's room now stood cold and dark. The respirator had stopped breathing for her. The display on the IV pump was blank. A chill wind whistled past him, and from the far corner of the room, the shadows shifted into the leering grin of the wolfish creature from the cave.

He snatched the lighter from his pocket and flicked it against his thigh. The meager flame dispelled the oppressive gloom, but cast a sickening pallor over the woman's ashen cheeks. While her face may have been bloodless, the bed sheets and front of her gown were stained a deep crimson, and a steady drip from the sodden cloth fell into a widening pool on the floor.

Anne-Marie was dying.

"Ben?" called Rebecca as she burst into the room. "Thank God! There you are. The whole building is out. We need all hands on deck to save as many patients as we can until we're back up and running."

"We're starting with this one." Ben set his lighter on the table beside him and started chest compressions on the redhead. "Grab a squeeze bottle and start breathing for her."

"Dammit, Doctor, we can't turn our backs on those with higher chances of survival than this one woman. We have to check on…"

"There are no other cases right now, Rebecca," he shouted as he lunged across the bed and grabbed the nurse's arm. He choked back his desperation before it seemed like madness, but judging from the shock in her eyes, it was too late for that. Ben let her go and winced when she rubbed her wrist, but he didn't have time to apologize. "You need to listen to me and do exactly what I tell you, Nurse Harmon. This is way bigger than just the power going out. If this woman dies, we are one step away from the end of the world. You can call me crazy or report me when this is all over, but right now, grab that damned squeeze bottle and help me keep her alive."

Ben couldn't look at her, but instead wiped the bead of sweat from his brow and then resumed compressions. He only stopped holding his breath when Rebecca took her place at Anne-Marie's head, fit the resuscitator mask over her nose and mouth, and began squeezing the bellows.

*   *   *

Clarissa's lungs burned and she coughed on the thick black smoke that filled the room. Steam hissed and the drone of sirens just barely drowned out the groans of the strained structure of the basement. Concrete beams cracked and steel supports bowed in the aftermath of the explosion. In the center of the basement, a twisted mass of pipes, wires, and metal sparked where she had last seen her best friend standing.

"Angie," she cried out, and she crawled onto the heap. She tugged at a piece of sheet metal but gritted her teeth as the searing steel blistered her hands. She grabbed a nearby pipe, and jammed it under the plate, trying to lever the debris away, but the weight was more than she could budge. Hot tears ran down her face. "Somebody help us," she shouted, but her there was only a whispered echo in reply.

Rubble shifted at the far end of the room, and Aiden's wing pushed aside some chunks of concrete and steel. She froze and crouched behind the mound as the creature freed himself from the pile of rubble and crawled to the hole in the back wall. Smoke rose from his burnt scales, and he held his hand over the wound in his stomach where Angelica had stabbed him. His snout lifted and sniffed the air, pausing only long enough to glance over his shoulder. She held her breath, but either he didn't see her or didn't care, and bared his teeth in a halfhearted snarl before he clambered into the tunnel and disappeared.

Clarissa stared helplessly at the mountain of steel beside her. Overhead, a piece of machinery chugged and sputtered, and a single blue-white spark fell from a lazily swaying cable onto the heap. Another fell, and then a showering burst shot forth, forcing her to cover her eyes. The machine wheezed once more and then erupted in a blazing cascade of white fire that streamed over the debris.

Chunks of broken equipment rattled and slid from the heap, and the unsure footing sent her back to the broken floor. Streaks of lightning flashed from deep within the pile, and the heavier pieces were tossed aside like confetti. Angelica blasted through the debris, gasping for air and then fell back into the crater on the floor with her eyes closed.

"Oh, thank God," Clarissa cried out and she forced a path through the mess to her friend's side. Angelica's face was bruised and bloody. Her hands were black with grease and soot, and her clothes were adorned with countless holes from the shrapnel that had shot through the basement. With a deep sigh, she opened her eyes, blinked a couple of times, and then coughed. She lazily wiped away a trickle of blood from her nose before letting her hand fall back to her side.

"You ok?" Angelica asked. Her voice was weak and hoarse.

"Thanks to you," Clarissa answered with a nod. "You look like you've been through hell though."

"Well, you're not too far off," Angelica replied. Her friend grabbed her hand and Clarissa pulled her to her feet. Her eyes found the hole in the wall, and she shook her head. "I really hate him."

"Aiden ran for the hills as soon as he could make a clean getaway. I thought he might come after me again, but he must have lost interest."

"He's a coward and I was able to hurt him pretty badly, but we aren't out of the woods yet." Angelica leaned over and placed her hands on her knees, catching her second wind. "I can't give him the chance to recover."

"How did he become that monster?"

"Shade poured as much dark magic into him as a mortal body can hold. I don't even know how much of his own mind is in there now."

"Apparently enough that he remembered how hard I hit him at the farm."

"You certainly left a mark on him."

"He wasn't alone," she said. A frosty sizzle rolled across the strange marks emblazoned on her skin, but before she could lift the edge of her shirt, the clang of heavy boots rang on the metal steps of the service stairwell. Clarissa turned her head away from the dazzling beams from several flashlights that zigzagged across the floor, but Angelica, she noted, stared straight ahead with the crackle of blue fire in her eyes. A burly shape loomed out of the darkness.

"Who's there?" called a deep voice. The shadows parted and John Harmon ran forward, followed closely by two maintenance technicians. His hand dropped away from the pistol on his hip and he sighed in relief when he approached them. "Clarissa? Angelica? Is that you? My God, what are you girls doing down here?"

"And what the hell happened?" said one of the techs. His steel-toed boot made a muffled thunk when he kicked the huge pile of scrap machinery. The man shrugged to his coworker, then clicked the button on the radio clipped to his vest. "Boss, this is Jack. We have a bad situation down here."

"We're going to have a worse one up here if you don't get those generators back up and running," crackled the reply.

"That's just it, sir. Not sure if we have any left. Nothing down here but a bunch of burned-up junk."

"Well, you better cobble one together pretty damn quick or we are going to start piling up bodies fast," said the voice on the other end. Jack looked at his partner and threw his hands into the air helplessly. The two men hurried off to inspect the rest of the damage.

"Angie, your dad told me quite a whopper earlier," Harmon said when he turned back to them. He gave them both a stern but questioning look and lowered his voice. "Did that have something to do with…all of this?"

"You know that my dad would never lie to you, John," Angelica replied. "I need you to trust him. And me."

"Don't get me wrong, Angie. It does my heart good to see you back in one piece, but I've got about a million questions for you, young lady." Clarissa hid her smile when John reached out to lay a comforting hand on Angelica's shoulder, only for sparks to leap out and zap his fingers.

"There isn't time," Angelica said. Clarissa stepped aside as her friend pushed past her and limped towards the tunnel blown through the back wall. Lightning flashed in Angelica's eyes and her voice was nothing less than the calm before a storm. "The creature that did this is getting away and I am the only one who stands a chance of stopping him. We can't afford for Aiden to slip through my fingers again, but I don't have the first clue where to start looking for him."

"The cave," whispered Clarissa.

"What cave?"

"There's an old mine that he and Shade kept me in." All the grim reminders of her time as Aiden's prisoner flooded her thoughts once more. "It's on the eastern slope of Alistair's Climb straight above your farm. It was some kind of shrine deep inside the mountain. They planned to sacrifice me there to draw you and Anne-Marie out."

"Clarissa, we played all over that mountain growing up. I don't remember any cave." Angelica looked over at Harmon. "You don't know of any place like that, do you?"

"Nothing comes to mind." John shrugged. "There are hunters' trails at nearly every switchback as you go up the road to the peak, though. They're all over those woods. You can't miss them."

"Unless you never knew it was there in the first place." Angelica smacked her forehead. "Oh, Anne-Marie. You clever girl."

"What are you talking about?" Clarissa squeaked as Angelica suddenly threw her arms around her and gave her a quick kiss on the cheek.

"You're safe now, Bumpkin. I wish I could erase everything that those bastards put you through, but payback is on the way." Angelica steered her into Harmon's arms then hurried over to the hole in the back wall. "John, please take Clarissa back upstairs and find my family. You've got to put some officers around Anne-Marie. I don't think Aiden is in any shape to make another try against her, but we can't let our guard down. You don't understand just how much her survival means to us all."

"Hate to break it to you, kid," Harmon said, "but if these crewmen don't get power running again, we may lose her anyway. The ICU looks like a bomb went off."

"Angie," Clarissa said, "let's grab your dad and we'll all drive out to Alistair's Climb."

"Even with John's siren blaring, it won't be fast enough. I can't give Aiden the time to heal himself."

"Then how do you plan to get there?" Harmon asked.

"Did you all forget?" The corner of Angelica's mouth curled upwards. "I'm still the best cross-country runner in Pioneer Vale."

"I wish you weren't going after him alone." Clarissa stepped forward and hugged her friend. "I should be there to help you, Hick."

"You never could keep up with me, Bumpkin," Angelica whispered in her ear.

Clarissa stepped back while Angelica raised her hands to the dark ceiling. Sparks flashed between the young woman's fingers and the flare of magic surging through her body lit up the basement. Her hair billowed on blazing currents around her face, and arcs of power flowed through her limbs. Engulfed by her own radiant blue fire, she floated over to the tunnel mouth and dropped into a runner's crouch. With a boom of thunder in her wake, she sprinted away with only a trail of fiery footsteps as evidence that she had ever stood in the room.

"What the hell was that rumbling?" called a voice from the corner of the room. The two workmen rushed back over to them. "Is the whole damn place about to cave in?"

"I don't understand half of what's happening," John replied, "but you guys get these generators back up and running. Call up the hardware stores. If you have neighbors who might have a portable in their garage then call them too. You've got to get the damn lights back on." He looked one last time at the fading blue-white trail leading out the hole in the back wall. "Our lives may depend on it."

"We need to get back upstairs and warn the others," said Clarissa. "If Aiden sneaks past Angie, then he will make another try against Anne-Marie."

"Don't count that kid out yet. Angelica's tough as nails, but you're right," John said. "Let's get you patched back up and then I'll radio for backup. We'll grab Will along the way and figure out a game plan."

His heavy boot steps echoed across the floor as he hurried towards the stairs. Clarissa wrapped her arms around her stomach as the terrible creature tattooed there burned and shook as though it laughed at their feeble efforts. A sob from her very soul wracked her body, for horrific visions of ancient memories that were not her own heralded the grim foreshadowing of what awaited them all if Angelica fell.

*   *   *

"Our years of conflict draw to a close, Sweetling." Shade seated himself on a rock that rose from the ground to meet his backside. He clasped his hands together and rested his elbows on his knees as he stared down with a slavering grin. "Your student rushes into the trap I have placed before her, and your frail mortal body fights for every breath. I fear you will not survive much longer."

"Good," spat Anne-Marie. She wiped the grit from her cracked and bleeding lips. "I hate long goodbyes."

"It must be agonizing for you, isn't it? To have fought me for all these years, losing so many you held dear? Barely holding me at bay, only to fail here at the end. That very power that you pledged to oppose me with now slowly kills you," he chuckled as he leaned closer. His black tongue slid out and licked his decayed muzzle.

"And yet still strong enough to bar you from entering my world, Shade." Her muscles vibrated and she felt her insides scrambling about. She clenched her teeth and looked into his cold eyes. "Perhaps it is my turn at last to be the sacrifice that renews your cage."

"I do so look forward to hearing your screams join the choir of your precious Firstborn. What a delightful cacophony that shall make when I have you at last."

"Too bad that Angelica released their souls."

"Released them? Oh, no, my dear. They are but scattered." The demon barked a staccato laugh and stretched out on the gray dirt beside her, baring his midriff to the sky as if he were a dog seeking belly scratches. He waggled back and forth, and showered her in a spray of black sand before he flopped over onto all fours. The levity in his gaze melted away as he loomed inches away from her face, and his leer was replaced by the savage snarl of a predator. "Their souls are mine, just as your own and that of your precious Angelica shall be soon enough."

"You haven't won yet, Wolf." She gasped as searing gray flame erupted beneath the leather bracer on her left wrist, and ripped away the armband that hid the terrible scar of the demon's handprint. A burst of lavender fire doused Shade's dark magic, but her heart immediately lurched in her chest and her breath caught in her throat. The wolf gingerly lifted her hand and let it drop limply by her side.

"All in good time."

"I will free my children from your grasp before I die. Though they may never forgive me for what I have put them through, I swear you won't keep them as your playthings."

"Oh, but you shall belong to them. Imagine their thrill when I give you over with each new dawn, and they are given the freedom to torment you at their leisure." His eyes rolled back in his head and his tongue lolled to one side. Shade ran his fingers along her cheek in a gentle caress, and then grabbed her chin with crushing force. "And then just before each sunset, I shall come to you as you lie in your final throes and I shall tear the last beat of your heart from your breast, your final thought knowing that in a few short hours, it will all begin anew for you. Forevermore."

"Angelica will stop you, cur. You have underestimated her strength at every turn. And by whatever inexplicable means, I have not breathed my last. Our final battle has yet to be fought."

"Then I would suggest that you strike in whatever time you have left, my dear, for in your condition, the odds do not favor you." The demon slicked back the fur of his head and then turned to the distant horizon. A thin smile crept across his face and he rose from the ground. "The finale is close at hand. The moment fast approaches when I shall step into my shrine beside your son, and take back my dark magic that he wields in my name. And Angelica shall scream in your stead."

Shade made a sweeping bow with the edge of his threadbare cloak, and one final wicked snarl flashed across his face. Black smoke swirled around him and when the scalding breeze blew away the last wisps of it, he was gone.

Anne-Marie snapped her hand at the fleeting shadow, but the feathery flame sputtered away, barely stirring the lingering ashes that followed her enemy's departure. Another bolt shot through her, and the taste of bile filled her throat.

"No! Leave her alone, you bastard," she screamed as the darkness closed in around her. The world spun, but she still clawed her way forward across the sand to where he last stood. The hard-packed earth simmered with the heat of his fading magic. "You haven't finished with me yet...."

A fleeting vision of Angelica standing alone before Aiden and Shade filled her mind, while the demon's dark chuckle echoed quietly in the distance.

CHAPTER 15
UNFAVORABLE ODDS - PRESENT DAY

A blue-white blur streaked along the old country road and swerved on to the dirt road that led up the side of Alistair's Climb. At the third switchback, Angelica stopped cold, leaned forward, and placed her hands upon her knees. Her breath came in short gasps, and blood dripped in a steady stream from her nose. Beneath her shirt, the faint scars that ran across her stomach from her very first battle with Aiden burned with a slow icy pulse. Despite the magic coursing through her, every ache reminded her of how much damage her body had endured.

But there was no time for a rest. She was too close.

Thunder not of her own making rumbled in the starlit sky above, and dark clouds rolled in overhead. A light patter of rain fell and tiny sparks flashed as the droplets kissed her skin. The hairs on the back of her neck stood up, and her supercharged senses picked up the unique, yet quietly familiar, signature of timeless magic close at hand.

"Where'd you hide it, Anne-Marie? Show me the path," she whispered. Cold rain washed down the back of her neck, and she took a deep calming breath. She closed her eyes, but saw the world around her with a clarity beyond mortal reckoning. She turned a slow circle and smiled when her teacher's illusion fell away. Leaves tumbled down in a lazy cascade and gnarled tree branches bent away from the lonely trail that disappeared into the woods.

Anne-Marie's spell didn't camouflage the long overgrown path so much as direct attention away from it, similar to the way both the Widow Stone and the waterfall sanctuary near Whisperwind had been shrouded from prying eyes. They were hidden in plain sight, but any bystander felt compelled to walk past. Angelica stepped cautiously onto the trail, studying the dark recesses ahead, but sensed nothing that didn't belong in the ancient forest.

After only a few steps beyond the overarching canopy, the droning buzz of flies and the pungent smell of rancid meat drew her to the brush beside the path. Poorly hidden amid the undergrowth, the grisly remains of some ravaged animal lie covered in a crawling swarm of black insects. While she was no stranger to the natural order of predator and prey, having grown up on a working farm seated at the edge of a thriving forest, Angelica judged easily enough from the scattered carnage that this forest creature hadn't been killed for food.

It had simply been torn apart.

"All the better to eat you with," she whispered. She hurried past the carcass and followed the path a few more minutes before it opened up into a small clearing nestled against the sheer cliff wall of the Climb above. Through breaks in the far treeline, the landscape fell away into a breathtaking mountain vista that stood like a sentinel overlooking the fields of Carmichael Farms, but the view that should have taken her breath away was scarred instead by the plumes of black smoke that still rose from the rubble of her house, blown apart by Shade's insidious might.

The wolf's presence permeated the air in the grove with the stench of soot and sulfur, but there yet remained a subtle underlying hint of lavender and honeysuckle. The familiar resonance of Anne-Marie's magic hummed about her, like this place had been the focal point of some powerful dweomer that had been set in place long ago and forces equal and opposite fought ever on in a never yielding standoff.

The crumbled remains of an old smelter stood near the entrance of a dark cave that carved deeply into the base of the mountainside. A foul wind moaned and shadows swirled around the black maw that swallowed up what small amount of moonlight pierced through the encroaching wall of tree limbs.

"No wonder Anne-Marie wanted to hide this place from the world," she muttered. Angelica wrapped her arms around herself and hugged away the chill. How had she lived so close to this foreboding place all of her life and never once realized it was here?

Cautiously, she approached the entrance and a crackle of lightning ensconced her fist. Thunder hammered the sky above and the storm's ferocity seethed around her. The pelting rain comforted her and brought a little more surety to her weary steps as the darkness around the tunnel entrance melted away.

Scattered tracks painted the soft earth inside the tunnel, including the paw prints of a massive wolf. Pressed deeper and more recently were larger three-toed reptilian tracks that gouged the dirt and loose stone. The trail was fresh, and steam rose from faint drops of black blood stained the rock.

Aiden was here.

The oppressiveness of the air reminded her of that fateful night in the library. The stench of their ancient enemy filled the tunnel and it only grew more foul with each step she took deeper into the mountain. Following Aiden's path was as simple as following the bloody streaks smeared against the walls. Dust filled the air, displaced by something large, like the Harbinger's wings, scraping against the ceilings and stirring the currents as it passed through the narrow corridor. Every instinct screamed at her to run. Collapse the tunnel entrance and seal this place up forever.

But even that wasn't enough of a guarantee. She had to be sure that Shade's threat was stopped forever. It was all on her now, even though Aiden, and probably the wolf himself, awaited her down below. Gritting her teeth, Angelica stepped forward.

There was no other choice.

*　　*　　*

The rising storm outside shook the hospital walls. Kim burrowed deeper into the blankets with Jamie into the corner of the couch. Her son squeezed her waist tightly and trembled against her in a fitful doze. Will sat nearby on a rickety chair and fiddled with the small flashlight he carried. His eyes drifted to the ceiling as the rumble subsided.

"Will I ever hear thunder and not think of her?" Kim asked softly. She absently stroked her son's hair. "Knowing that she is out there fighting monsters?"

"If that was our little girl, then that thunder was most likely a warning to whoever's butt she is about to stomp." Will chuckled softly but she wasn't oblivious to the worry in his eyes.

"I just want her home safely." Kim said when her husband placed his hand on her forearm. "It's hard to wrap my head around everything that has happened in these last few days. I want things to go back to normal again."

"You mean like before you discovered that you married into a family of witches and that the fate of the world rested on your daughter's shoulders?"

"Or that the boogeyman was real," she said, then regretted it immediately when his grin melted away and his hand slipped back into his lap. Jamie whimpered, and she kissed his brow gently.

"Yeah. That part too." They sat in awkward silence, with only the muffled shouts of the hospital staff reaching through the heavy door to the room. Will started to open his mouth when the door burst open and the powerful beam of a large flashlight blinded her. The silhouette behind it fell against the frame and wiped a meaty hand across its brow.

"Finally found you," John gasped. "Been looking all over the place for you guys."

"Oh my God," Kim said. "Johnny, are you ok?" Will jumped up and rushed over to his friend. He steadied the man, who nodded and waved him off.

"Will, I need your help."

"Of course, John. What's up?" John's eyes drifted from Will to her and then back again.

"It's Angie. She's in trouble."

*   *   *

His tongue snaked across the wicked burn scar on his arm when an alarm bell rang in his head. There was an intruder at the mine entrance. So, she had followed him, exactly as Lord Shade had promised. He saw the pulsing glow of her magic through the stone walls as clearly as if she carried a lantern held high. He hissed, and the sheen of coldfire wisped across the other wounds that her accursed lightning had caused him.

How his stomach hurt! The blade of energy she had driven into him had cut deeply, and her biting lash had left blistering creases in his hide. Dark energy soothed his injuries, but even here in his master's sanctuary, healing was slow to bring relief for theirs was the magic of chaos, not rejuvenation.

It matters little, he mused. He flexed his wings, spreading them out in a lazy stretch, and listened to the sinews crack. Once she found her way to this hallowed shrine, all of the power she could muster would not be enough to save her. He would at last fulfill the oath he had made so many ages past. The last of the Firstborn would die by his hand, and the line of the Guardians would see its end.

He dragged his black claws along the ancient stone altar, the air surrounding it still heavy with Clarissa's scent, so recently bound here as a sacrifice. There was something different about that one now. Just as he had readied to end her miserable life, his promise of vengeance had been revoked. Some greater implication was set upon her, although he suspected that once her new destiny was finally revealed to her, she would prefer death.

The scrape of shoes on stone sent a ripple of magic through the air, and the beacon that was his enemy crept down the slope of the shrine's entrance. His black tongue flicked out and played along the dagger-like points of his teeth. He slid deeper into the shadows behind the altar and with his wings folded neatly behind him, reached up and grabbed a spur of rock high along the wall. Talons dug into the stone, and with natural ease, he pulled himself into the darkness above. He spared a glance over his shoulder as the gloom swallowed him up, and the whites of his fangs gleamed.

"Coooommmeeee aannndddd pplllaaaaayyyyyyy, Ccoouusssiiinnnnn," he growled.

*   *   *

Anne-Marie stared at the sunless sky above her. Her body spasmed, convulsed, but refused to answer her call. Another Blood ran freely from the corner of her cracked and dry lips and spattered the ruffle of her blouse. She searched the once white linen, but there was no longer any spot that remained unstained. She fell to one side, curled into a ball, and fought against the fury of frustration that boiled within her. The wolf remained unchecked, while Angelica walked into his trap, and she was powerless to help. She might have even laughed at her plight if only she had strength enough to draw in a deep breath.

She was dying.

"You can't give up now, Annie." The mists parted and Jeremiah stepped forward and dropped to one knee beside her.

"Get the hell away from me, Shade," she spat.

"There's no wolf here," he said softly. "Not this time. With his attention turned elsewhere, I was given the chance to join you."

"You've already tried this prank. There may be precious little left that I may do, but every moment that I continue to draw breath, I buy Angelica more time," she groaned.

"Our granddaughter won't win this fight alone. You can't stay idle any longer."

"Tell me, demon. Were you hoping I'd unleash one final blast at your mangy hide and spend the last of my strength trying to incinerate you? Make your victory come so easily?" She rolled to her back, her arms crossed over the place where her wound existed in her mortal body. "Let me assure you that the thought has occurred to me. Why don't you just leave me be instead? You've waited for my death for nearly 400 years. A few more minutes should seem like nothing to you."

"Do you remember our first Christmas at the farm, Annie?" Jeremiah sat down on the ground, his legs crossed and his arms wrapped around his knees. "I had spent all morning chopping wood and building the porch railings while you busied yourself preparing that scrawny goose my father had managed to shoot. He had run off to Abel's to trade side dishes, and you fetched me to help you lift the bird onto the spit. Afterward, I wove a sprig of mistletoe into your hair so that I could steal all the kisses I wanted from you."

"How can you know about that, demon," she whispered. Tears filled her eyes as she embraced the remembrances of that day so long ago.

"With dinner over the fire, you drew me back to our room where we entertained ourselves the rest of the day with that clever bit of mistletoe. My father returned to find the goose burned and the two of us wrapped in nothing but fur blankets sitting on the floor in front of the hearth. We ended up eating a cold stew and boiled potatoes later that evening."

"And what came next?" Anne-Marie asked. Her voice trembled and her breathing came fast. He reached over and caressed her cheek. Her skin still intimately remembered every callus on his rough hands. She looked into his chestnut eyes that had melted her heart so long ago and lost herself in the crooked little lines at the corner of his smile that his beard could never hide from her.

"And we swore on our love for one another and our unborn family yet to come that not even death would keep us from being there for each other when we were needed most."

With a sob wrenched from her soul, Anne-Marie found the strength to pull herself into her husband's waiting arms.

*   *   *

The bones of the ancient dead lay in barrows along the tunnel and the musty reek of dust and ash filled Angelica's nostrils. The stench only grew stronger as she followed the droplets of black blood and the taloned tracks that led deeper into the cavern, until the walls and floor changed from rough-hewn rock to worked brick and stone pavers.

The air was freezing, but the bag on her hip suddenly warmed as the narrow tunnel opened into a high vaulted chamber. A sickly yellow glow leaked from the pouch that carried the shattered gemstone from the Holding Chamber. The light pulsed, slow and steady at first then faster and erratic, almost sentient with anticipation.

As if it had found its way home.

The staccato snaps of lightning in her hand pushed the darkness away, but cast grim shadows over the cavern. Several giant broken pieces of a statue carved like a wolf's head loomed in the entryway, while across the vast chamber, a raised platform with a stone table rose out of the inky gloom. Two torches in rusty metal sconces flared to life with the gray flame, and cast an eerie wavering sheen across the glistening blackened stains that ran down the altar's sides.

She approached the dais, and slowly mounted the steps. Shadows swooped around her, and phantom fingers tenuously reached out, although they posed no more threat than the haunting song of the wailing wind. With a casual flick of her magic, she burned away the ghostly manifestations, but a flash of movement and a thin scrape on the stone above her weren't lost beneath the sizzle at her fingertips.

She threw herself forward and rolled under the explosively swift swipe of Aiden's clawed hand tearing through the air where she had stood a heartbeat before. The Harbinger's heavy feet cracked the marble floor, and the wind from his wings fanned her hair. She scrambled back, but bumped into the altar slab. Her cousin spun, yet he stumbled slightly when he turned, for blood still oozed from the partially healed slash in his stomach she had given to him at the hospital. His pale eyes narrowed, and he hissed at her.

"Love what you've done with the place. And here I thought blood-soaked gothic was so passé."

Aiden roared and threw a thunderous punch, but she deftly tumbled to one side, and hopped over the platform's railing and dashed back to the center of the chamber. His wing swept backward and pulverized the stone. He was pissed off and off balance, and she meant to keep him that way. She cocked her head and placed a hand on her hip.

"Look, Aiden. Aren't you tired of getting bashed around yet? Just admit that I am stronger than you are, slither back to the fuzzball, and spend the rest of eternity licking his boots. Or paws. Or do you guys sit around and sniff each other's...."

"Yyooouurrr doooommmm aawwwaaaaiiittts," he bellowed. The Harbinger planted his foot, and his chest swelled with a deep intake of the shrine's dank air. His jaw unhinged like a snake's and coldfire churned within the depths of his throat. Angelica braced herself, a shield of lightning already growing between her hands, but Aiden jerked his head suddenly to one side and the great gout blew instead across the blooded altar stone. Bathed in an unending stream of unholy fire, the slab shook with an echoing roar of ancient evil, and filled the cavern with a dense sulfurous smoke.

The acrid cloud stung her eyes, and her tears reduced Aiden's massive frame to a bulky shadow lost in the mist. Angelica pulled the collar of her jacket over her mouth and nose, and drew a ball of lightning into her hand. Blindly she hurled the bolt into what she hoped was his unguarded flank, but the glare was so intense she couldn't tell if her shot had found the mark. Still, the roaring fires of his breath abruptly ended, and the smoke slowly dispersed. Her monstrous cousin stood on the dais, panting, and then quizzically turned his head to her.

"You missed," she said between coughs. She stiffened suddenly, for through the dispersing smoke, a telltale fiery gateway folded upon itself behind the glowing altar.

"As did you." The too-familiar timbre rumbled behind her and only lightning enhanced reflexes pitched her forward fast enough to keep Shade's vicious claws from removing her head. The heavy heel of his hand still thudded against her skull, and she pitched face-first against the side wall of the shrine. She dazedly crawled over a chunk of the broken bust strewn about the floor and tried to put some distance between her and the demon, but the Father of Nightmares stood tall over her. Wreathed in gray fire, eyes ablaze with his foul magic, he threw his arms wide, and howled a triumphant, "Hello, Sweetling."

"Cheap shot, Furball. Even for you." She wiped grit from her cheek and leaned heavily against the wall until she was back on her feet. Her legs wobbled and the walls of the shrine spiraled around her.

Shade glared at her, pacing back and forth before the dais steps. He was larger than he had been in his realm, standing taller here than she had seen in any of their previous encounters. Tendrils of living shadow snaked from his cloak, and he beckoned to Aiden who crept meekly to the chamber floor.

"Come, Apprentice," Shade called, then his voice dropped into a menacing whisper. "You have something that belongs to me."

The demon reached out and purplish-black bands, far darker than coldfire's typical hue, lashed forth and bound his servant's winged form. Her cousin threw his thrashed and screeched while bursts of shadowed energy tore away from his twisting frame. Metallic scales cracked and clattered on the marble floor as they fell away from his body like rain on a tin roof. The Harbinger's massive frame shrank before her eyes, and although he still bore the batlike wings, long iron talons, and glistening fangs, Aiden's face had regained a trace of his former humanity. With a thump, he collapsed on the dais steps.

Shade threw his chest out and roared as he once more became the true master of his infernal power. He tore away the threadbare cloak that draped across his shoulders. Power rippled through his muscles, and he punched his mighty fist into the ground with such force that she fell against the wall of barrows at her side. Shade clenched his fist and blew across his knuckles as flames rolled from the tips of his claws up to his elbows in an almost gleeful parade.

"Feels good to be back," chuckled the wolf.

"You look different," she said. "Have you been juicing?"

"Oh, dear child, you are about to realize, quite to your detriment I'm afraid, just how strong I am in this place."

"Yeah, pretty sure you made your point," she muttered under her breath. She rubbed the knot on the back of her head where he had hit her. Even though she had fought with him before, Shade had never hit her with such force. His strength was unreal, and with Aiden at his side, standing alone against them would take everything she had. She stepped cautiously towards the center of the chamber, watching the demon carefully, but wary as her cousin haltingly rose from the place he had fallen.

"I should thank you, I suppose." Shade flicked a claw towards the belt pouch on her hip. "I could always dwell within this sanctuary, bathed as it was for centuries untold by the blood of my master. But my power quickly waned the further from this place that I ventured. Thus were you and Anne-Marie able to defeat me at the farm."

"And here I thought it was our 'take no crap' dispositions."

"A meddlesome quirk that will carry you no further," he said. Shade's voice was soft, but the walls shook with the waves of dark magical energy that weighted his words. "By foolishly carrying those broken shards from your world into my Realm, the veil has become more tattered still and soon the ancient bindings that bar me from your world shall fall."

"You still need two dead Guardians for that, and, last time I counted, you're still coming up short there."

"Your deaths, inevitable now as they are, will allow me to roam without restraint. Through your ignorance, a doorway that had once been merely cracked has now swung wide, and I have brought with me such power that your world has not felt since the earliest dawn."

"Well, you better hope it's enough," Angelica snapped, "because I'm not down and out just yet."

She snapped her hand outward and a ball of lightning rocketed past Shade and barreled into Aiden. Her cousin drew a wing around his body, and deflected the arc into a barrow carved in the rock wall behind him, but the impact still drove him sideways. An eruption of splintered bone shards peppered the side of his face, and with a howl, he spun away with his cheek streaked in blood.

Shade sprang forward with claws out and yellow teeth flashing in the fading light of her blast, but her training on the practice grounds served her well. Angelica dove to one side and tumbled behind the broken statue, leaving the demon scrabbling across the slick floor. She spun back to her feet in a dead sprint toward the altar platform and vaulted over the marble handrail, rolling across the slab and keeping another obstacle between her and her enemies.

Shade's rage filled the cavern, and he effortlessly hurled a chunk of the shattered statue at her, but a reflexive fan of arcing magic caught the clumsy missile and knocked it harmlessly to one side. A whip of lightning uncoiled in her palm and she cracked it in a wide arc over her head, but her enemy charged undaunted. Her second snap wrapped the tether around the demon's mighty forearm, and smoke rose from his fur while black flesh blistered beneath. Shade's teeth bared but he grabbed the lash in his hand and planted his feet. With a sudden yank fueled by his immense strength, Angelica jerked forward and slammed into the stone altar with a whoosh.

"My turn," the demon growled. Coldfire blazed around him, and Angelica was forced to cover her eyes once again as the sudden glare dazzled her vision. A wash of tingling fire slowed down time around her and the flow of magic that thrummed through her grew sluggish. Two shadowy figures dashed toward her through the rainbow spots in her eyes, and she summoned all her strength to raise a feeble defense.

Iron claws raked against her magic, but her shield held and turned the blows aside. She stumbled backwards, however, from the sheer force of the attacks, for both enemies pressed heavily upon her. Her legs, exhausted and aching, buckled and she slipped to the ground between her foes. A thunderous kick to her ribs was followed by an audible crack and she choked on new blood that welled up in her throat. She gasped for air, but a slash across her back tore through the leather jacket she wore and sent new bolts of agony through her.

Angelica pitched forward, and magic surged through her fingers. She dug into the marble floor, and leeched the rigidity of the stone into a draping cloak that fell across her shoulders. The surface of the floor had become like a loose rug in her hands and she snapped it with her lightning-shrouded fists. The shockwave rippled through the floor and her attackers feet went out from under them. Shade fell headlong down the dais steps, while Aiden managed to catch himself with a flap of his leathery wings.

"Sorry to pull the rug out from under you, boys," she said.

Angelica started to raise her hand, but her rib screamed in protest. Quickly, she routed some of the fading strength of the stone from her back down through her side. A slow searing burn from within eased the pain, however. She hissed through her teeth, but from above she heard the sharper intake of Aiden's breath. Gray flames rose through his throat again, and only the barest of shields, scarcely the size of a dinner plate, sparked between them before Aiden's bolt of coldfire washed over her.

A deep battle cry rose within her and her scream echoed throughout the ancient sepulcher. Her arm, already weakened from their previous fight, went numb and her skin turned pale as the relentless barrage licked around the edges of her barrier. She shook with the impact of his heavy feet landing just in front of her, and the tip of a bony wing slammed against her head, tearing a gash across her brow.

A second shadow fell over her, and a ripping pain gripped her scalp as Shade lifted her into the air by her long ponytail. His shoulder pumped once and her ribs exploded in agony once more. The demon's roar beside her ear caused a pop within her head, a wetness down her earlobe, and the sudden dull muting of the battle around her just before she was slammed on her back onto the bloodstained altar. The wolf leaned in close, his hot breath steaming against her cheek.

"You're nothing more than a pup who has worn yourself out chasing your tail, child," snarled the demon. Hissing laughter fell from Aiden's scaly maw as he slowly ascended the platform beside them. With a light hop, Shade joined her on the altar and pressed his knee into her stomach. His crushing weight dug her broken ribs deeper into her body, and pink froth spewed from her lips. "What? No last witticisms of youthful impudence? A pity. I so hoped your last words might hold something for posterity."

"Go to hell," she spat.

"You first," Shade purred.

Broken and bloody, Angelica watched as the Father of Nightmares lifted his taloned hand skyward. Swirls of dark energy sucked the heat from the room as coldfire engulfed and transformed his fingers into an arcane weapon of menace. The dim light of promised death reflected in the wolf's eyes as his talons grew longer and sharper, banded in ancient power.

Angelica feebly scratched at the demon's iron grasp as The Nightmare Hand, in all its infernal glory, swept down towards her face.

Chapter 16
The Battle of Pioneer Vale - 1671

"Do you think they'll fall for this?" whispered Abel.

"Are you really asking me this now?" replied Kitchi. The young man crouched beside him took a deep breath and then pointed to the distant town wall. "Study their lookouts. They are skittish and jump with every word the forest speaks."

"Maybe they've spotted some of your friends."

"Not likely. None of my people stand where the soldiers are looking."
His friend's grin widened and clapped him lightly on the shoulder. "After all, we have been sneaking up on your farm since your folk settled here and you've never seen us."

"Glad you're on our side," he muttered. "Thought I'd be used to this sort of thing after the fighting I saw in my youth, but I am shaking like a new recruit. This never gets easier."

"Threatening another man's life should never come easily. The day that there is no one left to feel remorse for such an act is the day that Maheegan has already won. If this must be our course, though, then all we may hope for is that, when the smoke clears, we are all looked upon as people who spared those we could and fought our foes with honor and courage."

"Yep, I got a little hunk of bronze right here," he said, patting the medal tucked inside of his shirt pocket, "that suggests as much."

"May we all be such warriors with iron in our hearts, then," Kitchi said. "It's time. Are you ready for this, my friend?"

"Aye. Let's do this."

The young Nipmuc leader signaled to one of the warriors hidden in the bushes nearby and nodded his head. The man pulled forth a notched piece of wood that dangled from an arm's length cord, and he began to swing it in a slow circle. As the wind passed through the holes, a haunting flute-like wail arose and sent a shrill warbling through the woods. One after another, ghostly howls joined in until the entire town was surrounded by the unseen shrieking.

Startled shouts erupted from the watchtowers, and Abel waved to Chogan and Machk, one of Chief Rowtag's courageous men. The two Nipmuc warriors vanished into the underbrush of the forest while Abel burst through the treeline and bolted for towards the front gate.

"Hold your fire!" He waved his arms wildly over his head. A gun barrel peeked out at him from between the slats of the wall. "I am just a simple farmer from the outskirts, but I've got something from the depths of Hell's darkest pit nipping at my heels, man!"

"You old fool," replied a muffled voice from inside the gate. A mercenary dressed in the Reavers livery pushed it open but only enough to squeeze his head and pistol through. "What deviltry have you brought among us? Don't you know there are whispers of a witch at play in these woods?"

"Then she might just be who follows so close behind! Shadows edged in purple hellfire chased after me as I ran through field and forest." He stifled a grin, hoping that Anne-Marie and his other friends had given the

Reavers frights enough to prey upon their imaginations. "I pray you, lad, let an old soldier through the gate before she reaches out for us."

"Move yer arse, old man." The gate swung wider with a creak as the young mercenary pointed his shaking weapon down the dark road. "We can't risk whatever's making that racket getting inside the walls."

"I'm afraid you're too late for that, son." He whistled over his shoulder and unslung his old weathered rifle as two large shapes flanked him from nearby darkness. War clubs of wood and bone brandished by the stealthy Nipmuc men sang through the air, and the young watchman's eyes widened. Abel hurried forward and tried not to hear the dull thud and muffled groan behind him.

Chogan stepped up beside him and threw the gate as wide open as the hinges would allow. Machk's blood-curdling war cry froze the men in the courtyard before them in mute shock, yet the shout pumped strength and vigor through Abel's limbs that he hadn't felt since he had worn a younger man's uniform. He turned to look at the brave men who awaited his command at the edge of the treeline.

"Nipmuc battalion, charge," he yelled, then stepped boldly forward and fired his weapon into the stunned ranks of soldiers. The echo of his gun was quickly drowned out by the blast of war horns that erupted from the Nipmuc warriors hidden in the forest. The mercenaries broke ranks and bolted in a chaotic muddle searching for weapons, cover, or both.

"Your plan worked, Farmer," laughed Chogan. The three of them ducked behind some nearby crates while the first return shots whizzed past their heads. The warrior's knuckles whitened around the haft of his weapon, and Machk readied to spring into battle.

"People of Pioneer Vale," shouted Abel. Curious faces peered at him from behind ever so slightly pulled curtains on nearby windows. "Now is the time to stand against this rabble that would hold us under their iron fists. Join us and fight!"

"Let us make our ancestors proud," Machk yelled. The brave man rose, but Abel grabbed his wrist and pulled him back down.

"Stand fast, gentlemen," he said as he reloaded his gun. "Our job now is to hold this position until reinforcements are in place."

"I did not come here to cower behind boxes and barrels," said Machk. "I came to fight."

Ahead of them, skirmish lines formed up with practiced readiness, and the barrels of a score of firearms were leveled their way. A hail of gunfire tore into the log wall behind them and showered the three men with splinters and sawdust. A careening ricochet grazed the young Nipmuc man's cheek.

"So did they," Abel muttered. He sighted down his barrel and fired into the Reavers once more.

*   *   *

A keening wail like that of a banshee rose and fell as if some specter that once drew breath still felt the need to do so. Cyrus hobbled over to the watch post while his men nearby fidgeted with their weapons, their knuckles white as they clutched their rifles and sabers.

"Watchman, report," he shouted. "What do you see, son?"

"Sir, the forest is ...moving closer." Panic edged the young soldier's voice. Despite his injury, he mounted the stairs to the tower and shoved the watchman to one side. His discerning eyes studied the treeline beyond the torch lights. The woodlands were peaceful and the subtle sway of a few branches and brush was oddly soothing.

Yet there wasn't so much as a breath of wind.

When the rising moon broke through the clouds above, pale light glinted from dozens of gleaming eyes. Couched behind the foliage and covered in various hues of war paint, the local savages stealthily approached the perimeter.

"To arms, one and all!" he yelled, and pulled his pistol from his belt. "We're under attack!"

No sooner had the words cleared his lips when the crack of a lone gunshot echoed through the streets from the direction of the town gate. Frantic shouts and scattered return fire followed suit. A war horn bellowed from the eastern woods and a second answered from the south. The underbrush exploded with chaotic whoops and battle cries as scores of the local natives broke from their hiding places among the trees and charged forward.

"Captain," yelled Carter as he skidded around the watch tower's base. "The gate has been breached. It's only a small force but they've more on the way!"

"Get every able-bodied man to answer the charge. Skeleton forces to keep an eye from the towers in case they try to scale the walls." Cyrus dropped from the scaffolding of the platform and gritted his teeth as he landed sharply on the cobblestones. Fire bolted up his wounded leg, and fresh crimson blossomed through his trouser leg. He cinched the bandage tighter and lumbered forward.

A young soldier with a blood-spattered face bolted around Carter and ran at him. He skidded to a halt and snatched Cyrus' shirt with stained hands. The boy's eyes were wild and glassy, and spittle sprayed from his lips.

"This is all your fault," the soldier cried out. "The witch has sent her devils for our souls! Your defiance has doomed us all." With the speed of a man possessed the young Reaver yanked a knife from his belt sheath and drew his arm back.

The cold fury of battle-driven bloodlust flowed through his veins now, however, and the pistol in Cyrus' hand belched flame and blue smoke. The young traitor was blown off his feet and crashed into the mud while a pool of blood spread from the gaping hole in his chest into the sodden street. All eyes were on him, and the nearby troops reeked of fear. He casually smoothed the wrinkles from his shirt and scowled at the crimson smear on the fabric.

"Carter, make it clear that I will take it very personally should any more of our own presume to lay hands on me again. Rally our men and lead a charge up the main thoroughfare. We must retake control of the entryway before those savages overrun the town!"

He didn't wait for his lieutenant to reply but hurried down the street while reloading his pistol. The distant sounds of battle filled him with a dark rage. An anticipation of making all those who stood against him suffer. A hatred that sprang from the coldest parts of his barren soul.

"I'll play nicely no longer," he muttered.

*   *   *

A bullet whizzed past Abel's ear while he reloaded, raised the weapon to his shoulder, and fired once more into the throng of soldiers ahead. He paid no heed to the havoc around him but lost himself in a steady rhythm. Aim, fire, and reload. Aim, fire, and reload. Returned gunfire from the enemy skirmishers kept him and his Nipmuc companions pinned down as the Reavers slowly restored order to their ranks. Mercenaries atop the watch towers fired over the wall and the occasional cry from the field outside explained well enough the delay of Kitchi and their sorely needed reinforcements.

"Reavers, form up and advance! Retake the gate!" The voice was familiar, and Abel peeked over the barrel he crouched behind.

The grizzled captain limped forward, the black wolf's head proudly emblazoned on his yellow livery. Like a hunting predator, the man slipped between his men, a shadow of darkness that eagerly awaited his next kill. His lieutenant followed close at his heels, with a dozen soldiers trailing behind. The men readied to charge, and one cold fact stood clear to him.

There was no way the three of them could hold the soldiers back much longer.

"It seems that we are about to have unexpected company, gentlemen" he shouted. A firm hand fell on his shoulder, and Chogan knelt near him.

"Our time is now, Farmer. I am honored to have stood by your side." The warrior dropped his bow and slapped his war club into his open hand. "I will speak highly of you to the Great Spirit."

"Let's plan on not dying today, shall we?" he replied. Abel grabbed the man's forearm and pulled him down as another shot careened past their heads. "Keep down and make them come to us."

Another volley, more orderly than the random shots thus far, drilled into their barricade. The smell of gunsmoke, blood, and oiled leather grew stronger as the Reavers' line moved closer with bloodlust in their eyes. A bugle's sharp note pierced the air, and then with a roar, the mercenaries charged ahead.

A tumultuous thunder drowned out the soldiers' shouts as a horde of screaming Nipmuc warriors stormed through the open gate. Their bellowing cheers shook the mercenary line as they fell upon the Reavers like a wave crashing over a rocky shore. The mercenaries' ranks broke apart, but there remained a few of the more seasoned veterans that fell into defensive postures. The clash of scattered shots and the rasp of sabers sliding from scabbards mingled with the onslaught of war clubs and spear thrusts as the fierce men of both sides locked in mortal combat. With an exultant whoop, Chogan and Machk leaped out from behind the barrels' protective cover and joined their tribesmen.

"Go get 'em, lads," said Abel with a grin. He jogged behind them into the yard and studied the field to see where he was most needed.

A sudden kick hammered his back and he sprawled out on the ground. He rolled to the side just as a sword struck the dirt where he laid just a heartbeat before. He struggled to rise, but the unexpected blow had driven the wind from his lungs.

"I've got you now, traitor," spat one of the rough looking mercenaries. The man raised his sword high above his head, and Abel was lost in the gleam of moonlight on the deadly steel. Just as the blade started to drop, an arrow sprouted from the center of the man's chest, halting his attacker in midstride. A second shaft spun the Reaver in a half circle and dropped him lifelessly to the ground.

"Are you sure you aren't getting too old for this sort of thing, my friend?" Kitchi loped up beside him, grabbed his arm, and pulled him to his feet.

"Took your sweet time, my boy," Abel groaned. He dusted himself off and picked his gun up from the dirt. "I tend not to like my shaves that close."

"Well, we could retake your town a lot faster if you weren't sitting on your arse, old man," laughed Kitchi. "Besides, I still owed you for the bear."

Nearby a door creaked open and a gun barrel led the way out of the darkened house, followed shortly by the man holding the weapon. Around the square, other townspeople stepped from their homes, armed and determined to protect their town.

"Time to rally your people." Kitchi clapped him on the shoulder and rushed off to join the fighting. Everywhere Abel looked, he saw expectant faces waiting for him. He pulled back the hammer on his rifle and smiled.

"Do you stand with us, Valemen?" he shouted. A huzzah erupted from the gathering crowd, and several men and women fell in beside him.

"Then let's not let the Nipmuc steal all the fun!"

*　　*　　*

Forrester's pistol belched blue smoke and another screaming savage dropped his crude club and collapsed in a spray of blood. At his side, Carter's shot took another of the brutes down to the cobbles. Their superior weaponry had taken its toll in the opening seconds after the breaching of the town gate but would matter for little soon enough. The enemy swarmed around them, and his men had no time to reload firearms. The streets already grew slick with blood as both native and soldier fought tooth and nail against one another. It was brutal. It was primal.

It was beautiful.

Carter tackled another Nipmuc fighter ran at them with a purloined hand axe high overhead. The young officer elbowed his foe in the face and then buried his knife deep in the man's ribs. As the attacker gurgled his last breath, Forrester steadied his second in command, while the man gasped for air.

"Captain, we'll never hold them here unless we can form up a proper skirmish line. In this mayhem, we're just as likely to catch the townsfolk in friendly fire. Look around you, sir!"

The frightened shrieks of women and children blended with war cries and gunshots to create a horrific battle symphony. Whereas he knew such a chorus chilled his lieutenant's blood, Cyrus found it strangely uplifting to see these sheep cowering before what he had wrought, but a deeper discordant note joined the music. Marcus Brenner, the mountain of muscle that ran the tavern, and that young blacksmith, hammer in hand, led a charge from the Hirsute Huntsman's porch with shouts of challenge and outrage on their lips. Other townsfolk followed behind them and stood shoulder to shoulder with the Nipmuc assault against his men. Some had rifles in hand, while others brandished only tools and farm implements, but they all wore grim expressions as they found courage enough to engage his forces.

"It would seem we have traitors in our midst, Lieutenant," Cyrus growled. "Give the order. Now that these brazen turncoats have dared to stand against us, we shall take the fight to them all. Savage or citizen alike. We shall not fall back, nor show any mercy."

"Captain, you can't be serious. If you make enemies of the townsfolk, you'll lose any shred of loyalty you might command."

"The town is already lost to us, Carter." His vision danced as all before his sight burned with gray black flame.

"Kill every last one of them."

*　　*　　*

Allison slapped her hands against the small window's pane as a detachment of the Reavers opened fire on the charging townsfolk. Friends and neighbors fell in the streets, but her father waded into the mercenaries with his swinging fists clearing a path just as decisively as the pendulum strikes of Micah's smithy hammer as the two fought side by side. A firm hand grabbed her arm and dragged her away just as a stray shot shattered the glass.

"Come away from there, girl," shouted Dorothea. Her mother pulled her over to the door. "Help me throw the bar in place."

"But Da and Micah are out there. What if they need to hurry back?" Her mother stopped struggling with the heavy piece of oak beside the front door and put her hands on her hips.

"Do you think the front and rear doors are the only ways yer father has into our home? He built the Huntsman like a fortress, with secrets enough of its own, but we'll be safer still once you help me with this damnable beam."

The crash of gunfire exploded once more and spurred her to Dorothea's side. With a mighty heave, together they dragged the stout bar across the plank floor and levered it into the iron braces mounted on either side of the door. Dorothea groaned and leaned against the edge of one of the common room's tables.

"That'll hold the front room for now," her mother groaned, "but help fasten the garden door next. Better if we bar off trouble from all directions."

A crash from the back hallway stopped them in their tracks and a hulking shadow darkened the passage to the kitchen. Two rough-looking men clad in the Reavers' yellow livery entered the taproom from behind the bar.

"Too bad for you ladies that trouble found the back door first," said one of the brutes.

"Then I suggest ye hurry out the same way, sir," snapped Dorothea. The older woman uncrossed her arms and took a step towards the soldiers. Allison reached for her mother to pull her back, but her fingers barely touched the homespun dress before there was a flash of steel, a sickening thud, and Dorothea crumpled to the floor.

"Mama," she screamed. She stumbled backward as the two men casually stepped over her mother's fallen form and grabbed a carving knife from a nearby table. She brandished it in front of her as the mercenary wiped the saber against his trousers, leaving a bloody smear on his clothes. She had seen the man in the Huntsman over the last few nights, and the way his eyes lewdly roamed up and down her body, she doubted that the soldier's presence here was accidental.

"Should my father return and see what ye've done to my mother, there won't be a hole deep enough for ye to hide from him."

"Then wait until he discovers what I've done to you, girl." The man snorted and picked up a pitcher of ale. He took a long swallow directly from it and then handed it to his friend.

Allison swung the knife in wide swaths in front of her, holding the two men at bay as the cautiously approached her. Slowly she backed away from them until her hip rammed into the corner of one of the tavern's tables. She turned her head only a moment, but in that stumble, rough hands grabbed her arm. Something popped in her wrist, and with a cry, her fingers fell open and the knife clattered to the floor.

"Get away from me," she said through clenched teeth. She tried to push the Reaver back, but the soldier slapped her hand away and drove her down onto the table. Allison kicked and clawed but his crushing weight was too much for her.

"Be quick, Gregor," said the second Reaver. "We're missing the fight."

"I've got more than enough fight for you, bastard," Allison said. She brought her knee up swiftly into Gregor's groin and her fingernails raked a bloody furrow across the man's cheek. He twisted away in pain, but then a sharp backhand swipe rocked her jaw and the taproom ceiling spun above her as she fell against the wood tabletop.

"You'll wish you hadn't done that, bitch." The Reaver's breath was hot and foul against her neck. Blood pounded in her ears, and spots danced before her eyes. She squeezed them closed, struggling to get her wits about her, when she heard a dull wet crack and the oppressive weight bearing down on her was thrown aside. Allison pushed herself up on her elbow and shook her head to clear away the cobwebs.

"Get the hell away from her," said Micah. The smith stood over the body of the second mercenary. His smith's hammer was stained crimson, and the fires in his eyes burned hotter than any forge.

"So, the little smith finally found his iron," chuckled Gregor. The man brushed off his shoulder and straightened his vest where Micah's rough hand had dragged him away from her.

"I never lost it, sir." He slapped the hammer into his palm. "I had only hoped you and your fellows would prove smart enough that I wouldn't need to draw it forth."

"You'd have been wiser to leave us to our fun." The soldier spat on the floor, wiped his mouth with the back of his hand, and then waggled his saber in the air. "Guess we're about to learn firsthand just how well you sharpened my sword, boy."

"I assure you, sir," Micah said with a tight smile as he stepped forward, "I take great pride in my craft."

Allison's hair fluttered in the breeze as the Reaver's saber flashed past her, but Micah stepped in close and caught the descending blade with the handle of his hammer. The smith shoved the soldier back, dropped into a crouching spin, and cracked the head of his weapon against the man's knee. Bone crunched, and the man fell heavily against the mantle over the great fireplace.

"You'll pay for that, boy," growled Gregor. Although he limped forward, the mercenary was still an accomplished soldier and his flurry of slashes and swipes put Micah back on his heels. A glint of metal caught her eye, and Allison dove after the carving knife she had dropped.

"Leave us alone," Allison screamed with the blade now in hand. She grabbed the man's vest and stabbed her knife through the thick leather covering his shoulder. Her father kept his blades sharp, though, and blood sprayed across her hand. Gregor roared and drove the hilt of his saber into her stomach. She dropped to one knee with her arms clutched across her belly and her weapon skittered across the tavern floor.

"You bitch," Gregor cried out. His sword gleamed in the firelight as he drew back in what promised to be a deadly chop. Time around her slowed as the strike dropped closer, but Micah's hammer met the descending blade in a powerful rising arc. The clash of the two weapons rang out, and Gregor's sword shattered into a cascade of metal shards. He stared blankly at the broken sword and then up at the smith.

"I'll not suffer any weapons serviced by my forge brought to bear against my neighbors," Micah growled. "I weakened the steel of every weapon your friends have brought to me with hairline cracks through and through. They hold up well enough in sparring, but I ensured that the metal was too brittle for active use."

"I don't need a blade for the likes of you," Gregor spat and threw the hilt aside. With hands outstretched, he jumped towards Micah and closed his fingers around the young man's throat. The smith, caught by the soldier's sudden ferocity, was unable to bring his weapon to bear, and his face turned a ghastly shade of purple.

Allison ran forward and jumped on the Reaver's back. She wrapped her arms tightly around the man's neck, and pulled back with all her might, trying her best to get him away from Micah. The three of them thrashed at each other, one and all suffering wild punches, bites, and scratches until the mercenary's injured knee could bear no more weight. Together, they all crashed to the floor in a tangle of arms and legs, still grappling tooth and nail, and rolling across the tavern floor until Gregor's body suddenly stiffened and went slack.

Allison scooted away as Micah rolled the man onto his back. A broken shard of Gregor's waved garishly from his side. In the chaos of their fight, he had rolled over on the very weapon he had discarded. The smith took her in his arms and held her close and she squeezed him back tightly, comforted by the way his fingers ran lightly through her hair.

"It's over now. You're safe," the young smith whispered huskily in her ear.

"How did you even know to come back for us?" she asked.

"Your father and I were in the thick of the fighting when I saw those two break away and run behind the buildings. I knew where I was needed most." He smiled at her. "Still, after seeing how you handled yourself in battle, remind me never to get on your bad side."

"I guess we make a good team." Her smile mirrored his own, and without thinking, Allison pulled his face to hers and kissed him deeply. The deep rumble of a cleared throat made them both jump and they whirled around. Her father knelt beside her mother who leaned against his broad shoulder with a sly grin on her face.

"Seriously? You two are doing this now?" Marcus said. Dorothea smacked him on the shoulder. "Ow!"

"Let them be, you old fool," Dorothea admonished. Groggily, she pulled herself back to her feet and gently dabbed at the cut in her scalp. "I'd have at least let them come up for air before letting them know I was awake."

"Mama," Allison gasped and she ran over to the bar. "I thought that they had ended you."

"Lucky for me, the brute caught me more with the flat of his blade than the edge." She grunted. "But yer own grip might finish the job, girl."

"I'm sorry!" Allison blushed when she realized how tightly she was squeezing her mother. She let her mother loose and Dorothea gave her a gentle pat. Their moment of peace, however, was broken by the thud of booted feet drumming along the distant cobblestones and the roar of another volley of gunfire. Shouted commands echoed only slightly louder than the screams of pain from the chaos outside.

"I fear we must hope that fortune smiles on us a bit longer," grumbled the tavern master. "Everyone arm themselves.

"We've only begun to fight."

CHAPTER 17
IN THE CROSSFIRE - 1671

The flash of gunpowder from the falling hammer was unusually bright. Carter winced at the thin whine of rupturing metal from the nearby Reaver's pistol just before the weapon exploded in the man's hand. Blood sprayed across his face as the soldier held on to his bloodied fingers and the man's hoarse cry made a macabre harmony with the rising war cries that drew ever nearer.

The tide of Nipmuc warriors had been relentless, their onslaught fierce. His men fell back in a controlled retreat, towards the main encampment where several more of their fellows who had been ravaged by the sickness within the camp had been dragged from their bunks and into the fray. Most of them, however, were so green around the gills that they could barely raise a rifle to their shoulders. The air around the camp reeked of bile and worse.

"Fall back, but steady," Carter yelled, but he knew his words fell on deaf ears. What had been a planned defense was nothing but a rout and his remaining men were too weak to fight properly or with any discipline. They were lambs being led to the slaughter, and all he could do was try to save as many as he could. "Maybe we can reach the alleyways," he muttered to no one in particular, "and then we can get behind them."

A young soldier, little more than a boy with barely any fuzz on his cheeks yet, tried to aim at the charging wall of wild men, but his rifle barrel shook and sweat poured down his brow. He squeezed the trigger, but the shot went wide, and before he could even try to reload the raw recruit clutched his stomach, fell to one knee, and retched.

From the obscuring mist of gunsmoke rose a war-painted bear of a man. The Nipmuc warrior towered over the fallen soldier and brandished a spiked club over his head in a fierce two-handed grip. Carter lunged forward and a fast slash of his saber that spilled the man's abdomen open to the wind. The fearsome club slid from the savage's grasp and fell to the blood-slicked cobblestones.

"Time to move," he said, dragging the younger mercenary to his feet. "Let's get you out of here."

"Sir, my guts are all twisted up," the man wailed. He clutched Carter's leather vest, and pulled him down close. "What was Captain Forrester thinking? What evil has his ambition brought down upon us?"

"I'm not sure if he even knows." He wiped his brow with hands that reeked of blood and gunpowder. Sporadic fired shots and primal bellowing shouts amid the two clashing forces echoed all around him. "But I don't think we should wait around any longer to find out."

Carter slung the young soldier's arm over his shoulder and led him away from the melee. A burst of shrapnel peppered one side of his face and his eyes burned as they stumbled through the perpetual haze that filled the streets. They slipped into the entrance of an alleyway that yawned open before them, and he glanced over his shoulder at the madness left behind.

All along the ragtag line, swords snapped and muskets misfired, all followed by cries of outrage and pain from the soldiers to whom such misfortunes fell. The Nipmuc pressed forward into the gaps left breached as Reavers, many all but defenseless, fell in droves. Men he had come up through the ranks with and served beside for years were beaten down before the vast numbers of the ferocious native warriors. Although no stranger to the atrocities of such pitched battles, this calamity was different. Within the terror that plagued the battlefield, there was a subtle undercurrent of a presence that not only bred but thrived upon the chaos.

"We can't win this, Lieutenant," the young mercenary at his side whispered ominously.

"Then let's simply attempt to survive it." Carter eased him down against a wall, straightened his crumpled vest, and reloaded his spent pistol. "I want you to stay put. This alley may prove no safer than anywhere else but if you are found, you must plead for mercy if you can. Defend yourself if you must. I'll return as soon as I am able."

"Wait! Where are you going?" Weak but frantic fingers grabbed his sleeve.

"I'm going to put an end to this." The soldier's eyes widened, but then he nodded and released his grip.

"You've always been one of the few good ones I've had fortune enough to meet. Watch your back, Lieutenant."

Carter shook the man's hand, tucked his gun into his belt, and drew his saber. He then rushed to the far end of the alley that fed into a side street off the main promenade. The sounds of battle were less pronounced here, yet still close enough that he kept a careful watch. He crouched low and dashed for nearby cover, following every flash of movement as combatants raced to and fro at the edge of his sight. Finally he closed his eyes and breathed deeply.

Calm down, he told himself. Fear is your greatest enemy now.

A muffled cry broke from a nearby tangle of bodies, and a mop of dirty blonde hair with crimson-spattered cheeks peeked from beneath the brawny arm of a fallen Nipmuc warrior that was wrapped protectively around a Valewoman's waist. Unsightly puddles formed where they lay on the dirty cobblestones. When the girl's pale blue eyes dropped to his chest and she pointed a shaking finger at the blood-streaked wolf emblem on his livery, her silent accusation branded him in his soul.

"You're one of those soldiers," she whispered. "This is your fault."

"Yes, little one. I am as much to blame as the one who fired these shots." Carter grabbed the yellow garment and ripped it away from his leather vest and hurled it to the dirt. "Once I was a soldier, but no longer. Tell me. Did this warrior attack you?"

"We were trying to escape the crowd when three of your friends saw us and raised their guns." She stared at him for a moment and then shook her head. "This man ran from the alley, and jumped in front of us. He covered us with his own body, but when the guns went off, Mama still cried out and fell. She won't get up."

Carter knelt beside the girl and placed his fingers along her mother's neck. He needn't have bothered though ragged hole under her shoulder told him all that he needed to know. He started to wipe his hands in the dirt, but couldn't bear to clean the blood from his hands. It was one more grim reminder of a lifetime of horrible things he had done for Cyrus. There was no more honor or glory in serving him. The man had gone mad, changed into something despicable, and he'd be damned if would bear the responsibility for any more of that monster's sins.

"This is no place for you, child," he said. He held out his hand. "If you'll trust me, I swear on my life that I will see you safely away." Shouts and gunfire roared in the streets growing closer as the battle meandered back and forth through the town. Hesitantly, she wrapped her small fingers around his own and he scooped her from the ground. The small arms around his neck squeezed tight and trembled, but she buried her head against his shoulder. Carter spared one last look at the dead woman and brave Nipmuc warrior and hugged the young girl as much for his comfort as hers before he hurried out of the shadows and into the moonlit streets.

*　　*　　*

His leg kicked, and his ears twitched with the jangled laughter of children at play nearby. He didn't remember falling asleep, but the fleeting dream of a war-torn hellscape gave way to a clarity unlike any he had ever known before. The edge of his vision was tinged in a flickering gray-black hue as if the trees around him burned beneath his gaze. Beneath the overwhelming honeysuckle and lavender that corrupted the air, there was a comforting touch of smoke and ash that played havoc with his self-control.

The dulcet ring of giggling continued on. How he hated it. Hated them. A snarl crept across his lips as their mirth ached in his ears, and his tongue brushed across the sharpened points of his teeth that now lined his mouth. A surprise, but not an unwelcome one, he mused, just before he pulled the branches aside and looked through the underbrush.

It was her children, alive and well, and far less undercooked than they should be given the predicament he had last left them in. His mouth watered and he wiped the corner of his lips. Raw meat was far more savory anyway, came an unbidden thought from the dark recesses of his mind. He shook his head to clear such stray thoughts that he knew were more akin to his shadowy master. Still, he fought down the overwhelming urge to jump out and snap their scrawny necks, holding his place, silent and watchful.

His real prey had not yet arrived.

As if on cue, the bushes across from his hiding place rustled and a flash of coppery hair peeked through the leaves. A low growl rumbled within his breast as Anne-Marie pushed through the canopy on the other side of the glade. The woman dropped to one knee and held her arms out to the squeals of glee that rippled through the air, like a stone shattering the calm of a placid lake. It wracked his frame, and he dug his heel into the soft dirt, ready to pounce. A chilling rumble filled his throat, and he bared his teeth.

They only needed to creep a bit closer and they were his.

*   *   *

"What are you two scamps doing so far from Whisperwind?" Anne-Marie asked. A smile, too infrequently felt these last several days, warded away the chill in the evening air. Her boys squealed in delight and Thomas threw his arms around her neck while Aiden capered and skipped near the treeline. Their carefree laughter proved infectious to her and she sprawled in the grass with her youngest in her embrace.

Flower petals floated lazily through the air as her boys tossed handfuls into the air to cascade all around her. Birds chirped in the trees behind her then took wing with their song. A squirrel leaped from branch to branch, but she stiffened suddenly. Her magically heightened senses screamed to her that the forest creatures were not playing.

They were running.

Around the grove, the shadows lengthened and reached towards them with taloned fingers. A frosty wind howled through the clearing, and a flash of gray fire erupted within the depths of the forest. Blanketed in darkness, a figure with a silvery glimmering eye and toothy grin stood upright in the underbrush and peered back at her, yet beyond the shape having arms and legs, finding means to call it a man eluded her as he stepped into the moonlight.

Coarse black hair sprouted all along his arms and face. The being's nose and mouth stood pronounced, pushed into an ungainly muzzle by slender dagger sharp canine teeth. Only the crimson scar that ran beneath the black cloth eye patch gave her any recognition of who stood before her. His throaty growl fell over her like an unwanted caress, and his icy glare turned to Aiden who frolicked unsuspectingly so close at hand.

"Mama, you're squeezing me too tight," whined Thomas, but his voice was a tinny echo lost against the roar of the lavender cloak of flame she enshrouded around them both. She shoved the boy behind her and fire filled her palms.

"Aiden, get away from there," she screamed, and a spray of bolts hurtled from her fingertips through the air as the beast wrapped in the familiar energy of Shade's coldfire crouched to spring. The bushes exploded in a blast of heat that lit the evening sky ablaze, and drifting blossoms became a rain of cinders while ashes slowly scattered on the eddying winds.

Yet through the buffeting conflagration, the brawny man burst through the storm and grasped her older son's shoulder with cruel fingers. His gleaming teeth flashed under the flickering lavender light, and Aiden's mouth opened in a silent scream as the massive predator slammed into his back. Her son was knocked down into the curling embers of the pine needles that carpeted the forest floor, while the twisted shape that had once been Patch Erickson dropped into a crouch over her son's limp form and closed his hand around Aiden's throat.

"I should have snapped his little neck the last time I visited your farm," purred Patch. The timbre of Erickson's voice was subtly different, the low growl tainted with a hollow sepulchral reverberation as if spoken across some great chasm, or from another realm altogether. "All in good time, though."

"My family has endured enough of your threats, Erickson. Stand away from my son, coward, and face me," Anne-Marie said. With unerring precision, she hurled a torrent of fire into the fiendish man that drove him backward until his feet dug into the earth. Smoke curled from his raised forearm, though as Shade's magic held her flames at bay.

"Did you believe this place still offered you some sanctuary, witch?" Erickson snapped his arm around her lance of fiery magic, and his own dark energy from the Nightmare Realm entwined and snuffed her flames.

A backlash of magical force jolted through her limbs. Her limbs spasmed and a kaleidoscope of pain shot through her head, knocking her to the ground beside Thomas.

Patch puffed out his chest and howled into the night sky with a deafening roar. The muscles of his already imposing frame strained against his very flesh and the pink-hued saliva that dripped from his lips sizzled through the leaves where it landed.

"Thomas, run," she hissed, and the boy bolted for the shelter of the nearby woods. Patch took a step towards him, his distended head swinging wide to follow the boy, but a wall of fire sprang up between them. Boldly, she rose and called her magic in a winding trail back to her and the flames wrapped a tight spiral around her body in a twirling dance of power. So long as her foe still straddled Aiden, she needed his attention focused solely on her and her display did precisely that. "So I see that Shade went in search of more bottom feeders, and found you ready to lick his boots?"

"It didn't take much to convince me. There's good hunting, hereabouts." Patch's words dripped with venom and a wicked grin creased his lips as his soulless eye bored into her. "As I recall, it was just through those trees behind you where I killed your husband."

"My memory will prove longer than your own," she replied. Grief surged within her breast, and a brilliant beam of pure magic leapt from the nearby Widow Stone. She was set ablaze with power rekindled and the flames within her flared higher and hotter with every heartbeat. "I will become fire and wrath and everything savage that you and your allies fear. I am your worst nightmares made flesh."

"Then the joke's on you. I don't have bad dreams anymore." Patch lunged forward, closing the distance between them with uncanny speed. She caught the crushing force of his grasping hand on the leather bracer she wore but screamed when Shade's hidden handprint beneath it blazed with searing light. He grabbed and twisted the silver chain of the amethyst pendant around her throat until it bit deeply into her skin. "But what I am about to do to you and your children shall haunt you forever."

"My flames leave no shadows for you to strike at the unwary, and there is reason enough why Preston lives in dread of the moment when I shall burst through his door." She grabbed his wrist with her free hand and pulled the brawny man closer. Her nose nearly brushed against his thick chest, but she held him tightly when the Guardian fires blazed within the depths of her eyes. "Would you care to see why?"

Flames erupted around her, and her coppery tresses were held aloft in a crown of lavender fury. The air around them burned, while the heat that swept from her fire-swathed body ignited the boughs above their heads like ceremonial candles. Her lips curled as Erickson tried to break free, and she unleashed an inferno that raked across the man's exposed flesh, bathing them both in an otherworldly brilliance.

Her enemy's hair and beard fell away in glowing cinders, while his skin blistered and cracked beneath the onslaught. The air reeked with the smell of burnt flesh as he struggled within her grasp, but her magic held him in a grip beyond what even his demon-infused strength could overcome.

"Unhand me, woman," Patch grunted. His fist slammed against her arm, her face, her shoulder, but even though each blindly-thrown strike fell true, her coursing power easily batted the hits away. The faint metallic tang of blood on her lips, however, assured her that she would feel the weight of those blows later. With an open palm, she hammered him in the chest and threw him end over end across the clearing in a blast of heat and fire.

The brute staggered back to unsteady feet while smoke wafted from his scorched shirt and blackened skin. Erickson held one hand out as if that could hold her at bay but drew the knife from his belt with his other.

Deftly, he twirled it between his fingers and held the blade across his body between them.

"Keep that up, witch, and you'll brand yourself as much a monster as I am. Be wary of just how far your own darkness descends."

"Then I will drag you down to Hell with me," she replied. Flames trailed along in her wake as she stormed towards him. Between her fingers she drew forth a line of fire, thin and wispy yet taut like a rawhide cord. With a snap, she wrapped it around her hands like a blazing strangling wire, and her voice lowered into a hissing whisper. "You'll find the devils there more forgiving than I am."

Patch lunged forward with a swath of vicious slashes through the air, despite the burns and scorches scarring his body. Hissing coldfire trailed behind each swipe of the man's blade, but, undaunted, Anne-Marie twisted the fiery cord and stepped into his reach, entwining his wrist within her magic. Lavender flames lit the clearing as she seared his flesh, but a cruel smile appeared on Patch's face as he stood toe to toe with her.

She had let him get too close.

Erickson's elbow blasted the breath from her lungs and his weight carried them both backwards. Her legs buckled as his charge drove through her defenses and together they tumbled across the ground in a mad jumble of flailing limbs. His knee jammed into her stomach, and her jaw erupted in a flash of stars. The blurry outline of his fist rose into the air again, and she blindly she raked her nails against his charred face, ripping away skin in bloody furrows. She shoved him aside and tried to scramble out from under him, but his hands grabbed the tangle of her hair and pushed her face into the dirt.

"I wasn't given the pleasure of ending Jeremiah up close and personal, but I intend to stare deeply into your eyes as I end your miserable life." His breath was hot against her ear and cheek, and he flipped her over again.

Callused fingers snagged in the laces of her corset, and her back lifted from the ground while Erickson's knife gleamed in the moonlight above his head.

She crossed her arms in front of her face, and a wavering lavender shield sprang between her and the descending blade. The barrier blew forth a blistering wall of heat directly into Erickson's face. Although the man twisted away, and his strike was deflected by both her defending flames and pain, the wicked knife still plunged through and buried deeply into her shoulder.

Dark energy raced down the blade and her arm went numb. A primal scream of both agony ripped from her throat as Erickson twisted the knife and, and she slapped both palms against Erickson's chest. With a doubled surge of lavender fire, she launched him across the clearing and his knife sailed through the air into darkness.

Anne-Marie gritted her teeth and slowly pushed herself from the ground. The sleeve of her blouse was stained to crimson, and she ignored the soft patter of dripping blood that that ran down her arm and rained into the scattered leaves beneath her. She summoned a ball of flame to her hands and stumbled away from the man, for across the clearing, Erickson crouched and panted, his one cold eye gleaming with a hellish yellow glow.

"Still not enough, witch. You can blast away at me all night long if you wish, but we'll see who goes up in smoke first."

"Leave Mama alone," cried a shrill voice to the side of the clearing. To Anne-Marie's horror, a flash of dirty blond hair shot towards her as Thomas dashed from his hiding place in the bushes and crossed the ground between her and Erickson. Her heart lurched in her chest as wolfish teeth gleamed in the moonlight and the scar along the man's face turned to an angry crimson.

She snapped her wrist in an underhand blast as he sprang into the air, but her shot sailed harmlessly past him. Her second bolt scored a glancing blow to Erickson's hip, however, and knocked his leg askew, fouling up his charge. He planted face down in the dirt, but not before his grasping hand closed on Thomas' ankle. Her son fell with a shriek, and Erickson dragged the boy across the ground into his clutches. The muscles in the man's forearm rippled and gray fires flickered within Patch's eye as the crook of his elbow wrapped tightly around her son's throat.

"Let him go," she snarled.

"I think not," Erickson sneered. "Shall we see how much punishment this little tot can take?"

"I will not tell you again." Her shoulder thudded with the dull ache of every heartbeat. Violet rage tinged everything in view, and the heat of her magic rose within her.

"You can't win, Guardian. At Lord Shade's request, I will rip away everything that you hold dear just before I tear the final breath from your body. I wonder," he purred, as his hand clamped tighter around Thomas' neck. The boy's eyes bulged and his pitiful wails trailed off to the barest whimper. Erickson's face became lost in shadow until only the shine of his pointed teeth pierced the gloom. "Will the sound of your heart breaking ring louder than the crack of his little spine?"

"Enough," Anne-Marie screamed. She fired twin blasts of fire into the ground that streaked toward Erickson. Roots limned in purple flame burst from the ground and ensnared the man's hands, tearing away his hold on her son. Coldfire instantly rebelled against her primordial magic, but the overwhelming roar of her power shook the trees in the glade, and crushed his resistance. She took a forceful step forward, groaning from the strain, but drove Patch down to one knee. "Thomas, to me now."

Free from Erickson's clutches, her son bolted towards her, nearly tripping her up as he grabbed her around the waist. Although she wobbled, her unearthly will held strong and she wrenched Patch's arms out wide.

Sinew strained and popped, but her foe's maniacal laughter chilled her blood. Coldfire buffeted her and a backlash of dark magic washed over her body, dimming the radiant power at her command. While she still held him restrained, his strength grew beyond reckoning. Anne-Marie stumbled, and swept Thomas behind her with a roll of her hip, as Patch slowly rose from the ground.

The cracked skin of Erickson's face split and sloughed away. Blood streamed along exposed bone as the foul magic within him twisted his face into a nightmarish imitation of Shade's own tattered visage. Erickson's lips moved, but the sepulchral voice in her head was the cold gravelly growl of the Father of Nightmares.

"The veil between the realms lies in ruin, crumbling ever more as my forces slaughter your friends and neighbors. Their little rebellion will only end in death," he growled.

Visions of a fierce and bloody battle raging in the town square ravaged her mind. The bodies of townsfolk, Nipmuc warriors, and nameless mercenaries littered the cobblestone streets. She searched for any glimpse of Dorothea or Marcus, Abel or Micah, but all were lost in the pile of limbs.

"And your mentor darkens my doorstep once again, as well. No one you hold dear shall survive the fall of the last Guardian."

Her fiery tethers jolted as Erickson drove his feet deep into the soft ground. With filthy fingers that now looked more like iron claws, he dug into the dirt and dragged his possessed body closer to them. Gray flames licked around his broken and bloody muzzle and the world blurred around her. A storm of Henna's green motes flashed ever so briefly, bathing the worn stone walls of Shade's ancient shrine in a soft green glow before all around her abruptly plunged into darkness amidst the sounds of wretched screams, wet tearing, and slavering howls from the shadowy depths.

"Show me no more of your lies, monster," she cried. Her fires roared around her and dispelled the illusion cast over the clearing. Erickson had crept closer, towering over her, and her flames flickered under the unearthly chill of his shadow, yet she looked up with a grim smile, in the wake of the horror she faced, upon her lips. "The futures you offer as torment are uncertain at best."

"And yet I have shown some success thus far, Sweetling. Do you truly care to gamble on how uncertain those futures may be?"

"The vision of death that the demon promised me did not take place in these woods, you bastard. I will not fall here."

Her strength redoubled yet Erickson's baleful flames met her own with unyielding force. Embers rained all around the Widow Stone, and the collision of ancient magics shot the sky full of fire, but neither could so much as win back a single step from the other.

She spied a flickering shadow behind Erickson that crept up behind him with slow deliberation. The glint of cold eyes, the only thing that pierced the veil of darkness, narrowed behind the unaware man. Her lavender flame flashed on the sliver of metal that streaked through the air as the figure leaped upon the brute's back, and Patch jerked as the blade of his discarded knife plunged deeply into the side of his neck.

Anne-Marie twirled around and lifted Thomas away on a gentle wisp of flame from her left hand, dropping him lightly behind a nearby stump. When she gracefully completed her pirouette all pretense of gentility melted away into pristine savagery. She unleashed a two-handed blast of hell's own fury from her palms that slammed into Erickson's arched body.

The brilliant conflagration of lavender flame and coldfire gray spiraled around the thug's frame, raced along the blade in his neck, and illuminated Aiden's bruised and tear-streaked face peering over his shoulder. A cold malevolence filled the boy's eyes and his hand was dark with Erickson's blood pumping across the knife in his hand.

A jolt shook her arms, and a swirling morass of ancient power flowed through them all, melding them as one through the magic's storm. Anne-Marie's stomach twisted while the air around them created a shimmering bubble, and she knew at that moment that her child, her Firstborn, had somehow just entered the greater war with the Demonkin. The knife twisted in Aiden's grasp and Erickson weakly grabbed the boy's shirt, lightly tossing him across the grove where he rolled to a stop against her boots.

With his mouth gaping in shock, the man fell to one knee and coughed up a pink and black forth. His fingers pawed feebly at the handle of his knife, but the blade had struck true and resisted his attempt to remove it. A crimson deluge poured down his neck and chest, and he collapsed into the grass. The rise and fall of his chest grew more labored and shallow as the last shreds of coldfire faded around him.

Anne-Marie knelt beside her son, cradling Aiden as he trembled and rocked himself back and forth. Trails of lingering smoke drifted away on the night breeze, and the putrid smell of burned flesh overpowered the subtle scents of lavender and honeysuckle that normally filled the air. Her eyes never left Erickson's face, however, and slowly his head lolled over to face her. On his lips were the telltale beginnings of a snarl, but when his eye met hers, he gave instead a shallow nod. A bright pink bubble burst on his lips followed by a hoarse chuckle.

"Remember this moment, witch, for this is but the beginning of events that will haunt you forever." His head fell back to the ground heavily, and his eye glazed over, staring endlessly into the darkness above. Anne-Marie sighed and fell to the grass with her son resting against her aching shoulder.

"Aiden…" she began, but her son's already battered facade broke. With a sob, his arms tightened around her chest.

"What have I done, Mama?" the boy sobbed.

"You did what had to be done. He might have killed us all had you not acted."

"Will I become a monster now? Like him?" he asked with a nod towards Erickson's body, smoke still rising from the corpse.

"Don't be silly. You are still and always shall be my darling boy." She gently took his hand and together they crawled over to where Thomas huddled behind the tree stump with his eyes squeezed shut against the night. She cast one final glance at Erickson, and then took them both into her arms, sending just enough magic through her limbs that she might carry them back to Whisperwind. Stray threads of Henna's green motes flickered in her thoughts, and she knew she was needed elsewhere. "I will take you both back to the cottage, but you must promise me that you will not leave until I return. We have many friends still in grave danger, and I cannot tarry overlong."

She started down the trail, back towards Henna's home, hiding a groan of fatigue and pain. Aiden's fingers brushed the amethyst pendant and a sudden resonant thrum of power flowed through her from the boy's touch. She gave a quick kiss to her eldest's brow, and at last a tired smile found its way to his lips as he nestled against her. Her relief was fleeting, though, and she shuddered at what she could only hope was not a premonition of things to come as the moonlight punched through the sparse cover of the clouds above and emblazoned the bloody print of her son's hand over her own heart.

*　*　*

Cyrus crept like the specter of Death among the corpses that littered the market square. While many of those fallen were townsfolk and savages aplenty, far too many wore the Reavers' livery. Amid the chaos and cries of the ongoing battle, a shift in the wind, almost like a calling, sent a pulse of energy through his body that brought a spring to his stride. Instead of revulsion, he found himself smiling with savage amusement as he stepped over the body of one of his men.

Throughout the town, pockets of his soldiers still fought on, but the Nipmuc charge had turned the townsfolk to open rebellion. Although his Reavers fought bravely, most did so with broken blades or used their rifles like clubs, and all that remained bore pallid faces that marked them as victims of the sickness that had plagued the camp. The savages made increasingly short work of those so afflicted.

He raised his pistol and aimed at the back of a beastly man whose war club glistened with gore, but a strange caution swept over him almost as though the subtle buzz of an insect in the back of his mind stayed his trigger finger. He knew that his shot would end the mighty Nipmuc warrior, but he would only call undue attention to himself which would lead to his doom as well.

Instead, he hobbled into the shadows of a side road and leaned against the wall. His men were overwhelmed and he foresaw very few surviving the day. He intended to be one of those. The town stables were near enough, and it would be far more prudent for him to escape instead. He could always recruit new soldiers for, if he held any certainty, it was that men of the necessary disposition to flock to his banner could always be found looking for opportunity in this new land. Reinforced with such allies, his retribution upon these peasants who dared stand against him could be delivered in due course.

And one day he would return to show Pioneer Vale just how merciless he could be.

*　　*　　*

Abel's knees creaked when he stood up from the cover of his position behind a water barrel. The townsfolk fought valiantly alongside Kitchi's people and together they seemed to have the battle well in hand. The mercenaries had lost their taste for the fight, and while some threw down their arms in surrender, most had simply tried to break away from the engagement and run away. He jogged up beside Chogan, who helped one of the town's shopkeepers back to his feet.

"It's time to offer quarter to any of their soldiers who want it. We lose nothing by showing a bit of mercy."

"As you say, Farmer," said the Nipmuc warrior. He rushed off shouting to a knot of his tribesmen.

"Aye, I'll spread the word as well," said the other man. "Didn't realize these new allies spoke our language. Might have made things a lot smoother between them and us all this time."

"Little more complicated than that," he muttered as the Valeman hurried off. He turned towards the Huntsman, hoping that Marcus and his family were safely inside, as he hadn't seen his friend since the beginning of the fray. Wouldn't hurt to grab a quick one to steady my nerves either, if given the chance, he mused.

A shadow flitted through the alleyway beside the old tavern, and he squinted through the haze of gunsmoke. The fog parted just enough for him to see the Reavers' brutal commander, Forrester, lower his pistol and slink into the back streets. There was something dangerous about that man that went beyond his sadistic command of the mercenary company. Abel had seen the sort before and knew that there would be no surrender.

He double-checked his rifle, loaded and ready to fire again, and then hurried towards the path that led behind the Brenner's tavern. He moved along quickly and quietly, and his familiarity with the layout of the streets would easily put him ahead of the retreating commander. The townsfolk could handle the rest of the company. He would face this brute himself. After all, he smiled to himself, when you spy a dangerous snake in the corn rows, you don't keep the hens safe by lopping at the tail.

You had to cut off the head.

CHAPTER 18
NOBLE SACRIFICE - 1671

The air in the old mine crumpled, folded upon itself, and then ripped open in a flash of violet fire. Anne-Marie fell through the portal, bounced a wooden beam, and dropped to the cold stone floor. The stench of the place turned her stomach nearly as much as the magic that burned through her frame, and she retched into the dirt.

"Oh, that was so much smoother than last time," she groaned. She wiped the back of her hand across her mouth, and lay still for a moment, while every burning muscle quivered. Her head throbbed, and rivulets of blood trickled from her ears and nose, and yet, none of the effects struck her as fiercely as on her first attempt. Given enough time and training would she even feel them at all?

A wisp of fire flashed in her hand, and six plumes darted around the chamber, lighting up the various torches and lanterns that were scattered about the cavern. The sudden burst of light glittered off the towering wall of gold that rose into the encroaching gloom of the mine's shrouded ceilings. These untouched riches had caused so much of the Vale's recent strife and turmoil, courtesy of Preston's greed. Once the dust has finally settled, she thought, I swear I shall put this to use undoing the suffering caused by Shade's schemes.

"Henna," she called out, cringing at the ringing echo of her voice. In answer, a cascade of twinkling emerald sparkles flooded the foul tunnel at the far end of the chamber that sloped down to Shade's unholy temple beneath the mountain. Shards of gravel and the occasional bone crunched beneath her boots as she plunged once more into those infernal depths.

The narrow passageway soon opened up into the cavernous shrine, the vaulted ceiling lost to the writhing darkness above. Seated upon a broken stone pillar surrounded by her signature green motes that lazily circled her head, sat her mentor. The old Guardian's walking stick was loosely nestled in the crook of her elbow, and she cleaned her nails with a slim dagger that was typically hidden in the leather bracers beneath her now rolled-up sleeves. She breathed easier when Henna looked over her shoulder and smiled.

"I was wondering how much longer ye'd keep me waiting, lass."

"You'll have to forgive me. I had a bit of a run-in with one of the wolf's friends."

"A little worse for wear, but at least ye came out in one piece." Henna pursed her lips and then reached towards her. Her teacher's withered fingers lightly touched the blood-stained ruffle on the blouse she wore and a soothing warmth flowed into the stab wound on her shoulder. "I trust the same can't be said for the one ye tussled with."

"He received what he deserved." She shrugged and then lobbed two balls of flame into the darkest corners of the shrine but saw nothing amiss. "So where do you suppose he's hiding? He has to know we're ready for a fight."

"The mangy devil hasn't made his entrance yet," Henna said with a dry chuckle. "Most likely, he was waiting for you to arrive, dearie. Old fool probably still thinks he can take us both down at once."

"Can he?"

"Trust in old Henna, my girl." The wizened crone looked up at her and winked. "I've got more than these old leather bracers tucked up my sleeve."

A frigid gust of wind filled with the stench of decay blew across the chamber from the great obsidian altar. The lid of the old wooden chest that sat upon the stone squealed on rusted hinges and fell open with a loud clang. A ghastly radiance shimmered from within the heart of the pale yellow crystal that rested on a tattered velvet pillow. As the light intensified, the gem rose from its cushioned perch, and spun lazily in the air.

"He's coming," Anne-Marie whispered. Her breath puffed in the deepening cold, and she wrapped herself in a mantle of fire.

"Aye," replied Henna. The old woman's hands tightened around the gnarled staff in her hands, and she pulled herself to her feet. "Stay on yer toes, girl. He'll throw every trick in his book at us this time."

The shadows surrounding the altar gathered and shifted, drifting back and forth across the dais. She squinted at the sinuous movement that teased just beyond the edges of her firelight, until the outline of a pacing wolf took shape behind the stone. The torches around the chamber erupted in a burst of coldfire, bathing the cavern in the sickly gray light. Behind the altar, Shade's moldering visage peered into the hovering gemstone.

"After so many eons of waiting, don't expect me to be so subtle, crone." With a wave of his taloned hand, a wall of gray flame burst into life behind them, barring the tunnel to the surface. "Tonight, I will slake my thirst for your blood, and your final dwindling screams shall herald my freedom as I conquer your world for my dark master."

"Hush yer threats, ye addle-brained cur," snapped Henna. "At most, I might whistle a bar or two as we shove your flea-ridden self back into the infernal kennel ye crawled from."

"And how do you plan to do so?" Shade scooped up an old skull from the floor, held it with an almost tender caressing gesture, and then crushed it to powder with the clench of his fist. "With purple sparks and fanciful green twinkles?"

Anne-Marie drew her cloak of flame more tightly around her body. Shade stood differently this time than in any of her previous encounters with him. He was more ominous. More confident. The demon carried himself now with a subtle ferocity, his every movement smooth and full of staggering intensity. Gone was the fanciful prancing and banter that he had always put on like some capering harlequin. He had come to this evil place ready to fight, and his form grew ever more bestial when he dropped down to all fours with fangs slavering.

"He does love to prattle on, doesn't he?" Henna asked over her shoulder. "I hope ye got yer fill of that lovely tree line outside for ye'll be seeing naught but the hellfires of your own home when we finish here, Shade."

"You've still not accepted that your world is doomed, Guardian." A cruel sneer twisted his lips. "Your stubbornness will be the death of you yet."

"I swore when we first met that I would fight you until my last breath," snapped Anne-Marie as she stepped up beside her teacher. The Elder's Whisper that coursed through her body steadied her nerves in this wretched place, empowered even more by the rage and sorrow that engulfed her. "And I'm still standing."

She lunged forward and twin bolts of lavender flame slammed into Shade's chest and shoved the wolf backward against the black altar. With the precision of a surgeon, she drove her lances of fire deeper into the demon's core. He howled in agony, but his form wavered in the dim light, and the stone wall behind him became visible through his flesh. Anne-Marie's blast passed through his wraithlike presence, sending splinters of black rock through the air.

Shade sprang forward and rolled out of the firebolt's path. His feet became solid once more and struck the rough ground with a heavy thud. His mighty fist was bathed in coldfire, and he punched the stone floor, cracking the ground with his powerful strike that sent a shockwave throughout the cavern. The floor bucked beneath their feet and dropped the two women into a tangle on the stone.

"Ye might've given me some warning of what you had in mind, girl," muttered Henna. Anne-Marie rolled to her knees while the old woman raised a swirling shield of emerald light in front of them both. "Now that ye've started the fray, ye'd best hit him again, fast and hard."

"With pleasure," she said, and her hands spun in a wide circle above her head. A coil of flame ringed with jagged barbs spiraled around and sliced through the air. With a hissing crack, the fiery whip raked across Shade's chest and face, leaving dark scorches across his pelt. A second snap looped the snare around the wolf's throat and choked his growing roar into a whimper as she tightened the tether through sheer force of will.

Shade wound her line around his arm and yanked her forward and off balance. Coldfire raced down the length and lavender turned to gray as the demon snuffed her magic, releasing her hold just before his icy flames engulfed her hands. The air trembled where the two forces met and she threw herself over to one side as the magic between them erupted in a backlash of blistering force. Her foe was already on the move, vaulting through the air towards her with supernatural speed. She raised her arm up to call forth her defenses, but a second shadow blended with the demon's own as he pounced.

Henna darted between her and the leaping beast with a twinkling green shield radiating from the leather bracer on her arm. The wolf slammed against the older Guardian's magic with black talons that scrabbled at the edges of the barrier. His black spittle sprayed against the safeguard and sizzled away as Henna's lined face glowed with an emerald brilliance. Her white braided hair brightened to a platinum blonde, and her eyes held the ferocity of a far younger woman. With her bone-handled knife in hand, Viking's Daughter, tall and poised, drove the blade into Shade's ribs.

Anne-Marie skittered back and rolled into a fighting crouch while the force of Shade's roar nearly knocked her down again. Henna's knife slammed home once, twice, three times more with each stroke drawing a steaming jet of thick ichor from the wounds. Her teacher's skin blistered wherever the demon's blood sprayed against her, but Henna twisted the blade with gritted teeth. Shade's fist hammered against the woman's enchanted shield, and although the energy wavered, she nevertheless kept him at bay.

"On yer feet, lass," Henna groaned. "I'll not be able to hold him off forever."

"Aye, witch," Shade snarled. "Not for one second more."

Gray fire enshrouded the demon's forearm and his claws elongated into black iron daggers. His wicked maw snapped down, tearing away Henna's glittering shield, and his fangs clamped down on the wrist guard she wore. Green sparks splashed across Shade's sunken cheekbones, but the crunch of bone was somehow more deafening to Anne-Marie than the beast's guttural snarl. She readied a bolt of flame, but her teacher was too close, too entangled for her to find a clear shot that would separate the grappling foes.

Henna returned the attack with her own barbaric roar and plunged her knife home once more. The old Guardian spared her a single fleeting glance over her shoulder before the wolf's wicked claws, trailing gray fire like the tail of a shooting star, raked down the front of her mentor's dress, and tore four bloody rents in the fabric.

"Henna, no!" Anne-Marie screamed. Henna's fingers clutched at a tuft of black fur, before slipping loosely to her side.

"One down," Shade purred, turning his cold gaze her way. "One to go." With his wickedly enchanted razored fingertips plunged deeply into her friend's belly, the demon hurled Henna through the air towards her. His legs coiled and he followed close behind with a mighty leap.

But Anne-Marie's enhanced reflexes were as quick as the wildfires at her beck and call. She thrust her left hand forward, and an eldritch bolt borne of pure rage shot past Henna's form and hammered into the soaring beast's chest. Plucked from the air, Shade was blasted from his course and dashed against the altar steps. With her other hand, she wrapped Henna into a cushion of heated air, and ever so gently lowered the older woman to the ground. She fell to her knees beside her friend, but her heart sank as she took the woman's gore-slicked hand.

Gone was the youthful warrior maiden that had stood reborn by the Elder's power. The old familiar wrinkles gifted over so many years once more adorned the woman's face. The vibrant blonde hair had returned to wizened gray, although crimson spatters covered all. Blood soaked the torn dress she wore, and pumped from the vicious slashes in her belly. Green twinkles yet sparkled in her clear eyes, though and a pained grin crossed her teacher's face.

"That didn't go quite as expected," coughed Henna. She looked at the tattered edges of the garish wound and frowned. "Oh, bother. And I was so fond of this old dress."

"Lie still and let me see how bad it is." Anne-Marie summoned a healing flame to her hand, but Henna shook her head.

"There's no time, Guardian. I've one last lesson for ye before I breathe my last."

"Henna, please don't…," she began, but her friend grabbed her wrist with surprising strength.

"The crystal yet remains Shade's weakness. He was born of the Adversary's own blood, and through blood may we bind him to it once more." A low growl rumbled from behind the altar and Shade's shadow fell across the floor as he slowly pulled himself back to his feet. The old woman squeezed her hand. "I'm dying, girl, just as he promised me years ago and there's no stopping that, but I've strength enough to shove the bastard back through to his side of the doorway. I can use what's left of my magic to forge his cage, but it will be up to you to turn the key."

Tears burned in Anne-Marie's eyes and she ran the back of her hand across her eyes. "Tell me what I need to do."

"For starters, help me back to my feet, if you please, dearie." A waft of warm air and her guiding hand lifted Henna from the stone floor and held her upright again. Her mentor leaned heavily upon her and kept her crimson-stained hands pressed to her belly, but the old woman's jaw was firmly set and her eyes blazed like twinkling emeralds. "Just give me enough time to grab the cur by the scruff of his neck. Your instincts will guide you from there."

"Henna, he'll tear you apart before you can even get close."

"Fear not for me, Guardian. All will be well." Henna chuckled and patted her hand once more. "Remember me fondly, lass. The gem is now yours to keep a watchful eye over. As I told ye before, Anne-Marie Carmichael, you are now the Witch of Pioneer Vale."

"A dubious honor that you shall not carry beyond the hour," called Shade from across the cavern. Blood still dripped from the places where Henna had stabbed him, and wisps of gray smoke wafted from the slowly closing wounds. His eyes smoldered in the shadowy recess in which he stood, full of hatred and hunger. He stomped his foot and the ground trembled once more. "Although you may sting me a thousand times, witch, ever shall I rise from the ashes. I am deathless!"

"And I am Henna of the Vale, Viking's Daughter, and servant of the Elder Guardian, you foul beast," Henna shouted back. The older woman shrugged off Anne-Marie's steadying hand and strode forward. Defiantly, she walked up to the stairs of the altar's platform, looked up at the demon towering above her, and grinned. "Ye showed me years ago that I'd die in these halls, wolf, but ye ne'er foretold what it would cost ye in return."

Shade hopped lightly over the stone slab and his ragged lips peeled back from his yellow teeth. He drew back his fist, but an orb of swirling green light erupted around Henna, and before the demon could strike, the Guardian slapped her palm to his chest. Vine-like coils of energy unfurled and tightly wrapped around his limbs, pinioning the monster's arms against his body. A ripple of power coursed through the chamber, and scattered bones from the niches along the walls. The gray light of the torches was snuffed and replaced by a searing emerald brilliance.

"What are you about, crone?" Shade yelped. He thrashed as smoke rose from his fur wherever the ancient power touched his hide, but the blazing green bindings held him fast.

"Now's the time, lass!" Henna called over the tumult. The old woman's fist closed, and Shade's muzzle was drawn down even with her burning glare. "Do your worst."

Anne-Marie's magic seethed within her, and her hair blew wildly as the currents of Henna's power burst through the floodgates and joined with her own. Her friend's heartbeat thumped in time with her own, and the rhythm carried with it the echo of an ancient chant. Her vision burned through the gossamer threads between realms and into the demon's sickly yellow core. His own heart, for lack of a better name, pulsed and hammered as he struggled to break free, and a pale ropelike tether threaded back through his body to the floating gemstone.

And there she saw her course.

Anne-Marie lunged forward, and a spiraling torrent of fire pierced through both Henna and the demon. Lavender light entwined with Henna's jade strands and together they corkscrewed beyond Shade and enveloped the Adversary's crystal. The wolf was jerked by the infernal leash towards the yellow gemstone and he howled in pain and terror as her firebolt raked against it. Her fires found purchase in the heart of Shade's being, and she channeled all of her rage, all of her heartache, into unraveling his hold in this world.

Piece by piece, Shade's body ripped away in gray and purple patches that streaked through the air and vanished into the swirling depths of the crystal. The demon lashed out and sank his claws into Henna's arms, but the older Guardian grabbed his wrists and drove him closer to the altar. Her teacher's form wavered by bits as well, but, where Shade had become a force of violent panic, hers was a face of serenity. While figments of her own body flickered and faded away, green bars formed around the gem, and Anne-Marie shaped Henna's selfless sacrifice into the latticework of an enchanted cage.

Shade bucked under the flow of raw magic that raked over his body. Beneath the onslaught of her flames, his leg crumbled to ash, and he collapsed to one knee. The monster shoved, bit, and clawed but all to no avail for Henna's emerald bands held him fast. Anne-Marie pushed through wracking agony as the magic twisted through her, and ignored all of the lingering pain of her recent injuries, instead reveling in the vibrating echoes of power that coursed through her.

She screamed and pushed with all her might, while the older woman pulled the demon tightly against her by the lingering scruff of his pelt. Step after step, they drove his back against the gem, and Shade's eyes went wide in abject terror. The bones of the mountain trembled and quaked as the last wisps of Shade's body burst into a roiling cloud of smoke and coldfire. Ashes seethed around the crystal in a maelstrom of ancient power and were then sucked into the stone in a flash of green light.

Anne-Marie's flames flickered away and she wiped the glare that yet danced before her eyes. A stream of blood flowed freely from her nose and her stomach jumped as if it tried to escape the confines of her own body. A faint emerald glow pushed back the gloom, and the silent specter of her friend placed her hand on the crystal. The final bars of Shade's prison formed around the gem with a crackle and hiss.

"Henna…," she began, but her words caught in her throat.

"Farewell, my dear," whispered Henna's voice in the back of her mind. The Guardian's body faded to nothingness, and a blinding pulse of green energy washed through the cavern in a soothing warmth that gently pushed Anne-Marie a step back. When the last sparkles cleared away, all traces of Shade and Henna were gone.

The yellow crystal, the ancient drop of the Adversary's blood, still floated lazily over the pillowed chest but now sparkled with glowing green motes that encased the gem and dulled the sickly glow. The last sparkle winked out, the gem tumbled back into the box, and the lid fell shut with a dull clang. The torches along the walls of the shrine, ablaze during the fight with shimmering green light, now gave way to the simple orange glow of normal flame. With a soft hiss, Shade's barrier that blocked the tunnel out of the shrine guttered out, and Anne-Marie found herself alone at last in the great vaulted chamber beneath Alistair's Climb.

*　*　*

Cyrus clambered over the small wooden fence that surrounded the tidy, well-kept garden behind the Hirsute Huntsman, but his wounded leg betrayed him as he put his weight down. He landed heavily in the soft dirt between two rows of herbs, swearing under his breath. He quickly surveyed the streets to make sure that no one was nearby, but as he pushed himself back on his knees, the recent cuts on certain plants caught his attention. While he was certainly no herbalist, Cyrus had spent enough time foraging when he was a young recruit to know that these were not seasonings intended for the Brenner woman's cook pot.

"I'll string that scruffy bitch up by her thumbnails when I return to this hole," he muttered. With a groan, he stood up just as the farmer who had led the savage's assault against his men raced around the corner of the building with his rifle pressed smartly against his shoulder. Cyrus smirked and gave the man a respectful nod as the Valeman sighted down the barrel at him.

"Had you figured for more than a simple dirt digger. Master Harmon, isn't it?" He jerked his thumb at the garden around him. "Your friends were clever to play on my soldiers' superstitions. You've no witch at all, but rather just a touch of foxglove in the stew, hmmm? I can only dare to assume that the young blacksmith who you include in your hushed whispers is responsible for the recent fragility of our weapons?"

"You can draw whatever conclusions you like, Captain Forrester," Abel replied coolly. "I don't much care for any thoughts of yours, sir."

"Such ploys add a certain intrigue to the games of warfare men like us play," he said. He slipped his thumbs into his belt, feeling the weight of his pistol on his hip. "Cleverness, however, will only keep you alive for so long, and you should be warned, my good man, that you common folk cannot remain vigilant forever."

"I only need long enough to bring you to justice, sir," the old farmer replied. "Whether by Dorothea's handiwork or the courage of those who have rallied against the Reavers, your men are defeated. Show your followers that you can be a man of honor so that no more lives are needlessly lost. I will ask for your surrender only this once, Captain."

"Or what? You'll kill me in cold blood? You may be made of sterner stuff than these other sheep, Harmon, but I don't believe you're the sort with the necessary taste for murder." A flash of heat rushed through his hand, and a sneer unbidden teased at his lips. The clouds overhead blotted the moonlight, and the farmer's eyes looked askance for just a moment at the descending shadows. "How unfortunate for you that I am not so afflicted."

Barely conscious of the movement himself, Cyrus' hand moved almost of its own volition and drew his pistol like a bolt of lightning. He crouched ever so slightly and fanned the hammer on his weapon before either of them registered what had happened. The crack of the shot roared in his ears, and the acrid tang of gunpowder filled the air. Through the cloud of black smoke, the farmer's eyes widened as the lead ball struck true over his heart. Harmon's musket landed in the dirt beside him as the impact blew him from his feet. The strange sensation in his arm slowly tingled away, and Cyrus quietly slipped his pistol back into its holster, nodded curtly, and then towards the stables.

*　　*　　*

Marcus burst through the back door of the Huntsman and fell to one knee as his rifle barrel swept across the yard. The lingering cloud of gunsmoke drifted past but hovered just long enough over the familiar crumpled figure lying on the cobbles.

"Oh, no," he gasped. "Dorothea, fetch your remedies and hurry."

"Abel," his wife cried out and pushed past him. He chased after her and they both hopped over the low fence of the herb garden. Dropping down beside their friend in the dusty street, Dorothea fumbled in a small leather pouch and pulled out some linen bandages and a vial of some poultice. He could only lay his hand on the farmer's shoulder and give it a gentle shake.

"Not like this, old friend," he said softly, then fell back when Abel coughed suddenly and grabbed his wrist. Dorothea gasped and dropped her satchel, scattering bottles all along the street. The older man's eyes flickered open, and he groaned, gingerly brushing his hand over the powder burn on his jacket.

"It appears, sir and madam, that you must endure my company a while longer," he said with a weary grin.

"Allison. Micah," Marcus called out to the two younger members of their group. "See if Anne-Marie is about and fetch her to us if you find her. We could use her particular skills now."

"There's no need for that," said Abel. "I have been spared by powers other than hers." The farmer smiled and reached into the inside pocket of his coat, and pulled something forth in his closed fist. His rough and callused fingers opened and revealed his tarnished bronze medal of valor lying in the palm of his hand. The arms of the cross were wrapped around the lead ball that would have otherwise ended the man's life.

"You lucky bastard," breathed Marcus.

"I guess the old Nipmuc woman knew what she was talking about after all," Abel muttered.

"You durned fool. I thought we'd lost you," said Dorothea. She hugged the man and kissed him on his bald pate.

"I could never yet enter the afterlife with a clear conscience. I've still too considerable a tab left to settle with you good folks."

"Not that any ever expect you will," Micah laughed. Marcus steadied his friend and pulled him to his feet.

"Nevertheless, your next one is on the house, my friend."

"And you may rest assured I'll take you up on it, but we haven't earned our victory drink quite yet," Abel said as he grabbed his hat and picked up his rifle from the ground. He pointed down the road towards the stables.

"We still need to stop Forrester."

*   *   *

The chilled air of the shrine fell away as flames burst around Anne-Marie's hands. With a clap and quick twist of her palms, a much smaller portal ripped open in the space beside the chest on the altar and peeked into the serene sitting room of Whisperwind. The hearth fire crackled with the same twinkling green motes of light that peeked through the cracks of the ancient container's lid, and she sighed in relief. The cottage would be a far safer place for so dangerous an artifact, although she knew that she would have to take further measures to hide it away for good. She couldn't merely leave it on the mantle beneath Henna's dreamcatcher and war ax. It would suffice, for now, she mused and pushed the box across the distance on a cushion of air.

The portal collapsed upon itself with a whumpf, and Anne-Marie absently wiped away the trickle from her nose. She looked a mess, covered in blood, ash, and rock dust, but she closed her eyes and rolled a thin wisp of cleansing fire across her body from head to toe. The lesser cuts and scrapes closed up, the soreness from her recent battles eased, and her clothes were as fresh as if she had just taken them off the line. She shook with an almost trembling ecstasy in her magic's wake, but she held back from healing herself completely.

"I've not cast my last spell for tonight," she breathed softly. "I'll yet need a little more strength."

The lavender glow faded, and she made her way over to the tunnel entrance that sloped up to the mine. She gave the dim chamber one last glance in search of any sign that the demon lingered, but only the moldering bones of those long dead lying in their catacombs remained. Even the darkness of the surrounding shadows seemed to bow before her. She took a torch from a sconce and slowly ascended the long corridors out to the surface.

Moonlight outlined the main entrance ahead and the crisp, fresh air was a welcome relief. Anne-Marie dropped the guttering torch into a bucket and sighed. The sounds of birds and insects, absent for so long from this once barren place, greeted her softly with their curious melodies.

She raised her hands to the night sky, and, in gentle measure, rather than her too-typical raging inferno, the soothing warmth from a globe of magical flame drove away the evening chill. These fires were light and ethereal, uncertain phantasms and impossible for the untrained eye to see. Slowly, the globe expanded from her gesture, and the wispy flames enshrouded the surrounding treescape. Even the living rock of Alistair's Climb was pierced by her fire until her arms and legs trembled with the strain of her focused will. Her throat rumbled with ancient and eldritch power that was now hers alone to command, and her voice shook with the weight of such mystical force.

"Just as old glamours guard the location of Whisperwind, let this place also be shielded from sight. May any who stumble near these borders find their way clouded and their steps turned away to safer paths."

A pulse rippled through the woods with her at its center, and it rolled across the landscape for half a mile in all directions. When the last vibration of her echoing voice finally faded away, the very air quivered around her, but at that moment, the illusion was set. Exhausted beyond measure, Anne-Marie let her knees buckle beneath her and she wearily dropped into the soft grass. The stars twinkled above and she longed to simply lie here and catch her breath.

But there was not yet time enough, she thought to herself. For there remained one last shadow that held sway over Pioneer Vale.

With a groan, Anne-Marie pulled herself to her feet once more and brushed the grass from her skirts. She gritted her teeth and with a barely stifled cry, ripped open another fiery gateway in the air before her. The tang of gunpowder mixed with her brimstone, and the cries and clashes of battle shattered the peace in the now serene glade. Through tear-filled eyes she stared through the hole that hung before her.

And there, sitting like a silent bastion immune to the chaos all around, sat the manor of Preston Mathers. Fueled by sorrow and pain, Anne-Marie stepped through her ring of fire into the estate's courtyard, and the magical gate slammed shut behind her.

CHAPTER 19
FIRE AND BLOOD - PRESENT DAY

"Doc, she's gone," said Rebecca. "You need to call it."

"We can't give up on her, Rebecca," Ben groaned. His arms had moved beyond cramping, but he relentlessly continued with the compressions against Anne-Marie's chest. The nurse grabbed his wrists, but he shook loose and resumed his slow steady rhythm. "We have to find a way to get her back on her feet."

"Ben, this woman is dead," Rebecca pleaded. "We have to help those other patients who still have a chance."

"Who's in here?" The door swung open and the bright flash of a penlight lit up the face of one of the staff residents. Dark circles underlined the man's eyes, and he sighed when he saw them. "Hibble. Harmon. Thank God! Everything is going to hell right now. Get out here and help us work some magic."

"On our way, doctor." Rebecca turned back and shook her head sadly. "We're finished here."

Ben froze and a wild ragged laugh shook his body.

"Vicky, take over for me right now," he said and he dragged the young volunteer over to the bedside. He placed her hands on Anne-Marie's still chest, and then bolted to the door, shoving the resident out of his way. "Nurse Harmon," he said in a low voice that brooked no argument, "under no circumstances do you stop CPR on this woman until I get back. That's an order."

"Ben, this is going to cost you your career," Rebecca snapped back. "Don't crack up on us now."

"Under NO circumstances." He pointed his finger at the redhead lying on the table and sprinted into the hallway.

Ben dodged stumbling patients and staff members who crowded the hallway by the dim and wavering beams of flashlights. A pile of debris tripped him up when he tried to jump over it, and he fell hard to one knee, sprawling across the floor. He gritted his teeth against the bolt of pain that shot through his leg before he scrambled back to his feet and continued his madcap dash until he slid to a stop at the doorway of his office. He dashed inside and yanked on the handle of the top desk drawer, but it bucked in his hand as the lock denied him with a loud bang.

"Oh, come on," he muttered, and patted his pockets for his keys, but they were nowhere to be found. His mind flashed back to the ancient shrine up in the hills, and in frustration, he realized that they were probably lost in the mud during his struggle with Aiden Carmichael.

"This can't be happening," he shouted and kicked the desk, ignoring the shock that ran through his foot. He pawed through the papers and file folders that littered the desk but saw nothing that he might use to pry the lock open. Frantic now, he grasped the handle once more, planted his foot against the desktop, and pulled as hard as he could. The desk shuddered, but the drawer silently taunted him with only a slight bounce from his attempt.

"Please," he whispered to no one in particular, "Help me out here." A strange warmth flowed through his arms and Ben's fingers tightened on the handle. With another heave, the lock gave a final rending squeal of metal and snapped. He landed roughly on the floor, watching the contents of the drawer sail through the air. Time slowed to a crawl as the same vial of viscous fluid that had so mysteriously showed up at the hospital after Aiden's attack on the high school tumbled end over end above him. Lavender sparks flashed within its vibrant depths, but with reflexes that he never knew he possessed, Ben snatched the glass tube moments before it smashed against the tile floor. He gave the vial a quick kiss and pulled himself to his feet with the corner of the desk.

Ben leaned against the doorway and ignored his throbbing knee. He took a deep breath and plunged back into the hallway. The corridor was no less hampered than before, but an urgency flowed through him that spurred him past the crowds. His eyes and instincts led him along the clearest path, but around him the hall darkened, and eerie shadows reached out toward him as he sped forward. He held the vial tightly in his hand and breathed easier when the lavender flashes of light drove back the encroaching gloom. He forced his way through the last throngs of people and breathed easier when he reached Anne-Marie's room.

Vicky and Rebecca were still at work, although he could see the strain on the younger woman's face. The volunteer bit her lip as she steadily pushed on the fallen woman's chest, and they looked up in unison as he burst into the room. Rebecca scowled at him but kept counting off beats for the volunteer.

"My arms hurt so much," Vicky said as he stepped up beside her. Sweat glistened on her brow lit by the feeble flame of his lighter still sitting on the nearby tray.

"You're doing great," Ben said softly and he gently pushed the younger woman aside with a sincere smile of thanks. "Let me take over, now. Becky, give me a hand with these wraps so we don't pull her stitches open."

He leaned over Anne-Marie and began to gently peel away the bandages plastered to the woman's pale skin. Rebecca's eyes widened when purple sparkles glinted from the vial cupped in his hand.

"Is that what I think it is?"

"Yeah. That magic juice that she sent over the other day." He yanked the stopper out of the bottle with his teeth and spit it to the floor. "Let's hope it cures more than just that weird frostbite."

Ben poured the fluid onto the sutured slash that ran across his patient's abdomen. He snapped on a latex glove and gingerly massaged it around the stitches, lightly trying to push some of the liquid into the edges of the wound. The salve flashed with a soft lavender glow and then sank into the wound. He held his breath and searched Anne-Marie's face for the slightest twitch that she was coming back around.

Nothing happened.

*　　*　　*

Anne-Marie kissed her husband fiercely and deeply. The familiar rasp of his beard against her cheeks and the firm press of his lips renewed within her breast a magic that had always belonged to him alone. She ached when he leaned away and lost herself in the vibrant twinkle of his chestnut eyes.

"She needs you, Annie. Angelica can't beat Shade by herself."

"I don't think I have enough strength left to face him."

"Of course you do. You have never been weak a day in your life," he said. His calloused fingers lifted the amethyst pendant away from her neck. "This is the moment for which you have endured centuries of hardship. Everything that you have suffered for, and the reckoning that is owed to you all comes due in these next few heartbeats."

"I wish I had never accepted this burden. The cost has been so terrible. Where did I have the right to send so many children, including our son, into Shade's arms?" She buried her face in her hands. "I've made so many mistakes that I can never take back."

"The only mistake you have made is in doubting who you are. It is no coincidence that your magic manifests in flame, love. You believe that you are buying Angelica, our dear descendant, the time she needs to find her road to victory. That she is the one destined to defeat Shade. But have you considered the possibility that she is holding him at bay until you return and drive back his darkness? This is your fight, Annie, not the ones who stood beside you." He smiled at her. "The big bad wolf is afraid of you."

"So it's up to me to save the world?" She squeezed his hand, and the pendant's warmth bled through his fingers into hers. He laughed and pulled her close to his chest.

"As long as we've known each other, you've never given a damn about the fate of the world." He laughed softly into her hair, and then whispered, "There's nothing in heaven or hell, however, that could ever stop you from trying to save your family."

*   *   *

"Come on," Ben pleaded. He rubbed the back of Anne-Marie's hand but there was no color in her pallid skin. "Give me a sign here."

"Doc," said Rebecca softly. "I'm sorry. I know you tried your best, but I think we're just too late."

"This has to work," he muttered. He spun away from the bed and kicked a nearby chair across the room. He leaned on the countertop and whispered, "Only she has the power to stop her son."

"Nurse Harmon? Doctor Hibble?" gasped Vicky. "What the hell is that?"

"Oh, my God," said Rebecca. "You see it too?"

A warm breeze ruffled Ben's hair and he saw their shocked faces staring at the woman in the bed. He whipped back around to the redhead and his jaw dropped open.

Wisps of lavender fire raced through the veins beneath Anne-Marie's skin.

*   *   *

Angelica choked on the foul stench of the demon's breath as Shade's Nightmare Hand tore grooves through the air. The barest crackle of lightning wrapped around his wrist and slowed, but couldn't stop, the fall of his mighty arm. The tips of iron black claws scratched at the skin of her neck, so wickedly close to her artery and windpipe, yet a strange calm fell over her as the last gasp of air left her lungs. The rush of blood in her ears drowned out his triumphant howl and a sparkling cascade of spots that captured every color of the rainbow danced before her eyes. Red. Green. Yellow. Purple

An incredibly bright and dazzling purple.

A wash of heat and a dull boom followed a streak of lavender light that blazed like a comet through the darkened shrine. The press of Shade's weight was torn from her chest, and the wolf's piercing howl turned into a fading whine as he was flung across the dais. Angelica pitched herself the other direction and rolled off of the altar only to crash onto the stone floor. The burst of agony dragged her back from the brink of unconsciousness as the heated air hit her lungs. Magic surged through her body at the sight of the shadowy figure kneeling in front of a fiery portal, blinding in intensity and raging like the midday sun.

"I told you," snarled Anne-Marie as she slowly rose from the floor. Her grandmother spoke in a whisper, but her voice shook the room with the roar of the fiery maelstrom around her. "You haven't finished with me yet!"

The Guardian's eyes were ablaze and a swirl of her signature flame ripped the bloodstained hospital gown away in a cloud of cinders. Like a coiling snake, tendrils of fire wrapped around her in an undulating sensual dance and when they sputtered away, the Witch of Pioneer Vale stood battle-ready once more in her sleeveless tunic, corset, trousers, and boots. The grim determination on the woman's face bespoke a fury and raw hatred that Angelica had never seen before.

A shadow loomed above her, as Aiden perched upon the edge of the altar stone. His ear-splitting screech chilled the air as he spread his wings. Angelica hauled herself to her feet and lifted her palm just under her cousin's chin. A blue-white lance of lightning blasted like an uppercut and jerked his serpentine neck toward the ceiling. Her energy grappled with him, raised him from his roost, and threw him into the wall beside his groggy demonic master. With a loud snap, one of his wings bent at an unnatural angle, and the Harbinger's anguished wail reverberated in the shrine. She stumbled down the steps and fell heavily into Anne-Marie's arms.

"You're cutting these entrances a little close, don't you think?"

"I'm sorry. I was a bit under the weather myself," Anne-Marie replied. Soft and gentle fingers caressed her bruised cheek, and Angelica knew from the tears that her grandmother fought back that she must look like hell. "I've got to get you away from here."

"There's no time," Angelica said. She stepped out of Anne-Marie's embrace, but she nearly fell over when her cracked ribs ground against one another. Blood from so many cuts and scrapes ran freely across her face and spattered her clothes. "We can't give them a chance to regroup again. We need to fight them here and now. I have the crystal, but can't figure out how to fix it."

"You can't even stand. You'll not survive another fight." Anne-Marie's hand swirled in the air, and the sparks of a portal began to take shape. A dark shadow rushed between them though, and her ancestor was tackled away in a tangle of fur and claws. Angelica was shoved back and landed hard on her rump.

"No more running, witch," Shade roared. The cavern flashed with sprays of both gray and lavender flame as they tumbled across the stone floor. Angelica raised her hand, but the dazzling lights and chaotic thrashing of the two figures denied her a clear shot at the demon.

A vice-like grip clamped around her ankle and yanked her back towards the dais. Something in her hip popped loud enough to hear even over the deafening sounds of the battle before her, and two fingernails broke as she was dragged across the stone. She twisted her head around and screamed as Aiden's blazing eyes were scant inches from her face. His roar whipped back her hair and she threw herself down just in time to avoid the bone-crunching snap of his razored maw.

The Harbinger's left wing hung askew, and a fine spray of his spittle splashed against her skin. Blisters sprang up where the drops touched, and he opened his mouth wider still. She lashed out with her free foot, and the heel of her boot slammed against his chest, but there was little strength behind the kick now.

The winged beast's fist slammed down and her head rocked against the stone. The back of her neck grew wet and warm, and Aiden howled in what could only be demonic glee. She looked through her cousin's legs and reached out to Anne-Marie, but her grandmother struggled to hold Shade's slavering fangs away from her own throat in flame-enshrouded hands. Hissing laughter filled her ears, just before dozens of needle-sharp teeth dug deeply into her thigh.

She had never screamed so loud in her life.

*   *   *

Anne-Marie fought against Shade's weight, her formidable shields torn asunder one after another by the unending barrage of claws and gnashing teeth that his relentless fury threw at her. The demon's deafening snarls were broken by Angelica's terrible shriek and her enemy paused in his rhythm just long enough for her to drive home a bolt of her flame into his midsection that hurled him away from her. She rolled to her side in time to see the great monster that had once been her son tear his head away from the girl's leg in a spray of blood.

"You can't save her, witch," purred the wolf as he brushed her glowing embers from his hide. "One final sacrifice from your bloodline to add to my tally. You may as well turn your flames on her now, for she'll suffer far less by your hand than by your son's."

Her 10th great-granddaughter clawed her way across the cracked dais with the Harbinger looming like an angry god beside her. So horribly wounded, and yet possessed of an indomitable will, the battered young woman rose to her knees despite her injuries and stared at something clutched in her hand. When Angelica lifted her gaze to look at her, the girl's eyes were bright and full of fierce determination.

Aiden stepped towards her and flickering swirls of coldfire sprung up around him, casting a corona of gray shadows across the girl's upturned face.

*   *   *

Angelica couldn't feel her leg. Her ribs ached with every breath she tried to draw in, and her tongue scraped along the jagged edges of broken teeth. Aiden's venom mixed with her blood that spilled from the wound and burned against the edges of his wicked bite. A heavy footfall crashed down behind her and the shadow of her cousin's twisted wings blotted out the dim torchlight. From across the chamber, Shade threw his head back and howled into the vaulted ceiling of the mountain shrine.

"Angelica, move," Anne-Marie shouted to her although her grandmother seemed a world away, her voice tinny over the ringing in her ears. Her grandmother rose from the ground, staggering under the weight of her own injuries, but clenched her fists and wreathed her whole body in lavender fire.

A sharp pain dug into her hip and she reached under her body only to touch the rawhide drawstring of the old leather pouch. The weathered flap fell open and broken shards of the ancient crystal along with two crumpled wildflowers, one blue and one purple, spilled onto the stone floor. She coughed and blood from deep within her lungs splattered across the pile.

"Reforged in fire and blood," she whispered and then looked to her grandmother. "The fire of the Elder's Champion and the power in the blood of the Firstborn."

Sparks danced across her fingertips, and as she pulled herself up to one knee, lightning coursed through her body, blazing and thundering once more. With a backward flick of her fingertips, she unleashed a raging bolt into Aiden's chest that blew him through the altar, shattering the centuries-old stone slab and filling the air with slivers of rock and dust. Smoke rose from his still form as he lay among the rubble.

The power within her surged to new heights and her arms trembled as she fought to maintain control of so much raw magic. The roiling thunder of her heartbeat threatened to split her skull and her eyes glazed over with blue-white brilliance. The veil between this world and the demon's realm shredded away and in the corners of the ancient shrine flickering candles flashed with every color of the rainbow, slowly gathering closer. Watching. Waiting. Her grandmother had taught her that the power of the Guardians was without limit except for what her own body could withstand. Now or never, it was time to see how much she could bear.

"Anne-Marie," she screamed over the roar in her ears. "Hit me with everything you've got!"

*   *   *

Anne-Marie threw her arm over her eyes, shielding herself from Angelica's blazing conflagration. Blinding flashes of lightning shot through the bloodstained crystal shards in her granddaughter's hands, and her crackling magic poured from the girl's wounds, like cracks in a wall that burned hot from her very core. The unbridled power rocked the young woman's entire body, and the resounding strain of such primordial energy threatened to tear her apart.

As flames filled her hands, the shrine came alight with vibrantly colored wisps from beyond the veil, and slowly took shape. All of her children lost to this war, the Firstborn, slowly gathered around her. Memories of how she had turned her fires upon her descendants assaulted her. The echoes of their fearful cries as one and all had pleaded with her in their final moments to spare them from the wrath of her magic.

And now her dear Angelica begged for her to unleash that hell upon her.

Behind Angelica's quaking form, Aiden rose from the rubble of the shattered sacrificial table and clutched a piece of the broken slab in his clawed hands. His snarl was lost in the rolling thunder that surrounded the altar and he raised the chunk high above his head. To her side, Shade crouched with coldfire balefully dancing in his eyes, ready to spring at her once more.

"Do it now!" Angelica cried. Lightning fell like a queen's mantle around her shoulders and the timbre of her voice staggered them all. The pillars that reached up to the vaulted cavern ceiling cracked, and rocks fell from the battered walls. Her magic flowed into her arms and legs as she held forth the shattered gemstone. "Please!"

Unhindered tears boiled away to steam as the fires within her swelled, and then, with a soul-wrenching sob and a rush of flame, Anne-Marie turned her magic's full fury loose upon her granddaughter.

*   *   *

Lavender fire raked across her body, but Angelica caught the blast within the branching tendrils of her net of lightning. A deep resonance thrummed through the room as she grappled and bound the two elemental forces together. The combined magics built upon one another, the unspeakable forces she directed growing with an incalculable energy until the world fell away into a twisting spiral of light and darkness. She was only dimly aware of the others in the cavern as her body became a furnace of cosmic strength.

She held the fury of an exploding star in her hands, and the ancient crystal pieces melted under her gaze. The inky bonds of dark magic reached out, pulled together, grasped after its own likeness. Cold guttural bellow filled her mind and her stomach twisted with the same sickness from that frightful night in the library, but the comforting warmth of the Elder Guardian's gift held the terrors at bay.

Icy winds buffeted her and numbness made every movement a battle unto itself but each wave of her hands was deft and sure. Pressing forward, Angelica drew together the formless slivers and reshaped the shards into the single dagger-tipped gemstone that she herself had shattered so many weeks ago. When the last splinter found its place, the torn veil between Shade's shrine and the Realm of Nightmares fluttered back into place like a mended curtain dividing the two worlds once more. With the last of her strength spent, she gasped and a final sparking ember from her fingers reflected off the prize she held.

The reformed Holding Crystal.

"What have you done?" roared Shade. The demon thrashed and the previous wounds and burns that he had so casually shrugged off returned, bleeding and blistering. The demon stumbled, his shadow wavering, and he fell to his knees. His gaze, however, was as foul and even more sinister than ever, without a hint of the capering fool that he had so often portrayed. He reached towards Aiden and snarled, "Kill her, my Harbinger! Do not let them imprison us again."

Angelica couldn't tell one shadow from another, and the demon's command was nothing but a gravelly rumble in her ears. She shuddered and an icy numbness flowed through her body as the gem drained away her fading magic. Fiendish shapes that once danced around the corners of the shrine now cowered, but the darkness spread and grew thick in her sight. Like a lighthouse to a foundering ship, Anne-Marie's lavender glow cut through the fog ahead of her, but brighter still were the gathering iridescent rainbow of sparks that drew closer to her and revealed the ghostly faces of those who had come before her. Where once before she had met by looks of scorn and hatred, she now saw hope.

"This is the moment you all died for," she whispered. "Stand with us now."

Angelica fell forward, the cold cobblestones rising fast to meet her, but with a final push of magic and a sparkling flick of her fingers, the crystal shot from her hand with unerring accuracy.

*   *   *

"Angelica!" Anne-Marie cried out. Her granddaughter collapsed to the ground but not before a miniature yellow comet with a blazing blue spark of a tail streaked from her fingertips. With sure hands, she snatched the Holding Crystal from the air, but immediately fought against the demonic power of their ancient enemy that roared to life within reach of her flames.

The gemstone surged against her, twisting within her grasp, but she held it tightly in her fist.

She spun on her boot heel in response to Shade's throaty howl, as the demon leaped towards her with terror in his eyes and dull black claws snatching at the price she now held. The shroud of coldfire around him had dimmed, more subdued with this attempted pounce. The corner of her lip curled up and lavender flame sheathed her arm, stealing away his impact with her as she pulled the demon from the air by the matted fur of his chest. His teeth snapped, and his heavy fists fell upon her, but, with the veil restored, his strikes had lost much of their fury whereas the animosity of nearly four centuries only fuelled her strength.

"Releeaaasssseeee hiiimmmm," hissed Aiden from the sacrificial platform. Her son swung the marble chunk in a downward arc toward Angelica's defenseless head. With the wolf struggling in one hand and the crystal held in the other, her fires blazed in her eyes. Twin beams streaked towards Aiden, but the stone fell faster still.

A gray-black dome suddenly blanketed Angelica's body, and Aiden's stone blasted away from the barrier and shattered in a cloud of dust. He stood stunned just as her strikes slammed into his chest and threw him across the rubble once more. From the swirling shadows behind the altar, Phoebe stepped forth illuminated by a dimming glimmer of coldfire that ensconced her hands. The phantom child looked down at Angelica then back to her and gave a deep bow of her head.

"Let's finish this."

Anne-Marie covered her eyes as the shrine lit up in a scintillating array of colors while the wraiths of her Firstborn streaked forward in blurs that surrounded Aiden and Shade. The wounds and scars that they had borne since their final moments faded away, and she was greeted once more by the kind and innocent faces that she remembered from their earliest meetings. Their magic flowed freely and entangling vines, blasts of energy, and eldritch explosions buffeted both demon and his apprentice. Aiden staggered under the assault and was dragged to the floor, shrieking as the touch of the deceased Guardians burned into his scaly hide.

Shade fought back against them, though, and his coldfire ripped through their ethereal bodies as the spectral Guardians dove and swooped around him. Although he did little damage, the demon disrupted them enough so that neither could they gain purchase against him. She struggled to hold the flailing monster still, but the Father of Nightmares threw his hand out to his fallen Harbinger.

"Return what is mine," Shade yelled. The Harbinger's back arched with a sickening crack and a searing ray of raw magic punched through the scaly chest, lashing forth to bathe the wolf in a chilling radiance. Bones snapped and muscles ripped while Aiden screamed in agony. Leathery hide fell away in chunks that left raw skin and sinew beneath. The great wings fell from his back, and for one fleeting moment in his soft beseeching eyes, Anne-Marie saw her son that had been stolen so long ago. With his power stripped away and his true form restored, Aiden was helplessly lost under the press of the spirits that raged around him.

Her wrist jerked as The Father of Nightmares stood tall once more, his powerful frame bristling with renewed infernal strength. The demon's eyes blazed with hellfire and his black iron claws flashed down leaving a plume of smoke in their wake. Razor-tipped talons slashed across her shoulder and blood sprayed across her chest, as the ferocious strike drove her to one knee. Crushing fingers clamped around her throat, and her foe lifted her effortlessly from the ground. His muzzle brushed almost tenderly against her cheek, and his leathery tongue lapped a trickle of blood from her skin.

"Nowhere left to run, witch," he purred.

Like bursting fireworks, the air came alive with the splashes of color from the wraiths that suddenly surrounded them once more. Before Shade could strike again, her lost children seized him by the wrists, the legs, or around his waist and drew him away. Anne-Marie dropped lightly back to the stone floor as Phoebe's inky shadow threw an arm around the demon's throat and yanked back his head. Though her eyes still blazed with malice, the crooked smile on the girl's face was the same playful smirk that she saw in the looking glass every so often.

"You've been away from your cage for far too long," she whispered into the wolf's ear.

"I'll tear your soul apart," Shade snapped in choking gasps.

"No," Anne-Marie snarled. "You'll never hurt my family again, you son of bitch." She lunged forward with the dagger-shaped crystal and slammed the gem into Shade's black heart. Coldfire erupted from the wound, and the force from the explosion of ancient magic threw her across the shrine. She bounced against the cavern's far wall and dropped to the floor. Her breath caught roughly in her lungs, but she pushed herself up on shaky arms.

A keening whine from the gem pierced the air and a nimbus of coldfire leaked through the splits in the wolf's tattered hide. The wraiths, too, were tossed aside in the outpouring of flame and fury, and each one vanished in a puff of colored smoke. Shade yowled and thrashed, clawing at the gemstone buried between his ribs, but so powerful was the tide that even his hands blackened against the unholy fire.

Anne-Marie braced herself and launched another driving bolt into the exposed end of the crystal. Her aim was true, and the force of her blow shoved the gem deeper into Shade's body. Black ichor sprayed from his lips, and the tip of the yellow stone punched through the wolf's back abruptly changing her enemy's enraged bellow into the whimper of a wounded animal.

A blast of mottled gray fire blew upwards and raked the vaulted cavern ceiling with bands of ancient magical force. Stone cracked and rocks fell all around her in a cascade that only a hastily raised shield managed to deflect. Spouts of water burst through newly opened fissures that connected the deeply buried chamber with the lake at the summit of Alistair's Climb, and she found herself ankle-deep in seconds.

She stumbled through the rushing current, splashing down as she sloshed towards the dais when Shade's massive fingers wrapped around her wrist. Glowing coals outlined his muzzle with an ethereal light that slowly ate away the already moldering flesh. The chill of his coldfire washed over her as he pulled her closer.

"Dare not...to... dream, Sweetling," the wolfish demon hissed, "for I'll be... waiting." The embers of his eyes dimmed, his fingers went slack, and with a final howl that rose in a terrifying crescendo then faded to a lamenting whine, the Father of Nightmares collapsed into a billowing pile of ash.

The mountain quaked again and an even greater deluge of water and loose rock washed through the chamber. Anne-Marie held on to a spur of stone, sputtering for air as the waves climbed higher along the walls. She saw Angelica lying still across the stone steps by the dim light of the guttering torches, one hand already submerged in the swiftly rising water. She pulled herself along, using what strength she had remaining to fight the current.

In a prismatic flash, the rushing water broke around her, and the gleaming wraiths of her Firstborn appeared in a line between her and the altar. They each held their hands aloft and their signature colors spiraled to the cavern ceiling, forming up a veritable rainbow bridge that held the collapse at bay.

Phoebe appeared at the end of the line, kneeling beside Angelica, and beckoned to her. Her eyes were still alight with the dingy gray of coldfire, but the Adversary's flames dimmed as she stroked the fallen Guardian's cheek. Bright golden light, blinding and pure, tore away the shadows that surrounded her and the harsh lines of her face once more bore the innocent and cherubic look thought lost so long ago.

"Go quickly, Grandmother," the girl called. "We cannot hold for long."

Anne-Marie waded forward as quickly as the deepening water would allow, but the quaking ground and unsteady swells hid trip hazards below the dark surface that slowed her down. A falling rock clipped her arm, and she was spun around, landing with a splash upon the bottom of the dais steps. Behind her, two of the scintillating candles of her descendants winked out as the force of the collapsing ceiling overcame them. She scrambled over jagged chunks of broken marble and sobbed when she finally reached Angelica lying on the other side.

"Hurry, please," shouted May. Her voice was but a hoarse groan, and no sooner spoken before she, Mitchell, and Kathryn were torn away in wisps of light. Anne-Marie took Angelica's hand and squeezed it tightly as she choked on the dust in the air. She was so very tired, but, amid the chaos around her, she reached deep within herself, and the Whisper of the Elder found the girl's beating heart, faint but still present. Her granddaughter's eyes fluttered open and her lips quivered, but she hadn't the breath to form a single word.

The colorful lights at her back dimmed, one by one until only Phoebe's radiance lit the area around her. She shielded her eyes and looked back at the girl. She floated along strong and proud with fists still clenched at her sides, but her expression was serene and forgiving. A warm smile finally found its way to her face.

"Goodbye, Grandmother," she mouthed, her whispered words lost among the tumult, and then she too faded away.

With the light of her children gone, the chamber plunged into darkness, and she called forth the dimmest of flames, just bright enough to see the area. Water thundered into the room, cresting now over the topmost step, and washed across her knees in short order.

Rubble shifted beside the ruined altar, and Aiden gasped from under a fallen chunk of granite that had pinned his leg. Blood and rock dust covered her son's face, and his glazed eyes suddenly grew wide as he choked on the rising floodwaters. Bathed in the glow of her purple flame, he stretched his hand out.

"Mother," he shouted, sputtering as the rising water reached his chin. Blood stained the water around where his foot was trapped. "Please, help me!"

Each tumbling rock sent rough waves across where they sat in the dark shrine, and the earth bucked with every section of falling ceiling. Anne-Marie leaned Angelica against a sheltering slope of marble then crawled through the water to take her son's hand. She gave him a gentle squeeze and tears welled up in her eyes.

"For too many nights, Aiden, I dreamt only of how I might save you from Shade's schemes." She bent forward and lightly kissed his forehead before she turned around and returned to Angelica, cradling the girl's head in her arms. "I'll chase that dream no more."

"Mother, nooooo!"

"Goodbye, my son," she whispered, but her voice was drowned out by the din of the collapsing cavern all around. She waved her free hand, and a portal of lavender fire irised open. With a deafening roar, the broken ceiling gave way at last in a torrent of water and stone as the entire peak of Alistair's Climb crashed down upon them.

*　　*　　*

The ground heaved, and Will fell against the side of his truck, watching in horror as the mountain imploded. A stinging curtain of rock and dust showered him just before the wall of ancient trees blasted down the slope of Alistair's Climb, ripped loose from their deeply rooted moorings. A cloud of ash from the shattered peak blackened the sky for miles around.

"My God," he gasped. "Please tell me Angie wasn't in there." A radio squawked beside him.

"This is Harmon," John said into his mike as he rushed over and placed a steadying hand on his shoulder. The radio went crazy with the chatter as all the EMS services went on alert from the peak's collapse. "I am at Carmichael Farms. We're gonna need…whatever you can spare out here. I don't even know yet."

"We've got to get up there," Will said. He bolted across his field towards the hill, but he hadn't even reached the barbed wire fence before a flash of violet light burst in midair before him. A ring of lavender flame ripped open before his eyes and a flood of water and rubble rushed across the grass. Two figures spilled out behind the debris, and he sprinted toward a familiar tangle of black hair.

"Angie," he yelled. He slid through the muddy grass on his knees and scooped his daughter into his arms, but she was unresponsive and her skin was cold. "No, no, no. Come on, honey. Don't do this to me!"

A firm hand pulled him aside, and Anne-Marie laid her fingers on the girl's brow. Wisps of flame danced in her eyes, raced down her arm, and wrapped around his little girl. The blue tint of the girl's skin turned rosy and, with a start, Angelica gasped and tensed up against his chest.

"She needs rest, but she will be fine," groaned the redhead as she plunked back down on the dirt. She wrapped her arms around her knees and breathed deeply.

"Thank you," he said to her, then hugged Angelica. Although she was barely conscious, and blood ran in rivulets from her ears and nose, his daughter smiled weakly at him and gave his hand a small squeeze. He laughed with tears streaming down his cheeks, and just rocked back and forth with her. "I was so afraid that we'd lost you."

"Yeah, I wasn't too sure myself," she croaked.

"I'm fine also, thank you for asking," said Anne-Marie. Her face was drawn tightly and she winced when her fingers gingerly touched her shoulder. Will realized that her shaking arms hid from view her blood-soaked blouse and the four wicked slashes that ran across her collarbone.

"Johnny, help the lady out," he said.

"We've got folks on the way to help, Mrs. Carmichael," his friend said. Harmon knelt beside Anne-Marie and pulled a handkerchief from his back pocket. He shook it out and held it lightly against her wound, and the redhead nodded her thanks to him. "Looks like you ladies have been through the wringer. Once you're all patched up, we need to have a long chat about what has happened around here these last couple of weeks."

"I sincerely hope for your sake, constable, that your intentions aren't to take me off to your stockade." Anne-Marie arched an eyebrow. "I've had quite the day."

"You know what, ma'am," he said with a chuckle. "I think I am going to be buried in enough paperwork to last me a few years as it is. I can probably let you go with a warning this time."

"Likewise, officer." She gave John a wink and Will laughed when his friend's mouth dropped open.

Anne-Marie dragged herself over to where he and Angelica sat, and his daughter struggled to sit up. Will moved aside and let Anne-Marie lay down beside his daughter. In the distance, an ambulance siren echoed from the surrounding hills.

The two women threw their arms around each other, and when they parted, the older of the pair, stroked the younger girl's cheek. Will gasped when a blue-white spark entwined with a wisp of fire that trailed behind the caress, and tears ran down their cheeks.

"You chose me," Angelica said, her voice a choked sob. "Over your own son."

"My dear girl, after nearly 400 years of deluding myself," Anne-Marie answered, "there was never any other choice to make."

CHAPTER 20
THE LAST COMMAND - 1671

Kitchi burst out of an alleyway and stared into the face of utter chaos. The whine of a musket ball zipped past his ear, and he crouched low behind a wooden cask. Cautiously he peeked around the side of the barrel, but whoever had fired the shot had moved on to another target.

The few remaining mercenaries, only about twenty or so in number, had fortified themselves within the town stable and had at last managed to form up a strictly regimented firing line. Deadly volleys rang out in a rhythmic cadence with musket barrels belching fire and plumes of smoke like the steady beat of a drum. One half of the surviving troop would reload while their fellows took aim and fired into the Nipmuc tribesmen and the allied townsfolk who struggled to close the gap.

He nocked an arrow and smoothly drew back his bowstring, hoping that a well placed shot might distract the soldiers' discipline and allow his friends to disarm them. He sighted down the length of the shaft when the icy, but undeniably razor-sharp, steel edge of a knife pressed against his throat.

"Sticks and stones are no match for steel and powder, boy," said a cold voice behind him. A gloved hand reached past his shoulder and snapped the arrow at the fletching. "Stand up and keep your hands out where I can see them."

Kitchi slowly rose from his kneeling position, allowing the firm pressure of the knife against his skin to lead him. With his hands spread wide, he slowly turned to face his attacker. The tip of the long blade never wavered from his throat, however, and the man leaned closer towards him.

There was a smell about the soldier beyond the blood and powder that filled the air. The man reeked of decay, and the whites of his eyes were tainted with a yellow gleam. The grizzled Reaver favored one leg but even without the noticeable injury, the same one that he had delivered, he recognized the mercenary captain that had shot his grandfather.

"Murderer," he spat.

"I know you, don't I, boy?" A wicked grin crossed the man's face. "You're the one who put an arrow through my leg after I killed that old man. He must've been someone dear to you to get you all worked up like that."

"He was our shaman. My grandfather."

"He was my target. My enemy." The man tapped the point of his knife against Kitchi's chest. "And, oh, how I intend to repay you for this limp, you little bastard, but, first, you are going to help me end this little rebellion. Perhaps if you're lucky, I will only flay you alive in front of your people. Now move."

The soldier spun him by the shoulder and shoved him out into the street, bringing the hail of gunfire and war cries to an abrupt halt as both sides saw their leaders arrive. Kitchi winced when the outraged wail rose from the Nipmuc lines, just as cheers erupted from the mercenary camp. Chogan jumped from behind an overturned cart and stood ready to charge, but he held up his hand and waved his brave friend off. The big warrior would only throw his life away if he bolted into the open space.

To the left side of the main thoroughfare, Abel rounded the corner of a large building followed by a giant of a man and a younger, but only slightly less intimidating, youth wielding a worn hammer. The old farmer raised his rifle, and Kitchi felt his captor stiffen at the sight of Abel's arrival.

"Let him go, Forrester! I swear that if you hurt him, you'll not take two steps further."

"Didn't I kill you once today already, Harmon?" the captain called back. "I didn't think a stubborn dirt digger was worth a second round."

"You can end this now, Captain," Kitchi said. "You've lost and no one else needs to die today. Yourself included." The back of his head exploded in pain, and then was yanked backward by a handful of hair before he could fall.

"Shut up, savage," growled Forrester. "Or my next strike won't be with the hilt."

"Your men no longer share your taste for slaughter."

"My men will follow my orders without question. Observe," his captor said in a harsh whisper. "Reavers! The enemy stands before you! Resume fire!"

"Belay that order," came a shout from a side street. A lone man, dressed in tattered remnants of the Reavers' uniform, marched from the dark alley to the right side of the promenade. The soldier's face was haggard, drawn and pale, and splattered with blood. He clenched his pistol in hand and boldly stepped in front of the mercenary firing line. The man's eyes met his own and he gave Kitchi the most imperceptible bow of sorrowful respect. "This battle is over."

"Carter, what are you doing?" Froth from the captain's fury sprayed across the back of Kitchi's neck.

"Your orders have caused enough senseless killing for one night," said the young officer. "Cyrus Forrester, I hereby relieve you of command. I demand that you surrender yourself now."

"Lieutenant, remove yourself from the line of fire, and let the men slaughter this…prey." The pause and subtle shake of the man's head, as if he tried to clear his thoughts, was not lost on Kitchi. The man's grip on his hair lessened ever so slightly, as the younger officer took a step closer, and Abel aimed down the length of his barrel, stock still and without so much as a tremor in his hands.

"I will no longer support your actions," said Carter. "You have proven yourself an honorless disgrace and no longer fit to command this company."

"After all these years of service together, I would never have thought you would turn traitor."

"The soldier that I once held in such high regard has given way to the monster that stands before us now. Our contract with these people has been subverted and abused and your tyranny of blood and death ends tonight."

"Oh, Nathaniel, I am just warming up." Cyrus twirled the knife in his hand in a deft circle, and Kitchi felt the grip on his braid tighten once more. "Starting with this whelp."

The knife rose high into the air, but that was all the time that Kitchi needed. With the blade away from his neck, he stomped his heel down on Forrester's foot, then whipped his head backward, taking satisfaction at the deafening crack of the mercenary's smashed nose. He grabbed Cyrus' outstretched arm, tucked forward, and threw the man over his shoulder and into the street.

He had underestimated the man's weight, solid with years of well-honed muscle, and the momentum of the throw pitched him to his knees. Even with his deer-like reflexes, Forrester was up and kneeling in front of him with his knife still ready in his hand. Cyrus' eyes flashed with that pale yellow glow, and spittle flew from the snarl on his lips. The hammer of

Abel's rifle clicked, but the powder flared in a misfire that flashed on the blade as it reached the peak of the throwing arc.

Thunder roared and a bloody hole punched through Forrester's chest. The mercenary leader lurched to one side, and his blade clattered to the street from his limp fingers. The crimson stain spread across his linen shirt, and the blazing fires in the mercenary's eyes guttered out. Pink froth bubbled from his lips and when he fell over, a plume of smoke trailed from the pistol in Carter's hand.

"You bastard. May you ever be cursed in darkness." Forrester pointed a bloody, quaking finger at the young officer before his eyes rolled back in his head and the mercenary pitched forward on the cobblestones in a spreading pool of his own blood.

"I've only too recently seen the light, Captain," said Carter softly. He holstered his pistol and turned to the remaining Reavers, folding his hands behind his back. "Men, you are henceforth dismissed from all duties with the company. Arrangements will be made immediately for our departure. We are done here."

Cheers erupted from the townsfolk, and the Nipmuc warriors, most of whom were oblivious to Carter's words, quickly understood from their allies' reactions that the battle had ended. Whoops of joy, vigorous handshakes, and tearful embraces spread quickly through the market square. The remaining Reavers mostly stood dumbfounded, but their ranks slowly dispersed as the men fell back to the barracks area, and began tending to those wounded among their ranks.

Kitchi was hit hard from the side and was nearly knocked from his feet once more as Abel and Chogan both barreled into him with their fierce hugs. The farmer's friends and Chief Rowtag followed close behind and all stood in a protective circle around him.

"Kitchi, are you alright, my boy?" asked Abel. "My heart damn near stopped when my rifle misfired."

"You and I both, my friend, but aside from a few cuts and bruises, I am well." He studied the newcomers and nodded his head. "These must be your brave friends that you spoke of."

"Aye, the same." Abel pulled the others forward. "Marcus, Micah, and Dorothea. May I introduce the man to whom we owe the town's liberation? This is Kitchi, Chief of the Nipmuc people. A braver and wiser leader I have yet to serve with."

"I am honored and pleased to meet you at last," he said. He held out his hand but the bearish man slapped it aside and threw his arms around him in a hug so tight that his feet left the ground.

"We all owe you dearly, Chief Kitchi," Marcus said when he lowered him back down. "We hope that after tonight's trials, your people and ours will march together into a new age of prosperity."

"I also hope for nothing less, however, our friend, Abel, honors me above my place with his kind words. I am no Chieftain, merely...." A heavy hand clapped down on his shoulder, and the bellowing laugh of Rowtag thundered in his ear.

"Merely too humble is what you are, and that us a hallmark of a true leader," the warrior said. "Just as the good farmer, no...this fine soldier," he said with a nod of respect to Abel, "has said, there are none more worthy among our people to show us into this new dawn. It would be my great honor to follow your guidance and place the care of our nation under your watchful eye."

"Hail, Chief Kitchi," yelled Chogan and he pumped his war club into the air. Rowtag followed suit and soon the other Nipmuc and, eventually, the townsfolk joined in the chorus.

"Hail, Chief Kitchi," echoed Abel softly. Kitchi's cheeks burned while the assembled people cheered his name. His friend clasped his shoulders and gave him a rugged shake. "May the mantle never weigh too heavily upon your shoulders."

"I don't know if I am ready for such a task. Did you know this would happen?"

"Always suspected it would in due time. You are compassionate and courageous. You stand in no one's shadow. Didn't take an old Nipmuc wise woman to see that you had what it takes, my boy." Abel pulled a piece of metal with a lead ball wrapped around the bronze arms from his pocket and placed it in his hand. "You are Chieftain's Son no longer."

"Speaking of wise women," interrupted Micah, "has anyone heard from Anne-Marie? We may have won our fight here, but how did she fare against…you know?"

"Our victory here surely had to weaken the enemy she went to confront," said Marcus, "but if she has returned to the town, then I can think of only one place she might go."

All heads turned as one to Preston's estate at the end of the street just as a single distant gunshot rang out in the night.

*　　*　　*

Firelight flickered through a doorway down the foyer and to the left, as Anne-Marie softly closed the front door to Preston's home. She padded down the hall and called forth a small ball of flame, neatly hidden in her palm, and ready to mold it into either a shield or a weapon as needed.

Muffled curses, the rustling of shuffled papers, and the slam of desk drawers brought a grim smile to her lips. She had him trapped and to herself. Boldly, she swung through the doorway, and the light in her hand flared. Mathers jumped and dropped the handful of papers he had been stuffing into a battered leather satchel. His eyes grew wide for she cast a

311

fearsome sight, covered in dirt and blood with her magic openly dancing around her fingertips.

"You weren't going to leave without saying goodbye, were you?" She rolled the wisps of fire across her knuckles as she stepped forward. The sweat that beaded on his brow glistened under the soft flow of her magic. "After all you have done, there is no hole dark enough for you to hide in that I would not hunt you down, Preston."

"Stay back, witch," he sputtered. His eyes followed the dancing lavender flames. "I was right about you all along, but I just didn't realize it."

"You know nothing about what I am, you bastard," she said. Her voice dropped into a low growl. "But you are about to learn."

"And how do you think that will work out for you in the end, you foolish girl?" Mathers backed slowly away from the desk, edging towards the sideboard. "You remain a fugitive with an accusation of witchcraft hanging over your head. If you burn me alive, do you believe that the rabble will embrace you once they find you standing over my smoldering ashes, or shall they drag you to a pyre of your own?"

"The townsfolk like me better than you. I think they will be easily convinced who the real monster is."

"Are you so certain of that?" Preston purred. He took a crystal glass from a serving tray and turned it right side up. "Here you stand, threatening my life so casually. Flush with power that you could carve out your own empire with. Ready to eliminate anyone who dares oppose you. Perhaps, my dear, you and the wolf are not so different? The only question is who are you willing to sacrifice to keep the beast in check?"

"The only one who will suffer my wrath will be you."

"Ever the outlook of the tyrant, until the day another runs afoul of your 'best intentions'." He grabbed the crystal decanter and poured himself a drink.

"I know who I can trust," she snapped. "You, however, are all out of allies. Erickson is dead, and the wolf has been caged."

"I've never relied on others to make my fortune." Mathers swirled his glass, held the amber liquid up to the light, and downed the drink in a single gulp. "But, I forget my manners. Would you care for one?"

"You'll need more than a stiff drink to numb the pain I am about to inflict on you," she answered. A chill breeze swept through the room, and an icy presence swept through the chamber. Behind him on the wall, Preston's flickering shadow twisted and grew. The shape's fingers elongated into wicked claws, and the head became that of a snarling wolf. When he turned back to her, Preston's eyes gleamed with a baleful glow, pale and yellow, as he raised the decanter.

"You know that I always keep the good stuff," he said, his voice an echo of Shade's low gravelly rumble.

The shock of the demon's voice sent the room spinning. Every detail of the study stood out to her in dizzying clarity. The grain of the dark woodwork, the warmth from the crackling fire, and even the glint of candlelight caught on the brandy decanter in Preston's hand all harkened her back to her first meeting with Shade, a stage setting of the first vision the Father of Nightmares had shared with her.

The one where she was killed.

She fell against the doorframe, trying to clear the nightmare image from her mind, but the whisper was lost in that moment along with the fireball that she held. Too slowly, her thoughts cleared, but Preston was already on the move and snatched a pistol from some hidden recess beside the glasses. He chuckled as he pulled back the hammer and leveled the gun at her chest.

"You've much to learn about being dastardly, my dear," he chuckled. "I'm afraid, however, that I can't afford you the time to study the subject. As I'm sure you now can see, even though you may have waylaid Lord Shade, I am far from defeated."

"Drop the pistol, Mathers," she said. She snapped her wrists but her flames failed to ignite. The distant cry of a wolf echoed in the distance, while the shadows writhed gleefully around Preston upon the room's tainted walls.

"You've no power here, witch. Although I would love to stand triumphant and gloat over your corpse, I know that departure, before the rabble arrives, yet remains my safest course." Mathers waggled his fingers in a taunting wave, closed one eye, and took a step closer. "Just between you and me, however, let me assure you that this is purely personal and I fully intend to enjoy these next moments."

Everyone Anne-Marie held dear - her boys, Jeremiah, her friends, and Henna - all flashed before her eyes as Preston sighted down the barrel aimed at her. The demon's rampant laughter rang in her ears, and she wondered suddenly if the thud of the lead ball tearing into her body would feel as it had in Shade's tormenting vision. She bit her lip and the faint glow of violet light formed around her fingertips as Preston's finger tightened on the trigger. Before she could lift her hand, the room echoed with the thundering boom of a gunshot.

And yet, she felt nothing.

Mathers stared dumbly at her from across the room, and the gun fell from his fingers and clattered on the floor. A crimson bloom spread across his white linen shirt, and blood trickled from the corner of his mouth. His knees buckled and he staggered, bouncing heavily against the sideboard and shattering all of the delicate crystal before landing on the ground among brandy and broken glass.

A silhouette stepped into the flickering lamplight from a side hallway and crossed over to Preston's body. Anne-Marie squinted at the figure, but a lingering cloud of gunsmoke hid him from view. When he finally lowered the pistol and turned her way, Anne-Marie gasped when Corbin's haggard face was bathed in firelight.

"Were I a braver man, I would have done that long before now," he said. The preacher's eyes were red-rimmed, his cheeks hollow. His rail-thin frame trembled and he gave the gun in his hand the briefest of glances before he tossed it to the floor beside Preston's. "How much pain might we all have been spared?"

"Oh, Corbin," she whispered. "You were not here by chance were you? You intended this all along."

"These last several days have been spent searching the depths of my soul for salvation, and I found that the only way to repay my flock for so much misplaced trust in me was to deliver Pioneer Vale from the true devil that lived in our midst. Too long have I stood silent and watched this man grab power at the expense of so many innocents." Corbin walked over to her and took her hands, his eyes filled with tears of his own. "I'm so sorry for Jeremiah. He was the best of men and deserved better."

"You were with him at the end." Anne-Marie swallowed the lump in her throat. It wasn't a question. She already knew the answer.

"He came to rescue me from my own foolishness, but Erickson's ill will followed close behind. I saw in his final moments what a pure and noble man your husband was. Kind and courageous. I admired him and was ashamed of everything my life had been to that point. He asked but one thing of me as he breathed his last. 'Save her', he said."

"And so you have," she said. Tears rolled down her cheeks knowing that Jeremiah's final thoughts were of her.

"And yet did I place you in mortal danger with my false accusation that Preston demanded in exchange for his silence of my transgressions." He reached into the inner pocket of his coat, pulled out a sheaf of folded pages, and pressed them into her hands. "I pray that this will absolve you to the good folk of the town."

"What's this?"

"A feeble gesture of penance and atonement. I dare not linger, for undoubtedly someone already comes to investigate the gunshot, but when the crowds arrive, tell them the truth of what I've done here, and show them these pages. Every misdeed I have ever committed is laid out by my hand. Perhaps in time, the town will eventually forget me." He went back to the doorway and picked up a leather satchel that he had dropped there. "I wish that your family had never suffered to know me."

"Corbin, you need not run. There are more than enough in Pioneer Vale who hated Preston enough to stand with you. He tried to take control of everything with his mercenaries. With this," she said as she waved the papers in her hand, "you can find your forgiveness."

"But I could not stay and forgive myself given all that I have been accomplice to," said Corbin. A sad smile crept to his face. "You are a bold and compassionate woman, Anne-Marie Carmichael. May you remain so to the end of your days."

The preacher bowed his head and then disappeared back into the hallway, melting away into the shadows. Shouts from the front courtyard grew in volume as curious townsfolk reached the manor, and she knew they would join her shortly. She unfolded Corbin's letter and fresh tears fell anew as she read the newly penned entry at the top of the page.

"Tonight I have murdered Preston Mathers so that I might free myself from the secrets he held over me. My need for his silence forced my hand to assist him with his crimes against the town of Pioneer Vale and the Carmichael family in particular. Herein lies my full confession...."

CHAPTER 21
HOMECOMINGS - PRESENT DAY

"Dereliction of duty, my ass," Ben muttered as he read his dismissal paperwork. He juggled the cardboard box full of his personal effects under one arm, and then, with a snort, crumpled up the paper and tossed it over his shoulder. He half-turned and yelled back at the hospital building. "Compromised the lives and safety of my patients? Are you kidding me?"

A few puzzled faces peered out the windows at him, and he felt the heat rise in his cheeks. He spun back around and walked towards the lot's entry. He nearly dropped the box he carried when he saw his beat-up pickup truck sitting in his usual parking space. He hurried over to it and ran his hand along the familiar dings and scratches that he had never taken the time to get fixed.

"You'll need these," said a voice behind him. "I found them in the mud near the mine entrance."

This time, the box slipped from his arm, but a cloud of lavender flame caught it like a cushion, and lifted it gently back to his waiting hands. He turned around and shook his head. Anne-Marie leaned against the tailgate with his keys lazily twirling around one finger while wispy flames danced along the knuckles of her other hand. Her coppery hair was pulled back into an unruly ponytail, and she was clad in blue jeans, work boots, and a flannel shirt with the sleeves rolled up.

"Looks like you've recovered from your injuries well enough. You'll be tilling the chickens, or slopping the fields, or whatever it is you farmers do for fun around here in no time." He opened the truck's passenger door and set his belongings on the seat. "Seriously though. It's nice to see you up and about."

"I had the most remarkable doctor looking after me."

"Well, that's apparently debatable," he scoffed. "And what's the deal with you sorcerous types always sneaking up on me?"

"Force of habit, I suppose." Anne-Marie smiled at him. "Three and a half centuries of avoiding the public eye."

"You should stop hiding. The world should know about what you two did for us."

"I will be around, as much as I ever was. Watching from the sidelines." His former patient slid her hands into her pockets and studied the people nearby going about their daily lives. "Shade's defeat left a powerful vacuum, and I suspect in time his siblings may rise to fill that void."

"So, this isn't over yet? You and Angelica are still on duty?"

"We are Guardians. That mantle demands we remain ever vigilant, but a message has been sent to the dark powers. We'll be safe enough for a time."

"You really don't know how glad I am that you are on our side. I can't imagine anyone else as brave as you are."

"A pale mirror when held against those who have stood beside me over the years. I am ever indebted and grateful to the old families of the Vale. Just as they had in the past, it was through their selflessness and courage that Shade's evil was held at bay. The Harmons. Brenners. Robillards." She tilted her head and raised an eyebrow. "Reynolds."

"I don't get accused of being heroic that often," Ben snorted. He shook his head and looked at his feet. "I learned something while watching you and Angelica fight so fiercely the other day. You weren't fighting for the sake of the world. Everything that you gave a damn about was right there on that farm."

"My love for my family is what led me down this road so long ago. They mean everything to me."

"I had that once back in New York. Seems like another lifetime now, but ever since you vanished from that hospital room, I've been thinking about getting a second wind. Wondering if they might forgive me and let me start over. Got a lot of rotten branches on my family tree. Not just me personally, but through generations. Who knows? Maybe I'm the one who can start to clean up some of the old messes."

"I believe that you are off to a fine start, Doctor. I suppose that means you will be leaving shortly?"

"Yeah, I don't have much to pack up. I'll probably be gone in a couple of days. Roll out of town with the little bit I showed up with." He scratched the stubble on his chin. "Despite the whole being nearly killed by an otherworldly demonic wolf, I'm truly grateful to have gotten to meet you all and fill in some of the gaps in my history. I guess that you had some rocky times with my ancestors, but I hope that you and I are parting as friends." He awkwardly extended his hand to her, which she glanced at before the corner of her mouth curled into a smirk.

"I never got the chance to thank Corbin for saving my life that night. I couldn't forgive myself if I missed such an opportunity again." Anne-Marie pushed his hand to one side, leaned forward, and kissed his cheek. "Farewell, Ben, and thank you for everything." She spun on her heel and walked towards a nearby van.

"I don't suppose you could throw a little magic my way to make sure I don't screw up again back home?"

"I could," she called over her shoulder, and then winked. "But I don't think you will need it." She disappeared behind the parked vehicle, and with a flash of purple flame, Ben knew that she was gone. He tossed his keys into the air, deftly caught them, and then climbed into his truck.

*   *   *

Anne-Marie placed her teacup in Whisperwind's farmhouse sink as night fell over the ancient forest outside the window. Crickets sang their evening song as the setting sun painted the sky with its own lavender flame. From the sitting room, the ever-burning fire popped and crackled merrily. She closed her eyes and simply breathed.

With the snap of her fingers, the air rippled behind her and the hidden staircase that led up to the second floor shimmered into view. Her boot heels clacked on the wood treads but the echo seemed less hollow tonight. The shadows were not so foreboding, and the cottage felt more like home than it had in ages.

She turned to the right at the top of the stairs and quietly opened the door to Angelica's room. A scintillating light enshrouded the young woman and twinkled through the spectrum, always pausing a heartbeat longer on a crackling blue-white radiance before cascading off into another rainbow surge. Her gravest wounds were already well on the mend and within a couple of days, she would be fit enough to get up and move around once more.

"Rest easy, my dear one," she whispered. "None of us would be here tonight without your courage." The slightest hint of a smile found its way to the unconscious girl's lips, and Anne-Marie backed out of the room so that her granddaughter could sleep. She went back to the other end of the hallway and pushed open the heavy oak door that led to her bedroom.

The wood-paneled walls were the only feature of this chamber that belonged to Whisperwind. The furniture and other trappings were antiques from a bygone time, all pulled from her favorite memories of when her husband and boys were the centers of her world. Gone but never forgotten.

A warmth at her throat and a soft glimmer of purple light emanated from the neckline of the flannel shirt. She lifted the gossamer silver chain and let the amethyst pendant that Jeremiah had given her so long ago spin at the end. Did he have any idea that day what his simple gesture of love would lead to? She brought it gently to her lips and then unclasped it from her throat.

Across the room, a simple weathered wood picture frame hung from a thin wire upon a hook that held the old sketch of her family sitting at the table in the Hirsute Huntsman. She looked fondly upon the faded drawing that their dear friend, Abel Harmon, had drawn for them on that Market Day so long ago. She carefully added the silver chain to the hook and the purple crystal swung back and forth across the smiling figures of her and her family until it came to rest at last over the image of her husband's face. She smiled as he hoisted his mug into the air in an eternal toast.

Thrown over the chest at the foot of her bed were the leathers and linens of her Guardian garb. Her shoulder still ached where Shade's claws had torn through her body, and while the tears had faded already from her skin, deep rents in the fabric and leather served as sore reminders. The aches and bruises would fade, and she could mend her clothes easily enough once they were given a thorough cleaning. Idly, she wondered when next she might need to wear the outfit into battle again. Musings for another day.

Anne-Marie sighed, pulled the scarf from her hair, and shook the snarls out of her coppery mane. She stripped off the boots, jeans, and flannel that she had worn today, and tossed the dirty clothes into a pile and then padded barefoot across the wood floor. With a groan, she pulled back the quilt and slid into her bed. The cool sheets and downy mattress welcomed her as she wearily laid her head on the fluffy pillow. Sleep quickly overtook her, and for the first time in over 350 years the cries of her descendants, her children - her Firstborn - were silent.

The ghosts were free at last.

*　　*　　*

Clarissa flipped on her bathroom light and skidded across the tile floor on her knees. She barely got the toilet lid raised before she retched. Her stomach twisted and cramps curled her into a ball on the floor. Her mind reeled from piercing growls, moans, and shrieks in some guttural language that she somehow knew were not of this world. Her skull felt like it was about to split and she pressed the heels of her hands into her temples.

"Leave me alone," she whimpered. "What do you want with me?"

The walls of her bathroom peeled away but instead of her house and yard, there was only a rocky wasteland. The sky ran red like blood and mounds of debris burned across the landscape. Creatures soared through the crimson clouds in the distance, and their echoing cries recalled the Harbinger and her frantic dash through the hospital hallways. Shadows crouched at the edges of her vision and swirling dust devils of ash billowed around her. Although she covered her eyes, grit found its way past her lashes and blinded her with tears.

"You poor thing," said a dulcet feminine voice. Although soft, the words reverberated with power that touched something familiar deep within her core. "Left behind by those you dared to trust. Made a pawn in a game whose rules were never explained."

The shadows parted in a flutter of movement at the corner of her eye. Bathed in coldfire, her face lost in shadow, a shapely figure emerged from the mist. There was a sultry sway to her walk that made the jewels adorning the sheer bodice roll like a ship on the tide and the silver belt around her waist bucked like a wild horse. Sandals of gold laced up the bronze skin of her sculpted legs and her fingernails were painted the deepest of ebony.

The skin of Clarissa's stomach burned and she fell to her knees. Fire blazed beneath the edge of her tee shirt, and she peeked under the hem while the woman drew closer. The shimmering dragon that was emblazoned on her flesh writhed and with every jolt that shook her body, the creature's form twisted, shifting little by little into a fiercer version of itself. Longer teeth. Sharper claws. Broader wings.

"The Guardian has forsaken your friendship in exchange for her power."

"Angie wouldn't do that to me," she cried. Another torment wracked her body, and she squeezed her eyes closed and rocked on the ground. "She'd never use me like that."

"Indeed she has, but you have been marked by the One, and found worthy to avenge yourself of the wrongs you have suffered."

"You want me to join the Adversary and betray my best friend. I want nothing to do with him." Her muscles spasmed once more, and blood seeped through her shirt in the pattern of the beastly tattoo she bore.

"Embrace what you are offered, Clarissa, for The One offers you that which has not been seen since the earliest of days."

"You mean since Aiden Carmichael. He would make me just another unsuspecting servant," she spat. The heat within her spread, and a thin shroud of gray flame fanned out around her. "I will not be his slave."

The menacing woman's laugh echoed all around her and the temptress stepped closer. The darkness melted away, and Clarissa gasped when the face revealed beneath the golden gem-studded crown was her own. With eyes rimmed by kohl and lips stained as black as her nails, her double, wreathed in unearthly beauty, gave her the most lascivious of smiles.

"Never a slave, sweet Clarissa," she purred. "You shall be His queen."

With one final wracking scream, she threw her head back as her shirt burned, cinders swirling in the air around her head. The dragon on her stomach smiled wickedly and then sank into her body. The world around her shifted and the colors of the landscape became more vibrant, as a comforting warmth settled through her.

*　　*　　*

Angelica's ribs gave her just enough of a pinch to remind her that she wasn't completely healed yet. While the week in Anne-Marie's care had fixed the worst of her wounds, including repairing her broken teeth, she was still a walking tapestry of bruises. Better than dead, she mused.

She winced as she lifted the burned-out husk of the book from the library's floor. The leather cover cracked at her touch and a shower of cold embers fell to the carpet. She dropped the tome onto the table where it crumbled into ash.

"Guess this one isn't much use anymore. I think I broke its magic when I slammed the gate shut."

"You're fortunate the recoil wasn't more powerful," Anne-Marie replied. The older woman looked around the study and placed her hands on her hips, head shaking slowly back and forth. "We'll be sifting through the ashes of this mess for days to come."

Angelica shelved the last of her grandmother's magical books, and then gave a nod to the bookcase. She plopped down into a well-cushioned reading chair while her grandmother picked up a tea cup from the side table and reclined in the chaise before the library's hearth. She toyed with the end of her ponytail and then stared into the dancing purple flames in the hearth.

"He nearly got by me," she said softly. "Almost made it into our world."

"And yet he failed."

"It was like he was hiding behind a doorway in another time, just waiting for someone to crack it open for him. Whoever had written that journal that I was reading knew I was here."

"Transcending time is a power unlike any I've ever heard of before. We should probably add that into our own grimoire. At the very least, it poses a new mystery in the war and has revealed another example of just how dangerous our enemy is. We may have to determine when the Adversary is hiding, rather than just where," Anne-Marie said. Her grandmother sipped the steaming brew and crossed her feet. "Still, it is a concern for another day. I sense that there's something else on your mind. Speak, child. I'd rather not use fire and flame to drag the thoughts from you."

"I wasn't sure how to bring up what happened at the shrine, or if you even wanted to talk about it." She bit her lip and then took a deep breath. "I mean, Aiden was literally a monster who tried over and over again to kill us both, but in the end, you still lost your son. I can't imagine what you must be feeling."

"I had always believed that with Shade's defeat, his hold over Aiden would fail as well and that I might be reunited with my boy one day. I was instead forced to accept that my son was lost to me ages ago." A sad smile crossed Anne-Marie's face, but she looked up and winked. "I saved who mattered most to me."

"Thank you for not letting the demon rip my head off."

"Just don't make me regret it."

"I'm not making any promises," she replied. She looked down at her hands and rolled a spark of lightning across the backs of her knuckles.

"For the first time, I understand why you had to hide away in the woods. How can I possibly go back and pretend to be a normal high school student when I know about the threats out there just waiting to take a shot at a world full of defenseless people?"

"That you can ask such a question shows me that you were never a typical high schooler, to begin with, child. You have grown so much during our short time together. Where I once knew a brash and headstrong child, before me now is a courageous and compassionate woman. You are, and always have been, exceptional." Anne-Marie gave a coquettish shrug and flip of her hair. "It's in your blood, after all."

"But modesty gave us a hard pass," she said, quaking with subdued laughter. "You've been the best role model I could have ever asked for. If I stayed with you a lifetime, I wouldn't be half the woman that you are."

"A lifetime with me would rob the world of your own light. You have already proven yourself a fearless defender to those who need you most, Angelica, and they will be fortunate indeed to have your watchful eyes looking over them."

"Even after the rampage at the hospital? People are going to talk about what happened. Should I be worried about torches and pitchforks?"

"Few enough actually saw anything that would place you there. Anonymity has ever been our greatest advantage, and soon enough the rumors of that night will fade and become just another facet of our legend."

"What about the other Guardians? Shouldn't we find them and tell them what happened here?" Angelica nodded at the ash pile on the desk. "Let them know that the Adversary is making moves against us now?"

"In time, we shall look to the old wives' tales and folklore and find others like us. What hidden corner of the globe would refuse the aid of two battle-proven Guardians? However, let the world wait for us a little longer. Shade has been cast back into the ooze that spawned him." Anne-Marie rose from her chaise and slapped her palms together. With a flash of lavender flame and a twist of her wrists, a portal ripped open in the air near them. "There are others closer to heart and home that await your return."

On the other side of the gateway, the moon cast its soft light upon the quiet front yard of Carmichael Farms. Stacks of fresh lumber sat in neat piles waiting for the rebuilding of the old farmhouse. An RV camping trailer sat in the gravel driveway, and the door swung open. Three shadowy figures stepped into the night and were promptly swallowed up in the surrounding darkness. One broke from the group and wandered over to the solitary corner post of the old front porch, the only part of the original structure that remained after Shade's blast had demolished Angelica's home.

The figure gently ran a hand along the post, then climbed the step and leaned against it with arms folded over their chest. Angelica wiped away the sudden tears, while her mother, revealed by the moonlight, took up her usual spot where she waited every day for her children to get off the school bus. She glanced at Anne-Marie, whose own eyes seemed glassy and distant as she regarded the same scene, but doubtlessly seeing a different memory.

"Maybe looking back through time isn't such a difficult magic to master after all," she said softly. Anne-Marie said nothing and she reached over and squeezed her hand. "You know that you could come with me. You're still part of this family, and after all we've been through together, I'm pretty sure we at least owe you dinner. And like 350 years of birthdays, Mother's Day cards, Christmas presents."

Anne-Marie's reverie melted away and her 10th great-grandmother laughed before she looked back at her. "One day, child, but after four centuries of hiding away, I am not quite ready to test those waters. Perhaps once my..., forgive me..., *our* urban legend is no longer the talk of the town you shall find me on your doorstep. Now go on. Don't make them wait any longer."

Angelica studied the portal's writhing flames. "You are going to have to show me how to do this trick someday. I still can't get it right."

"A witch should never reveal all of her secrets." Angelica looked at the RV and then back again.

"It's Guardian."

"So it is." Anne-Marie gave her a mischievous smile and an exaggerated cackle. "But let's not tell that to the locals, dearie. Now run along before I turn you into gingerbread."

She gave Anne-Marie one last embrace. "Promise me I will see you soon," she said softly.

"My dear, I could never make a more solemn vow."

Angelica hopped through the portal, which spiraled shut with a familiar whumpf. Gravel crunched loudly under her boots as she started up the driveway. She cast one last glance over her shoulder but only the ancient forest stood behind her. A campfire sprung to life by the trailer and the light shone upon the faces of the three people who meant more to her than anything in the world.

"There better be a s'more over there with my name on it," she called out. She ran forward, greeted by their shouts of surprise, and soon found herself engulfed by the warmth of her family's embraces.

She was finally home.

CHAPTER 22
PROMISES TO KEEP — 1671

Anne-Marie brushed the strand of hair away from Jeremiah's face and gently kissed his brow. The pyre she had built for him stood on a small stone outcropping in a grove that she had found a short walk from Whisperwind, still enshrouded in the mystic woods that kept her new home hidden from prying eyes. She considered once more if she should have brought the boys along to say farewell, but after all they had endured yesterday, the serenity of the cottage was probably better for them. She would break the news of Jeremiah's passing to them another day.

The rising sun reflected off the surface of a small nearby pond fed by a gurgling stream. A scintillating cascade of light burst across the gently lapping water. The warmth felt good against her skin and drove away the last of the lingering chills that had followed her from the dark depths of Shade's domains. Birds chirped softly in the boughs above the bier in an almost reverential homage to her husband. Although she ached down to her bones from all the magic that she had channeled recently, she opened herself once more to the comforting flow.

"The first of many castings for the new day," she whispered to herself. "But perhaps the most meaningful." She closed her eyes and the heat of the dawn melded with the lavender flames that sprung up around her. As lovely as this clearing was, Anne-Marie intended for it to be a monument to the man she loved.

The husband she had lost.

Her mind drifted away to her memories of the Nipmuc sanctuary and the beauty of that hidden refuge filled her thoughts. She knew how much Jeremiah would have loved to have seen the thundering waterfall. To have gone fishing by the lake. To have hunted alongside the boys in the forests. He deserved nothing less.

Her feet lifted slowly from the ground, carried aloft by the growing power within her body. Her copper tresses became a billowing fiery crown in the dawning daylight. She stretched her hands high above her head, fingers grasping at every thread of power that she could weave to her will. When her eyelids cracked open just a sliver, the world before her shimmered with the dazzling golden sunlight and the purple radiance of her magic, unbridled energy awaiting her command.

With a snap of her hands, fire roared out across the glade. The still pond sloshed water along the banks, and birds scattered from the tree branches, their once peaceful melody cut short by surprise. The ground itself began to quake, but Anne-Marie reached deep into the bones of the earth and took hold. Rocky outcroppings shot skyward as she wrenched the ancient stone from eons-old beds.

The babbling stream was likewise carried to new heights, its natural course diverted and amplified by the raging power that Anne-Marie wielded. The once gentle trickle became a torrent of water that crashed down from on high in a magnificent waterfall that caught the morning sun in a prismatic spray of grandeur and overflowed the small pond into a shimmering lake of crystal clear water.

Her flames rolled across the surrounding foliage as well. Scrub grass grew soft and lush and of a vibrant verdant green. Dandelions and thistles bloomed into lavender and honeysuckle, the scent filling the air. Oaks and pines changed into orchard trees worthy of an Edenic garden as her magical fires ran their course.

The last embers swirled into the air, spinning in a lofty, lazy spiral, that Anne-Marie sent with a gesture into the dry kindling at the base of Jeremiah's pyre. Her eyes flashed violet once more, and a tongue of flame caught the stacked wood alight, blazing into a lavender bonfire that quickly wrapped Jeremiah's body in a shroud of primordial power.

From across the void, she sensed a fleeting presence, intimately familiar to her, bound to her through a love more intense than any magic that she could bring to bear. She called out to the spirit, and to her surprise, it reached back. She spun around to the pyre, watching the flames twist faster and faster around Jeremiah's unresponsive form. Brighter and brighter the conflagration burned, until even Anne-Marie had to shield her eyes from the glow. With a cry to the heavens, she granted all of her might to the presence that hovered so near and dragged it across the veil. The air thundered and she was hurled to the ground, rolling across the grass. The echoes faded away, lost in the roar of the new waterfall, and the last of the wood from the pyre crumbled to ash.

Yet a lavender flame, not at her beck and call, still burned.

From the cinders rose the shape of a man clad in living fire. The being looked down at its hands, turning them over and back, then looked around the glade, finally resting its gaze on her. There was a nudge in her mind, unusual and foreign to her, yet strikingly familiar at the same time. And then she heard his voice.

"This…place? For…me?" he whispered, like the soft crackle of a hearth fire, in her head.

Anne-Marie held her hands over her mouth and sobbed with joy. All she could do was nod. The elemental stepped closer to her on shaky legs and then knelt beside her. His fingers caressed her cheek, but his touch was no warmer to her than that of the man this being had once been. She had no idea how she had done it, or what power she had drawn upon that hadn't ripped her apart in turn, but she had managed to manifest the love that she and Jeremiah shared and had breathed life into it. She knew it wasn't truly her husband's spirit, but rather the embodiment of his purity that the magic had brought back to her.

It was the essence of him that she would have hated losing the most.

"It is for us, my love," she choked out at last. "I can visit you here still, and though you may not be who you were in life, it is at least a way for me to still hold you close."

The fiery being nodded slowly, and then slowly wandered away to explore the new home that she had created for him. Fatigue washed over her and Anne-Marie stretched out languidly on a bed of grass softer even than the downy mattress they had shared back at the farm, lulled by the gentle lapping of water along the lake shore. He soon slid down beside her, his fiery body pressed tightly against hers, and a strong and comforting arm wrapped around her waist.

Her aching muscles and drowsy lethargy were soon forgotten when she felt the familiar tickle of Jeremiah's beard and the wispy flames of his lips touch the bare skin of her neck.

*   *   *

Alawa dropped a few more berries into the basket by her feet and wiped her brow. It was a relief that her sweat was from honest work for the first time in what seemed forever, rather than from the oppressive fear that had held sway over her people since the mercenary attack. Even the sky had cleared up overnight and the heaviness in the air had lifted at last.

It was a sign that something good had happened.

A handful of children fished in the pond below the great waterfall and suddenly burst into cheers. One of the boys shouted in triumph as he held a wriggling trout aloft on the end of his spear. They would eat well tonight, she thought to herself.

Leaves rustled behind her and she dropped into a fighting crouch, her knife in hand and her back pressed against a nearby tree. She breathed easier when Chogan and Rowtag stepped forward with their empty hands held before him.

"Chogan," she scolded. "You nearly got stabbed. You should know better than to creep up on me like that."

"Forgive us, Alawa," he said. "We did not mean to startle you." Dozens of Nipmuc warriors fell in behind the two men, many carrying baskets full of food and supplies.

"These look like spoils of war. Does Pioneer Vale still stand?" She looked anxiously through the growing crowd, but couldn't find the one face she sought. Her tribesmen gathered round and cheered as they distributed the bounty brought to the sanctuary.

"Indeed it does," Rowtag bellowed. "These provisions were sent by our new friends to help you get back on your feet. They wanted to show not only their gratitude for our assistance but insisted on sending what help they could offer to our people being watched over by our chieftain's dutiful wife."

"I don't understand. These supplies are welcome indeed, but I have taken no husband, and certainly not a chieftain. Have these townsfolk been misled somehow?" A strong, yet gentle hand took her wrist and twirled her in a circle. She brushed her hair from her eyes and her knees wobbled.

"That's because I haven't yet had the chance to ask if you would have me," said Kitchi as his strong arms held her close. He stepped back and slid a bracelet of braided wildflowers onto her wrist. "Would you do me the honor?"

Without pause, she threw herself into Kitchi's arms, and together they toppled to the ground in their embrace. Alawa kissed him fiercely and ignored Rowtag's joyful booming laugh behind them.

"I think she accepts," roared the brawny man.

"I was afraid I'd never see you again," she whispered.

Kitchi's finger gently lifted her chin. "I will remain by your side as long as you'll have me." They kissed again and the cheers of their assembled tribesmen thundered louder than the waterfall behind them.

"Tonight we shall feast for we have many things to be thankful for," shouted Rowtag. "Our newly formed alliance with the settlers, an end to Maheegan's darkness, and," he said with a grin, "an upcoming wedding!"

*   *   *

"Master Brenner," said Micah. The young smith wrung his hands together under Marcus' stern glare. "In the absence of my own Da, I had hoped to tell you how much you've been like a proper father to me through these recent days, and how deeply grateful I am for all of your guidance and support. And though I'll never be a part of your true family, sir, with your blessing, I'd like your permission to court your daughter, Allison, if I may be so bold."

"Mister Robillard," said Marcus. The dull slap of his heavy hands on the weathered bartop echoed across the taproom and he leaned across the polished wood. "You do understand that in these particular times, what a busy man I am, yes?"

"Of…of…of course, sir. Plenty of clean up around the town."

"And yet here you stand, wasting my time when I have repairs to make, game to clean and dress, and a thousand other tasks that require my beck and call."

Micah's shoulders sagged, and he lowered his head. Marcus held back as long as he was able but his restrained laughter burst like a dam, and he let loose in a raucous bellow that shook the counter he leaned upon.

"Sir?" The young smith scratched his head, confused by the unexpected laughter.

"Micah, my boy, you've had my blessing from the moment you stood in Alison's defense during the attack. If it's marrying that you've a mind to, lad, by all means, go and ask my girl."

"He doesn't need to, Papa," said Allison as she appeared behind Micah. "The taproom isn't so wide that I couldn't hear what ye two were discussing."

"Have you an answer for me already, then?" asked the young smith.

"Aye," the young woman said. "It would be my pleasure."

"Drinks on the house," Marcus shouted, and he gave another resounding slap to the countertop as the two kissed. He turned to the open doorway into the kitchen area. "Wife, grab us a bottle of my best stock! It looks like the Brenner family is growing again!"

His mirth was cut short by a retching noise from the other side of the doorway, and he dashed into the kitchen in time to see Dorothea poised over a bucket. Slowly she wiped her mouth with the back of her hand and shook her head. Marcus' jaw dropped when he saw her hand resting beside the same cook pot that she had served the sickened soldiers with.

"Oh no, love." He rushed to her side and cradled her in his arms. "Please tell me that you didn't forget what you put in that bowl."

"Don't be daft, Marcus," she replied with a roll of her eyes. Allison pushed past him with a mug of water, which his wife gratefully accepted. She took a long sip, swished, and then spat it into the bucket. "I know well enough what I may nibble upon from around my own kitchen. No, this is something different. It reminds me of…."

"Not the winter fever from a few years back," said Micah. "That laid up half the town."

Marcus studied his wife, and his jaw slowly fell open as a broad grin crossed her face. She reached over and cupped his hairy cheeks in her palms. "You don't mean…?"

"Aye," she nodded and then kissed him. "Feels just like each time I found that I was carrying one of our girls."

*   *   *

Abel watched the young officer shake hands with one of the Reavers who shouldered his pack and turned toward the town gate. Several other mercenaries continued the tasks of breaking down the soldiers' camp and the man stood tall and straight, hands folded behind his back, and watched what was left of this company go about their duties. He approached and cleared his throat, waving his hat in the air when the fellow turned around.

"Good morning to ye, sir," Abel said. He gestured towards the nearby soldiers. "You're the commanding officer of these lads now, yes?"

"In name only. Forrester's Reavers are no more," the soldier replied. He snorted. "Lost about a quarter of what we had left to desertion overnight, but I suppose there isn't any reason to try and hold them together now. I am Nathaniel Carter." He extended his hand and Abel grasped it firmly.

"Abel Harmon." He put his hat back on his balding head. The morning sun was already promising to be brutal today.

"I have heard that you are the newly elected mayor of Pioneer Vale. I suppose congratulations are in order, sir."

"Dubious honor if you ask me," Abel said. He shook his head. "Everyone thinks that since I brought the Nipmuc to the town's rescue, that I suddenly possess some great wisdom. Truth be told, I think their new chief put the idea into somebody's mind and I got tricked into taking the post. I should have let that big bastard of a bear eat him."

"You strike me as a man of honor, Master Harmon, and I hear that you are a veteran from days past. Once I thought that I served under such a commander. I'm sure that the town will thrive under your guidance. Please let the citizens know that we shall be gone before nightfall."

"About that," Abel said and folded his arms across his chest. "What if you didn't need to? Twas a bold thing ye did here yesterday, son. The town owes you a word of thanks as well."

"I think you will find them more thankful still once we have left." Carter stared at him then shook his head sadly. "What Forrester attempted here was a disgrace to every reason that I became a soldier."

Abel scratched at his stubbled chin. "A good soldier knows when to follow his conscience instead of his orders. You were given a difficult choice and should take heart that the call ye made saved lives."

"I've an equally difficult choice ahead. Without the company to tend to, I'm not entirely sure where I'll end up next."

"There is always land to develop and settle," Abel said. "Should you or any of your men of like mind feel up to it. Knowing that we had a few more neighbors who knew how to handle themselves in a scuffle could certainly put some folks at ease." The young officer stared thoughtfully at the men scuttling around the encampment.

"Do you truly believe that the townsfolk would so quickly dismiss what part we played here? Our ranks were full of the sorts of men that most would not be comfortable living beside. Men of shady backgrounds who were often on the wrong side of the law."

"As well as some eager young men who still respect you and look to you for direction. There are enough already within these walls who have come to this new land in search of second chances to erase the sins of their pasts. Find fresh starts." He extended his hand again. "I see no reason why you boys aren't entitled to the same opportunity. Don't throw it away."

Faces, young and old, beardless and rugged, ran to and fro past them. One soldier, barely past the cusp of manhood, snapped a salute their way, which Carter answered with one of his own. The Reaver commander turned back and then once more grasped his offered hand in a firm shake.

"Let me extend the offer. Maybe a few worthy recruits remain, after all, sir."

*   *   *

Aiden bolted upright as a log popped in the hearth of the old cottage, and he bit his lip to keep from crying out. Sweat poured down his face, and his chest thumped. The nightmare faded away from his memory just as quickly as it had come, with only fading images of blue lightning and falling rocks that stole his breath away.

The purple fire crackled again, dancing merrily, but he kicked away the heavy blanket that his mother had thrown over him and Thomas. His brother smiled in his sleep, his chest rising and falling slowly, and barely stirred as Aiden climbed off the old couch. His bare feet hit the wood planks of the floor, cozy and warm from the radiant glow of his mother's strange new fireplace. His stomach growled and he tiptoed over to the table where a bowl of fruit sat. He set his eyes on a juicy-looking apple when a small noise caught his ear. He paused and cocked his head, then heard it again.

The sound of a dog yipping from somewhere behind the fireplace.

"Puppy?" he called in a hushed whisper, careful not to disturb Thomas. He stepped closer to the hearth, and another distant bark brought a smile to his face.

His mother had told them to get some sleep while she went about her work. She had waved her hands in the air, and when she had touched the stones above the mantle, the fireplace had split open and a hallway had opened up behind the flames. She had stepped through unharmed and disappeared into the darkness. She must have found a puppy for them and was keeping it in a secret kennel.

"How can I open this?" he said to himself. In answer to his words, the flames flashed again, but this time they were a grayish-black rather than the pretty purple that his mother seemed to like so much. It didn't matter though. Once more, the secret hallway behind the fireplace opened wide, and he hurried through the space, sparing his sleeping brother only a brief glance before moving deeper along.

The short corridor led to a long spiral staircase that plunged far below the cottage. Torches flickered along the walls and cast long shadows across the stone. Aiden shivered, but another echoing yelp from below found his feet hurrying down the stone steps.

Down and down the stairway twisted, with a flat space breaking up the path every few turns, and each with a short hallway branching off. He stopped to catch his breath at one when a flash of purple light drew his eye to the left. His mother stood in what must have been another kitchen, for he saw a large black cook pot hanging on a hook over a cold fireplace. She pulled glass jars out of a wooden box and placed them one by one on a wall of empty shelves.

He started to call out to her, but the puppy barked once more from farther down the stairway. She probably wanted to surprise him and Thomas with it later and might get upset if she knew he was sneaking around. He'd just go have a peek and act surprised when he saw it later. Quietly, he padded away and went further down.

The shadows ahead of him danced like a wagging tail and he rushed towards the next landing. It was much colder in this short hallway than the other passageways, but that was probably from being so far underground. Like in the old cellar back home. He shook his head and studied the heavy wooden door at the end of the hall. It stood slightly cracked open and a strange yellow light drove away the gloom as it gleamed around the edges. Gently, he pushed the door open and peeked inside.

"Puppy? Where are you?" he called softly then froze as he stepped into the room.

In the center of the chamber, a glowing yellow rock spun lazily above a stone pedestal. Flashes of green light streaked across the face of the stone every few heartbeats, but something shimmered from deeper inside, and Aiden crept closer. He heard the bark once more, but this time it felt like he heard it inside his head. There was nothing else in the room so he leaned in close to the stone.

"Puppy, are you in there?"

A distorted canine muzzle, tongue lolling out of the side of its mouth, swirled from the heart of the crystal gemstone. The poor pup had bugs crawling over its snout, and there were gouges along its cheeks that must hurt, but, although the image was cloudy, a wide smile creased the face. Aiden heard the echo of a deep chuckle rumble in the back of his mind.

"Hello, Sweetling," purred Shade.

*   *   *

Anne-Marie tapped her quill against her chin with ink-stained fingers and then placed it on the stone table top in her new study. She leaned her head on her fist and her fingers toyed with a strand of her hair. She tried to stifle a yawn, but there was no stopping it. Carving out the chambers behind Whisperwind's fireplace had thoroughly exhausted her, but she had shaped the cozy cottage more into a workspace that suited her needs.

No, not mine alone, she mused as she looked at the page before her.

Her mind drifted back to the battle with Erickson, and how Aiden had been caught in the crossfire of the Elder Guardian's gift and Shade's coldfire. The collision of those two magics, equal but opposite, had opened an untapped reservoir within her child. Was it his destiny to learn of the war with the Adversary, something that she herself only had the most basic awareness of? Was the magic and knowledge even hers to pass along, or did she only make assumptions that one day her Firstborn child might become the master of Whisperwind? Such a gift was both blessing and burden, yet there must always be someone ready to stand watch over Shade's possible return. She stretched her aching back and read what she had written again.

Of course, there were provisions made for Thomas as well. Carmichael Farms needed a caretaker, and her penned words would provide him ownership, once he came of age and create a legacy to pass along to his own children one day. There was plenty of work to be done before it would return to its former self, however. The barn was a total loss after Erickson's fire, but at least there was more than enough gold under Alistair's Climb to pay for the materials and labor to get the job done. A wave of her hand could easily take care of the heavy lifting, but too many questions would arise in the small community, and she had only just put to rest the suspicion that her witchcraft was all a lie. Better to keep it that way.

She took a pinch of sand in her fingers, and, with a wisp of fire, sprinkled it over the drying ink. Infused with her magic, the script on the page glittered like a rainbow after a summer storm, vibrant and bright, and subsided into a soft glow that pierced the gloom and held the shadows at bay.

Set down by my hand is this Covenant of the Carmichael Descendants. In days yet to dawn, when the shadows encroach once more, let this serve as the clarion call for the

Firstborn of the successive generations of our family to stand against the ancient danger that threatens our homeland...

Anne-Marie yawned again and then blew out the candle on the desk. As she left the study, a warm rush of power flowed through her, and she smiled knowing that her promise, her covenant, already stood sentinel against the darkness yet to come.

THE END